I0565171

Anxious Gravity

For Raina

A heaven on earth I have won, by wooing thee.

— William Shakespeare, *All's Well That Ends Well*

Anxious Gravity

A Novel

Jeff Wells

SIMON & PIERRE
A MEMBER OF THE DUNDURN GROUP
TORONTO › OXFORD

Copyright © Jeff Wells 2001

All rights reserved. No part of this publication may be reproduced, stored in a
retrieval system, or transmitted in any form or by any means, electronic, mechanical,
photocopying, recording, or otherwise (except for brief passages for purposes of
review) without the prior permission of Dundurn Press. Permission to photocopy
should be requested from the Canadian Copyright Licensing Agency.

Editor: Barry Jowett
Copy-editor: Julian Walker
Design: Bruna Brunelli
Printer: Transcontinental

Canadian Cataloguing in Publication Data

Wells, Jeff, 1959-
    Anxious gravity: a novel

ISBN 0-88924-299-2

I. Title.

PS8595.E5566A75 2001   C813'.52   C2001-902250-6
PR9199.4.W44A65 2001

1   2   3   4   5   05   04   03   02   01

THE CANADA COUNCIL | LE CONSEIL DES ARTS
FOR THE ARTS | DU CANADA
SINCE 1957 | DEPUIS 1957

Canada

ONTARIO ARTS COUNCIL
CONSEIL DES ARTS DE L'ONTARIO

We acknowledge the support of the Canada Council for the Arts and the Ontario
Arts Council for our publishing program. We also acknowledge the financial support
of the Government of Canada through the Book Publishing Industry Development
Program and The Association for the Export of Canadian Books, and the
Government of Ontario through the Ontario Book Publishers Tax Credit program.

Care has been taken to trace the ownership of copyright material used in this book.
The author and the publisher welcome any information enabling them to rectify any
references or credit in subsequent editions.

                                                  J. Kirk Howard, President

Printed and bound in Canada.

www.dundurn.com

Dundurn Press   Dundurn Press   Dundurn Press
8 Market Street   73 Lime Walk   2250 Military Road
Suite 200   Headington,   Tonawanda NY
Toronto, Ontario, Canada Oxford, England   U.S.A. 14150
M5E 1M6   OX3 7AD

It came from mine own heart, so to my head,
And thence into my fingers trickled;
Then to my pen, from whence immediately
On paper I did dribble it daintily.

John Bunyan, *The Holy War*

For Word

I

A joke is the epigram on the death of a feeling.

Friedrich Nietzsche

0

ideon Frye was my uncle, my mother's elder brother, a gunner in a Lancaster bomber during the Second World War. He was my grandmother's favourite, his incendiary death in the night sky over the Eder Dam in '43 only compounding her prejudice. To me he wasn't much more than musty clothes and nondescript oddments packed tight, in a swampy-smelling trunk tucked behind the furnace. That, and a few hand-tinted photographs set in silver frames on my mother's bureau before she moved out, was all he was to me. But he was also the reason I was named Gideon.

One photo was from wartime — my uncle smiling broadly and squinting into the lens, stripped to the waist, lying on the wing of his plane with his palms cradling the back of his head. I suppose less was expected of a man's body in those days, and perhaps the prospect of a sudden, bloody death made scrawny guys less inhibited about taking off their shirts, but it's a wonder a fella could go to war and still look like a pushover.

The other picture had been taken shortly before he'd left for England, and served him better. He was wearing spiffy black oxfords, brown, wide-wale corduroys, and a rumpled white shirt beneath a copper-coloured wool vest my grandmother had knit. He was grinning as though it were V-E Day, with his spindly arms thrown around his Mom and his wife, with his 10-year old sister, my mother, in the middle. They were standing in a crowded midway, beside an amusement ride that resembled an open, inverted umbrella with candy cane striping. Buckets hanging from its metal joints were filled with girls pretending to be scared paired with boys pretending not to be. My grandmother told me how the umbrella would open and close as it creaked about, the buckets swinging wildly from the horizontal to the perpendicular with the movement of its joints. "Aye," she said, "that was a fine ride. Biggest damn umbrella ever's been."

Before the war my uncle had designed amusement rides. He was just 20 when his idea for the Devil's Umbrella was sold to Francis Suchmann Pastimes (later to become KrazyWays Inc., one of the North American midway's seven sisters). It wasn't long before he received the green light for his first rollercoaster, the Eager Beaver, to be erected on the grounds of the Canadian National Exhibition. Frye had no interest in engineering or cost feasibility; Suchmann paid others, poorly, to worry about that. All he had was an intuitive sense for what made people drop a quarter to cheerfully wish they were dead. In those days of blitzkrieg, that counted for something.

And it had to be intuitive. From his childhood Gideon had refused all rides, including his own. "Our Gid didn't like to be spun about," Nanny said. "He had a tender belly ever since I dropped the cat on him that once." She also told me, with the smile of someone who couldn't quite believe she once cared about such nonsense, that she'd fiercely objected to the name "Devil's Umbrella." But the decision had rested with Mr Suchmann, so she hadn't held it against her boy.

I remember a very heavy, very black, leather-bound Bible in my uncle's trunk. It was Nanny's. There were two inscrip-

tions on its blotting paper. The first: "Dear Alma: 'Be not overcome of evil, but overcome evil with good' — Rom. 12:21.
Love Sarah — Christmas, 1922." (I wish I'd thought to ask
who Sarah was.) The second was dated July 13, 1935, "on the
occasion of your 16th birthday. 'He will not suffer thy foot to
be moved: he that keepeth thee will not slumber.' — Ps. 121:3.
Love always, Mum." Pressed between the pages of Second
Corinthians was a yellowed clipping from the *Toronto Telegram*:
"Mimico Lass Beats the Beaver":

> Young Elfie Wheatmore may be many things, but
> queasy she most definitely is not. As visitors to the
> Canadian National Exhibition can attest, riding the
> Eager Beaver but once takes a stalwart belly, but for a
> girl of 18 to test her intestines from sun up to sun
> down, every day but Sunday for three weeks, takes the
> kind of stamina that could teach Mr Hitler a thing or
> two about the indomitable Canadian spirit — should
> he have the stomach for it!
>
> "The Beaver's different every time," Elfie told us. "If
> it wasn't, I would have stopped long ago. I bore easily!"
>
> Elfie's devotion to the Eager Beaver caught the
> eye of Exhibition officials, who arranged for Elfie to
> meet the amusement's designer, Toronto's own Mr
> Gideon Frye. Frye, 21, is something of a sensation in
> the world of the midway, where many old carny
> salts have taken to calling the local lad "The Wizard
> of Ahhhs."
>
> "I'm delighted, of course, that Elfie finds my little
> ride so compelling," said Frye. "It's for people like her,
> after all, that I'm doing this sort of thing."
>
> Elfie's day ended with — what else? — a spin on
> the Beaver. This time accompanied by her new friend,
> "the Wizard." One guess who didn't look green about
> the gills at ride's end!

It was, apparently, my uncle's first ride on his — or anyone's
— coaster. But it was also the first time he'd fallen for a girl.

By the time they were engaged, Elfie had cajoled him into riding the treacherous Port Stanley Hog's Back and the notoriously untrustworthy Aldershot Axis Smasher. Thanks to Elfie, my uncle had outgrown vertigo like he had his Paddington Bear, which my Mom had inherited and kept on her night table into her 60s. Soon after they married, he enlisted in the Royal Canadian Air Force. Soon after his death, she rode the Eager Beaver to the crest of the first drop and stepped into the sky.

It was in all the papers, my Mom said. But she hadn't saved any.

1

"**Y**ou an' me, Gideon," my grandmother wheezed between slurps of her gin and tonic when I asked for a subscription to *TV Guide* for my 13th birthday, "we're different than them others, eh?" *Them others*, I understood, were my father and mother — a pair of old-school Trotskyites with little time for capitalist eye candy. Until, that is, my Mom hitched a ride with Jimmy Swaggart on the ever-metaphorical Road to Damascus, and Dad suddenly couldn't get enough of Canadian football.

From my bowel's first untoward movement (a scherzo, I'm told, conducted against a heavily-scored volume of Deutcher's *The Prophet Armed*), to the Sunday morning she flew away from us to live for a time with her sister in Birmingham — and particularly from the moment of my mother's conversion from Marx (and my father) to Christ — my grandmother and I had been a Grand Alliance of non-aligned souls. Her tiny sitting room down the stairs, always stinking of potpourri and a smoking picture tube, was the one place in the house I could rest in peace. It was the free space in my Game of Life; out of bounds for parents trying to raise my consciousness about the fall of Allende, and later, the resurrection of the dead. When my parents fought, I preferred Nanny's room to my own because it was usually the furthest removed from their state of permanent revolution, and the volume on her Zenith console was always cranked up so she'd have a shot at following her "stories." And since she'd often fall asleep while I was visiting, I was often left in my own company. I usually watched her television.

I started seeing a lot more of her the spring that Nixon resigned, after an old classmate of my mom's, someone with whom she'd long been out of touch, invited her to a Swaggart crusade at the CNE Coliseum. I remember the days before, the anxious lines on my father's face. Attendance, he argued, was "anti-revolutionary," and he offered to picket the rally with her in protest. ("What's wrong with us?" he whined. "We don't go to the barricades like we used to.") My mother confessed she'd always sort of enjoyed Swaggart's singing voice and why shouldn't she go and what was he afraid of, anyway?

He should have had his reason, ever since Mom accepted his proposal with, allegedly, an off-handed "What the hell?" It embarrassed me, even as an adolescent, to hear them tell that story. I knew even then that considering marriage demanded a tad more *gravitas*.

Dad used to say Mom looked like a vanilla sundae in her wedding dress. The wedding photos are more dulled than his memories; Mom looks like two modest scoops poured into a caramel-coloured sugar cone. A tiny smile plays with the corner of her lips that could have meant *I love you* or *I can't believe we're doing this*. They tied their slipknot in Calgary, for the benefit of his parents and a Jasper honeymoon.

While she was out, my father found time to watch *SWAT* with me. He even asked my grandmother to come up and join us, which was unusual, as he typically coped with her presence downstairs by embracing her upstairs' absence. She declined.

She was happy to be left alone with her gin and imported sweets once I'd told her there was a *Sanford and Son* listed she hadn't seen.

It's one in the morning and I'm Barney Rubble. I'm walking through a scene with the Great Gazoo when Flintstone stumbles onto the set, refreshed after happy hour at the lodge, and promptly knocks me out with his lunch (Bronto ribs, naturally). When I come to, Fred's doubled over me, blubbering his "bosom buddy, life-long pal" routine, but I'm in no mood for that. I look up, from his toes that swell like ripening grapefruit to the shiny tips of his starched black hair, and tell him I'm one pissed Cro-Magnon. "Don't *fuck* with me, Flintstone!" Gazoo whispers something to Wilma that makes her laugh (What's going on between those two, anyway?), and I wish Betty were here. I awake with a start to an argument between voices I barely recognise. Mom and Dad.

The next morning when mother shook me awake for school, she said with a tremulous smile and gooey red eyes that she had died to the world; Christ had made her a new creation. She'd been renovated, she said: "What yesterday had been an abandoned flop house has become a temple of the living God!" I didn't have a clue what she meant, but I knew enough to be scared.

Dad was mortified. God had never been an issue for him. He'd always taken his disbelief on faith, and would have presumed the Road to Damascus to be nothing but a hoary Crosby/Hope comedy. But once his wife was born again he became a student of atheism to turn her head and trust her heart would follow. "Jesus was a good man," he'd say. "A revolutionary, even. But to believe everything in the Bible! That the world's 6,000 years old ...." Mom would begin by smiling indulgently, quoting the latest Scripture she'd committed to memory, but often wound up screaming that he was going to Hell and she wouldn't be held responsible for it. It was times like these that I'd decide it was time to visit Nanny.

"A man forced his pig and it died," she'd often say without elaboration, once I'd settle into her musty, lemon sofa beside a bowl of calcified fruit drops. I never knew what she was talking about. I was just glad to be there, out of the reach of old Phil Ochs LPs or a gospel "translated into the idiom of today's youth" my folks would try to fob off with a promising, "close your eyes and hold out your hands." Unlike my bedroom, which could only be locked from the outside (though thank Christ it never was), my grandmother's basement suite was an inviolate demilitarised zone.

Tabula rasa and *erasa;* we *were* different than them others. Faith, secular and religious, was rolling snake eyes throughout my adolescence, as it was for my grandmother ever since she'd heard her son had fallen from Heaven. I got a boost from my grandmother's cranky disbelief — it helped me say "Thanks, but no thanks" whenever I felt pressed to choose sides.

We didn't talk much, even when she was awake. She might ask what they were fighting about now, or if there was anything good on. If we tuned into a rerun of *Bewitched* boasting "that bloody bugger," the second Dick, she'd likely mutter some Edwardian imprecation of quaint gibberish, ask me to pour her another g&t, "there's a good lad," and keep watching until she fell asleep. We were more comfortable watching bad television than was good for someone of either our ages; certainly far more than my folks, what with their educating the masses and, later, my mother's preparing the way of the Lord, and all.

Nanny left for England when I was 14, but I felt 5 that morning at Terminal One; red-eyed and clutching a bag of licorice allsorts she'd bought for me, not knowing when I'd see her again.

Less than six months later — around the time of the Mayaguez incident — my parents split up. One evening, while Dad was recounting the problems jiving the chronologies of the synoptic Gospels, she walked out and into her old classmate's apartment. All she'd taken was her Bible and tampons; four days later she returned with her friend for the rest of her things. A month later she had a rented bungalow and I went too, because everyone expected that of me.

Left with scant sanctuary from my mother's grasping faith —
not to mention my roaring antipathy towards her for the melt-
down of our nuclear family — my father's politics suddenly
seemed a liberal, inviting alternative. Though weekly Mom
would cajole me into joining her for Pastor Vern Filmore's
three-point, 40-minute sermons, I slowly began to cultivate a
secret life of subversion that I thought would make my old
man swell like the Red Flag seized by an eastern gale.

It began with my Radio Shack short-wave radio — an old,
didactic gift from my father to wean me from American television. I'd hardly used it before, but within a month of moving
out I'd graduated from the white noise of the police band and
was regularly tuning in to Radio Peking. I spent hours, some
evenings, twiddling the dial for gossip from Mao's China. The
Great Helmsman was still alive then, and the news was intoxi-
cating and strange. I toyed with my geometry homework
while listening to reports of campaigns to educate the masses
by the examples of exemplary peasants. I hummed along with
the heroic operas of the Long March, celebrated the weeding
out of capitalist roaders, and nodded sagely to the warnings
against Brezhnevian revisionist hegemonism. Occasionally I'd
listen to Havana and Hanoi and, on rare nights, quite late
when I wasn't masturbating to the grainy memory of my science teacher's panties when she crossed her legs on a classroom stool (*"why Mrs Pocaradi, I had no idea…!"*), I'd pick up a
weak English transmission from Albania. It sounded as distant
as Alpha Centauri.

It was 1975: Nixon was gone, Angola was free and we
could still believe that Pol Pot meant well.

I embraced communism only when my Mom no longer
approved, so it felt properly wicked and delicious. She found me
out on account of my having requested a programming guide
from Radio Peking. One late afternoon after soccer practice, I
clopped home in muddy cleats to find her sitting at our kitchen
table clutching my mail from the People's Republic. The rice
paper envelope had been slit and resealed in a clear plastic

pouch stamped with the mark of the Royal Canadian Mounted Police. "What will the mailman think?" I remember her moaning.

She didn't know what to make of me. Her bilious self-assurance that it was "just a phase" only encouraged further acts of civil disobedience. I took down my Guess Who posters and entered my period of socialist realism. Agitprop collages with block red caps began popping up. "SOLIDARITY WITH THE WORKERS AND PEASANTS OF SOUTH YEMEN!" wheezed one. "USA OUT OF NORTH AMERICA!" another bawled. My bedroom was a Marxist Magic Kingdom where I could liberate Alaska and deliberate with my fantasy cabinet. (*Minister of Finance, Milton Acorn?* My eyes watered at the thought.)

I wasn't surprised — though I was surprisingly hurt — when upon my 15th birthday, upon the counsel of Pastor Filmore, Mom chose to trust the Lord for my soul and let me live with my father, who had decided he wouldn't mind having a little fellow traveller around the house.

I didn't mind, either. It was good to sniff about the only place that had smelled like home to me.

It stank of solidarity forever.

To credit my father, my nascent Maoism was never much of an issue to him, even though, down to his Troskyite bones, I was committing egregious heresy. He dismissed it, largely, as youthful ignorance and overzealousness; something I would undoubtedly outgrow given the right literature and emotional muzak. After all, I was only fifteen, and discounting an hour spent on the American side of the Falls six years before, I'd never left the province. How could I be expected to appreciate the vanguard role of the urban proletariat or be on guard against the Stalinist fallacy of socialism in one country, let alone know the essentially reactionary nature of the petty land-owning peasant masses? Besides, he seemed honestly happy as hell to have his son back.

At this time, I was working after school and on Saturdays in a musty shoe store on Mount Pleasant Avenue. It was where I had my first close encounter with a woman's privates.

Mylo's Discount Shoes typically drew mature women smelling of mothballs and perms, searching out sensible shoes to fit their insensate feet. Our shop specialized in the hard-luck cases: the women the chains wouldn't look at once if given the chance, who had bunions like hazelnuts but still wanted to cha-cha-cha. There was a sense of mission about Mylo's that I picked up naturally. If these hobbled souls had faith enough to brave the smouldering cigarette butts, the pools of bitters piss and rotweiller excreta of our store front, then I wanted to be able to tell them with confidence, "Take up thy bed and walk." Mylo's was the problem foot's Hail Mary, and I saw us — sometimes — as miracle workers, helping our customers make it to the grave on their own two legs. Other times, the Great Commission meant nothing more than 20% off the top. Mylo's served no men, and few women below pensionable age, so when a slender, late-20s beauty with a close-cropped black bob strolled in, bare-legged in two-inch heels, a black skirt and red halter that clung to her with sweat, she did not go unnoticed.

I may have just turned 16, but I had a cock that, like a colicky babe, cried hysterically for attention every half hour. She smiled at me; I blushed and twisted awkwardly to hide the bold new crease in my pants.

With me in the store were Barry Myron, grandson of the "My" in "Mylo," who was working his way through a degree in endocrinology, and Nick Granakis, the thick-lipped, pooch-faced assistant manager who had been selling shoes since he'd left the Greek army half his fifty years before. The three of us were occupied with other customers, but Barry and Nick began to rush their sales, each hoping to be the one to serve her. She just browsed, occasionally scratching the back of her neck and smirking in the mirrors at nothing in particular.

Nick beat us to her, but the woman was still "just looking." Barry was so distracted that he fit a left walking shoe on a decrepit regular's swollen right. (She liked it, however, and eventually bought two pair.) My customer finally strolled, and when I asked the dark-haired beauty if I could help she promptly smiled again, sat down and stretched a leg between mine. "Fit me for a pump," she sighed. I found a foot scale and crouched before her. When I dared to look between her legs, I saw she wasn't wearing any panties. *Omigodomigodomigod*: the first live, naked girlie-equipment of my life.

I might have shown her a dozen shoes but I wasn't counting, or even giving much thought to what I showed her. The store's selection, by design, wasn't sexy, but with each fitting I'd hold her higher on the back of her calf, letting my hand slide slowly over the contour of her heel as I'd slip it into the shoe. She stayed long enough for the crowd to thin, and through much of it Barry and Nick sat staring at us, whispering to each other and shaking their heads. Eventually Nick left, looking clammy and agitated, for his usual lunch across the street at Mr Submarine, and Barry muttered he was going downstairs to "rotate stock." We were alone, and couldn't be seen from the doorway or windows thanks to a rack of canvas sandals reduced to clear.

I licked my lips and looked again between her legs. Did she know? Of course she did. Her carnal smile bearing down on me said she did. But nothing like this had happened to me before. Could I trust my good fortune? I wanted to let my tongue trace her salty, soft leg till I found the sticky sweetness where one thigh met the other, but I was still afraid the moment I stuck out my tongue for her she'd run screaming for the cops. (It didn't even occur to me that she might get in trouble too, for corrupting the morals of a youth.) Pussy lips practically in my face, sweetly singing "Come on-a my place," but I wasn't convinced one hundred percent that they were singing to me.

Barry bounded up the stairs, looking noticeably more relaxed, and the woman soon said sorry, but we had nothing she wanted, and was gone. She couldn't have been in the store for more than 30 minutes, but it was enough to imprint a new erotic ideal upon my id. Until then, busty, big-lipped vixens with Farrah-hair had cavorted in my night-sweats. Now, it was time for slender, leggy brunettes from the Louise Brooks' School of Sexual Pathology to assume the lion's share of my fantasy life.

I happened to see her again a couple of months later when she came by to see Steve Loeb, son of the founding "Lo" in "Mylo," my boss and, coincidentally, her husband. She smiled at me in passing, an unspoken admission of something shared, but there was no carnal spark. Still, I blushed and twisted at the waist again. I found a job closer to home soon after and never saw either Loeb again, nor discovered if he had known of or even planned her adventure. I didn't think so at the time, but now I'm not so sure. Now, as an adult, I know what we're capable of suggesting.

And even though it had come a bit late, and I'd balked at loosening the final ribbon, it was a hell of a birthday present for a 16 year old. She'd given me the perfect gift: a story to tell back to myself when no one else could hear.

My father's small, radical clique of disaffected ex-NDP Wafflers and Spartacus League die-hards came and went, drinking acrid coffee ground from the beans of Honduran co-ops and bitching about Trudeau's wage and price controls. They'd suffered a big blow when the Yanks fled Saigon, and now numbered in the low severals. Before mother's conversion my Dad had begun to think them ludicrous. By the time I returned home, he had become their leading light. I supposed he was warming to desperate causes.

With the tenacity of pubescence I began to find the life of a teenage communist a hard thing. Were the Beatles right? Would I really not make it with anyone, anyhow? When, one evening, my father showed more interest in defending the suppression of the Krondstadt Rebellion than in the score of my soccer game, even when I'd been prepared to lie that I'd scored the winning goal, I quietly decided enough's enough. Behind my bedroom door, under the ferrous gaze of Che, I called Mom and told her I was interested in her church's summer youth retreat. Her jaw must have hung slack and dumb at the news, as though she were about to receive the body and the blood.

"You're not having me on, are you?"

"No, no. Might be a nice change. For a change."

"Well then, praise God!" Unintentionally, it seemed I'd answered a prayer. "A boy your age needs some fun. Not to mention food and fellowship." She giggled, nearly hysterical. "The three f's!"

Hanging up I turned on the radio, switching the band from short wave to AM, dialling away from Radio Tiraña and tuning into CHUM's Top 30. I pulled something by Isaac Asimov out from beneath a collection of Mao's poetry, stretched back upon the bed and fell asleep to Paul McCartney and Wings.

Why doncha listen t'what the man said?

2

The Cliffside Baptist youth retreated to 100 acres of Muskoka scrub 90 miles north of the city; an investment property of a Hong Kong émigré who'd given his life to Christ in a recent "I Found It!" campaign. There were four counsellors and two dozen campers: mostly God bullies who wore *Jesus, the Real Thing* t-shirts and rattled off the names of born again athletes as though introducing the home team's starting line for the Judgement Bowl. One or two others were my friends, and a few more near-friends, who agreed that, like the swarming black flies and our peeling noses, fellowship was a nuisance tag-along to the fun and food.

Our tents were pitched on a narrow, weedy carpet between shallow Lake Oompah and an outhouse that had the barbed reek of thriving faecal coliform. The boys preferred, like boys of most faiths might, to disappear into the bush to piss on the dogwood and wipe their asses with handfuls of mature maple leaves. The few girls held their noses and voided their bowels with fearsome modesty.

Up the road half a mile there was a field cleared for us. Most afternoons and evenings, between Bible Study and camp-fire singsperation, we'd be there, playing interminable games of softball. The preaching didn't convince me God was good, but so long as He let me hang out in the outfield with Patti Hula I didn't mind him overmuch. Christ and Marx could have been a law firm from the end of the world for all I cared: from that unnumbered inning when we split a pack of banana-flavoured BubbleYum, Patti was my Alpha and Omega. She was a year older and almost a foot shorter than me, with shoulder-length hair as red and rich as a Saviour's blood. Her breasts were small — half a mouthful, I imagined. She was handsome, not beauti-ful, and then only just; but she hooked me with her loopy grin out there near the ragweed and gopher holes. More than once I shouted "It's yours!" just to watch her trifling nipples poke at her sweaty-T as she stretched to catch a pop fly.

Patti came from what was politely called an "unchurched" family, and didn't know Eve from Adam. She'd been invited by her friend Marinda Learner, who undoubtedly was hoping for an easy conversion and another crown across the Jordan. It didn't look good for Marinda. The Word of the Lord neither hardened Patti's heart as it had the pharaoh's nor melted it like Simon Peter's. She was curious, certainly, and listened with considered attention to the stories from the life of Elisha, though she would do the same for snippets from any unfamil-iar heroic fantasy. Hobbits and prophets, Christ and Frodo, magic rings and resurrections from the dead — she absorbed it all, but that she was expected to accept Jesus into her heart left no sensible impression.

Every night I'd strategize to plant a big wet one, or even a hard one, on Patti Hula. She wore a roomy vinyl poncho in foul weather, almost big enough for two, so maybe I could say, "Got a hand under there I can hold on to?" Maybe not. If it were hot and there were no counsellors in sight, I could offer to massage oil into her shoulders while she lay by the shore

with her eyes closed and her lips slightly parted. *If it were hot* ....
The thought of sweat pooling in the small of Patti's back while
I kneaded her freckled flesh reminded my hand of a rhythm
never far from my mind.

Coward that I am, we didn't touch until the final campfire.

Our evening conflagrations were set on the lip of a cliff
almost a mile from the lake: a Precambrian wall 60 feet high,
poking through the mossy earth like an old shark's tooth.
Though the cliff stood at right angle to the world, along the
winding footpath from the shore and our tents, the slope barely registered. The clearing was a dirty circle of ragweed 80 feet
across, proscribed by adolescent spruce and a licorice night
sky. There was a sickly-looking bush half over the cliff's edge
next to which, once the girls had retired to their tents, some
male counsellors would stage urination contests, not noticing
the dirt they pissed out of it's arthritic grasp.

Pastor Filmore was to arrive our last night in order to
deliver the closer: our final campfire message. It would stink of
sulphur and Christian gore, full of If-you-should-die-tonight
logic, crafted to literally scare the hell out of us, and the
bejeezus into us.

"Last year out at Burke's Falls all that Lake of Fire stuff ter-
rified me so much I nearly got born again and again and
again," Terry MacRury told me after breakfast on the morning
of our last full day. "It's not like his sermons back home. Here
he really let's it all hang out."

Filmore had been scaring kids shitless for ten years' worth
of these retreats, almost all of them held on the sprawling
grounds of a well-appointed evangelical camp outside Elmdale.
But rents were up and collections were down, and for a time it
was feared the Cliffside retreat would be downsized to an
evening of nanaimo bars and gospel records in the church
auditorium. Filmore, I was told, thanked God frequently in his
sermons for providing the property through the charity of a
recent convert, though he'd visited the site only once.

We'd expected him to arrive in time to share our evening
chili and Tang, but when the last spoon of Laura Secord but-
terscotch pudding was licked clean and he hadn't shown, camp

leader Drew Tallboys called the other counsellors aside for a whispered huddle. I sidled up to Patti, who was waiting with Marinda for a pair of dragonflies to leave their mosquito net so they could grab some snacks and flashlights for the campfire.

Sarcasm sloshing everywhere, I muttered, "Gee, I sure hope he isn't lost."

"Say it ain't so," Patti smiled. She wouldn't mind either way, but it was nice to hear her play along. Marinda frowned and sighed heavily. Then she knelt down, plucked a half-buried stone and tossed it at their tent flap. One dragonfly buzzed towards the lake, the second towards a weaving, screaming Marinda.

Five minutes later, after a brief prayer, the huddle broke. Tallboys announced that Curtis Drieger — coincidentally, winner of the previous night's pissing contest — would remain at lakeside to await Filmore's unmistakable burgundy Buick LeSabre. The rest of us would accompany Tallboys and two other counsellors up the footpath to the cliff for our campfire.

The first 30 minutes each evening we humiliated ourselves for Christ's sake with nonsense songs. I preferred Yano Leimerman's lesson on Paul's use of the aorist imperative in Ephesians 6:13 to one more chorus of "Rocco Ate My Taco." Singing was bad enough. The broad, spastic gestures by the light of a gibbous moon made it unbearable.

These were not selections from the Baptist hymnody — they came later — and there wasn't even one vague allusion among them to the propitiatory work of our Saviour. "Rocco Ate Mt Taco" could just as easily be sung by an assembly of abjuring Shinto youth, or a pimply gang of pointy-eared Trekkie conventioneers while awaiting a celebrity Q & A with George Takei. We were a mandala of mock flagellants and nutty professors, exorcising our demons of frivolity by exhaustion and embarrassment, in order to be *good* and good and tired for the gospel songs, sermon and sloppy confessions of thought, word and deed that inevitably followed.

Everyone but Patti and I had finished eating and were beginning a crowd pleaser called "We're from Nairobi" when I noticed two figures stamping towards the clearing.

We're from Nairobi and we're on the best team
We do the watusi we're seven feet tall.

Patti still had a couple of marshmallows melting on her
whittled maple twig, and I had room for at least one more
Shopsy's dog, so I coolly lifted one from Tallboys' bag while
he kept on singing and thrashing and impaled it to half its
length through the circular seam of its prick end.

The cannibals may eat us
But they'll never beat us
'Cause we're from Nairobi and we're on the ball.
Sing along! Sing ALONG!! SING ALONG!!!

I'd refused to join in since Leimerman had led the group
through the opening number, "Rodney the Round-Eyed
Chinaman." It was an ugly doggerel of pigeon English which
frequently required both hands pulling one's eyelids tight or
forming the point of a coolie's hat above one's head. I chose to
protest silently, eating early and often throughout the song,
filling my hands and mouth as much as possible. She might
just have been hungry, but Patti did the same.

"We're from Nairobi" called for us to leap up at the end of
each verse, beat our arms and stomp our feet wildly, and chant
"*Ungawa! Ungawa! Ungawa! Ungawa! Ungawa! Ungawa!
UngaWAWA!!*" It was a favourite of the counsellors.

As the second verse began, Drieger ambled out of the
darkness, while Pastor Filmore stepped softly into deeper shadows. He disappeared to my right, in the direction of the counsellors' piss-bathed bush. I ate my hot dog and didn't think
much of it, until during the chorus I heard the scrabbling of
rubber soles on rock and a shower of gravel off the cliff face.

"Um, I think maybe —"

"Pastor?" Drieger looked puzzled as he entered our circle
and the fire danced in his eyes. The singing stopped. "Pastor
Filmore? He was right behind me ...."

"He's fallen over the cliff!" Terry's voice was a mix of horror and delight at having scooped the rest of us.

"Oh, my Lord! *No!*"

Patti was on her feet and with me as we scampered to the edge of the rock, where Tallboys fell to his belly and slithered until his head and shoulders were suspended in space. He cupped his hands to his mouth and bleated Filmore's name. Then we all called.

"Shut up!" Tallboys snapped. But there was no one answering. No sound at all.

"Drew," said Drieger calmly as he knelt beside him, "we've got to go down there."

Tallboys nodded. "You and me." He threw himself erect, ran to the circle and grabbed the nearest pair of flashlights. He whispered a brief something to Yano, who had been hanging back close to the fire, and disappeared with Drieger.

"Everybody now, come on, back away from the edge there," said Yano with a tremulous voice. He wasn't built for life in the bush — his arms and legs were marked with appalling bruises from turning over in his sleep — but as a recent graduate of Overcomer Bible Institute, Yano commanded respect as the camp's uncontested spiritual leader. (Though he wouldn't join the other counsellors in their pissing contests, he also refused to cast judgement upon them, deciding it was between them and the Lord.) In the gross physicality of Muskoka he seemed like a skittish house cat left with strangers for a weekend, looking for a low table to crawl beneath. "Let's gather around the campfire and pray," he suggested.

Patti moved towards Yano on the opposite side of the fire, and I moved towards Patti to close the circle. I barely noticed when Patti took my hand. I glanced at her and saw her eyes were shut tight, her mouth open and moving without making a sound.

"Oh Lord," Marinda began uncertainly, and then was racked with sobs. "Please, Lord —"

"Jesus," whimpered Terry. "I just —"

"Please let Pastor Filmore be okay."

"Yes, God." It was Patti. I knew it was her more by the tensing of her palm than by the sound of her voice. It was remote and humourless. It was as if I'd never heard it before.

"God," I managed to say after a long silence, "just make everything better." Yelps of amens and tears surrounded me. Then I squeezed my eyes shut.

I opened them at last during Yano's scripturally-rich yet rambling prayer, at the sound of voices and cracking twigs outside our small circle. I squinted through the smoke and falling cinders and could make out three figures in the flames, burning yet unconsumed. The large shape in the middle had his arms outstretched upon the shoulders of his two companions. As he approached, I saw across his forehead a dark slash of blood. His shirt was ripped at the belly where it had snagged on a branch. At first his face seemed expressionless, but as he drew closer I realized it had jammed at a singular moment of astonishment. Yano poured a cup of grape Freshee from his thermos and rushed to his side. Patti squeezed my damp palm even harder.

"He landed between two huge boulders!" Tallboys shouted. "A little to either side and he'd be dead for sure!" He handed Yano the flashlight he'd grabbed, who then set it down within the fire circle.

"You used *this* flashlight?" Patti breathed. "It's mine. I've been trying to get it to work for days." She took her hand from mine and pressed it to her forehead. "It's a miracle," she whispered, trying to understand.

"I'm a miracle," Filmore mumbled as he passed us, a dribble of blood streaking his cheek and spotting the grass at Patti's feet. Then he stopped and looked back at me with wide, vacant eyes.

"You," he said, feebly pointing. "I was coming up behind you. Sneak up. Surprise. You weren't singing. Meant to surprise. Supposed to be funny. *Jesus...!*"

Five minutes later I knelt with Patti and two others beyond the circle of the fire, where the black flies were thickest, and asked Jesus to enter my dumbfounded heart.

3

"So basically," I said, taking a deep breath full of sock dust lifted from the crusty, amber shag carpet and borne upon the buttery steam of fresh popcorn, "that's how I came to know the Lord."

I scooped a few kernels onto a paper napkin which was so oily I could see through it to the arm of the lavender sofa and passed the bowl to Dylan Geisler, a jumpy sophomore who had been crossing and uncrossing his legs all evening. All we'd heard from Dylan had been a timorous "Praise God" when Tibo Fung described his exorcism in the Marshall Islands. Dylan whispered thanks and held the bowl tightly in his lap with both hands, and didn't eat from it.

"Wow," Joel Kajinsky murmured, bobbing his head like a lazy oil pump. Half of the two dozen other heads of the other occupants of the fourth floor of the Abner Henry Residence for Men did the same. "Heavy conversion, brother. Why'd you decide on Overcomer?" Donny Loveless, our floor leader, glanced at his Timex and rested his forearm immodestly upon the hip of his acoustic guitar.

Overcomer Bible Institute — in the world (though just barely, so it seemed) but not of it, artifact of dustbowl revivalism and factory outlet of global evangelism — God's big house in south central Alberta. I was there because I'd asked Jesus to help me pass my final high school geometry exam and the answer was "No." I accepted my 27% as a sign that Christ wanted me at a Christian college. O.B.I.'s academic admission requirements were not nearly as demanding as its measure of godly character.

"Because of its strong missions emphasis and commitment to the Word," I told Joel.

"Excuse me, bro'." It was a serene voice that I didn't recognize, addressing me from a doorway obscured by a brass lamp and pressboard bookcase laden with 20 years of Reader's Digests and maybe 20 pounds of raw turnips. "Why did your pastor jump off the cliff? Did the Lord tell him too?"

I twisted my neck towards the doorway. Stretched against the white casing trim was a sallow, spindly young man in a red terry robe, his slender fingers folded together at his groin around a sandy brown vinyl Bible. His thinning hair was the colour of his scriptures. His features were rudimentary and wholly forgettable.

"He didn't jump. It was an accident."

"Oh, right. *Accident.*" He spoke it as though the word lied against God and Heaven. "Sorry, brother. Guess I missed that part. We were late getting in from Calgary." Open-air evangelism, I imagined; O.B.I.'s Friday night crusade on the 12th Street Mall. Two Christian service points towards graduation. Two points of 50. "Still, no accidents with the Lord, eh?"

"He was trying to sneak up on me and this girl because we weren't singing. I'm not sure exactly what he was planning; just fooling around. Breaking the ice, I guess."

"Praise the Lord ...."

"It's like God made him fall just for you..."

"Kinda funny your church is called Cliffside," said Ferly Norman, the short, red-haired running-back of the senior football team. (Everyone called him "Tennessee" because he had an aunt in Nashville, though he'd lived all his life in Saskatoon. The name was his idea. He refused to answer to Ferly and we respected that.) There were nods and grunts of agreement all around our circle.

"It's the name of the street the church is on, but for that to be a coincidence .... I mean, the odds must be pretty wild."

"Astronomical," someone swooned.

"How about one more song before we pack it in?" Loveless suggested, picking over the salty husks of an earlier batch of popcorn. "Before I forget, remember to grab some turnips on the way out. Remember to thank the Newtons. A card, maybe, would be nice."

"'When the Roll is Called Up Yonder'?" Jerry "Nebraska" Cheeseman — my roommate and proud Nebraskan — suggested.

"Just three verses. Only 10 minutes before lights out."

In the dream Jesus says, "Fear not, I am with you always," and I believe him. I believe him even as our heavenly ascent is arrested; even as the bottom falls out of the world and I squeeze my eyes shut against the hole we're tearing in the sky. The air as we drop chafes my face and in the strange roar of metal, wood and wind I can't tell if I'm screaming, and I can't imagine why I wouldn't. I want to cover my ears but my hands are not about to let go of the steel bar that spans my lap. Is Jesus still there? Has he lied to me? I cock my head towards where he's supposed to be, dare a peek, and there he is: head snapped back with a laugh, thick curls blowing freely, his arms and wounded hands thrown carelessly high, all for the lovely hell of it.

In the Overcomer handbook, on page iii, I read this:

Welcome, Soldier!

That's right: a soldier in the army of the Lord! First you enlisted by confessing Christ as Saviour. Now it's time for boot camp, where you'll learn how to better wield your weapons of the faith. ("For we wrestle not against flesh and blood, but against principalities, against powers, against the rulers of the darkness of this world ...." Ephesians 6:12)

You've probably heard all kinds of stories about Overcomer. (No, we don't have blue sidewalks for men and pink for girls!) It is true, though, that we are a Bible school with a difference; a difference for which we make no apologies. What sets us apart from many other institutions of Christian learning is our philosophy of education, which encourages a personal RELATIONSHIP between the student and God's precious Word. Given this, it is important that worldly distractions be kept to an absolute MINIMUM. Still, you'll find a cheery atmosphere and many new friends with whom you can grow in the Lord.

I folded it back among the socks and cookies of my shoulder bag, then switched off the overhead light which had obscured the prairie night outside the bus. I'd read it many times already, and this was my first Alberta sky, one week before the dormitory floor "sing 'n share."

My father had driven me to the airport without many words left besides "Take care" and "I hope you know what you're doing." I'd expected him to fight my conversion like he had my mother's, but apart from a fit the first time he saw me bow my head over a plate of gluey macaroni, there was nothing. Before I could ask him — before I knew that I could — he had paid for my flight and tuition.

The Greyhound from Calgary made five scheduled stops before Three Trees and two after, but we didn't need to ask each other, "Are you going *there*, too?" — though we did. It was easiest to single out the male students. Our fabrics gave us away (too many double-knit polyester trousers; too little denim), or our haircuts (too short or too long or just right: whatever, they'd been paid too much attention), or our reflexive, embarrassing way of being in the world: a smug, godly *Nya-Nya* that said, "I know something you don't know." Female Bible schoolers were tough to spot. Every woman in Alberta dressed alike and looked equally God-fearing to me.

Airdrie; Crossfield; Acme .... The Christians had collected in the back of the bus, and by the time we reached Carbon we were singing all four verses of "Amazing Grace" with guitar accompaniment. I sang, too, but softly, not wishing to be a righteous nuisance to the half of the bus which didn't share our destination in this world and the next. From across the aisle I watched a beautiful sophomore named Monica close her eyes and raise her open palms to heaven (though only to shoulder height, so as not to draw attention to herself), while a track of tears glistened on her cheek like a scar from a duel with the Devil. That first night, as I turned back to the window and the cold dank of the world, the wheat fields seemed as strange to me as lunar seas.

"Uncle Corey used to have this expression at the dinner table — I ever tell you boys about Ol' Corey? — Anyhow, he used to say, 'Not as good as skinned cat'."

"Jeepers, Jerry," Montana whooped. "We're *eating*." (Kansas, Montana, Tennessee .... In four years not once did I meet a student nicknamed Yukon or Manitoba or Prince Edward Island, though I did meet a guy from Fredericton who called himself "Dallas.")

"No matter what he was served, whenever we'd ask how it was, that's what he'd say."

"Did he ever eat *here*? Anybody know what *this* is?"

"So anyway, we all got a little tired of hearing this —"

"Why didn't you just stop asking him?"

"So just before Corey's next visit Dad went and caught this stray cat."

"No *way*!"

"Mom wasn't sure what to do with it, but figured the meat'd look like chicken anyway. So when dinner came around there we were, right, all with barbecue chicken in front of us except Uncle Corey. We could hardly keep a straight face, watching him shovel it down. Good it was a big 'ol tab; he couldn't get enough. When he was sopping up the plate with the corn bread Dad asked him how it was. 'Great', he says. 'Not as good as skinned cat, of course.' Well, we all start hooting, and the look on Corey's face ... man, I wish I had a camera. And then of course he *pukes* right there."

This was my first supper in the O.B.I. dining room, and the last meal I intended to share with my roommate Jerry Cheeseman. The day before I arrived on campus, he had tacked a huge Ol' Glory Stars and Stripes to the wall at the foot of the top bunk, and taken the bottom bunk for himself. "Don't mind the flag, bro'," he'd told me before introducing himself. "They call it North *America*, right?" Jerry was an unabashed John Bircher who could not wrap his head around the idea of Canada. He loved Canada — what he'd seen of southern Alberta looked just like home — but our untimely Thanksgiving, three down football and universal health care seemed either whimsically foreign or perilously un-American. Gingerly, I let Jerry know how I felt about the stars and bars being the first thing I'd see between my legs by the dawn's early light. He suggested we switch beds. I agreed, not expecting him to continue his habit of kneeling next to the lower bunk for prayer. After his evening's devotions my sheets were often damp with his salty cries unto the Lord.

Jerry had a poster of Rembrandt's Christ on the road to Emmaus taped to the cupboard above his desk. A faithful reproduction, but for the Lord's crew cut. ("Nothing in the Bible proves Jesus had long hair. I'm not saying he had a crew cut. We just don't know. When he comes back I bet he will. Not that I'll actually place a wager. The Devil's a gambler, Daddy says.") All this and his "skinned cat" yarn confirmed him as a crypto-hillbilly cocksucker (though not in so many words: I'd been saved, thank God, from such a vocabulary). He was someone who could be trusted with neither big ideas nor small, furry things.

"So roomie," Jerry drawled, hitting the lights the night of our first floor meeting, "What do you make of Delbert Moon?"

"Which one was he?" In the long shadows of the lower bunk I pulled the sheets and blanket to my chin, brushing my penis back upon my belly.

"The late guy, who asked about that stuff with your pastor."

"Oh yeah." Careful so as to not inflame my loins, I flipped my cock down against my right thigh before folding my hands behind my head. An elbow was moistened by a stain of Cheeseman's tears and I rolled to my side in disgust. "What about him?"

"He's a funny guy." Jerry paused for my, "Funny how?" but I said nothing. He waited so long that I was nearly asleep by the time he added, "A *real* funny guy."

"Funny how?" I finally mumbled, but Jerry didn't answer. He was snoring a minute later.

My roommate aside (who was, I'm sure, my father's nightmare of what I would become), I was thrilled to be at Bible College. I threw myself into my studies and obedience training. I wanted to melt into the mould of God's plan for my life, which he'd known (and God *was* a he; the he*ist* He) since before the foundations of the world. I was delighted to be suddenly subject to the rules of sober men (and they *were* men; and by God they were *sober*) whose selfless, sole concern was that I and my classmates grow into the disciplined officer core of the Church Triumphant's shock troops. My hair is too long, and has to be off the collar and behind my ears? Off it comes. I'm to be woken daily at six for a 30 minute spell of private prayer, and I'm to be asleep by 10:30 (11 on weekends) after another half hour of compulsory devotions? Hey, I'm awake — I'm asleep. No *folk* music, not even Burl Ives, let alone rock and roll? I'll take my Heavenly Father over Big Daddy 10 times out of 10. (And even now Bob Dylan — *that* Bob Dylan — was singing about Jesus and the End Times and being born again. *How much am I,* I thought, *on the right side of history?*) I'm permitted to speak with female students on the O.B.I. grounds, but only so long as we're walking, and walking in opposite directions? I don't have a problem with that; I can do without. *I can do* *without everything but the Truth,* I wrote in the flyleaf of my Bible my first night on campus, *and without everyone but Jesus.*

Overcomer Bible Institute had been a baby of the Great Depression; conceived, delivered and breastfed by the Reverend Charles Kaye Barstowe of the popular *Glory Hour* radio program. As a young Baptist minister in rural Alberta, Barstowe believed he had heard the call of God to evangelize China, and was to sail with his wife and child for Shanghai when, as described in his book, *At Home with God*, "God stopped me with a cow":

> We'd brought in nearly all the Derby's crop of bar-
> ley, such as it was, when a great ruckus drew us to the
> barn. "Father! Edwin! Pastor! Come quick! It's Libby!"
> Derby's youngest lad, Pelton, cried at the top of his
> nine-year-old lungs. When we arrived upon the scene
> Pelton's eyes were wide as saucers, and he was jumping
> up and down as he shouted, "Libby talked! Libby talked!"
>
> "What do you mean, boy?" The elder Derby, as
> flummoxed as I, asked with the patience of Job.
>
> "I was cleaning out her stall, just like you asked,
> and she lifted her big face towards me and said
> 'Proverbs 16:9.'"
>
> "What do you mean?" the good farmer repeated.
> "Our cow's quoting scripture?"
>
> "She didn't quote it," Pelton explained. "She just
> gave the reference."
>
> "'A man's heart deviseth his way, but the Lord
> directeth his steps,'" I recited.
>
> "Cows can't talk, you crazy pug!" said Edwin, tear-
> ing a strip from his little brother.
>
> I said nothing while the family argued their
> heifer's loquaciousness. Finally, Derby sent the chil-
> dren away so as to confer with me in private.
>
> "Perhaps it is true," he ventured cautiously. "If God
> could speak through Balaam's donkey, I suppose He
> could speak through my cow. Perhaps it's a sign that
> you're meant to stay."

"Brother Derby," I began, "I have no doubt that God could speak through a rheumatic cockroach if He saw fit. I think, however, that young Pelton is the author of this 'miracle'. You know of course that he's quite good chums with my boy Matthew, and he's dreading the thought of our sailing.

"Furthermore, I believe that Miss Ibbotson's lesson last Sunday drew heavily from the 16th chapter of the Book of Proverbs. Ask him about this before we call it the Lord's work. If he confesses, let your correction be gentle yet firm — he meant well, though his little heart came close to blasphemy."

I waited in the barn while Derby repaired to the house to confront his son as to the cow. As I suspected, Pelton owned up to it all, weeping mightily upon his father's breast for forgiveness. (Which he was given — along with a tender paddling, of course.) I was in no shape for self-congratulations, however, for shortly before Derby returned to collect me the cow suddenly dropped dead, falling upon my legs and breaking them both. Regardless of whether God had spoken through the animal in life, He spoke clearly through her in death: my travel plans were immediately cancelled.

Within the year Derby surprised Barstowe with a deed to one quarter of his land, with the provision that he build a Bible school upon it. (In his mischievous *Your Shoes Are Too Big, Lord*, the late, self-ordained Reverend Beau Hammond of the Beiseker Four Square Christian Academy hinted that Derby's cow had been demon possessed. During the autumn of '43 the issue was more hotly debated in some prairie evangelical parishes than the timing of a second front or the true count of Hitler's testicles. To most believers of the day, Barstowe satisfactorily answered Hammond's charge with his famous *Glory Hour* sermon, "The Milk of Divine Kindness." Shortly thereafter, Hammond disgraced himself with a pair of war widows and returned to his native Montana, where his ministry flourished until the summer of '57 when three boys, drunk on their first guns and beer, mistook him for a scavenging, flannel-vested moose.)

Barstowe was still alive during my time on campus, though he'd passed the mantle of presidency to his son a decade before.

The years and the harsh prairie winters had shrivelled him like a failing star — a brown dwarf, not a black hole — and he seemed to have collapsed upon himself until all that was left was all that was necessary for him merely to be. Judging by the photos in his book and on the library walls, Barstowe had had a pinched and aged face — a face perpetually expecting a fist to be thrown at it — since his high school days in Lethbridge when he played goal for a junior hockey team, and each puck that struck his unguarded nose drew blood by the permissive will of God. *Holy* shit happens. "The determined set of his modest frame, when filled with the Spirit, has scared many a sinner to heaven," read the back cover blurb to *At Home with God*, but as his body twisted and withered to at last match his face, Barstowe grew quaintly freakish; becoming both more humane and less than human. Watching him and his wife of half a century carefully measure their steps from bungalow to church and back again, I'd sometimes reflect on the tenacity of God's grace or the persistence of godly love, but mostly I'd be reminded of a set of novelty ceramic salt and pepper shakers grown precious with age.

In the fourth floor washroom, early in the morning after our Sing 'n Share, Delbert Moon took the sink beside me, cocked his smooth head at a sharp angle and said, over the soft buzz of fluorescence and electric shavers, "I dreamt of you last night."

"Really?" I laughed, nervously, then squirted a ball of shaving cream into my hand and spread it thick across my neck and cheeks. "What was it about?"

"Not much," he answered flatly, pulling a disposable razor from the pocket of his scarlet robe while he stared absently at the mirror. "I just remember bits and pieces. It began with a birthday party for my sister on the lawn outside my house. Mom's place, actually. You show up with a big chocolate cake,

and just as my sister Lori's made her wish, a giant bear jumps
out of it and chases us all inside. I start running around, making sure all the doors are locked and the windows shut. Then
— I'm kind of fuzzy on what happens next — but after a while
I'm standing on this tiny island in the middle of nowhere with
you and an old man with a beard and pyjamas."

"No kidding?"

"Oh no. An Old Testament prophet, I think. The sea's rough
and filthy. I'm trying to keep clean and dry but there's no way. I
feel dizzy and think my head's bleeding, but you tell me I'm
OK. I say something like — I forget what, exactly — then you
give me a plastic whistle and the old man pulls out a bucket of
Kentucky Fried Chicken and we all eat. That's when I woke up."

"Whew. Pretty wild."

"I know. Amazing, eh?" Delbert leaned closer and chuckled
while he ran hot water over his blade until the basin steamed.
"I wonder what it means?"

"I haven't a clue."

Moon winced, as if he'd nicked himself, but his razor was
still in the sink. I twist my face up and away from his so I
could better shave my neck and put some distance between
us. His breath smelled sweet and ruined, like a butter tart in a
garden compost.

"Sounds funny." I smiled gamely. "Especially the chicken."

"Sure, sure, there's some humour in it," Delbert agreed, lath-
ering his cheeks. "But I wonder: maybe there's something else
going on." He must have glimpsed my unease because he
laughed curtly and shook his head, and then explained himself.
"Don't worry, bro'. I don't mean any of that Freudian garbage.
Freud and Jung," he spat, pronouncing the J as harshly as he
might for "Jesuit" or "Jehovah's Witness." "Reich — Have you
heard of *him*? — full of demons, all of them. We may as well
burn their books, because they're burning themselves right now."
He shook his head with revulsion, and then looked at me with a
slight, incongruous grin. "Sorry to go on like this. Anyway, all I
mean is, I wonder what the Lord's trying to tell me."

"Oh ...." That's what I was afraid he'd meant. After all, I
knew Freud only second hand, thanks to the Montgomery

Clift movie and bits on *The Carol Burnett Show.* "Don't you think
— I don't know — it could be just a dream, right?"

"*Just* a dream? Have you ever had *just* a dream? 'And it shall
come to pass that I will pour out my spirit upon all flesh; and
your sons and daughters shall prophesy, your old men shall
dream dreams ....' Joel 2:28. I think we always need to listen
for that still small voice, even in our sleep. Maybe *especially* in
our sleep. It's scriptural. It's like God's shortcut to our hearts.
Plus, this being the last days and all ...." Then softer, conspiratorially: "Not everybody here goes for that kind of talk. This
kind of talk, I mean. No one says anything, but a lot of people
suspect I'm some kind of Pentecostal or something." He shook
his head slowly, rolled his eyes and smiled.

"I'm sure God can use dreams," I said carefully, and in the
mirror caught Donny Loveless's concerned glance as he shuffled behind us before turning towards a urinal. At sinks on
either side of us and in stalls quietly feigning a shit, there were
godly men confirming their judgements of Moon and shaping
their judgements of me. There was a hush about us. The walls
wouldn't take our words, but they were absorbed by the
porous souls of holy ghosts. I wished Delbert hadn't singled
me out for conversation. I wished he hadn't told me his dream.
Most of all, I wished he hadn't dreamt of me. "The thing is, if
we really believe the Bible to be God's final Word, don't we
have to be awfully careful about how we interpret stuff?"

"Oh, absolutely, absolutely," Moon nodded vigorously,
drawing his razor with long strokes down his slender,
unlathered neck. There was silence between us until I wiped
my face dry. Then: "What's your schedule like today?"

"Well, Delbert, it's pretty crazy. Lots of stuff. Dean says I
need a haircut before classes Monday."

"Come by my room if you've got a minute. How's after
breakfast? It won't take long. There's something I'd like to talk to
you about. After breakfast then? Got something for you, too."

"Really?"

"Don't sweat it."

My room could have been any other in the Abner Henry Residence for Men. An olive, all-weather carpet stretched across an uneven floor 12 feet square, separating a pair of stacked, pine bunks bracketed to gyprock and a chipped, silver radiator beneath a small, screenless window that had been painted shut. Against each of the other walls a formica-topped desk squatted beneath pressboard cupboards and pressed against a narrow, oak-panelled closet with a door scuffed from years of radiator strikes. A cheap tuna-coloured loudspeaker — wired to the dean's office and without an off switch or volume control — was screwed into the plaster over the door. Every wall was antique white, and every ceiling washed in a stormy ivory stucco with a stingy splash of homely copper spangles. At night, in moonglow and the high-beams of infrequent traffic, it resembled the empty starfield of a hyper-extended universe.

The week of my arrival, I gathered with the other frosh in O.B.I's tabernacle for a special exhortation from Dean Blier on the godly principle of stewardship. He admonished us to "live as sojourners, calling no land but heaven home," and referred us to page 44 of the school handbook, where we read that room damage would earn us five property damage points. Twenty points could mean suspension; 30, expulsion. If we wanted to decorate our rooms we needed to use an adhesive putty called "NoMar," which was the colour and consistency of a dry wad of grape bubble gum and, taste aside, about as useful. In four years, the only friends whom I never heard grouse about the property damage rules were from Singapore, and therefore, I supposed, somewhat accustomed to pernickety despotism.

Despite the risk, few left their walls bare. In my first week I hadn't seen an unadorned, occupied room until I visited Moon's.

Delbert was sitting at a desk with his Bible open to Revelations, wearing a shirt the colour of unstirred yoghurt. His pants were a flared Tory-blue wool blend — too heavy, I judged, for this time of year, though his room seemed unusually cold — with ringmaster-white pinstripes as thick as pencil lead running up his shanks. Dressed like that, it seemed odd he was barefoot.

There were no posters on the walls, no books on the shelves, and the only bedding I could see was a rolled up khaki sleeping bag at the head of the top bunk. There was little evidence he lived there. He was an over-dressed extra on an under-dressed set.

"Hi bro — breakfast's over, huh?" He tucked a yellow felt highlighter in his breastpocket and folded the Scriptures shut. I nodded. "I hardly ever eat breakfast. Don't like to rush devotions. Come on in and close the door. Pull out the other chair." He read my face like I read Dagwood Bumstead's, and smiled as though he saw a halo of question marks. "I know. I guess I like things tidy."

"I guess. Where's all your stuff?"

"I don't need much — not like I used to. What I have, I keep out of the way. I refuse to be tyrannized by thinghood. I won't be possessed by possessions. Cluttered room means a cluttered mind. I like both of mine to be shipshape."

"My place is a mess already," I said as I sat. "Mostly my roommate's stuff. Books and socks and boot polish everywhere."

"I see, I see," Delbert grinned and nodded too sharply. "I've got a room all to myself. Where are you from, Gideon? *Gideon* — you've got such a neat name. He's one of my favourites from the Book of Judges. 'The Lord is with thee, thou mighty man of valour.' He's right up there with Deborah and Barek — way cooler than Samson. Casting the fleece to test the Lord — I mean, we do stuff like that all the time — but then, reducing the number of his army so the whole world would know that it was God's victory .... Now that's a real hero. You're fortunate to have such a neat name."

"I'm named after my uncle. He designed amusement rides. You ever heard of the Eager Beaver?"

"I *loathe* my name. 'Delbert' is my thorn in the flesh. Wish I had something historical. Martin Luther Moon, maybe."

"Church History's the best, man, I love that class. And Sophia Faulkner's a great teacher. I guess you must have had her too, huh?"

Moon leaned back, resting both elbows behind him on his desk, then crossed his legs and craned his neck to stare hard at his curled toes. And then ignored me.

"I mean, I can live with Delbert, if that's God's will, but my parents weren't Christians. Certainly not when they named me, anyway." He flashed a brittle smile. "My father was a drunkard and a complete whoremonger. Don't be shocked; I choose my words prayerfully. He was in Vietnam when I was born. A Canadian volunteer. Heard about them? Not many have. I don't grudge him his war. I'm still proud of whatever it was he did over there. It's just I wish he'd never come home." He took a deep breath and raised his eyes, briefly meeting mine. "Mom's a believer now, praise God. Only a couple of years old in the Lord. Only since Dad died. I know it sounds terrible, but it was the best thing that could have happened to her. Whether it was the best thing for him, I can't say. I just hope that he called on Christ before he lost consciousness." Moon took another deep breath and shrugged, then flashed me a strange, soft frown. "Maybe I shouldn't be telling you all this but it feels right to, and 'if our heart condemn us not, then we have confidence toward God.' Right?" I nodded, but he didn't wait for it. "Where you from, brother?"

"Toronto."

"Right, right. I remember from the other night." He shifted in his chair, raising one buttock and then the other just enough to sit on his hands, palms up. His thumbs poked out and occasionally drummed on his cheeks. "I was there once. I used to subscribe to *Maclean's*."

The static crackle of the loudspeaker interrupted Delbert. The Dean cleared a throat jagged with feedback, then informed us of an opening for the Sunday crusade team to Drumheller prison (worth 10 Christian service points), and confirmed that, henceforth, ties would not be required in the library on Saturdays after four p.m.

"Sodom," Moon sighed. "Toronto, I mean. Sorry, I know it's your home — it's just all those prostitutes, drugs and *theatres* everywhere. Man, it must take as much grace to live a godly life there as it did in pagan Rome — or like it still does in Rome, for that matter, what with the Pope and dirty Italian movies and all. It's a real fiery furnace, eh?"

"Oh, I wouldn't say —"

"I'm from Shadrach; up Peace River country? I couldn't even find it on a map, so don't feel bad. You'd think we'd know about fiery furnaces, but we got, like, six churches for 300 people and just one of them Catholic. Nobody blinks at a six-day creation, Noah's Ark, the whole biblical ball of wax. It's not right. There's no scandal to the Cross. Some people like that, but not me."

"Why?"

"When everyone's sanctified and set apart it's easy to forget how freakish we must seem — *should* seem — to the world. And I'm not just talking about folks out in Toronto, but to the liberals and papists in Edmonton and Peace River. It reminds me of something I heard the Keaton twins say... I can't remember exactly right now, but it was good. You ever heard the Keatons preach?"

"I don't think so, no."

"No? You don't know what you're missing, brother. Siamese twins out of the Amazon jungle, totally on fire for Jesus. It's really something to hear them preach the Word. My, my, my ..." He shook his head and snorted. "I think freakishness, if you want to call it that, is a spiritual gift. We should stick out like sore thumbs." Moon drew his breath sharply, then twisted his neck to stare vacantly out the window at a queue of jaded grain elevators. "No; we ought to be healthy thumbs. Christians ought to stick out like healthy thumbs on the mangled hands of the world."

Mentally, I was practising excuses for leaving when he said, "You must be wondering what I wanted to show you, right?"

"Sure," I shrugged. "Lay it on me."

"It's really just a little thing. Actually, it's got something to do with our conversation in the washroom. Remember? Just remember for a second." He leaned towards me slowly and dropped his voice like it was the other shoe. "Feeling embarrassed?"

"*Embarrassed?*"

"Ashamed I should say. Convicted, maybe?"

"No," I drawled slowly. "I can't think of anything."

"Hmmm." Moon took a deep breath but gave up just a tiny sigh. He arched his eyebrows and drooped his shoulders, and I felt as though I'd punctured him. "Okay. No problem; don't worry about it. It's not as though you're very old in the Lord — no offence. I have something you might find interesting."

Moon gave his desk's top drawer a couple of firm tugs. "A little stuck," he mumbled, curling a corner of his lip into an apologetic smile. Then he twisted in his chair and pulled harder.

The drawer, when it finally opened, was crammed with creased and mangled papers, at least a dozen pens (a good half of which, I assumed, must be dry), two Bible highlighters, a set of precision screwdrivers, a rusty garden trowel and maybe three bucks in pennies. As he strained to stretch his slender forearm towards the back of the drawer, I heard a muffled jangle which sounded like several vials of pills.

"Ah ha!" He took out a stained and dog-eared red pamphlet, closed the drawer with his elbow and pressed it into my palm.

"*Heck No! The Secret Sin of Minced Oaths,*" I read. "Hmm. Minced oaths? Sounds interesting." He frowned. "Interesting but, you know, like, sinful. So, what are they?"

"I didn't think you'd know," Moon beamed. "When you weren't embarrassed, I was hoping for your sake. They aren't things that worry most people, even Christians, but — well, let me tell you about them and you can decide for yourself. Now you take a word like 'heck'. Say, for instance, I show up for Mr Gurney's Doctrine class and he's got a pop quiz on soteriology. If I groan 'Oh, heck', there's not many around that would consider that foul language, even though we all know what 'heck' stands for, don't we?"

Delbert folded his hands behind his head, staring at me as though he didn't know a rhetorical question when he'd asked one.

"It stands for 'hell', doesn't it, Gideon?" I nodded, just to let him know it had sunk in. "Worse than heck, though, are words like 'golly' — a contraction of 'God is holy' — 'gee' for 'Jesus' and 'goshdarn' for ... well, I just don't want to say what, but you can imagine, I'm sure. And that's precisely the problem: you *can* imagine!"

"Oh," I said. But what I'd meant to say was, *Oh?*

"The best you can say about a minced oath is that its a loophole: a way to swear without saying bad words. But how do you think the Lord feels — believe me, I don't mean to preach at you, brother; every time I point a finger I've got three pointing back at me — when we twist his name to make it foolish, just to comfort ourselves that we haven't actually blasphemed? Why not curse and be honest about it? Better yet, why not acknowledge we'll be asked to account for every idle word? The hateful thing about minced oaths is that they follow the letter of the law, not the spirit, and 'the letter killeth, but the spirit giveth life.' I'm not making this up. It's all right there," he said, pointing at the pamphlet, "and there," pointing to the Bible.

"Pretty heavy stuff," I sighed after a moment's silence. Could he be right? He could be crazy, but I'd read enough Bible to believe he could be right *and* crazy. "I don't remember what I said."

"'Gee', if I recall correctly."

"Oh." Worse than 'heck', though no 'gosh darn'. I felt like shit. "Sorry. I didn't mean to offend you."

"Don't worry about it. Don't be hard on yourself." Moon knitted his brow and smiled grimly as he slowly, gracefully let a hand fall on my knee.

"Okay then. I'll try not to be."

"You've been a Christian now, how long? Not long, right?"

"Not long."

"You're still a babe in Christ. No offence."

"None taken."

"Just a babe." Now, I was offended. "Read the pamphlet and pray. I'm not asking you to take my word for it. I trust God for that."

"Alright. Thanks, Delbert." I wanted to leave, but Moon's motionless, leaden hand fixed me to the chair just as I used to press together freshly-pasted model parts while the glue set.

"Got something else that might interest you." Moon stood to open a cupboard and, as though he'd raised me up himself, suddenly I was standing at his side.

His cupboard was overstuffed with paperbacks and cardboard boxes. Most of the books were arranged in neat piles with their spines aligned on the left; some were filed, two deep, in vertical rows; others lay at odd angles over the piles and rows like a layer of frosting squeezed from across the room. The boxes, I imagined, held more books. I was startled, not surprised, when I realized they were all copies of the same book.

"Like to read? You read much? Ever see this?" Moon grabbed a copy from the top of the nearest row and handed it to me. Its cover was a coarse charcoal sketch of a pair of empty sandals against a lurid taupe and purple background. The book smelled bad, almost mossy, as though the sandals could use a pair of Odor Eaters. The book was a *Your Shoes Are Too Big, Lord*.

"Take it. I've got others. I think you'll find that the name of Beau Hammond isn't exactly honoured around here — you'll see why in the 8th chapter — but I find it a great devotional aid. If we're going to 'rightly divide the word of truth' then we're bound to make some unpopular choices. And I'm pretty unpopular," he chuckled mirthlessly.

"Okay. Thanks, then."

I squinted at the tract and the book in my palms, smelled the cover and felt a headache coming on.

"Why do you — I mean, all these books ...."

"My uncle — he's not really my uncle; more like an uncle in the Lord — my uncle has a little publishing company in Red Deer. He reprinted *Shoes* a couple of years ago. He always figured someone had it in for Hammond. I'm not saying it was Reverend Barstowe. All I know is my mother's going to heaven because of this book."

"Wow. It must be good."

"Precisely."

I thanked him again and told him I had to run. He said he'd like to talk again soon; perhaps we could have devotions together sometime? I said that sounded fine.

I knew he was nuts, but that didn't mean he wasn't right.

4

God is not a magician, but a Harry Houdini: a cosmic escape artist cheating Death and the Devil with a twinkle in his eye. The world wiggles with enchantment: a bothered nose, dripping blood like an Amityville faucet, recalls the blessed spigot tapping the veins of the sinless Son of Man. A smudge of rainbow in a puddle of gasoline pictures God's promise and threat that never again will the world be destroyed by water. Next time, it's fire.

Christ wears our flesh more comfortably than a politician dons hard hats and headdresses at election time. Of course, having once ascended to the right hand of the Father He reigns forever, but He doesn't neglect his constituency. He still cares about all his flock's lost loves and odd socks. Take the time to pray — always more expedient than writing your member of parliament — and every wrong will be righted and every hurt avenged in one world or another. Nothing is too trivial to escape the attention of a personal saviour: a comforting thought for a teenage fundamentalist with a clean conscious; a thought that sometimes haunted me at three in the morning.

When home for Christmas my first year of Bible School I began to suspect that my stereo, specifically my tape deck, was demon possessed. As Lucifer and a third of the angels fell on account of pride, and as my equipment — down to its three fat knobs for volume, balance and tone — was a 15-watt exercise in humility, I thought it judicious not to jump to conclusions. I only owned one Black Sabbath LP and had gone off Alice Cooper since my conversion. (Though as I anticipated Christmas break, I'd softly sung "School's Out" to myself a couple of times.) Most significantly, I never played anything backwards. But if there was one area of my life that I hadn't surrendered to the Lord (two, including my monkey-boy libido — Onan the Barbarian, another sweaty-palmed virgin for Christ), I had to admit it was my love of rock music.

Overcomer's music policy was strict but fair, forbidding as it did almost everything composed since the death of Sousa. This meant leaving my scratchy Stones albums at home for the school term. (I'd left *Frampton Comes Alive* in my mother's basement for the long, *long* term.) Rumours of Bob Dylan's baptism in Pat Boone's swimming pool lifted my spirits, encouraging me to hope that someday O.B.I. might come to accept that redemption could have a back beat. Until that great day, I determined that while on campus I would faithfully observe the music policy. Christmas vacation was another matter.

Of course I wanted to see my family, but I hadn't heard "Tumbling Dice" for three and a half months. In early December, during a pop quiz on the Pelagian theory of sanctification, I even found a moment to fantasize of my earthly reward: a big bottle of Coke, a family-sized bag of barbecue Lays and my precious, unscathed copy of *Exile on Main Street*.

Things took a turn for the unearthly my second night home. *Exile* was cooling on the turntable and I was lying on my bed nodding off to *Your Shoes Are Too Big, Lord*. Beau Hammond had just defended his dropping out of a B.C. Baptist seminary as "all I could do to salvage my soul. I'd been Daniel in a den of perverts, antinomians and closet hyper-Calvinists," when the *Best of the Doobie Brothers* fell from the cassette rack that stood on top of the receiver, and broke apart on a blue cotton throw rug at the foot of the bed. The sudden clatter at the margins of my sleep was startling, but I didn't suspect the machinations of "Ol' Sooty Face" (Hammond's words) quite yet. The cassette rack was no more than an inch from the stereo's edge, and I figured that even 15 watts could have danced a tape that distance. I returned the Doobies to the rack, which I moved a couple of inches back from the corner, closed the book, jerked off remorsefully and fell asleep.

About four o'clock that morning I awoke to the sound of rolling, deep-throated laughter coming from my speakers.

I moved reflexively to turn off the stereo, but froze in the dark. There was no warm, green glow from the wave band indicator — I hadn't left it on. Listening to the chortling *basso profundo*, I sat upright and clasped my arms around my shins, telling myself I was awake. The laughter lasted about forty-five seconds, but it faded so gradually I couldn't tell the moment when it became a fearful memory. After a while I turned on a light, wondering why I'd sat in the dark through the whole thing, prayed, then tried to read more of Hammond but was too rattled. Still, having a book in bed with me settled my nerves some, but by the time I was relaxed enough to read it I was too sleepy to turn a page. With the foggy rationale of someone who, despite everything, is suddenly and truly tired, I decided to worry about it in the morning. (Though I also decided against turning off the light.) When I rose about six to take a piss I was ready to believe I'd dreamt the whole thing. Almost, that is, until I noticed my *Best of the Doobie Brothers* tape, shattered again, lying at the foot of my bed.

I was flustered, though not as spooked as one might expect. Since Filmore's fall from the cliff, and particularly since my growing acquaintance with Delbert and his peculiar, sacred obsessions, I'd been feeling an encroachment of supernatural powers upon my person; as though I were Ground Zero in an intimate, other-worldly war. This wasn't a big deal — it was nothing but the Christian life. The air hung heavy with the cloud of witnesses from Hebrews 12:1, and was so charged with angels and demons that when their spiritual brawling finally opened a second front in the material world I practically said, "What took you so long?" I heard no more laughter, but over the next couple of nights, despite my moving the cassette rack further away from the edge until finally I laid it on it's back nearly a foot from any vertical, the tape (and inexplicably, only *that* tape) flew to the ground three more times. Though my wallpaper didn't drip blood or even peel worse than usual, and though I saw no apparitions and heard no voices telling me to get out of the house, after fourteen weeks of Bible School I found it both effortless and uncomplicated to believe that Satan must be picking on me.

Perversely, I confess, I felt flattered by the attention.

I imagined a boardmeeting in the bottomless pit, with a middle-management succubus pointing to a pie chart of my soul while he detailed a scenario to stop me before I won all those headhunters for Christ. "We can get to Gideon through our music," he'd tell the others, who would nod their scarlet heads and scribble notes in their asbestos spiral binders. "He's particularly fond of the opening riff of 'China Grove'." *I'll have to tell Moon about this when I get back,* I thought. *He'll be so jealous.*

One evening I approached my father — his left hand deep in a tin of mixed nuts and his right clutching the latest *Worker's Vanguard* — and nonchalantly mentioned that I suspected some sort of demonic activity in my bedroom. He looked up at me slowly, pushed his glasses back against his bridge and popped an almond in his mouth. "Count your blessings," Dad sighed, tugging at his moustache just as a car honked in front of our house. It was his carpool. "Rally at the consulate," he explained. "Exorcism." He shrugged and smiled wanly, then stood and left the room. What must life have done to him, I wondered, and made a mental note to pray extra hard for him later that night.

After *Jeopardy* I almost called my mother for counsel, checking myself only when I considered that she'd probably blame the evil visitations upon my Father and insist that I move back in with her. Besides, I was certain that she would be paralysed by any inference that I was rooming with Lucifer. She'd likely live in expectant dread of my hissing at the crucifix of some astounded Catholic priest, or my head spinning as though my spine were a string of rosary beads. No, she could never know.

During *Maude* I called Pastor Fillmore, and he told me quite calmly that he had two other possible cases of demonism on the go, and could he possibly get back to me, no later than mid-week? I was equally alarmed and disillusioned that my predicament wasn't as novel as I'd thought. Perhaps this was just a run-of-the-mill haunting; a rite of passage for the common Christian rabble — nothing to write home about. Left to sort things out, I saw two courses of action before me: a radical purging of my record and tape collection, eliminating everything that smacked of syncopation (which was everything except a Steve Martin comedy album), or just deep six the Doobies. Since their tape seemed to be the focus — and given that Filmore's indifference had led me to believe that it wasn't such a big deal — I found the latter course most prudent. Just to be safe, I also scrapped *A Wild and Crazy Guy*.

Say what you will, but that was the end of it.

When Filmore finally got back to me he was glad to hear that the disturbances had ceased (though he sounded nonplussed I hadn't trashed *all* my albums, and perhaps slighted that God hadn't needed him to cast out a demon after all. He alluded to his having put the devil to chase on other fronts, but didn't offer details.) After chatting amiably for a while about the power of the blood and what I wanted for Christmas, Filmore asked whether I might be interested in scoring quickie Christian Service points over the holidays.

"You know Johnny, don't you, Gideon? Johnny Cicero? A short fellow, but stocky — tough and leathery — an ex-biker, actually. Sings in the choir."

"Oh right — I know who you mean." Barely. We'd shaken hands a few months before, when he'd heard I was leaving for

Bible School and had wanted to wish me well. All I remembered was a squat, fleshy man in a corduroy suit that matched
his tan, with a grip that could splinter my palm like a pistachio
shell. A raw pistachio.

"Johnny does lots of work with a nifty little street mission
downtown called *Wise Up!* Heard of it? Been with them ten
years now. Johnny's director of their open-air campaigns. He
often gets some of our young people to help out. Surprised
you haven't yet. Anyway, he asked me to recommend a young
man who might give his testimony on Christmas Eve."

"Oh?"

"How about it?"

"Well ...." The man of sin inside me, my Old Adam, said
Nomotherfuckingwayleavemethefuckalone. The new man said *Get thee
behind me, Satan.*

"How many points does Overcomer hand out for street
evangelism?"

"Five. I'll do it."

"Good stuff. I'll call Johnny. And, Gideon," Filmore
added with *sotto voce,* "I wouldn't say anything about the
Doobie Brothers and all that, son," he suggested. "What
Johnny's looking for is a basic conversion story. 'Once I was
lost and now I'm found' kind of stuff. Devil talk could, you
know, distract from the greater miracle of God working in
your heart. Besides, we don't want to give Ol' Sooty Face any
free publicity, eh?"

This, then, was how, while balancing on a folding chair in
the open air at the corner of Yonge and Dundas, I came to
meet Oppie Szabo.

Cicero called the evening of the 23rd to confirm the arrangements, and was as blunt as any man should be who'd been
making the same phone call for 10 years. He told me to meet
him at 4:30 in the Cliffside parking lot. ("a.m. or p.m.?" I
inquired. *"What?"* he barked. "Never mind.") Then he asked if I
was nervous. "Well, I guess," I answered. "Good," said Cicero,
and that was that, besides telling me to be on time and to dress

"for the street." He'd hung up before I had the courage to ask him what he meant.

Snow had been falling since mid-morning, and was beginning to choke the parking lot when I arrived at 4:20 on Christmas Eve in my oatmeal wool sweater, beige double-knits and blue vinyl coat. The mission van was already there with the motor idling; it had been parked long enough for its tracks to almost fill with snow. Cicero rolled down his window and spat out a pink wad of chewing gum, folded his copy of the *Toronto Sun* away on the dashboard, then stretched across the passenger's side and opened the door.

"Hop in. You got the death seat. The girls'll be along soon."

"Girls?"

"Augusta and Sally," he answered, as though I should know them. "They do the singing. Good kids."

Cicero seemed remarkably underdressed for winter, wearing only frayed jeans, a stained maroon sweatshirt and a ragged denim jacket, the back of which I would discover he'd embroidered with ruby-coloured sequins that spelt "Jesus is Lord." His thinning black hair was pulled back and tied off in an unnecessary ponytail, and beard stubble spotted his cheeks and neck like iron filings do a bar magnet. *A leathery man*, Filmore had called him. That and more. He looked like cowhide, with the cow still inside.

"Glad to have you with us, Gideon." His voice, sweet like a Macintosh seeded with razor blades.

"Glad to help out, Mr Cicero."

"Johnny. We don't stand on formalities. Not on the street."

"Sure, okay."

And that was all that was spoken between us until Augusta and Sally showed up. In the meantime I admired his diploma in New Testament studies from Swift Current Bible College, which he kept taped to the back of the van's sun visor.

"You gals've done this before," he said, once they'd arrived *just* on time and found their seats, "and Gideon's an OBIer. There's not much a punk like me can tell you college kids. You know where we're goin', and you know why we're goin' there. Any questions?"

"I'm just wondering about the order of things."

"I'm gonna start, then Augusta and Sally'll sing a few songs, then I'll say something more, then the girls again, then you, and then me again." He sounded like Bob Hope, outlining a Christmas special to Johnny Carson. "Sally, I might ask you to use the felt board, but we'll see how the Spirit leads. That'll probably take us to seven or so. Then we'll do an invitation to know the Lord and see if anyone needs counselling."

"And um, about how long should my testimony be?"

"Oh, whatever. Not long. Fifteen minutes or so'd be fine. Sally, you got a playlist or something I can look at?"

"No — sorry, Johnny," Sally said. "We didn't think that was necessary."

"I know. I've never asked for one before, but you haven't been on the street with me since October and, well, now it's *Christmas*." I glanced over my shoulder at Augusta and Sally. They looked as clueless as I felt.

"What'dya plan to sing?"

"The usual," Sally answered, "plus a few carols."

"Yeah," Cicero sighed and scratched his head. "I thought you might. Sorry, I should have talked you sooner. It's not your fault. I just would rather that no carols be sung." He released the brake and put the van into gear. "Jesus ain't a baby no more."

Cicero was the only Christian I'd met who didn't object to the materialism of Christmas; his problem was with its *spirituality*. "It's nothing but a Babylonian feast day," he explained on the way downtown. "Egyptian, too. December 25th was celebrated as the birth of Horace, the son of Isis. I'm not telling you nothing you don't know when I say that Christmas was a compromise of the early church to accommodate pagan culture. 'Yule' is Chaldean for 'infant'. Not too many people know that." Baal, Moloch, Osiris, it didn't matter which gods of which godless nations were invoked: they were all in it together so far as Cicero was concerned. He objected to Christmas ever having been introduced into the Christian calendar. In fact, he despised the notion of a Christian calendar altogether. It was nothing but "veneration of the moon and cycles of the earth, pure and simple": another concession of the first popes to the earth and sky cults. "I've got a saying: 'Santa' is 'Satan' spelled sideways. We gonna preach Christ *crucified*, baby!"

Then Johnny fell silent until we crossed the Don River, when he decided the time was ripe to share some stories from the street. It sound like a warm-up exercise; one I imagined that Augusta and Sally must have heard many times, for they weren't listening now, as they whispered alternative selections and chord changes to each other before we parked in an emergency snow removal zone.

The girls. To me, a pair of strangers in the Lord. They attended an Associated Gospel Church on Kingston Road that was infamous for icing the dirtiest hockey team in the East Metro Christian League. Augusta, I learned, was a Trinidadian in her sophomore year at York University. The previous winter a Youth for Christ representative had rescued her from Pentecostalism; an affliction she'd so come to dread, I gathered, that she now avoided feeling much of anything just to be on the safe side. She stuttered when she spoke, which wasn't often, and wouldn't meet my eyes the whole evening, but she sang without stumbling and without emotion. Sally was a stubby, husky-voiced blonde in a blue parka with a face like one of my grandmother's old apple dolls. I thought she'd probably make a wonderful grandmother herself, if only she could find someone to get the ball rolling. Augusta and Sally: I never did learn their last names.

"I didn't believe there was a God before I believed there was a devil," Cicero said as we exited the van. "I used to live in outer darkness — no different than some of the people that'll be out tonight. That's why I keep coming back. Soul-winning's my life, and my mission field's the asphalt jungle."

Johnny, I hear, also had a wife and three children. But they were already saved, I suppose.

"I'm really glad to be here tonight to tell you what the Lord's done for me."

It was nearly seven by the time Augusta and Sally closed their last set with "When I Survey the Wondrous Cross" (upon

Cicero's recommendation, after his late scratch of "Silent Night"), and my 15 minutes finally arrived. The snowfall had stopped during Cicero's second call to repentance, and what remained on the ground had either been churned to slush by ten thousand pairs of Kodiaks or spotted the pavement like a field of dandelions gone to seed. Johnny had assured me that I needn't stand on the chair if it would make me uncomfortable. "Naturally the girls don't use it," he'd said. I took that as a dare. When I stepped up there were perhaps a dozen people standing in a ragged crescent around it, almost half seemingly friends or groupies of "the girls" (a couple of them I recognized from their church hockey team) come to provide them with an assured audience. Now — with a wave, an embrace and a chuck on the shoulder — three of them and then a fourth began to drift away. My mother had made me a similar offer but I'd begged her to stay home, promising to drop by later so together we could weep through *It's a Wonderful Life.* (The Wayne Rogers, Marlo Thomas version.) Facing Yonge and Dundas — the Caesar's Palace for Canadian open air evangelists — with the lurid fluorescence of the Eaton Centre glowing red and green at my back, I was sorry she wasn't here.

Much of the sidewalk traffic was done with and home for the holidays, but there remained lots of straggling workaholics and frenetic mall hounds for me to harangue. A number of them, laden with bags and looking unseasonably ugly, would pull a Moses and part the crusade team from our congregation in order to beat the lights. At the Dundas curb just beyond our little band, a fresh clique of commuters formed every ten minutes or so to await the next streetcar. Mostly they pretended we weren't there, but a couple of faces would turn towards me, and another couple of ears.

"You've just heard Augusta and Sally sing about a 'love so amazing, so divine ....'"

Giving my testimony was no big deal. At Bible School, "How did you come to know the Lord?" was as common a question as "What kind of soup is this?" and "Can we take our ties off yet?" But now at this gig for *nonbelievers*, I felt like a stand-up Christian suddenly unsure of the strength of his material. "Lord," I whispered during Augusta and Sally's last song, "please, make me *interesting.*"

After all, it's not as though this were the only show in town. Less than half a block south an African Methodist preacher was in full flight, his voice carrying up the street like a snowball with a pebbled heart. I was also competing with the Salvation Army thrash and bugle corps dug in at the northeast corner of Dundas, who were storming through the scripturally suspect "I Saw Three Ships." Then there was the warty street vendor peddling flags of the world and wind-up, cymbal-crashing monkeys; a pensioner playing chess for chump change, who looked like a Santa who'd lost his bag of toys; and our ever-engaging and truly world class assortment of demented and derelict urban garden gnomes. All of that, over-dubbed with an aural collage of a thousand fleeting mono-logues, attitudes and conversations.

Most critically, I was competing with the example of Johnny Cicero: a man who'd sinned — "sinned grandly," he boasted — and so had a larder full of lurid anecdotes with which to flavour the gospel. My life before Christ just hadn't been very spicy. What kind of a witness was I, when almost everyone in earshot who wasn't asleep in momma's arms must have been more seasoned in vice than myself? I was parsley to Johnny's curry: *nolo contendere.*

"I'm here today because I want to tell you how that same love has changed my life."

The wail of an ambulance graciously interrupted me. Black ice and a choked intersection slowed its progress north on Yonge, and as heads turned towards the street mine turned to Johnny. He pursed his lips in a playful frown and nodded encouragement. Two fire trucks and a Mr Pong's Chinese Food delivery car followed straightaway, and I waited until they passed before trying again.

"Like I was saying ... you've been hearing a lot about the love of God this evening. I'd like to share with you some of what that love has meant for me."

"Preach it, brother!"

"Glory to *Jai*-sus! Praise Gawd and Halleylooyah!"

"Can somebody give me an amen?"

Two young toughs, full of roguery and eggnog, taunted me in tacky TV Evangelese while sprinting behind my back and across Dundas for an idling westbound streetcar. Besides one chippy defenceman who lingered long enough to mask his laugh in a cough, my humble flock didn't flinch. Behind them at the eastbound stop, however, five or six were curious enough to cast sly, sidelong glances towards the punks, to me and then back to their paper or bootlaces with a smirk and chuckle. But for one, the rest behaved as I used to in math class when I'd neglected an assignment: *Don't react and avoid eye contact — you might get called upon.*

That single exception was a young woman in candy cane coloured tights and a black leather jacket that was at least three sizes too big for her. Her head was bare, and her squid-ink hair had been given a brush cut much like many a floor monitor's in a Bible School boy's dorm. She wore no gloves, and though I could see her breath and her hands looked chapped, she didn't even warm them inside a jacket pocket — even the one that was without a cigarette. She wasn't smirking like some, and she didn't have her back to me like the others. No — she was smiling right at me.

Though on my bad days, these days, I believe that in the end we're all just carbon deposits, to be mined like the dinosaurs by creatures which we can't imagine, on that day a stranger's smile was enough to transport me to the bosom of Abraham. Suddenly I didn't worry if I was dull. I wouldn't have minded if everyone dismissed me as just a gangly Bible-thumper who couldn't whistle even a single song of experience. Everyone but this one young woman. Perhaps most remarkably, I no longer cared about the Christian service points. Suddenly it was so much bigger than that.

As when the Lord flashed his backside to Moses on Sinai, so when I beheld that smile I caught a glimpse of a hallowed and uncommon knowledge: *This is where I'm supposed to be.* I regretted none of the doors I had closed or ignored in my 18 years to bring me to that speck and blink of space and time: the chair on which I stood was the fulcrum about which the

Wheel of Heaven spun out God's perfect and peculiar will. In an instant, one kind smile from this stranger (a rather attractive young woman, I couldn't help but notice) had become blessed assurance that I was performing my Father's pleasure. She might smoke, dress like a tramp and even have been with a man, but all I knew and cared for was that Jesus loved her and wanted me to tell her so. I was as humble a mouthpiece for the Holy Ghost as my stereo had been for Beelzebub, but the woman's smile was a smidgen of rainbow to me — a promise of a covenant she didn't even know. *It's okay,* she might mean by it, *don't let those punks get to you;* or, *Sure it was funny, but I'm listening;* or even, *Amuse me til my streetcar comes.* But God was whispering through her scarcely parted lips, *This is the reason I've led you here.*

"I used to be a communist. Actually, a Maoist — not that that matters. I was disrespectful to my parents; full of wicked thoughts. Like many of you, I'm sure, I was desperate for something to give meaning to my life .... Desperate, that is, until I found the answer in the one who's birth we'll be celebrating tomorrow." Out of the corner of my eye I thought I saw Cicero wince. Oh oh: *Christmas.*

"I didn't come to that answer easily. I had a rebellious heart and lots of distractions. I was doing lousy in school — geometry, especially." I notice a few smiles and nods of empathy. "But when I gave my life to Jesus, he changed me. I don't mean my problems suddenly vanished — I failed geometry — but at least I knew my problems happened for a purpose."

"So, how come you failed geometry?" It was a boy in the back, maybe 15. Maybe struggling himself with the curriculum.

"Ah! Well you see, I would have been able to get into university if I'd passed. But the Lord arranged things so I'd only be able to get into Bible College." I flush, with something like pride, at the tittering.

"Couldn't you have made it up at summer school?"

"Well yes. *Technically.*" I imagine Cicero hanging his head, and I glance over and he's done precisely that. "I didn't really want to do that. And God doesn't allow us to be tempted beyond our ability to resist." A rumbling of muffled snickers, and I press on. "All problems are sent to test us; to draw us closer to the Lord. Even geometry problems. So today I might not know how to calculate the circumference of a circle, but I've learned that Heaven has glories that cannot be measured." Cicero raised his head and turned sharply towards me. He looked confused. The smile broadened on the face of the woman in tights and leather.

Perhaps if I'd been saved a little later in life — say, with six more months of puberty under my belt — my testimony would've been as savoury as Cicero's. But this was great; no exaggeration, no apology. My heart was racing. I thought of Polycarp, the third century bishop of Smyrna, and recalled Amphora Faulker's impassioned sketch in Church History 101 of his glorious, sticky end. I heard her syrupy, southern drawl recount his hymns of praise as the flames licked his body, the streams of blood from the stabs of impatient centurions, and their astonishment as the blood doused the fire. I thought of Dylan, ass-deep in Pat Boone's shallow end, squeezing his hands tight across his narrow chest and falling backwards into new life. All of us were fools for God. *Be not afraid of them that kill the body .... Fear him who hath power to cast into hell.*

As the son of a Trotskyite, I'd had many opportunities to contend with public humiliation. Now, while I played this dinky part in premillennial history, this was my first time to use that experience in the service of the Lord. I felt the Holy Ghost tickle the base of my spine and I practically swooned, steadying myself only upon the weight of my burden for a single immortal soul. Here I was, then: a tiny link in the ancient chain; the great chain of being a Bible-thumping pain in the ass.

"I'm not talking about a religion; it's a relationship. The most intimate you can imagine." The several sniggers from the curbside crowd emboldened me. "I thank God he saved me before I fell too deep into the ways of the world, because I know that all it offers can't be compared to one mo-"

"So, you're like a virgin?"

If the question had been asked by anyone but the woman in tights and leather, I would have ignored it. But this was my stake; my centurion's spear.

"Yes, I am a virgin. A virgin and unashamed."

"You haven't missed much."

It was as though the hour had struck: a long dash following five seconds of silence. After a startled hush, the shoulders of those who'd seemed to have been hiding from my math teacher began heaving with laughter. A couple of chunky guys in bomber jackets started hooting. Soon, Augusta and Sally and almost everyone else were either chuckling or grinning shyly. Even me. The only two who weren't smiling were Cicero and the woman.

"I know: I haven't missed a thing," I said as the laughter tapered down to titters. "The Bible says that 'God so loved the world that he sent his only begotten son, that whosoever believeth on him should not perish, but have everlasting life.' What I want to ask is, what have you missed?"

"And Jesus wants an answer!" Cicero jumped on my line like a cat upon a pigeon's neck. I hadn't finished, but the spark in his eyes made me feel like a bundle of dry kindling, and the throbbing vein at his temple was a telegraph that told me to step the hell down fast. He was up on the chair and preaching before I'd touched ground. "That's why we're here this evening: to tell you about the bridge that God built with the flesh of his only begotten to bring us all back into his holy fellowship."

"Praise 'em, eh? Fine job, boy," whispered a middle-aged Asian woman with a bad cold as I backed out of the semi-circle. "There's no shame in saving yourself." Then she blew her nose, examined the tissue and walked on.

Now, I didn't know what to make of it. I enjoyed the rush of being a fool for God, but I didn't expect that afterwards I'd feel nearly so foolish.

"We're all born in sin, cut off from God," Cicero boomed, and he motioned for Sally to raise the felt board. It showed a familiar enough scene, straight out of my Principals of Soul Winning textbook: two fudge-coloured cliffs separated by a deep valley and orange licks of hellfire. Above one cliff hovered a pale yellow crown, and upon the other stood a black stick figure that looked like an airport sign indicating the nearest men's room.

"Jesus said 'I am the Way, the Truth and the Life,'" he continued, slapping a swollen scarlet cruciform right in the chasm's middle, it's crossbeam bridging the gulf. "'No man cometh to the Father but by me.'" So no one would miss the point he walked the stick figure across to other side.

I backed away a little further from the crusade, my brow creased by my longing to learn the mind of God. Pacing slowly towards the Dundas sidewalk, idly kicking the snow into dirty coolwhip, I noticed the woman in black leather approach me. She was smiling again, rather shyly, now.

"Sorry if I embarrassed you. It wasn't personal. I just pull that shit sometimes."

"No problem. It's okay." I tried to quell the flutter in my voice, but I again felt the thrill of all things working together.

"Too bad about geometry. I had to go to summer school three fucking summers in a row for French and all I can say is *Où est la salle de bain?*"

"Hmmm, yes. Well, the Lor — "

"*Scott!* Sorry, it's my fucking boyfriend. Been waiting forever for the — Shit! *Scott! Where the bloody fucking hell are you going?*"

Down Dundas West, about a 100 feet away, stood a young man, his body frozen in mid-stride towards the Eaton's Centre as he faced us with a stupid grin. He was wearing baggy pants that looked like quilted terrycloth, a red checkered flannel shirt and a buttonless, much distressed, grey leather greatcoat that reached the tips of the tongues of his tattered Doc Martens. He would have been shorter than his girlfriend but for a green mohawk gelled into five, 10-inch spikes.

"Scott's a musician," she confided as he loped towards us. "Thinks he is, anyway. Calls himself Scott Mission. Least he has since the Santa Claus parade. His real name's Poors, so he figures it's kind of a pun. He thinks he's funny, too. Oh, fuck it," she sighed. "Ignore me. I'm just pissed he's late. He's the bassist for the Bangkok Lady Boys. Heard of them? They suck dick, but he's sure they're gonna be the next Masturbation Death."

"No kidding?"

"Yeah," she nodded, and took a drag on her cigarette. "Don't be scared. He's not exactly harmless, but — Scott, sweetie," she shouted, "where the fuck have you been?"

"Alarm didn't go off," he rasped in a reedy voice. "I thought we were meeting at the subway."

"Well, we know better now, don't we, ya sweet, dumb bastard?" As Scott ambled closer she smiled, tossed her cigarette into the street and stretched out her arms as though she were about to feel her way across a darkened room. After their embrace and sloppy kiss, Scott kept one hand around her waist while the other fished a pack of Marlboro's out of his coat pocket. He was staring at me as if he'd never before seen blow-dried hair.

"I'd like you to meet my street preacher friend — sorry, what's your name?"

"Gideon. What's yours?"

"Oppie."

"*Oppie?*"

"Yeah, that's it. Like Poppy. Just hold the 'P.'"

"Street preacher?" Scott cried. I nodded, and gave a little shrug and smile to tell him that I was still human. He let loose with a phlegmy laugh that quickly became a hacking cough. "No shit! You're just in time. Oppie an' me need saving, baad!" And he squeezed her ass.

"Bastard!" Oppie said, slapping his arm. "Behave yourself. He doesn't need you to embarrass him, too."

"Why? What'd you do?"

"Tell you later — just be good."

"Be good?" Scott leered at me. "But that's not enough — is it, brother? It's not enough just to be good, is it?"

"No, that's right." Suddenly I was in a wind up, about to cast my string of pearls. "The Bible says, 'Our righteousness is as filthy rags.' Everybody falls short. That's why Jesus came; so that 'we might be made the righteousness of God in him.'"

"Have you been born again?"

"Yes. Have you?"

"Why make the same mistake twice?" Scott smirked as though he'd caught my pearls on one of his spikes, then he wiped his mouth. His fingers poked out of his coat sleeve like little piggies in a blanket. He lit a cigarette and then leaned towards me, his gelled points quivering, and put his hand on my shoulder. "You probably wouldn't think to look at me, but I'm into God."

"Great. What does that mean, exactly?"

"I like talking religion and shit. My folks are Catholic. I've read the Bible — more than I can say for them."

"Well, good. That's good."

"Pretty hot stuff. That Song of Solomon — I mean, Whew! I can dance to that."

"Scott, *must* you be such a prick?"

"I don't know; I guess. But Jesus, Oppie, I'm just joking. God should be big enough to take a joke, eh?"

"Don't pay any attention to him," Oppie told me. "He's always like this."

"So save me — in twenty-five words or less."

"I can't do that," I smiled beneficently. "That's up to God. I can't argue you or anybody into Heaven."

"So it's up to God then, who gets into Heaven?"

"Well, that's one side of it. But it's also up to us. The Bible says, 'Whosoever will come unto me I will in no wise cast out.'"

"No *wise'*?" he laughed. "What the fuck kind of way is that to talk?"

"Anyway," I said, pressing on. "What the Word tells us is we've got free will. It means that on one side, God chooses us, and on the other, we choose God."

"Why do you think God gave us free will?"

"Because he loves us. Because he wanted creatures who could love him freely."

"Where's the freedom in that?" Scott coughed as he poked the air with his Marlboro. "If we don't make the choice he wants, then he sends us to hell? If that's freedom, I'll take Door Number Three, Monty. Shouldn't God love us whatever choice we make?"

"But the thing is, God's holy. He hates sin but loves the sinner."

"Uh huh," he nodded, taking a puff while weighing which plank of the Creed he should splinter next. "So I guess you think we've got immortal souls or something?"

"Can you imagine not existing?"

"Tell me, what was it like before you were born?" He was leering again. "You didn't exist then, did you? Why is it so tough to accept that someday you won't? I think, maybe, our life energy or something goes on in some form ...."

"Ah, well, there you go." I felt the hint of a smirk begin warming my face.

"But your soul's got personality, right?" I nodded. "Let me tell you something. My Dad was in a bad car crash a couple of years ago; had a real serious head injury. Personality doesn't even make it out of this life, brother."

"But — I'm very sorry about your father — but there's a lot of comfort in knowing that God loves him."

"Right," he spat. "And if I treated my lover the way your God treats his, I'd be thrown in jail."

"Scott, our streetcar's coming."

"Merry Christmas, preacher."

"Merry Christmas. Nice meeting you, Scott, Opy."

"*Oppie!* Ritchie Cunningham used to be Opy."

"Oh hey, just a sec, would you mind if I gave you something?" I reached inside a trouser pocket for a couple of gospel tracts entitled *This Was Your Life* that were stamped with Cliffside's address for soul-winning emergencies.

"Ooh, cartoons," Oppie squealed, and took them both. Scott was preoccupied counting exact change.

Once they'd boarded the streetcar I returned to the crusade. Cicero was still heralding the Day of the Lord, but he'd finished with the felt board and it now leaned against the chair. The cross still bridged the great gulf, but the golden crown and the black stick figure had both slid to the ground and the grey slush.

II

Experience has proved the toad to be endowed with valuable qualities.

If you run a stick through three toads, and, after having dried them in the sun, apply them to any pestilent tumour, they draw out all the poison, and the malady will disappear.

Martin Luther

1

January 26, 1979

Finally, out of the Infirmary! (Worst flu ever. A week's way too long for little but cups of pasty Tang and National Geographics with all the breasts blacked out. (I know they mean well, but it makes me wonder if the reason our Dining Hall breakfast eggs are always scrambled or hard-boiled is that they don't trust us with easy-overs and sunny-sides up.)

But that's okay; at least I'm beginning to trust myself. Every night about 8, when one of the nurses would come around to offer talcum-powdered backrubs, I just said a polite "Thanks, but no thanks." Of course they were only doing their jobs, and I know they were totally innocent, but the prospect of some female contact — particularly if Inka Ebbers was on duty — excited the other guys so much that I thought it prudent to be a humble witness of restraint. (Praise God, it's been nearly four weeks since I abused myself!)

I shared a room with Chester Babbs. He joked he has no problem avoiding pre-marital sex, because he doesn't plan to marry.

Chester's funny, but he's definitely on my prayer list for February.

January 28

Amazing service this morning. Pastor Barstowe preached. First time I've heard him, and best sermon I've ever heard on Leviticus 10. (I wonder: how often have I offered strange fire like Nadab and Abihu?) He had three alliterated points with three subpoints each and went on for an hour and a half. He must be my grandmother's age. (God, that I might have a half portion of his blessing!)

Sat down front with Delbert. He likes to be "in the line of conviction." Every time I've sat with him he's wound up weeping by the end of the service. He sniffles quietly and doesn't really make a scene, but next time I'll suggest we move back a few rows.

January 31

Langdon's World Religions class isn't precisely what I'd hoped for. He's a godly man for sure, and all his years on the mission field make for some gripping anecdotes, but I guess I was expecting to learn something. Can't blame him, though. For a guy with only a high school diploma, and that by correspondence, he's done OK for himself. (In Jesus' name, I rebuke the spirit of sarcasm!)

Today he mentioned that when he was in the Philippines he learned to smell demons. I can't say it surprised me to learn they smell pretty bad. Now, I'm sure, a few people'll be self-conscious whenever they pass Langdon in the hall. ("Aren't you glad you wash in the blood of the Lamb? Don't you wish everybody did?")

Can't believe I just wrote that. Maybe I'm still a little sick. Not that that's an excuse. God forgive me, anyway.

February 2

Dreamt about the Rapture last night. It happened during high school gym. Mr De Soto had gathered the class around the trampoline to watch me demonstrate a double back flip which he knew I couldn't make. The trumpet sounded while I was stalling, taking gentle warm-up bounces. When I was about to pass through the ceiling and into glory I glanced down, and De Soto called out sharply that he'd have to mark me absent. I remember how relieved I was. I knew that flip would have killed me.

February 5

Miss Faulkner finally passed around a sign-up sheet for her long-promised second semester dinner parties. I'm going in a couple of weeks — the first slot available for guys. I know Chester and Tibo signed up for that night, too. Not sure who the fourth is. Chester's pretty excited. Says she's supposed to be the best cook on faculty. I don't care if she serves beans on toast. (Blah (I guess I do!) She's the most interesting person here. Where was she before her conversion? University of Alabama? Georgia? Somewhere down there for something like a dozen years, and now another ten or so at Overcomer.

In the eyes of the world our faculty and graduates must look singularly unequipped to prosper. Handicapped, even, from ever earning living wages. To think, Faulkner abandoned a tenure and her colleague's respect so she could impoverish herself for Christ's sake at a non-accredited Bible College. Now that's a testimony!

If she's still teaching Greek next year, I think I'll take it. If not, then it's on to Principles of Chalk Art.

February 6

Morning chapel sure was wild.

I've known since last Wednesday that Dean Blier was scheduled to address only the freshmen guys today. Now I know I haven't been imagining all those sophomores snickering at us.

Before Blier told us the text of his message he demanded that we all take notes. Then he asked us to turn to Proverbs 6:25 ("Lust not after her beauty in thine heart; neither let her take thee with her eyelids.") and calmly announced he was going to speak about "the spilling of seed." Ouch. "I thank God He spared me," he added quickly and with much emotion. (I really should pray tonight for the Lord to help my attitude towards the Dean.)

Basically, he's not for it. Neither am I, but even though it's been a month and a half since I last touched myself with lewd intent it's not as if I haven't wanted to. Sure, I wouldn't accept a backrub, but I've committed masturbation many times in my heart.

The girls, it seems, heard a devotional study about etiquette. (I guess they're just not challenged like us guys in the sexual realm.) At lunch Wendy Weibe asked me about our chapel. "Pretty much the same," I said.

It's not like I believe in situation ethics, but I thought a little lie was called for there.

February 8

Letter today from Mother. Nanny's coming home! She's leaving England in the Spring, God willing, and will probably take my old room. I'm not sure why the change of plans — the details were kind of vague, and Mom didn't seem completely thrilled about it — but as for me, it's an answer to prayer. I haven't seen her since my conversion. Sure hope she'll be able to notice a difference in me. I want to be a good witness.

Allan and Mark were handing out liqueur-filled chocolates during Life of Elisha. I didn't take one, but passed them to someone who did. Does that make me a better person? Or just as guilty as them?

February 9

Finally heard why Joel Kajinsky didn't return after Christmas. Tonight after supper Danny mentioned that he just got a letter from him. It seems as though he'd meant to come back — he'd said goodbye to his folks and was all packed and everything, even — but then his car wouldn't start. Joel took it as a sign that God didn't want him to go, so he unpacked and within a week was engaged and assistant manager of a miniature golf course outside Kamloops.

Danny asked me what I thought, and I told him that I didn't want to judge Kajinsky, but his methodology sounds dodgy. He agreed. I mean, it's like Our Father, the Car or something. Deal with it: bad guys don't always have transmission trouble. And that's not because God's impotent to strip their gears or whatever. That's just how it goes in a fallen world.

I wonder what Joel's devotional time is like these days. I wonder how his car's doing. Not that it's for me to judge.

February 10

The Holy Spirit's been speaking to me about doodling too much in Doctrine class.

2

vercomer's been blessed down through the years with a bountiful share of stalwart ladies of faith. Almost from the day we turned the sod there was dear Glenda McGully, O.B.I.'s first euphonics teacher. An ex-flapper not unfamiliar with what the world could offer a maid, she proved herself cherished of God and a veritable lighthouse of divine love, heroically warding away many a soul from the shoals of concupiscence. The McGully Music Building, consumed in the fire of '49, was named in her honour. And who could forget saintly Valerie Hall, dean of girls for more than three decades? Or old "Praying Maggie," our cheery Dining Room hostess since 1958? Now, in later years, the Lord has favoured us with the likes of Amphora Faulkner ....

Charles K. Barstowe, *At Home With God*

"Church hist'ry is not for the faint a' heart."

Those were the first words I heard skip through Amphora Faulkner's unpainted lips, my first Church History class on my second day of classes. Her hickory-smoked voice — a hash of ripe innocence and suggestion unlike anything I'd heard since the cancellation of *Petticoat Junction*, and wouldn't hear again until *Designing Women* — concentrated my mind like the pinch of a patrician dominatrix. Just once, after a long night polishing a paper on Mexican Mariolatry, did Faulkner's lush harmonics lull me to a podgy sleep, my head nestled on the desktop crib of my arms. When I awoke to a suddenly hushed classroom with a smattering of heads turned towards me, and Faulkner's odd, forbearing smile (a worldly sneer mellowed by deathless mercy) fixed upon me like a Romulan tractor beam, she rapped her pointer at the chalk words "Diet of Worms" and drawled, "Well, Mistah Gast?"

Some might jest that Overcomer's good fortune is witness to God's using the foolish to confound the wise. Well, amen and so be it, but "ignorance is bliss" is not found in my Bible, brother! In this regard, we rejoice that Miss Amphora Faulkner has joined our fellowship, and has come with such a high scholarly pedigree.

Her father, Therman Faulkner, was a well-admired archaeologist of the Holy Lands. As for her mother, some readers may recognize her pen name: Sophia Sybil Downey, the author of the popular *Sniffy Boots* series of children's books during the war years. Amphora's adolescence was spent in libraries and upon Mesopotamian flood plains, and the precocious young girl grew to treasure a great love for the life of the mind. This passion, alas, was without knowledge that her mind had been given to her for a greater purpose, and for the enjoyment of a life everlasting.

After years of secular higher learning (the finest education the world could offer — or so she supposed), Miss Faulkner was well on her way towards becoming a leading light in her field of Roman imperial history. To that end she spent twelve years in the Classics department at Georgia State. When she found Jesus in 1969 and, in her words, "Stopped cheering for the lions," she determined to devote her life to the cause of Christian schooling. That God-kindled devotion lead her in 1971 to become, almost single-handedly, Overcomer's history and Greek departments.

Charles K. Barstowe, *At Home With God*

Faulkner was 52 my freshman year; a cracked Southern Belle with fuzzy jowls and a budding widow's hump, yet my interest in her wasn't as virtuous as I pretended, especially to myself. Her class might have been a scholastic Zanadu on the lone prairie, but — ashamedly, yet perhaps most portentously — Faulkner also bore the most pendulous breasts in Western Christendom.

It seems crazy now to think that a woman wouldn't know when a man — even a God-fearing one — is talking to her tits, but my consciousness was raised, such as it was, long after my cock. Until then I nurtured a lazy eye for decollage, and my lingering gaze became a steady compass to trace bosoms beyond measure onto my onion-skinned imagination, to be catalogued at leisure by the higher faculties of my lower nature. Even with my heart set upon charting a righteous after-lifestyle, Bible School was the same story, and Church History the same chapter and verse. Faulkner, of course, never dressed immodestly. (*Nobody* did. Ever. Even in the men's residence our housecoats had to cover the knees.) But it didn't matter what she wore. It's alarming how little a breast-fixated fundamentalist requires to make him walk bow-legged once he's been shaken from a fantasy by a call to the blackboard.

She was not a heavy woman so much as spacious; much like Montana used to be, I imagine, before cultivation and the incorporation of Billings. Faulkner's was a big sky belly of unorganized territory, and it rolled on for country inches in an awesome swath of amber waves until her breasts swelled up like the Lewis Range; so grand you feel their bulk almost bury you, even though you've barely left Missoula. She might have ploughed under her sensuality when Christ took possession of the deed to her heart, but my furtive lusts figured that a decade of lying fallow had only nourished that still-fertile loam.

Faulkner's clapboard bungalow sat with four of its kind on a small button of frozen gravel called M'Cheyne Circle, which by chance and locale — and because no one bothered pronouncing "M'Cheyne" — was known to all as the Navel; a cul de sac off the Spurgeon Way, the asphalt Jordan which sundered the academic buildings and tabernacle from the gymnasiums, playing fields and small dairy farm. Her home resembled the small, uninsulated cottage my family had rented for several summers just five convenient miles from the bracing undertow of Wasaga Beach. Its knotty wooden siding was roughly the shade of Chester's frayed safari jacket, which he wore beneath his plaid poplin coat the night of our dinner party.

The four of us — myself, Chester Babbs, Tibo Fung and Nathan Weaver (a spindly, vexatious and improbable pal of Delbert Moon's who I hadn't expected to return after Christmas and who had the annoying and sadly not uncommon quirk of communicating chiefly through Monty Python routines) — arranged to meet in Chester's room at six and walk together to Faulkner's. Each of the others had some reason to dread being the first at her door: Chester still hadn't submitted his Fall term paper — hadn't even chosen a topic; Tibo was a caustic loner, which I thought odd for someone who'd been exorcised just the previous summer; and Nathan had answered too many questions with "Nobody expects the Spanish Inquisition." I joined them at Chester's because he'd asked me, and I didn't want to appear stand-offish.

Babbs had been slavering a semester and a half for this meal, hunger being one of the few appetites a single man could righteously fulfil. A steady diet of Dining Hall rations, the bright spot of which had been two weeks-worth of frozen pork pies salvaged from a providential train wreck, had whittled his pride down to a kiddie portion. He'd already greased his stout ass onto the sticky vinyl chairs of nearly half the faculty's kitchen tables, but this invitation had always been the brass onion ring. By the time we left the dorm, the morning snow and the midday rain had consolidated into sheets of brittle phylo pastry.

"Johnson had duck when he went," Babbs reflected in an oddly poignant, reedy voice. "Best ever, he said. Of course, that was last month, but man ...." He shook his head slowly, and shaved his voice to barely a whisper. "I do love my crispy duck skin."

"Steak'd be alright," Fung allowed. "Rare, so you know where it came from, but not so bloody you think it's still there." He added quickly, as though he'd forgotten to gripe. "Hope this won't take all night."

"I really don't care what she serves, or how long it takes," I sniffed. It was true. Given that most nights held nothing more exhilarating than a guilty boner before sleep on a mattress damp with the prayers of a dumb shit named after a dumb shit-shovelling state, this meal was the gala of my semester's social calendar. Suddenly I felt terribly alone. I hadn't made many friends on campus, and though I didn't like the ones I had, I felt an appalling desperation to keep them. So I squeezed my sniff into a sniffle, feigned a couple of coughs and added with brio, "Duck sounds great, Chester."

"Spam," cackled Nathan.

Approaching the corner of Spurgeon and Navel, Chester tensed. We were being hailed by the scent of something unholy: scorched fish sticks or one of Langdon's devils. *Smells like Tibo's exorcist missed something*, I joked to myself even as I felt guilty for doing so, while whatever it was hung in the air like a rusting Ski-Doo on the spring crust of a lake. Fung grumbled a scornful "Great" and Weaver hissed "Luxury." Once we'd passed the Blier family's stubby split-level the stink faded, along with the muffled strain of a scratchy Bill Gaither Trio album which seeped through their basement storm window. Soon we picked up the faint but complex fragrance of a righteous meal in the making.

"This smells like the place!" Babbs yelped, and trotted ahead of us with a laugh that sounded to me like fingernails scraping a smorgasbord.

But for Babb's belaboured breathing we were silent on the stoop, kicking snow from our boots whether they needed it or not. Pale lights shone through pearly shades on both sides of the door. Her doorbell chimed the first bar of Beethoven's Fifth, seemingly arranged for emery board and garburator, and as I rang it I felt the others fall into line behind me, as though they considered me a convenient shrub in an idiot's game of hide and seek. Then the screen door scraped opened before a swell of muggy air, rolling kitchen smells and Amphora Faulkner, wearing an about-her-Father's-business-like navy skirt with a mid-calf flounce, and an unfamiliar pastel-banded cardigan that strained to check her urgent bosom.

"Evening, gen'lemen. You're right on time. Even you, Chestuh. Come in an' mind Pertinax." A tiny, glistening smudge of grease reflected a sliver of porch light at the coiled brim of her mouth.

A scruffy orange and black tabby weaved between our legs, and Weaver mumbled something about having spent four hours burying the cat. Pertinax managed to reach the thatch welcome mat and catch a whiff of the night before Faulkner latched the door shut. While we pulled off our boots (Weaver's big toes, long overdue for a pedicure, had sliced through his dogshit-brown nylon socks) and I bumped my head on a dangling Spider Plant, Faulkner chided the cat with a sugary "Bad baby. Good girls don' go out this late." Pertinax curled into a sulky ball, next to a potbellied terra cotta vase with a clay mole at its middle that squatted just inside the doorway. At the end of her hall, Faulkner pointed us towards her modest bedroom, where we were told to toss our things.

Almost everything I saw in her house seemed to pick a quarrel with its roommates. In the putting green living room, a chocolate corduroy chesterfield stretched impudently before a black melamine coffee table, not giving a damn for the blue leather recliner and almond swag lamp across the deep pile maroon carpet. A splendid walnut case displayed soapstone carvings and Andean pottery alongside a set of novelty souvenir mugs from the Banff Gondola Ride and a mint condition Michelin Man piggy bank. A laminated reproduction of

Brueghel's Last Judgement hung between a pastel pair of knobby praying hands and a strangely beautiful map of the U.S.
made of dyed macaroni and crushed sea shells.

Nothing fit. In fact, nothing fit so perfectly that it was like
one of the more desperate proofs for the existence of God —
there just had to be an intelligence behind such brilliant chaos.
Didn't there?

Bookcases were everywhere. In her plum-coloured bedroom, a collection of nesting, egg-shaped dolls rested atop a
headboard bookcase, above a queue of Penguin classics whose
black spines were softened and streaked by the cracks of constant bending. I pitched my coat onto Faulkner's lavender
duvet and lingered after the others to scan the titles. There
was *The Satyricon*, which I knew only from some terrifically
unerotic stills from Fellini's film that were picked up for a Sex
in the Cinema spread in an old *Playboy* of my Dad's. Loeb editions of Tacitus, Dio and Suetonius — the last word for
enquiring Roman minds — filled the top row of a narrow oak
cabinet. On her dresser's doily was the *Augustan History*, something which I, having skimmed it once for the naughty bits,
thought of as a lost work of Dr Seuss: *And to Think that I Saw it
on the Palatine Hill*. Rome seemed at home in her bedroom.

"No trouble finding the place, I hope? It *is* rather hard to
get lost around here — in every sense of the word." Faulkner
grinned and waved us into the living room. "Make yourselves
at home. Dinner's almos' ready. Can I get anyone anything to
drink? Coffee? Freshee? Milk?" We agreed that milk sounded
great, and with another smile she withdrew into the kitchen.

"How long you think this will be?" Tibo whispered as I
squeezed between his knees and the coffee table to the sofa's
middle, since Nathan had staked out its other end and Chester
had collapsed heavily into the recliner with a handful of blue
corn chips. I replied with a curt — though I hoped not unkind
— shrug, while Weaver muttered beneath his breath, "That's a
rather personal question." Babb's chair was angled slightly
towards an obsolete Zenith console set beside a case of first
edition *Sniffy Boots*. Televisions were rare on campus. Broadcast
transmission had just missed sin's shortlist of commission and

omission, and most staff erred on the side of caution. Her set might have been a primitive black and white job without cable and remote control, but to my hungry and habituated eyes, its antennae were gamely splayed more like a pair of Bunny legs than rabbit ears.

I tugged at the neck of my ivory sweater, lacquered a corn chip with guacamole and popped it in my mouth. Her house was hot — hot enough to warrant a mumbled minced oath to myself — and the worst of it felt to be burning a hole through the couch and into my kidneys. Glancing over my shoulder, I saw a radiator set inside a crude wooden frame between the couch and window, on top of which sat a pot of African Violets, a couple of cacti, an Aloe Vera and a succulent Pitcher Plant that tempted a bloated and sluggish housefly. I began fearing sweat stains and body odour, but for most of the night I forgot to be bothered by it.

"Maybe it's duck," Babbs suddenly blurted in a rapturous whisper. "I bet it's duck. Or chicken, maybe ...."

"You lose, Chestuh." Faulkner entered the room carrying a tray of four slender, warty glasses which she set on the table beside the copper bowl.

"Oh, that's alright," Chester granted with a hungry leer and giggle, though his cheeks were stained with embarrassment. "Chicken's really my favourite."

"It's turkey. I thought for sure turkey'd be your favourite." She gently nudged a tan suede ottoman a little closer to Fung, then crossed her legs at the ankles as she sat with an air of Just Plain Folks. "Sorry, Chestuh, that was a joke but it wasn't nice. I won't pick on you any more tonight." Babbs shrugged and moped across the carpet to collect his milk and more corn chips. I reached for my glass and wondered why Faulkner's mouth was bothering me so much.

She had a rather meagre mouth for a woman of her age and amplitude. A good mouth, just not drawn to scale. It's modesty was offset in classroom light, but tonight her mouth seemed smaller; a convalescent wound that had only just begun to heal. Apart from her mouth, Faulkner's familiarity underscored the unanticipated strangeness of her home.

"Turkey? Sounds great!" I couldn't pass on the chance to flatter with a smattering of banal pleasantries. "That's a lot of work for a Tuesday night."

"I don't teach on Tuesdays."

"Good rule," Chester blurted. "I don't go to classes, either."

"Turkey's not much bother, though," Faulkner continued, ignoring him. "Besides, I enjoy giving my students a break from the Dining Hall. I know Maggie Banks does what she can. I just can' see that it's good to eat so many frozen meat pies." We all chuckled, and Tibo's mood seemed to lighten. "I ate often when I first arrived. Of course, back then, the sexes weren't allowed to mix like now."

"They are?" Chester's eyes were as round as bathtub drains. "Since when?"

"More than before, that is. You can sit together at lunch. Isn't that right?"

"We can't choose who we sit with," Tibo grumbled.

"They use student ushers," continued Chester. "They point a butter knife wrapped in a dish towel to where we've got to sit."

"And we've gotta wait for the girls to finish before taking off," Weaver added. "We're even expected to clear the table afterwards."

"My, my," Faulkner sighed after a while, her eyes glinting. "I had no idea of the hardships you boys face."

"You know," I sputtered, "I think it's really great, having us over like this. It's neat seeing you out of school. There's lots of stuff I'd like to know that I can't ask in a classroom."

"Like what?" she smiled, and leaned slightly forward with eyebrows arched.

"Oh, like, you know .... How did you become a Christian?"

Faulkner threw back her head and hurled a laugh to the stucco ceiling. Her tongue flicked out of her tiny mouth for a moment, curling upwards to briefly lick her incisors before her gaze sank to rest on the bowl of guacamole.

"Oh, I can tell you're someone who's not backward about being forward, Mistah Gast! Pardon me. It's jus—" She shook her head, as though to shake the smile from her lips. "It's nothing. Now, well, I — My folks were Episcopalians, you know. I was raised in the church, an' for years I thought that was what God required. In my teens I stopped caring about even that, and it stayed that way until '68, when I was researching Roman literature down at GSU. I was going over Pliny the Younger's letters to the Emperor Trajan, seeking instruction on the proper way to put believers to death. Something struck me like a dart. I could have read similar evidence in the Bible a hundred times an' it wouldn' have mattered, but a pagan witness, someone out-side looking in, carrying no brief for Jesus .... Well, suddenly Christ wasn't just idle talk. That was the beginnin' for me." She exhaled heavily and scratched her chin. "That, an' a patch of unpleasantness in my personal life — well, who hasn't had that? — it made me receptive to the Lord for the first time since I was seven an' played Martha in a Sunday School pageant."

"Wow ...."

She suddenly squinted at Tibo and then at me, tugged at the neck of her sweater and asked, "It's hot, isn't it?"

"Oh, it's not bad," I stammered. I glanced around the room for consensus. They were as blank as a shaken Etch-A-Sketch, especially Chester, as though once the topic had shifted from food he'd lost interest. "It's nice for a change."

"I turn the thermostat way up in the winter for my othuh babies." Faulkner nodded towards her plants. "It gets so hot, sometimes I almost forget where I am." She raised her glass to her lips but didn't drink. "How'd you boys come to know the Lord?"

"Well," I began, "I used to be a Maoist — "

"Oh right!"

"You know?"

"You're the one whose pastor fell off of the cliff, aren't you? We don't get many ex-Maoists, you understand — ex-Mennonites, more likely — and that story's already made the rounds of the faculty lounge a couple of times."

"Wow. I had no idea."

"Well, it's a darn good testimony, son."

"Delbert would get you for that," Weaver yammered impulsively, chuckling in his milk. The more he worked his own material, the more I pined for the Dead Parrot sketch.

"Pardon, Nathan?"

"Delbert Moon," he elaborated. "He's always going on about minced oaths."

"Oh right. Mistuh Moon," she said slowly, wringing an extra syllable from his name while she smoothed the folds of her skirt. "I had him a couple of years ago. Nice boy, though I recall he did get exercised over some rathuh esoteric points of life in the Spirit." She took a sip from her glass before stifling a startling burp with two fingers to her lips. "You won't tell him I said that, will you?" We shook our heads. Now I was in her confidence.

The kitchen fumes reheated by the radiator had begun to make my eyes water, so I rubbed them discreetly. When a moment later my eyes blinked open, the world was gone.

"Power's out again," Weaver offered helpfully.

Faulkner indulged herself to a delicate groan before I heard the floor creak and padded footsteps saunter to the window's edge.

"You don' need to move," she assured Tibo as she braced her left hand on the sofa's armrest and stretched her right towards the blind's draw string. Another groan — this one, not so terribly graceful — and the blind flapped home like an office temp at five o'clock. The snow's reflection of moonlight cast the room in grainy, low contrast grey that evoked the grim cheer of a Fifties sitcom. Still, it was enough light to let us see again; at least to see what we expected or wanted to find. Babbs could count his corn chips, Fung could squint at his watch, Weaver could stare at the holes in his socks and I could study the side of Faulkner's face. Her head hung heavy in space like an immense and lonely planet.

"Lights out all around the circle. Most of the campus is dark, too. No telling how long they'll be out. Fortunately everything's practically done." She stood away from the window, put one hand on her hip and brushed a grey curl off her brow with the other. "Been a long time since I've eaten by candlelight."

Fifteen minutes more of awkward silence and more awkward chat before Faulkner led us to the dining room. The lights were still out, but my eyes had adjusted sufficiently to the dull candle glow to tease the cat, pretending I was about to set my foot down on his head. He didn't even move.

"Gideon, would you be so kind as to return thanks?"

I cleared my throat and bowed my head, but since the lights were out, I decided, for a change, to pray with my eyes open.

"Dear Lord, thank you for being so good to us — "

"Yes, Fathuh."

"Thank you for Miss Faulkner and her kindness in having us over here tonight." I felt Chester shift anxiously in his chair. The turkey's skin was crackling, spilling its fatty juices the longest yard from his nose. My prayer was making him squirm for longer than it takes to say "Rub a dub dub, thanks for the grub."

"We pray you'll bless this food to our bodies, and our bodies to thy service, in Christ's name, amen."

I rested my eyes on the pastel stripes of Faulkner's sweater, which spanned her chest like the bands of Jupiter. Over her shoulder I could make out three rows of pine shelves slung above the sink, heaped with cookbooks, a *Family Circus* compilation and what looked like a Greek-English lexicon. That was as far as I could see by the light of the stumpy beeswax candle. She made sure our glasses were full and told us to help ourselves. I passed on the yams.

"By the way," Faulkner said after a few minutes of mumbled compliments and sundry chewing sounds, "who knows what today is?"

"Tuesday?"

"Excellent, Nathan. Half marks for that. It's *Shrove* Tuesday, to be exact. Know what that is?"

"Aren't we supposed to eat pancakes?"

"If I were a Catholic girl, Chestuh, and I'm neither Popish nor girlish, that might very well have been your doom." I smiled to myself. The peachy fuzz of Faulkner's cheek glistened from a smudge of grease, but her nose had the steep solemnity of a Mayan sacred place. "Shrove Tuesday is the last day before Lent in the Christian calendar. You know Mardi Gras? Same idea, but rather more intemperate. Last party before the Easter season, when we're asked to abstain from natural pleasures."

Faulkner leaned back in her chair and stretched her legs beneath the table, pressing the cold toe of her canvas deck shoe hard against my shin. *She must think I'm a table leg*, I presumed, though for a few shameful moments I pretended that my professor was hot for a bout of footsie. I tried not to flinch, first in order to stoke that impure thought and then — while my leg tightened uncomfortably into a cramp — on account of embarrassment. *If I budge*, I reasoned, *she might think I was up to something prurient.* After what seemed like a night in Gethsemane, Faulkner reached for the mashed potatoes, shifting her foot in the process. When she moved, she moved away sharply, without a glance or an apology.

We'd nothing but bones before us and the promise of hot gingerbread and cream when I remembered we can't buy milk, we can only rent it. I excused myself, noticing Tibo scowl as I stood, as though I were cutting out on the *pro forma* offer of helping to do the dishes. Stumbling towards the bathroom I borrowed a small candle that was pooling red wax on a hallway bookcase. I felt for the door and found the lock as I shut it behind me.

I glanced in the mirror. My face was burning in the flickering orange flame. Sweat broke on my brow like the oils of the basting turkey. I looked like a man in the shoals of the Lake of Fire, drowning within sight of the T-shirt concessions. Behind me, I saw a pair of pantyhose hung to dry on the shower rod. The shadows in the candlelight made it look like a long, black veil. I swallowed hard.

An abrupt, hormonal rush tilted my centre of gravity to below the belt. My slumbering crocodile brain had snapped awake, and I felt it slither towards a window of opportunity. I felt horny and nauseous and short of breath as I fumbled with my belt. I recalled my father's definition of supply-side economics: "The Invisible Hand, home alone on a Saturday night, with a bottle of baby oil."

I stared at the pantyhose. *They've been against her legs — her naked legs.* That which I would not, I yabba dabba do. I lifted the toilet seat, unzipped my fly and flew out of the starting blocks, beating the clock in another three-legged race.

Whoa, brother, think what you're doing. Two months without an orgasm! Think of Polycarp. No, think of Origen. He had an answer, eh? If thine eye offend thee, and all that. Don't feel the blood warmth, the stiffening in your palm.

"Gideon, are you all right in there?"

"Huh? Oh sure, yes, fine."

"I jus' worried you hit your head in the dark."

Spinning like the Ur galaxies that soiled the unblemished Nothing, my semen clouded the toilet bowl. I felt sick. Protestants don't enjoy a Catholic division of labour with respect to the wages of sin. Venial, mortal, makes no difference to us. Every misstep warrants recall of the entire production line come business hours on Judgement Morn. God's love means never having to say I'm worthy.

With a yard of three-ply I wiped myself and buried the evidence at sea. Then, shaking with my spent and suddenly stupid-seeming lust, I whispered "God!" as a prayer of contrition and unlocked the door. I was afraid I smelt rude and obvious.

"Jus' in time for *Uno*, Mistuh Gast."

"Nudge nudge, wink wink, say no more."

"All I'm asking is, if you had your own Fortress of Solitude, would *you* hang out with a cub reporter?"

"I know, I know," I granted, planting my palms on the circulation desk. "But lest we forget, Jimmy was Superman's *pal*. Some things between guys aren't easily understood."

Kelly Deneault smirked as she stamped return dates inside the back covers of *Hebrew the Happy Way*, *Those Curious New Cults* and *That Hideous Strength*. I was the first to check out any of them. That made me feel special.

"I *know!* A cub reporter? Like, what *is* that?"

"Yeah, and he was always getting into trouble," Rory Zuckerman, her paunchy library supervisor and O.B.I.'s only Jew for Jesus, interjected. "I could never get a handle on that guy. He sure had his problems, eh? I mean with friends like that, right? It was like he needed round the clock care. Mr Mxyzptlk, for instance —"

"Oooh," Kelly cooed, "I'm impressed."

"'The imp from the fifth dimension,'" I added hastily. Rory got on my nerves when he got like this.

"One and the same. Well, he was always changing Jimmy into a werewolf, or a human porcupine or something ...."

"I think the porcupine was Miss Gzptlsnz's doing," Kelly said smugly without raising her eyes as she closed the last book, before allowing, "but your point's well taken." *Jeepers*, I thought, *this gal knows her stuff.* "Once — correct me if I'm wrong — Jimmy was turned into a 'giant turtle lad.'" She piled my books neatly, the paperback centred atop the two hardcovers — my three poor excuses for seeing her — and then, with the flat palm of her ruddy right hand, slowly pressed them towards me against the grain of the scratched walnut desktop. "So tell me," Kelly cooly sang, almost whispering, as she met my eyes with an innocent, almost teasing smile. "Could you respect anyone who's been a giant turtle lad?"

It was late February before I found there was more to Kelly than a pair of fetching calves. She'd begun working the Tuesday and Thursday afternoon shifts for Sarah Funk — a good librarian, great with child — and on the grounds of a glowing review in *Christianity Today* I happened to borrow *The Man of Steel and the Son of Man*. (I was a fan of Godpop typology that gussied up Christ like a paper doll in a cultural theory that had a dotted line along its cutting edge.) Kelly groused she'd found it a waste of time, and then listed all the reasons she found it more scriptural to compare our Saviour to the Silver Surfer.

We soon established a twice-a-week routine of baiting each other with superhero trivia. It was an unforgiving habit; hard to break and holding scant promise of trading up to a trifle harder, perhaps even dangerous addiction. Delighted though I was to talk to her — thrilled, really, for any cross-gender bending of the rules — and even though *Superman's Pal, Jimmy Olsen* truly had been my favourite comic book until I was old enough to shoplift my first copy of *Vampirella* to avoid a dirty look from a judgemental cashier, by mid-March I'd grown anxious to move beyond our cute quarrels about whether the Avengers could take the Justice League. But since campus boy-girl talk was never cheap, neither was it small, whatever was said. I knew of two sophomores who dropped out and wed on little more than a half dozen clandestine heart to hearts about the original cast recording of *Fiddler on the Roof.* (Both their soundtracks had been confiscated. *L'amour fou.*)

"Okay, okay," I conceded, like always, happy just to flirt. "I accept Jimmy's a jerk. The green plaid alone ...." Kelly snorted a laugh. "But you tell me, what about that special wrist gadget Superman gave him, so Jimmy could call for help?"

"What about it?" sniffed Rory. I liked Rory, but only as a librarian, and whenever he drew Kelly's attention I wanted to stuff his mouth with microfiche.

"Yeah — so what?" Kelly added. "That guy was such a pest, always distracting his so-called best friend from saving the world. Would a real friend do that?"

"You don't give Superman enough credit. It cost a lot to be his friend. Anyone would look bad standing next to him, right? But he must have thought a lot of Jimmy to give him that thing." Kelly didn't look impressed. I didn't glance at Zuckerman. "I guess what I mean is ...." My voice sank to a confidential whisper as I leaned across the desk. "Wouldn't it be *so* great to have one of those?"

"I'd rather have the Fortress of Solitude." Rory nodded thoughtfully at Kelly's words before slipping away to do some reshelving.

"I thought girls just read *Archie*," I sneered like an infatuated delinquent, who measures his mystery boners by the number of schoolbooks he knocks from the arms of his beloved.

"It's funny. I only read *Archie* after my conversion."

Suddenly, Kelly's gaze was snagged on something that unravelled her smile like a cat's cradle when the doorbell rings. She glanced at me briefly with *omygawd* eyes, cleared her throat and made an effort to look busy sorting index cards. Before I smelled his Old Spice, before he sidled up beside me at the desk, I knew the Dean must be near.

"Good evening, Kelly. Gideon."

Blier had caught us at this a couple of weeks before. He hadn't spoken; only scowled painfully, as if our bending the rules had somehow thrown out his back. Blier bore infractions of the student handbook just so. Not that strict compliance to the legal letter was at issue, as we so often were told. The principal was discipleship, and the godly behaviourists who drafted the handbook only worried how best to imprint a pattern of submission and godly fear upon the arhythmic hearts of today's troubled youth. Kelly and I needed no reminding that "library privileges shall not be abused for the pursuit of proscribed relations" (boldface, middle of page 22), and as a sheep before its shearers is dumb, so we had been judged and found wanting a good dressing down. I felt for the Dean. We all must have been such a disappointment.

"Everything alright here?" This was clearly a proscribed relation, so he was just toying with us. Blier sounded anguished. He hated having to do this.

"Fine — great."

"There, you're all set." Kelly slid the books even further towards me, almost onto the floor. "Enjoy."

I hurriedly gathered them up with one hand, hoisted my knapsack with the other, stammered "Good Afternoon" and ran the hell out of there. I'd expected Blier to call me back, and when he didn't I was tempted to glance back, but instead just wished Kelly well and dodged through the crowded library foyer. I picked my way among clots of students, mission displays, a papier-mâché empty tomb done to scale (the Easter gift of the senior class) and the world map that bristled with pink and blue pins for O.B.I. graduates serving overseas.

The pins represented active alumnists only. The retired and deceased were regularly removed, and the martyred were honoured with heart-shaped, golden broaches. The map wore eleven broaches. None had been added since the Congo rebellion. Some days I read it closely, as though it were a treasure map, of treasures found and never lost. I wondered about Larry Teller, Class of '48, who'd heard the call to plant a church in Amazonia and blessed God with a precious and gummy end. I wondered where my blue pin would eventually stick, and whether there'd be a pink one next to it. I wondered how joyous my death would be, and how sticky.

Once outside I leaned against a balustrade and tossed the books in my sack, which I then slung over my shoulder and started down the Spurgeon Way. The campus was enjoying another gracious chinook. ("A temperate kiss of God," Fiona Smiley, English teacher, called it — rather intemperately, I thought. In *At Home With God*, Barstowe described chinooks as "one more manifestation of divine forbearance," as though the Scripture about rain falling on the just and unjust should have been caught in proofreading.) Snow that had been heaped nipple-high the week before had melted to my ankles. Now runoff clear as a baby's pisswater was pooling in the sidewalk hollows before spilling into rivulets that coursed well past the tabernacle.

The sky was cloudless and consummate and screamed Jesus Loves You. I could have craned my neck to Heaven and yessir, there He'd be, nodding as if to say, "So? Who did you expect?" A gospel quartet was rehearsing nearby, and I quickened my stride to keep pace with their medley of Sunday School favourites.

> One door and only one
> and yet its sides are two;
> I'm on the inside
> on which side are you?

When I'd just passed the tabernacle's south entrance and was better than half-way home, a spindly figure wearing a yoghurt-coloured shirt and a pair of blue double-knit trousers with white sidewalls darted out from behind a corner and an unmade bed of tulips. He must have come from town, and was pressing against his belly something big and boxy in a white plastic bag. He began to turn towards the dormitory, and if I hadn't been walking so quickly he might have missed me.

"Gideon! Hey, brother!" Delbert Moon twisted to face me, almost losing his balance. He set the white bag on the sidewalk and steadied himself, wiping his brow with a slender, pale hand while he waited for me. "This is truly providential," he wheezed.

The bag was from Three Trees Home Hardware, and was stretched taunt over something the size of a toaster oven. He lifted the bag as I drew closer, and again held it hard against himself as we walked together.

His excitement at seeing me was disheartening. By design — my design — we hadn't seen much of each other in recent weeks. I had nothing against him. I'd seen the light on minced oaths and I even liked him, after a fashion. It was simply a matter of social expedience for me to put some distance between us. Being Delbert's friend had meant he was practically my only friend. I felt a spasm of guilt, but I'd been on campus long enough to learn that even Christians play at supply-side fellowship.

"Been downtown, Delbert?"

"Uh huh. Needed some things." His plastic bag was so tightly drawn around the box it was practically sheer, but he held it so snugly I couldn't tell what he'd bought. "Quartet, eh?" He nodded towards the practice room. "Good stuff. Going to the concert? Neat weather, eh? Meteorologists, climatologists, whatever they call themselves these days, they can tell you what a chinook is, you know, but they can't tell you *why* it is. That's what really matters." Moon chuckled softly and shook his head. "The only weather they should worry about is whether they're ready to meet the Lord, you know? Swell to see you, Gideon. Where you been? Haven't seen you lately."

"Yeah, I know. I've been real busy. You know — doctrine paper."

"Funny seeing you. I was going to look you up when I got to the dorm. What time is it now? Three thirty? Four? The thing is, could you drop by later? Tonight I mean? You going to the concert? Before the concert, how's that?"

"I thought it was compulsory."

"Right, sure. So before the concert? I've got a favour to ask. I'm afraid I can't really explain it now. You're eating at the Dining Hall, I presume? So how about six thirty-ish? How does that suit you? Six forty-five-ish?"

"No problem," I said breezily, stifling an urge to contradict myself. Guilt can land us in the deepest shitbath. "What's up?"

"Lots and lots," Moon giggled, squinting at the sky. Then he turned towards me and, smiled broadly before shaking his head again. "It's nothing to discuss here." He poked my shoulder with an index finger. "Don't worry; you're not in trouble."

"Are you?"

"Oh nononono. Nothing like that."

"A hint?"

"Nope. It's just something ...." Delbert stopped himself with a strangely frail smile. "Wait and see. Wait on God. Hey, now *there's* an idea! See you tonight. Sorry, I'm in a real pickle, time-wise. Lot's to do, lot's to do. Later, bro'!" And he sprinted ahead of me, awkwardly embracing his white plastic bag and whatever it stretched to hold.

When I reached the dorm I got a V-8 from the Coke machine outside the mailroom — Blier had replaced its soft drinks with fruit juices and vegetable cocktails; surely breaking the terms of its lease, but only in our best interest — and collected my mail. Besides a few corrected quizzes and a brief essay distributed by campus post I found a postcard from my grandmother and a manila envelope with the stamp of Cliffside Church.

The postcard was a photo of the Shifnal Giant: an ancient, chalk outline of a Celt in battle stance sketched upon a green hillside in the lake district, and favoured with a five-metre erection. The rudeness didn't bother me. (Or not much. I was bothered enough to assume that my grandmother hadn't noticed, or maybe didn't recognize it.) What really put me off was its aboriginal strangeness. I could hardly blame the Celts. Wrong time and place, and that's all she wrote for 'em in the Book of Life. I always found my comfort level higher when studying the anti-Christian rather than the non-Christian. To be against something at least admits its existence, and the reminder of generations living and dying without a few scraps of Gospel made me anxious.

I leaned against the wall and turned the card over. Usually she hadn't much to say. By now, I expected "Hope you know what you're doing" as much as her mention of how much she missed her shows. But here she said she planned to buy a home once she returned. She would invest in lottery tickets so she could afford something big enough for two, in case I ever needed a place.

I didn't bother opening the Cliffside envelope until I reached my room. Since January, when Filmore launched his biweekly newsletter, church mail was too familiar to get excited about, especially with articles like "Remembrance Day Rummage Sale a Boon for Boat People." But this time the envelope held something else besides. There was a smaller envelope, addressed in fine green ink and in a woman's hand to the church and to my attention. I tossed the newsletter on my desk ("Paul Henderson talks about Heaven" was the lead), sat on my bed and tore at the seal.

February 25

Gideon,

Bet you didn't expect to hear from me! And who's "me," you ask? Think back. Christmas Eve, outside the Eaton's Centre, a harpy in black leather. Is it coming back now? Need more help? Oppie, remember? I don't even know your last name, but your first is weird enough that I figured if I wrote to your church (the address was on the back of the pamphlets you gave us) a letter would reach you sooner or later.

So, why am I writing? I thought you'd be curious to know the name of my new pet rabbit (Sid), that I saw my first (and hopefully last) Leafs game last night, and my wisdom teeth are impacted. Let's see — anything else ...? Well, if you're interested, on January 12 Scott and I (and I'm not kidding!) both accepted Christ as our Saviour. (Seems like a lot of people say "personal" Saviour, but that sounds redundant to my untrained ears. What do you think?)

I wanted to let you know because you played a very important part in our discovering Jesus. It wasn't what you said, or the pamphlets. (They were kinda dumb, doncha think? But they must work on some people, so praise God I guess.) Really, it was more the memory of your humility and your sincerity that stayed with me, and provoked our wrestling with God for the first time in our lives.

Scott and I have started attending Showers of Blessing Assembly in the Annex. We're going to Wednesday night Bible classes and a discipleship session on Saturday afternoons. Scott's even trimmed his mohawk and taken up volleyball. Takes all kinds, eh?

Please pray for us, okay? Though Jesus could return any moment, I know we need to live as though there's still a long time to go. That means lots of temptations to overcome. I'd like to ask for your intercession on four things in particular. One is smoking. We're trying, but trying's not the point. We both know it's sin, and we're trusting the Lord for the victory. Another thing is my language. I hope you've forgotten, but my mouth is pretty foul. Some words seem still too easy for me to say. The third is Scott's music. He's still with the Bangkok Lady Boys. He's trying to be a witness in the band, but he knows it's no place for him anymore. Trouble is, he still enjoys playing. Please pray for him to do what's best.

The last thing is celibacy. So far, so good, but God help us!

Guess that's all for now. I hope to hear from you. Thanks again, from me and Scott, for just being there. (Wherever "there" is!)

Love in Christ (see, I'm already diggin' this spiffo Gospel jargon ☺).

Oppie Szabo

I read the letter three times before folding it back in the envelope and pressing it between First and Second Kings. I'd stained it with a couple of heavy teardrops, causing some ink to run, making it more precious. I didn't wipe my eyes; I loved how raw they felt, so red and wet. Then I closed my Bible, its gilt-hemmed pages crackling like a fresh bag of potato chips.

I was Scrooge the morning after: the Spirit had done it all in one night. Oppie and Scott, born again believers. I hadn't forgotten them, but I'd forgotten to pray for them since — When? Mid-January? The time of their conversion — and now I could see my name on heaven's game clock: it was still early in my soul-winning season and I'd scored two assists. (The Holy Ghost, that glory hog of the God Line, always bagged the garbage goals.)

I knelt by my bunk, pressed my face into the quilted blanket and stretched my arms until my fingertips were chilled by the wall's cold plaster.

"Lord," I prayed in a voice muffled by bedding unwashed since Halloween, and with my breath hot on my face, "thanks for stooping to use me. Your grace is — " I laughed abruptly, and enjoyed its resonance upon the quilt. "Your grace is *so* incredible. I sure haven't been trusting you enough. I haven't expected miracles. Not really. Forgive me for giving up on Oppie and Scott. Thanks for leading me to them; for the honour of playing a small part in their finding you. Thanks for not giving up on them — or on me." I rubbed my nose dry and lay still for awhile.

"Oh, Jesus," I finally sighed, as I would to only a lover or a God, "I just hope that even when I mess up, and I will, you won't give up on me."

I drew a deep breath and held it till my lungs burned.

Inhaling, exhaling: I mean, *really*. Both were gross indignities. What were they but humiliations for our own good; constant reminders of our corporeal punishment. Breathing was a page from God's biochemical handbook, written to bore sinners into physiognomic submission. And Jehovah is more ambitious than a Bible School dean: he expelled us all and still expects obedience. The body is such a heavy cross.

So respiration was a must, like wearing ties to class, but a day drew nigh when the Elect would discard their bodies like so many pistachio shells and be as the angels, neither inhaling nor exhaling, neither married nor given in marriage. No more pissing, shitting, farting, puking — no fuss, no muss, no more stubborn grass stains — once we'd shaken off our animal sacks seeped with blood and come and fluttered free to the right hand of our Elder Brother and our destiny: junior partners to the prosecution and the judgement of the damned.

But for now, the best I could do was permit myself a modest smile and the thought, *mission accomplished*. I released my breath slowly as though to teach my lungs a lesson, then crawled onto the bed and laid on my back. I folded my hands across my chest like a dutiful corpse dead to the world, and fell asleep.

4

awoke with a slight headache and sore throat at 7:30. A dull buzzing — the whir of an electric razor, I imagined — had bled into my dreams. I'd missed dinner and was late for my visit to Delbert, but all I managed was a mumbled "Gotta get up" through pasty lips, before closing my eyes and indulging myself to another twenty minutes. I was in no condition to judge the quick, let alone the dead, and didn't snap wholly awake until I rolled on my side and squinted at the clock on Nebraska's desk. My headache was gone but my throat was still sore. I didn't regret skipping the Dining Hall — it was asparagus-on-toast night — and a peach nectar from the vending machine sounded like just the thing. I'd grab one on the way out the door once I'd checked in with Delbert. Perhaps he hadn't left yet, and though I wasn't sorry about standing him up I thought the decent thing would be to let him sit with me for the concert. That's what guilt wrung from me. Since we were late, at least we'd have no choice but to sit at the back.

The hallway hummed with the contented drone of Christian men pumped on sugars and starch, laughing, talking hockey and knotting ties, running to the toilet for a quick dribble and shave before the concert. Beneath all of this purred that same electric buzz that had pricked my sleep.

Finally on my feet, I noticed that a yellow slip from the Dean's office had been slid under my door. "You have an appointment Monday, 3 p.m.," was all it said. A yellow slip was like an amber street light: both a warning to slow down before you hurt someone and an incentive to accelerate until you killed yourself. Mine was probably for getting caught with the lights on 15 minutes after curfew. Cramming for an Apologetics test was the reason, but it was no excuse. You never wanted a yellow slip, but it was never that heavy. Not like a red one. A red slip was the invitation to get your affairs in order.

The hall was quiet when I locked my door and ran a hand through my Chad Everett, wishing I'd thought to check the mirror. On the way to Delbert's room I made up my mind to use his, and was probing my pockets for a comb when I realized the buzzing was coming from his end of the hall. I thought nothing of it, and little more than that when I stood at his door and knew that the buzzing issued from its other side. I was only curious when I noticed an envelope taped below his room number, addressed to me in his tiny, delicate script. I didn't begin to worry until I opened it and found nothing but a key, but I was still more inquisitive than concerned. I knocked, waited, then rapped a little harder, calling his name. Finally the buzzing stopped.

"Gideon?"

"Uh huh. What's the key for, Delbert?"

"The door," he said sharply. "You alone? Use it." And so I did.

The air tasted sick; as clammy and stale as a salami sandwich left in a high school locker over the holidays. Delbert stood across the room, staring into the mirror that was screwed to his closet door. I assumed he was auditing his pimples. He didn't turn to greet me.

Except for a pair of cotton briefs with a smear of butter-scotch at the crack, Delbert was naked. His skin had a curious patina, a sweaty gloss that tossed back the wavering flores-cence of the ceiling lights like the shimmer of moon upon a lake's burial dress. The air had a ticklish aftertaste, as though moments before it had been charged with eccentric electricity. If I touched anything, I imagined my hair would stand on end.

I hadn't seen Delbert naked before. With one shower room for three hundred men, I'd seen plenty. At Bible School as everywhere, always, cocks were objects of secret pride and public shame, though we could only guess what they were good for and why God had cursed us with their blessing. There was a fat upperclassman, a singer with the King's Ambassadors, well regarded for his evangelistic skill with pup-pets, whose baby prick was a thimble of uncut neglect. After he'd dry and dress and leave, someone would say something — not a joke: too pointed; not "cock" or "dick" or "penis": too dirty — but a triple entendre, an obscenity with a crust of spiritual allowance. If you laughed it was only because you had a filthy mind. There was a stumpy, round-shouldered sophomore, legally blind from birth, but with a cock that rode his leg better than half way to his knee. Strange; not so many quips about him. Once he'd left I sometimes heard some good humoured, self-conscious attempt at penile self-criticism, but never once did someone dare to mutter, "Why do *we* care?" It hadn't occurred to me before, but I'd never met Delbert in the showers.

He had an unusual, piebald back, as pale as filleted halibut for the most part, but dusted with several darker, tan-coloured patches. One zig-zagged from the dimples above his tailbone to his left kidney; another was a smudge between his shoulder blades the size of a jelly donut. His hair was wet and slicked back, too thin to perfectly cover the back of his scalp. A white towel hung loose about his slender neck, while below it beads of sweat and water gathered to brave the moguls of his cervi-cal vertebrae. Both his hands were raised to his right forehead, out of my sight, and his elbows blocked for me the reflection of his face. Delbert didn't budge. He didn't move at all.

"You in? Shut the door, please. Hurry." I wanted it left open, the room was so stifling, but I respected what I thought was modesty. As I closed it, Delbert added, "I didn't think you were coming, so I started without you."

"Started what?" I squinted vacantly at his mottled back and made a sour face. "You know, it's really stuffy in here. Before we go, maybe you should open the window. Sorry I'm late, but we'd better hurry. You should get dressed." I didn't care about the concert; I just worried about missing compulsory events. And there were more of those in a day than ugly dicks in the showers.

I leaned against a bunk post to wait for Delbert to finish whatever occupied him, and was suddenly impressed by the rare, relative untidiness of his room. His sleeping bag was rolled up as always, but his clothes were carelessly strewn over the bottom bunk and his shoes had been kicked against a closet door. One desk was bare apart from his brown vinyl Bible, open to the Book of Jeremiah, but the other was littered with a crumpled plastic bag, an empty Black and Decker box, some Styrofoam packaging and several sheets of instruction. What looked like a library copy of *Gray's Anatomy* sat on the radiator beside his thigh, and a blue plastic beach pail nestled between his big toes. As I noticed it, I heard a dollop of something drip into it.

"I should've waited, but you were *so* late and I was *so* anxious to get started. It's my own fault, I guess."

With his hands fixed upon his forehead, and keeping his feet in place as though playing Twister with himself, Moon turned slowly towards me. No, his hands weren't against his head, they met above it, and were holding something that was pressing hard against it. Something shiny, metallic — a pimple remover was my first thought, but this looked too big. A caulking gun? That didn't make sense. No, but gun shaped. A gun? Somehow, that didn't occur to me. A power drill. *A power drill?* I didn't get it. I squinted at him, leaning forward, hands on hips, stumped for how to caption this picture. Then the threads and specks of blood on his hands and cheeks came into focus, and the single clot the colour of cherry nectar that seeped from a hole in his brow no broader than the face of an aspirin. From the centre of the hole poked a shiny horn, the metallic bit, about two inches of it, one end nestled in the drill socket and the other disappearing inside his skull, as though it were a straw and his brains the choice of a new generation.

"Not a pretty sight, eh?"

"Delbert! Holy *crap!*"

"Gideon," he clucked, his gory brow wrinkling in a frown, "no need for that kind of talk. Remember, you're a Kingdom kid." His frown disturbed the clot, which shook free another drip that trickled down his cheek in a crazy, bloody course till it collected in the corner of his lips like acid rain in an abandoned eaves trough.

The drill had sliced a neat hole through Delbert's skin, punching into his skull about three inches above his right eye, with God knew how much drill bit still inside. Blood freckled his pale flesh like burst mosquitoes on a bug lamp, but given what he'd done to himself I was astonished there wasn't more.

I remember the plastic pail, the old orange one in the basement next to the water heater, that my mother used to haul to my sick bed when I'd wake her in the night squirming with flu or Halloween candy. She would sit with me, drumming her fingers on my maple headboard until I had finished purging. Even if it was just a head cold, even if I hadn't felt nauseous and had just wanted to piss off a day of school, her plopping the puke bucket next to my pillow was usually all the motivation necessary to fill it frothing to the brim. Leaning over the lip of my mattress, staring so deeply into the pail that I could count the plastic rings on its bottom as though it were a cut of old growth pine, I knew instinctively how much nature hates a vacuum. I learned that when you stare into the puke bucket, the puke bucket stares back.

When I saw the pail at Delbert's feet I remembered all my close calls and false alarms; all the sour notes of my adolescent maladies. If I'd noticed it earlier, the pail would have told me all I needed: that someone here was ill, or giving it his best shot. The hole in his head just filled in the blanks.

My dry mouth hung open as though I'd broken my jaw, all my words withered and blown away, and Delbert just stood there oozing, moving gingerly to shrug his shoulders while a sheepish grin splayed his lips. Despite the blood, the bucket and his pierced skull, my body's frightful wisdom found his grin the scariest sight. Indignation cleared my head like a whiff of cordite, and I spun about and pitched myself towards the door.

I threw the door open and dashed into the hall, shouting loud and long for help. When finally I paused to gauge a response all I heard was the rattling echo of footfalls in a stair-well and the slam of a storm door blown shut by the wind. And then again from Delbert's room, the hum of the drill.

He'd turned afresh to the mirror, and was staring deeply, peacefully at the drill work as it showered his scalp with the fine white powder of pulverized bone. He resembled a figurine in a shaken Christmas snow ball. Delbert stopped drilling as I re-entered the room. This time, I didn't shut the door behind me.

"I *thought* you'd be shocked." Delbert broke into another sly smile as he glanced at my reflection. Blinking away flecks of pow-der and blood, he giggled. "I mean, of course, right? But don't worry. I'm glad you're here. I'm almost through and everything's pretty much okay, though I think my arms are falling asleep."

I managed to gasp, "What are you *talking* about?" and almost immediately followed that with a cackle of hysterical astonishment. I pressed a finger hard against my brow, hard enough to hurt me back to earth, and I steadied myself by grasping the bunk post. "What have you done?"

"It's kind of complicated," Delbert said with a pensive squint, as he slowly craned his neck to face me. "First thing, I guess, was this *incredible* dream I had last week." His eyes rolled heavenward, and he smiled sweetly at its recollection. "I really don't want to get into it now, but believe me, you — well, you wouldn't believe it. The Lord really spoke to my heart, you know? He sort of straightened a few things out. It's all rather personal. *Oops.*" With a fresh speckle of blood spotting the carpet he shifted his feet to bring his body in line, nudging the pail along so it might catch the next drop.

"But *what* are you doing? Look at yourself!"

"What? Skin grows back. Till then I'll use a bandaid. No biggie. Seriously, it's not like I'm *dying* or anything. Truth is, you don't look so good yourself. Sit yourself down, 'kay?"

Delbert's cheeriness rattled me. He was preposterously serene, and even with a shaft of metal sunk in his skull he still thought to watch my tongue. For a moment, I even hoped he might know what he was doing.

Through it all, a crazy tape kept playing in my head: *So this is what a guy who's drilled a hole in his head looks like.*

"Can you please put that down first? I'm not dealing with this very well."

"No. I don't think so."

"Why not?"

"You know, it's kind of funny. The skull's a serious piece of work." He shrugged and gave a little sigh.

"What are you talking about?"

"Actually, I'm a little stuck."

"You're *stuck?*" My voice cracked along with my courage. I collapsed upon his bunk, doubled over, nursing my temples with two cold hands.

"Well, I don't know for sure, exactly. I've tried to take it out, but it's very tight in there. I don't like the sound it makes scraping the bone. Makes me kinda queasy." It was difficult to tell with all the smears of blood, but Delbert seemed to blush. "But no problem. From all I've read, it should pop out easily enough once I'm through."

"All you've read?" I managed to snort. "What are you reading? What are you talking about? What *is* this?"

"Like I said, I really don't want to go into details. Not about *why* I'm doing it, anyway." Delbert paused a moment to suck his teeth and tap his feet. When he began again, he sounded like a Sunday School lesson. "You take the Bible seriously, don't you? Sure you do. What do you think of Moses, Isaiah and Hosea? Great men of faith, right? And how did the world treat them? What do you think Children's Aid would have told Abraham? While the Lord tarries, devotion is going to look a little crazy. If it doesn't, then maybe —"

"But Delbert, there's crazy, and there's drilling a hole in your head!"

"— then maybe we're not really listening to God. But I'm not asking anyone to understand. That's not my business. This is between me and God — I'm just being faithful the best way I know how. God wants to make me an example." *God told me to.* Who can argue with that? Who should? As the rain falls on the just and unjust, so God's Word comes to the wise and the mad, and in the language of their understanding. God asks strange things of us. Incommunicable things. "Who am I to ask the Lord to explain Himself. It's *his* skull. I mean, for *goodness* sake!"

"So," I said after a long silence, in a hollow whisper, *"are you trying to kill yourself?"*

Delbert's eyes swelled as though the question had stunned him, as if I'd wounded him by suggesting such a thing, and when he replied his voice had an exasperated, bitter edge.

"Christians don't kill themselves. Not *real* ones. I'm not drilling *into* my brain. For goodness sake Gideon, isn't it obvious? God willing, it's just a little hole." He took a long, awkward moment to wipe his mouth on the towel which hung about his shoulders. The blood that had dappled his cheek was smeared together like a port wine stain. "You still don't get it, do you?"

"Get it? Get what?" I shook my whole and heavy skull. Suddenly, it felt so monstrously full.

"All I'm saying is, this is part of God's plan for me. I'm not saying it's for *everybody.* It's not like I'm telling *you* to do it." He took a deep breath and shifted his weight. His hands, I imagined, must be very tired. "And honestly, this looks much worse than it is. Doesn't even hurt. It's just bone. I mean sure, cutting the skin smarted, but it's pretty thin there. Kind of like getting inoculated."

I've got to get help, I thought, but what I said was, "Why did you ask me here?"

"Because God wanted you here. It's funny," he chimed, "I really don't know why. I guess it made sense to have someone spot for me, you know, in case I got into trouble. But I was sure you wouldn't understand and that you'd try to stop me. I prayed about it this morning, but I felt confident that the Lord wanted you to be with me. It's probably God's will that you were late. But I don't know why you're supposed to be here. You know," he added, with a self righteous twitch of the nose, "maybe you should ask him yourself."

"God can't possibly want this," I muttered softly; so softly I thought perhaps I'd only meant to say it.

Once Delbert decided his revelation would fail to convince me, he tried another angle. He thought I needed to hear that four out of five doctors recommend carving an ass for a constipated mind.

"You know, it's actually very therapeutic. It'll be a good aid to meditation. It helps focus your thoughts." He made it sound as natural as a fart, as supernatural as a prayer.

"I should hope so," I sputtered.

"What's the time?" He wore a watch, but he wouldn't twist his wrist to check it.

"About quarter after eight."

"Really? We've got to hurry up. We're missing the concert."

"You can't be serious! Delbert, missing a barbershop quartet's got to be the least of your worries."

"But it's compulsory," he whined, nervously rapping the fingers of his left hand upon the drill's motor housing. "I really looked forward to hearing them."

"You're going to be expelled anyway. If you survive, that is. You've got to know that, don't you?"

"You got a steady hand, bro?"

"Huh? Why? What?"

"I think we're going to have to try to break through. There's not much left."

"Forget it." Mutilation or apotheosis? Count me out, brother. "I've got to get help — "

"I'll just start it up again when you've gone. But my arms are *so* tired. I figured I'd be through by now. I didn't think the bone would be so thick and tough." His words were punctuated by the thunk of another drop of blood, this one hitting the target. "Maybe I should have practised."

With the shiny prick of the drill poking in his skull, its motor humming like a idling vibrator, I noticed for the first time that Delbert's own candy was stiffened in his shorts. He didn't even blush. He was in the holy of holies, the bedchamber of his Beloved, a place beyond shame and vulgar lusts. This was sacred self abuse; he was making his body a living sacrifice. This was a sloppy kiss of innocence and experience, the blood slobbering his lips like a lover's ejaculate. Delbert grinned broadly. He was getting off and he didn't even know it. I stood, but just to take my eyes off his crotch. I made no move towards him or the door.

"Delbert, there's no way I'm going to help you do this. But until I think of a way to stop you, or until help arrives or something, if you'd like me to pray with you ...."

"Thank you, Gideon," he sniffled with a tremulous croak. "That's, well, just so Luke 10 of you. I'd really like that. We haven't prayed together for quite a while. But really, you can't believe how heavy my arms are. If you could hold this thing for a moment, you don't even have to do anything —"

"No no. Sorry. Can't do that. I mean, I just won't." Then suddenly, with the clarity of a *Jeopardy* home contestant, the situation resolved. "I'm going into the hall and pull the fire alarm."

A shudder slowly rolled over Delbert's body as he shut his eyes and squeezed out a tear. He breathed deeply, blinking at my feet with a muted smile, even as they moved towards the door.

"Whatever," he eventually whispered. And squeezed the trigger.

"*Fuck!*" He couldn't hear me.

Once I'd thrown the alarm I rushed back into the room like a superhero and made a grab for the drill. Immediately I realized I couldn't fight Delbert for it without making a worse mess of his head. He knew it too, and was grinning about it. I fought the mad impulse to push with all my might, and drive the auger bit through the cottony-soft tissue of his cerebellum. It could have been so easy. All I'd have to say would be *Oops*.

My hands were warmed by the handle, and tickled by the vibrations. I pursed my lips, closed my eyes and prayed. When we met no more resistance the drill slipped out effortlessly, without intention. There was a strange gurgling from the hole and Delbert staggered back. An alarming arc of blood spouted from the wound, splashing my trousers and the carpet. As he crumpled upon a swelling halo of blood and bone shavings I dropped the drill, grabbed my wrist and waited for Superman.

III

In those days cats and dogs will be enemies, swords will cut better than radishes, fields and mountains will be out in the open, and the taverns will be well frequented.

Master Pegasus Neptune,
a Venetian *cantastorie*

1

He didn't die.

Much blood was lost — by the time help arrived, a lavish amount — but astonishingly, he'd suffered no brain damage. *No brain, no damage*, I was surprised to hear someone joke just a couple of weeks afterwards. It startled me because that was the only joke I heard, and there should have been dozens more. No one was speaking about it. I expected an official announcement of some kind, maybe something from the Tabernacle pulpit or a posting outside the Dean's office, but there was nothing. Certainly word spread somehow. Within a few days, all but a few reclusive staff members working on the tiny campus dairy farm must have heard the rudiments. Yet you would hardly have known it.

I needed to talk about what had happened, but everybody seemed afraid to listen. For much of the rest of the semester I sensed my classmates were embarrassed or suspicious of me. I felt infectious, but of what, I didn't know. But it was as if I'd received a catastrophic diagnosis and all they saw now was contagion.

I visited Delbert in Foothills Hospital just after his *pro forma* expulsion. (The Dean had denied him permission to return to campus. He was instructed that a parent or guardian would have to clean out his room. He asked me to do it. Delbert was one of the disappeared, now.) He'd called me the day before, sounding, it seemed to me, more reasonable than he ever had, and asked that I bring one of his copies of *Your Shoes Are Too Big, Lord.* He looked wan, just like always, and half his forehead was pasted over with an extravagant bandage, but he was buoyant, not manic, and claimed he felt "Great, really. Super, you know?" I believed him. I didn't want to believe it, but it made me wonder, at least for the bus ride back to campus, if maybe he'd done the right thing.

For some time I thought of transferring to another Bible College. Later, when I felt more together, I thought of dropping out. And for a while it looked as though I might have no choice. Blier conducted his own investigation, calling me twice to his office for debriefings. He eventually determined that there was little more I could have done, but I was left with the impression he'd reached the conclusion rather grudgingly. But Pastor Filmore had fallen off his cliff just for me, so God could bring me to himself. And I'd failed Geometry so He could bring me here. So here I stayed.

I began spending more of my free evenings in the library periodicals room, hugging the corner of the men's musty velour couch, unwinding with the literature of the evangelical fringe. "The King James Version the *only* Bible?" "Dinosaur bones evidence of fallen angels?" Wacky stuff. Even with Delbert and his drill, Overcomer seemed an oasis of moderation.

I enjoyed laughing at those even more extreme than me, but I felt the laughter turn bitter and my heart begin to calcify with cynicism. I gave it up, and like everyone else, started picking over weeks-old issues of *Maclean's* which the staff had

conscientiously sanitized with black marker, so every bikini or
odd topless shot in the "People" section was daubed with similar sombre, Hutterite-like modesty. A couple of times I thrilled
to find an image they'd missed, and passed it on to my new
peer group who had the nerve to look up "fellatio" in the big
Oxford dictionary. When I'd finished with the *Maclean's* I'd turn
to the *Calgary Herald*. It was there, in my third year, that I first
read the Keaton twins were coming.

2

I remember the quarter-page ad that ran on the religion page, and its photo of David and Jonathan in matching white blazers as sickly pale as unattended pimples. They stood back-to-back, their arms folded across their chests beneath the display type "THE KEATON TWINS SAY, 'LOOK TO JESUS!'" Twins? That couldn't be right, I thought. Compared to his brother, David seemed scrawny and weathered, seemingly five years his senior, with a few more crinkles around the eyes and much sparser black hair — maybe a couple of fistfuls off the top — and a complexion that recalled the baked appearance of the homeless. He was smiling, but only just, while Jonathan wore a broad grin that sculpted his pumpkin face with an almost oppressive cheeriness. David looked like an Anchorite; Jonathan, like an anchorman.

The Keaton's were to lead a week of revival meetings at one of Calgary's more cavernous Christian Alliance churches. Just a week, but in the militant cells of the confessing Body, God is no respecter of schedules. "One day with the Lord is as a thousand years," wrote Peter, so you can imagine how interminable a week can seem. Few must have been surprised when the week became a month of olde-tyme, fire-breathing, Holy Ghost-fuelled shit disturbance.

By the second week a bus departed our campus every evening full of students and staff, eager to spelunk the well-lit cavities of their God consciousness. I barely gave the Keatons a thought, let alone a prayer. It was only when I read Pastor Filmore's announcement in *The Solid Rock*, almost a half-year in advance of their Cliffside summer crusade, that I realized they were Siamese twins.

Much of the newsletter's next issue was devoted to their biographies, which was lifted whole and without attribution from their promotional materials. The lead article was entitled with oblique perversity, "What God Hath Put Together":

"Just like home delivery of the Atlanta Constitution!"

With his patented hearty chuckle, that was how Virgil Keaton liked to describe how he and wife Enid first came upon the twins. The devoted couple had already spent twelve rich years in Brazil with the Global Gospel Fellowship, and were crowning their mission service by planting their third church along the Madeira River in the Amazon basin when they literally stumbled across the boys at their door one morning in 1957.

It has often been said that if the twins did not share kidneys and liver, they would need a blood test to prove they were even related, let alone brothers! They looked to be from six to twelve months old; or rather, one looked to be six months, the other about twice that. Both were obviously Indian children, though the contemplative David (the self-described "runt!") had a noticeably darker complexion than Jonathan, who in turn exhibited a markedly more, shall we say, "exuberant" deportment. But brothers they were, and more than brothers. Joined from shoulders to pelvis, back to back, a perfect 180 degrees, they were certainly twins, alright. Twins, who could never look each other in the face.

Where they had come from was a mystery. The word went out among the villagers, then up and down the river, but none were found who would admit to ever having seen or even heard of such novel children. Meantime, the Keatons cared for the boys as though they were their own. Virgil had been preparing a Bible series in the first book of Samuel when the boys were found, so right from the start it seemed the most natural thing in the world to call them David and Jonathan. Virgil and Enid had never been blessed with children, so after much searching for the boys, natural parents as well as plenty of prayer and fasting, these tillers in the Lord's field came to see the boys as God's extraordinary grace.

When the Keatons final tour of service was complete and they returned to Atlanta, David and Jonathan were examined by top surgeons to determine the chance of survival if separation were attempted. David most certainly would die, they were told, and it was quite likely that both would perish. After more waiting upon God, Virgil and Enid decided the Creator had joined David and Jonathan for a reason — a reason they were not privy to — so they chose not to proceed with the operation. That reason soon became evident, as the boys soon found salvation as easily as you or I find a plug nickel on the sidewalk. Before Virgil and Edith passed into glory they rejoiced to see their sons devote their lives avidly to the Lord's work, and their crusades become a cause for much glorifying of the untold, manifold mercies of the Lord.

For two years, ever since I'd watched Delbert Moon reno-
vate his skull, I'd cultivated a wariness of Christian sideshows.
There were too many Gospel midgets and born-again devil
worshippers about for my liking. Too many freelancing carny
barkers trumpeting the One Way as if it were a midway, baiting sinners with the snare of their tragedies and moral quirks,
neglecting the Word made flesh for word upon word about
their own mangled selves. It never crossed my mind that they
might be in it for the money. Demonstrably, most weren't
wealthy enough to be successful hypocrites. Often, they
weren't even snugly middle class. What worried me, and what
I came to presume until shown otherwise, was that their egos
were sluts for congregational hand jobs.

Take, please, the former Satanist, fundamentalist stand-up.
Judging by the tapes Chester Babbs lent me ("You gotta hear
this dude! He's *hilarious!*"), his billing was the funniest thing
about him. His only sense of timing was the conviction that
sinners would soon run out of it. Ten minutes of grievous,
take-my-sin-please cornball, a salacious ramble about his salad
days as high priest of Satan and a half-hour altar call did not
make for side-splitting stuff. But dying-to-self is easy; it's comedy that's hard.

Others were less odious, but more pathetic. Like the moti-
vational gamin with Audrey Hepburn eyes, paralysed from the
neck down when she was struck on her bike by a drunken cabbie. Her boundless spunk filled halls with Christians anxious to
watch her paint an inspirational watercolour with a brush
clenched between her teeth while the cabbie, sober and dedi-
cated to Christ, warbled "He Touched Me." The campus book-
store stocked a half dozen of her audiocassettes, a calendar
and three volumes of autobiography. According to the dust
jackets, she was barely 23.

Not surprisingly, these people never came to Three Trees.
Few strayed from the American midwest, and for those who
did, Overcomer was too grounded in stolid, prairie
Anabaptism to extend much welcome. (One of my reasons for
pride in the place.) So long as I kept reading the religion page
of the *Calgary Herald*, I expected to find a notice with the all-

bold, all-cap banner, THE MAN WHO PIERCED HIS SKULL FOR CHRIST. HEAR HIM SHARE THE PAIN, AS HE SHARES GOD'S PLAN FOR YOUR LIFE.

But then I got bonked by a volleyball, and O for a thousand tongues to sing my great Redeemer's praise!

3

Mary Christmas had a wicked serve, but that was as far as it went. Her wickedness was well contained by the volleyball court in the girls' gym of Overcomer Bible Institute. A tapestry the length of two and a half Oldsmobiles graced the bubblegum-pink cinderblock at the south end, just above the basketball hoop, admonishing us to present our bodies as living sacrifices. Though she wasn't wearing a tank top but rather an Amy Grant T-shirt, still, by the press of her bra against Amy's forehead I could, with some effort, imagine the wholesome form beneath Mary's Maidenform bra.

Not that I tried. Not right away. I'd gone to watch Kelly Denault, whom I'd had obsessed about since she passed me a sweet potato between her knees during an icebreaking frosh mixer two years before. As I'd taken the yam, gently yet with a man's resolve, Kelly blushed and smiled shyly. Our calves were familiar for only an instant, but that instant held the magic of words I could never pronounce, though knew well enough to look up in a good, unabridged dictionary. Afterwards, someone gave us balloons.

In two years on campus, rubbing leg joints was the sum of my secret life. Inter-gender hanky panks were neurotically discouraged, yam passing being permitted under only the strictest supervision. A senior couple — an engaged, senior couple — were expelled for holding hands in the library stacks. As a sophomore, watching the new crop of freshmen troop back to the dorms wearing satisfied smiles and tell-tale vegetable stains on their cords, I'd grin and sigh wistfully, "It doesn't get any better than this."

And it almost didn't. Two years should be time enough for any obsession, particularly a silly one. But this one hung on, to my chagrin, like a tenacious fart. I saw a lonely future looming, one of furtive glances, unfurnished rooms and bewildered prostitutes. ("I haven't got a sweet potato, darling. Is eggplant good for you?") Frankly, I was in over my head with Kelly's calves. And from whence cometh the help for a fundamentalist fetishist? Since it was not yet too preposterous for me to pray, "Lord, show me a sign," and I was still believer enough to expect one, a lightening bolt would have been a start. I settled for a volleyball in the face.

Later, Mary told me the serve had felt struck by an unseen hand; a hand that didn't play by the rules of Man. It struck me flush on the nose and dropped at my deck shoes. "Oof!" I gasped, more shocked than hurt. *Oh Lord, is this thy spheric messenger sent to try thy servant for gazing upon thy handmaid's gams?* And then Mary sprinted across court for the ball, apologizing, smiling like a crescent sun moving out of eclipse. She rejoined the game.

Kelly could wear sweats for all I cared. Mary was an angel. Her face shone with the *shekina* glory of the Lord. Everything shone. Perhaps I needed to sit down. But lightening bolt or no I had my sign, and though God had my heart, I hoped the Three-in-One would be gracious enough not to mind sharing a ventricle or two with Mary.

I hadn't met her before that afternoon (With whom, I fumed, had she passed yams?), but I'd been telling obvious jokes about her name since I'd seen it on a sign-up sheet for Friday night mall evangelism in the Fall. She was tall, slim and seriously tanned, with a ponytail of straight walnut hair that reached almost to her waist. Before the game had finished, before I'd even tossed off a brotherly "Praise the Lord," I had decided on Joshua if it were a boy and Sarah if a girl. Oh, chaste *agapé*.

"You and Mary, huh?"

It was the November of my Junior year, and it was Tibo Fung, whispering conspiratorially to me one morning in the hallway outside the dormitory washroom. He was fiddling with the knot of his candy cane tie, and his breath was still hot with breakfast porridge. It was the first time someone connected me to Mary. This was the blessed confirmation I needed to learn that we were, in fact, connected. Until then, I thought I was fooling myself.

Since Overcomer's social contract had been drafted to inhibit the circulation of premarital pheromones, students of dissimilar gender were permitted to mix only in manageable numbers, such as anything more than two. There was simply no leaving a single male alone with a single female. Over the years, and against the objection of those who thought it meant compromise with the World, some allowance was made for our God-given heterosexuality. A concession introduced my sophomore year was to permit juniors and seniors a single date per semester. The date could go no longer than three hours, and no further than dinner at the home of a married staff member. All you could hope to touch was a big tumbler of RC Cola. If the date was successful, the couple could request that their relationship be "recognized," which was the official designation of going-steady status. These couples could also sit together for Sunday lunches and exchange mail twice weekly. They were the Big Virgins on Campus.

There were, naturally, some who found their way around the rules. Sympathetic staffers might excuse themselves for a few minutes so a favourite couple could hold hands, kiss or pray together. But if the rules found their way back to the couple, discipline was harsh. Characteristically, partners found in an "unrecognized relationship" were subject to expulsion, followed by much prayer that the Lord would condescend to shepherd them back to Himself. Astonishingly, and with some perversity, this segregation extended even to brothers and sisters, though they were granted the additional dispensation of a ten-minute phone call to each other's dormitory once a week.

Mary was a freshman, and therefore ill prepared — in the estimation of the Social Life Committee — for the insinuation of a social life, even for what passed for one at Bible school. There could be no date until her Junior year; no sanction for me to naturally explore my thesis that maybe, just maybe, she dug me. All we had was body language, which wasn't saying much. Eye contact was the only kind the handbook conceded, and that surely by oversight.

But Tibo knew. *Me and Mary.* I wasn't making it up.

Furtively I glanced from side to side, more as a show of intrigue than genuine confidentiality. The only ones to keep in the dark were the Dean, a few puritanical stoolies who couldn't get kissed even if it were a course requirement, and Kelly Deneault. (Though our flirting had never born fruit, other than the one bruised yam, I thought of her now as a lover scorned. *Delta Dawn, what's that flower you have on?*) As for the rest, I wished they had but one nose that I could rub in it. Or better yet, I should rub Mary's nose; the one that began beneath wide, dun-coloured eyes and ended succinctly above a mouth that was so often curled in a virtuous, sensuous smile. That nose. A nose for rubbing.

"How do you know?"

"Everybody knows. She took your scarf at the hockey game."

"I got it back."

"*Scented,*" he leered.

I grinned self-indulgently. She'd done that, hadn't she?

The night of the deciding game in the intramural final she'd walked the aisle behind me and, without stopping, had yanked the thing right off my neck. When I got it back at the end of the game it smelled just like her. (Or what I imagined was her; I couldn't get close enough to tell.) Edgy stuff for Overcomer, where loose lips sink scholarships. But I was so proud she'd taken that risk for me that I couldn't drop it. I wanted Tibo to tell more.

"*Everybody* knows?"

"It's so obvious, man. I saw you two at lunch yesterday."

The only meal at which the sexes were allowed to mix was lunch. The random order of the boy/girl serving lines determined our tablemates. Student ushers guarded the beverage counter to deter queue jumpers. When, by chance or grace, Mary and I were seated together, we were both so hot and jittery that we barely touched the creamed asparagus on toast.

We were sitting across from each other in the library reference room, just days left in the first semester. Books and papers were scattered on the tables before us, but our eyes rarely fell to them. After some time, she sighed deeply and walked out of the room, holding some sheets of paper. I followed her into the foyer, hoping to catch her at the water fountain for a word or two of dizzy banalities. I couldn't see her, so I took a long drink myself. When I turned around, she was right behind me.

Her face was flushed. Before I could mouth a glib hello she said, "Check out *A Manual Grammar of the Greek New Testament.*"

"Dana and Mantey? I've already got a copy."

She looked stricken. "Just *do* it," she hissed. "*Please.*" Then she quickly collected her things and left.

I went to the stacks of linguistic texts and found the book, picked it up and rifled the pages. My heart skipped like the mountains in Psalm 114, because in the middle of the section on the imperative mood I found several crisply folded sheets of paper. Without removing the sheets I took the book to the circulation desk. Kelly Deneault was on duty. I think I mumbled a thanks before rushing off with my first dispatch from the Other Side.

December 14

Darling Gideon,

You know what? I love you! I've been telling myself "I love Gideon" over and over for weeks, and now I want you to hear it. How many times can I say "I love you" before I get bored? I don't think I can count that high!!!

It's funny. I have so much to tell you, but I'm finding it so hard to know what to say now. But just writing your name makes you seem a little closer. *Gideon.* It's kind of funny, isn't it? Here you are in front of me, and I miss you so much my head hurts. I know the Lord wants me here, but sometimes I think maybe He has something special for us, too. Do you sense that too, my darling man?

It's really funny. We really haven't had any chance to get to know each other, but you feel *so* familiar to me. Just now, looking up and seeing you smile at me makes me feel *so* cosy. You make me shiver in a nice way.

What are you going to think of me? Can you *possibly* feel the same as I? I think of you all the time (maybe even more than is good for me!) and everywhere (probably places I shouldn't!) God willing, maybe someday we can *really* be together. I pray for that every night.

What do you pray for, Gideon? Tell me. I'd like to know. I'd like to pray for it, too.

I'm putting my address at the bottom of the letter, so you can write me over the holidays if you want to. I want to tell you things. Nothing profound or stuff like that. Just the ordinary junk a girl wants to say to someone she cares for. (And for me, that's someone like you!) I'll give you my phone number, too. Winnipeg's not all that far from Toronto. (See? I've done *my* research!)

What kind of a name is Gast? German, maybe? It suits you. I used to wish my folks had named me something else. Kids can be so cruel. But I don't mind anymore. In fact, I think it's kind of cute!

Now I'm going to fold this up and leave it for you. Am I doing wrong? Have I displeased God? I hope not. He's been showing me some really neat stuff at Overcomer, and I sure am glad I'm here. In fact, I've been thinking I should have come here two years ago, so we could have been in the same class. Or maybe you should just have failed a couple of times. (Ha ha that's a joke.) There's nothing like knowing you're where the Lord wants you.

I love you, Gideon! Are you bored with me yet?

                            Mary

I read the letter on my bunk. Then again standing up. Then at my desk and twice while I paced my room. I read the letter a dozen times before I sat still and absently flipped the pages of the Greek grammar, trying not to worry about catching my breath, or how I might stop the tingling in my hands and feet. She thinks of me in places she *shouldn't*? What does she do when she thinks of me? Was it anything like what I did when I thought of her? "Really be together" — what was that about? *When the original agent which produces the action signified in the passive verb is expressed* .... I make her "cosy." I make her "shiver in a nice way." *The imperfect itself denotes only the appeal of the will* .... I was her "darling man." *The indicative may be used to express an impulse* .... I closed the book, giggled impetuously, squeezed my eyes shut and burst into tears. Everything was so perfect I didn't need to masturbate.

I had no roommate my junior year; no by-the-Good-Book buddy whose heart had hardened with uncharitable compassion, who might turn me in for the good of my soul. So long as I kept the letters hidden I was safe behind my locked pressboard door. I dreamed my dream. But I fretted anyway.

How *could* she love me? She didn't know me. Maybe that was it. It seemed too good to be true, too crazy to be right. But so did the forgiveness of sins and the resurrection of the dead.

December 22

Dear Mary,

I thank God for you every day. I know we haven't known each other long, but I'm full of confidence that the Lord wants us to know each other better, and for a long, long time. I sense you feel that, too.

I hope you're having a wonderful holiday. It feels good to mail you a letter like a normal person, and not leave something for you in an old book. I've told my family about you, and they're looking forward to meeting you. Do you think we can work something out this summer? That would be terrific.

It's nice to be home, but I miss you even more when we're apart. (Does that make sense?) As I told you in my first letter to you (That seems like so long ago!), I live with my father, a Communist, who's not yet saved. My grandmother is not saved, either. She was in England for a few years. Now she lives with my mother, who is a Christian. My grandmother's health is not too good.

Please pray for her, okay?

Sometimes I'm scared, when I think of how much you suddenly mean to me. I wonder, What are we doing? But then I take it to the Lord, and you know what? He gives it right back to me and says "Enjoy!"

Love,
Your "Darling Man"

I enclosed my Christmas present: a heart-shaped pendant on a thin silver chain. My mother had picked it out of the Consumer's Distributing catalogue, and my father put it on his VISA. The next day, I received a parcel from Winnipeg containing a silk tie the colour of candied cherries and a *Reader's Digest* subscription. The magazine was a gift from her folks. She'd been talking about me.

Christmas morning I called her, waiting until 11 o'clock to allow enough slack for the Earth's rotation. I wished I'd waited longer. Mary and her family were just getting up. She sounded strained, perhaps even surprised to hear my voice. No wonder, since she'd hardly heard it. When I told her I loved her, all she said was "Me too." I felt nervous and vulnerable the rest of the day, as though the soft spot I'd had as an infant had suddenly reopened, and again my forehead visibly throbbed with my cerebral pulse.

Things improved again when we returned to campus. Quickly, surreptitiously, we fixed a pattern of letter drops every Wednesday evening. With an economy of words at the water cooler, and after some experimentation, we agreed to leave our correspondence in the flyleaf of *Amongst the Rosicrucians*. Romantically, she'd left me her first letter of the new year in a copy of *Surprised by Joy*, and though I followed her by only 30 seconds, if I'd have been 10 seconds later I would have had to pry the book from the hands of an obdurate Korean sophomore. In its favour, the last return date stamped in the back of *Amongst the Rosicrucians* was March 11, 1941.

January 14

Dear, dear Gideon,

I can't believe how good it is to see you again! Oooh, I wish I could kiss you right now!

I know I sounded kind of weird on the phone at Christmas. Believe me, it had nothing to do with you. The truth is, thinking about you was the most fun I had all vacation!

I haven't told you about this, because I didn't want you to worry or anything, but I have an old boyfriend back home who still can't accept that it's over between us. We started going out before I accepted Christ. Ismail is not a Christian. I never loved him, but I was a different person then. But please don't be jealous. I honestly never felt anything for him like I do for you.

During vacation Ismail kept calling. He's a nice guy — we met at a track meet — and I wanted to share more of my faith with him. I told him I wanted to be his friend, and that was it. Anyway, the whole time home was depressing and confusing.

But not now! Now, here I am, sitting here on the girls' side pretending to study. When I look up and see you're already smiling at me, I feel fine. It's funny. I guess the one good thing of the vacation was to learn how important it is for me to *see* you, even if we can't hug or even really talk.

How's Greek going? What's Faulkner like? You're *so* smart!

I love you!!!

Mary

I didn't know what to make of that. Whenever I read it — which was often, until I received the next one — I felt in turn good (She wants to kiss me!), miserable (Will I ever kiss her?) and alarmed (Ismail?). Distances, whether a thousand miles or dozen feet, were killing us. If we wanted to be together, we needed to start that summer. For my liking, the farther from Ismail, the better.

And we had other worries. When Mary's next letter said the Assistant Dean of Women had made an appointment to see her I thought that was it, and that in a week's time we'd be on the bus to the Calgary airport. A few days later, though, she confided in passing — literally, so as not to arouse suspicion — that Miss Friesen's only concern was that Mary's room was not quite tidy enough.

Then there was Kelly. She worked in the library most Wednesday nights, and whenever I could bear to glance in her direction she seemed to be looking back at me with sour, dark eyes. But all that changed when Joel Kajinsky invited her out on a dinner date at a staff home. And with the magnanimity of a man in love, I wished them well.

It wasn't until three weeks later that I found the solution.

February 4

Dearest One,

Hi, honey! Too bad about lunch. Just one spot ahead in line and I could have sat with you. On the bright side, I bet that would have ruined my appetite, and it was pretty good ravioli today, don't you think?

I've got some big news for you. First of all, remember I told you my church was starting a summer pastoral internship program? I just got a letter from Pastor Filmore, and he says that the board still has to approve it but it's pretty much a sure thing. In fact, he's invited me to be in it! I'm pretty excited about it. It's going to be a big summer at the church. I just learned that the Keaton brothers are going to be there. Remember that crusade in Calgary? You didn't go, did you? I wonder what they're like. (Do you know they're Siamese twins?)

Secondly (and this might be the *bigger* news), in the same church newsletter I saw that the street mission *Wise Up!* is looking for a full-time student worker this summer. It doesn't pay much, of course, but it would just about fulfil your Christian service requirement. (I know you're only a freshman, but wouldn't it be great to get it out of the way?)

I've attached a copy of the article. I really want to be with you this summer, and I think you want that too. If the Lord agrees with us then I'm convinced He'll find a way for it to happen. When I read it, I just had the feeling this might be the way.

I haven't asked them yet, but either my father or mother might be willing to put you up, at least for a while. Actually, my mother's more likely. (And even though I'd love it, I don't know if it would be a good idea for us to stay under the same roof. I love you, but we both know there are desires which cannot be righteously fulfilled.) I'll ask, if you're interested.

> All my love,
> Your "Darling Man"

Six weeks later I find Mary on the sofa outside the dean's office. When she sees me she springs up, too excited for discretion, and yelps she's got the job.

"Really?" I squeal. People are staring at us. I want to hold her. I want to squeeze her for the first time.

Mary nods, and then motions towards the sofa. "Why don't you sit down and take a load off your pants?"

"Par-"

She knows what she's said, but she's too stricken to correct herself. I blush, mumble that I'm late for Homiletics and hurry off. Engorged with holy blood, I'd never known guilt to feel so guileless.

4

I'm the one in the lime-green, poly-blend three-piece vestment, one hand clutching my best Bible and the other enveloped by the moist and pulpy fist of Pastor Filmore. We're standing beside the church sign, almost on the sidewalk, in front of the knotty willow with *Eat Me* carved in its bark. It was the first Friday of June, the end of my first week, and the first day my name was added to the Cliffside roster.

CLIFFSIDE BAPTIST TABERNACLE

"A family place"

Sunday Worship: 10 a.m. and 7 p.m.
Wednesday Bible Study: 7:30
Mary & Martha Prayer Circle: Tuesdays 8:00

Youth Group: Thursdays 7:00

College & Careers: Fridays 7:30

Minister: Vern Filmore, B.A.
Ass't Minister: Charles Jesperson
Minister of Visitation: Trevor Rylie
Youth Minister: Drew Tallboys, B.Th.
Sunday School Principal: Marilyn Moss
Student Intern: Gideon Gast

Sunday Morning Sermon: "Sin now, pay later"

All welcome!

The photo is still tucked into the frame of the mirror above my mother's bureau, behind her inexhaustible jar of Noxema, between a yellowed notice of my birth and the snapshot of my uncle relaxing on the wing of his Lancaster.

It wasn't supposed to be just me. If it had been, God knows better than anyone I wouldn't have applied in the first place. (As much as I wanted the job, and as much as I want anything, it's always nice to have a few warm suspects to hide behind when the inevitable shit unavoidably flies.)

It was no secret, actually, many board members had serious qualms about throwing more hard-earned tithes after young people, especially since the calamitous "Jesus Fest" the summer before (a mucky Altamont for marginally evangelical headbangers that nearly cost Tallboys his ministry). A cautious, moneyed faction led by Peter Wong preferred spending funds less whimsically, and made a strong case for reshingling the sanctuary roof. They almost won the day, until an impassioned, eleventh-hour pitch by Filmore. ("That's what they pay him to do," Oppie said when I told her the news. "To tell everyone how wrong we are." When she started talking that cynically, and after she switched churches and boyfriends again, I began fearing her faith was falling off the rails.)

The original deadline for internships was published in a church bulletin as April 31, corrected the following Sunday to April 30 and then extended to May 15, by which time only myself and two others had applied and been promptly accepted. Almost immediately, one backed out when an opportunity unexpectedly arose behind an A&P pastry counter. Undoubtedly it paid better, and her boyfriend worked in the meat department, but she said she'd prayed long about it and knew "God wants me there," so who could argue? The other applicant was a late and reluctant scratch when he contracted mononucleosis, the dreaded "kissing disease," a cause for profound embarrassment and pride within the celibate community. In mid-May, soon after I learned I was the only intern left, an uncommonly laconic Filmore invited me out for a coffee and Egg McMuffin to gently inquire whether I, too, might want to withdraw from the program.

"Absolutely not!" I beamed. "I'm persuaded the Lord means for me to be at Cliffside." He smiled wanly. I'd mistakenly thought that was what he'd hoped to hear. The five other salaries were soon shuffled to Capital Expenditures where they paid for new pew cushions and a flat of shingles.

My day was supposed to look like this: a 9 a.m. prayer meeting with the assistant pastor (a full hour was allowed), followed by a study of church doctrine with Filmore and a round of nursing homes and hospitals with sprightly septuagenarian Trevor Rylie before lunch. Afternoons were to be spent either in door-to-door evangelism or something described as "Sunday School preparedness." The first day went pretty much like that. Most of the next one did, too. On Wednesday, Charles Jesperson was five minutes late for our prayer meeting and brought along the *Globe and Mail*. "You had 'Your Morning Smile' yet?" he asked. He recited the pun to me, which reminded him of a story about his granddaughter, who looked like Churchill, which recalled the Blitz. Thursday he took me to McDonalds, and our only prayer was a silent *rubadubdub, thanks for the grub*. Filmore's doctrinal studies lapsed into a debilitating recitation of the church handbook, portioned out at one paragraph a day, punctuated only by "Any questions?"

Friday it was sausage McMuffin and hash browns, this time with Trevor Rylie. I never discovered how Drew Tallboys spent his days. I rarely saw him around the church, and only a couple of times at the drive thru.

Afternoon soul winning was Hell. I was exhilarated when I found no one home, and the people who had time for me were typically Christian widows with azure hair and broken televisions, who despaired of ever again having someone to bake for. A notable exception was a slim black woman in her early thirties, clad in a scarlet bikini and glistening with lotion and sweat. She'd been sunbathing in her backyard and had barely heard the buzzer, but — just as *Penthouse Forum* would have it — invited me in for a neighbourly glass of Freshee. Without lifting my eyes from the alarming press of nipple hard against her swatch of nylon, I stammered my regrets, pressed a sticky Gospel tract into her palm and speed walked back to the church, commending myself, cursing myself. Before I arrived, I'd already fabricated an alternative ending for one more story that never was.

After that, I rarely trusted myself to stray far from church property. Or at any rate that's how I flattered myself.

Increasingly I felt abandoned to my own amusements, much as Filmore seemed shipwrecked on his. Besides the Happy Meals and the woman whom my mundane imagination came to call the Bikini Lady, much of my internship is a blur. A blur with a boner and fries.

The kiss opens her throat like a well, and I'm a penny tossed for a preposterous wish.

"I've been wanting to do that for a long time."

"I've been wanting you to, too."

I'm the one lying next to Mary on the flannel tartan couch in my mother's living room, one foot pressed on the floor just like Hollywood demanded in the days of the Hayes Code. We'd warmly embraced at the airport two hours before — kissed with our tongues, even — but we hadn't braided our bodies together until she fell back on the itchy seat cushion and pulled me down beside her. Discounting my fantasy life, which was essentially the sum of my erotic experience, I was more aroused than I'd ever before allowed myself to be. Yet I was mindful to the saintly cloud of witnesses, so it didn't occur to me that I might unfasten one teasing button, or slip a hand beneath her blouse to raise goosebumps on her belly.

Mother had met Mary before she'd dashed to Tuesday night prayer meeting, where she would thank God for a nice Christian girl in my life and await the supernatural rush of endorphins which would assure her she'd done right by inviting her into the house. Before Mom left we'd gone calling to my grandmother's basement apartment, but she'd already fallen asleep to *The Joker's Wild*.

"This is so neat." I brushed hair from her forehead, just because I could. "I love lying here with you."

"Mmmmm." Mary's eyes moistened. "I think we've been together a long time. We just didn't know it until now."

I wanted to say something to tap a vein of ecstatic sobbing; something for the Oscar clip from the movie of my life, but all I could splutter was, "Gosh, I really like the way you talk."

Mary smiled and nuzzled against me, and with the charm of our new familiarity wiped her eyes dry against my cheek. "Tell me something special. Something you haven't told me before."

I arched my eyebrows and gently kissed the tip of her nose, making her giggle. "Something special, eh? Hmmm, okay ... do you know what the capital of Upper Volta is?"

She laughed again, as I'd hoped she would. "No! I mean something about *me*."

"Ohhh," I drawled, "is *that* what you want to hear?" Mary squeezed her eyes shut and nodded expansively. "Alright then. Have I ever told you how much I love your ... toes?"

"Nope." She nestled closer. "Go ahead."

"I know it's weird, because I've never seen them, and we're not supposed to notice such things at Bible School. But your feet seem so nice and slender I'm sure they're ten little beauties. I'll write a ballad for each one someday, promise."

She dug the big toe of her left foot into the heel of the white cotton sock on her right, and pulled it off. Then the other.

"You can look at them now, if you'd like. I don't see any deans here, do you?" She lifted one Wrangler-clad leg without bending the knee, nimbly pointing her toes towards the mantle and my mother's paint-by-numbers rendering of Christ throwing out the money changers. I held her foot. It was very pale and slender, and the skin felt soft yet close to the bone. Her toenails were trim and brushed with clear gloss. She looked like the future to me.

"Very nice."

"They don't believe you," she protested, wiggling her toes. "They want you to *prove* it."

I'd never been asked to kiss someone's toes before, and I wasn't convinced I was then, either, but Mary expected something of me. I pecked her baby toe as though I were its Daddy, wishing it sweet dreams.

"Oh no, not like that!"

"How do you want it?" Just hearing myself say such a thing made my head swim.

"I'll show you." She rolled off the couch and onto her knees before me. "Give me your foot," she instructed, and I sat upright and offered her my left. (The hole on its argyled heel was not as egregious as the one on the right.) She cradled it gently in one hand and eagerly stripped it with the other, then met my flushed face with an indulgent, almost wicked grin.

"Sorry," I said, blushing. "I'm not one for pedicures."

"Don't worry, my dear," she answered, before whispering tenderly, improbably, "I like the way you smell. If there's any dirt I know it's yours, so I'm sure it'll taste ever so sweet."

Then, in a delicious, wet instant — one I might have predicted, but could never have imagined — my big toe was immured in the sopping warmth of Mary's mouth. I felt as though every joint threatened finally to come unstuck, and I sank back into the couch, moaning and rolling my eyes in reply to her mumbled, "You like that?" wondering if this, *this* at last was sex, and whether God might mind ever so much.

She dragged her incisors along the ripples of my toeprint and friskily bit the grimy nail, and then again took me in and made lazy, slobbering circles with her tongue around its base, tickling me where it flicked the tender flesh between my toes. She giggled as she felt me shiver, and it was then I opened my eyes and stared at her. My rude angel, my Mary Christmas, my Dirty Word made Flesh. I had coveted her from the gymnasium sidelines, from the margins of the men's portions of every room and lecture hall we'd shared, from the lonely world apart of my dormitory room. And suddenly the miracle of her immanence, her irrefutable incarnation took my breath over the hill and far away. The same mouth I'd prayed to kiss had actually, finally opened for me, and not for my mouth only. There it was: a ruddy and frank solicitation, an imperfect circle tracing a shimmer of spit along the shaft of my toe. This was so much more than I'd dared hope when I'd entreated the Lord for Mary's lips. This was the prayer I hadn't asked, because I hadn't known to ask for it. And if I had, I'd have thought only a devil would answer.

"Oh my gosh, Mary — this feels so ... so *neat!*"

She glanced up, her eyes half lidded, her mouth full of me and coiled in a vulgar smile. So this *was* sex, I swooned, thanking God for my hands, and for the lanky walnut hair in which I wound them.

With a loving kiss upon my ankle, Mary set down my foot and drew herself towards me. She rested her arms on my thighs and I squeezed her gently between my legs. It felt right and good to do that. I pulled her closer and kissed her on the lips.

"You really got off on that, didn't you?"

She made it sound dirty. I didn't like that, but I *liked* that.

I nodded dreamily.

"We're going to have fun this summer, my darling man."

"Looks that way. God's giving us something *amazing* — don't you think? It just blows me away." I took a deep breath and shook my head again, this time because I needed to. "It'll be a great summer. The best."

Mary grunted a warm agreement and dropped her head to my lap. I gave a start, alarmed and embarrassed by the animal lump in my pants, and she quickly raised her head again.

"I'm so sorry about your folks. I think it's so sad that they aren't still together. It's a shame you don't all live together."

Then she lowered her voice and studied our clasped hands. "On a more *personal* note .... I'll be lonely when you leave tonight."

"My father would be lost without me. Of course, he may be lost *with* me, too." Then I tossed my head as though I were trying to throw it away.

Mary gave me a quizzical look.

"Sorry. It just bugs me I can make jokes like that."

"I'm sure God doesn't think twice about it," she replied matter-of-factly, snuggling closer and massaging my palms with her thumbs. "You know, I think you take things too seriously. The Lord can't mind us having some fun." She leaned into me and we kissed. "Jokes are okay. Relax. Tell me how I can help you relax, okay?"

"Promise."

"Good."

"I love you."

"You'd better!" she screeched, pinching my ears until I yelped. Then she added, "Nobody's sucked your toes before, have they?"

"No. Not counting myself." She chuckled at that, which unaccountably depressed me.

"It's fun, isn't it? There's other things we can do, too. You'll see. We *are* going to have fun together, you and me."

Suddenly my cheeks flushed, as I surprised myself by finding the nerve and the desire to say, "Is this something you've done, you know, a *lot?*"

Her body stiffened between my legs. "What? Toe sucking? Oh, no! Only once or twice, and not for a long time. You're the first since I've been a Christian. But it's so *different* with you! With you it feels, I don't know, like when — I hope this doesn't sound blasphemous! — like when Jesus washed the disciples feet. Do you know — Does it feel like that to you?"

I squeezed her elbows tightly, reflexively, as part of my full-body wince for having said something so careless. "I know what you mean. It *does* feel that way. Sorry. You're wonderful. That was a stupid thing to say."

"No it wasn't. But don't worry. I'll love you even when you say stupid things."

"Promise? I'll give you plen-"

"*I know what yer doin'!*"

"Oh! Nanny! Mary, this is my grandmother."

I hadn't heard her climb the stairs but there she was, steadying herself on the landing, pressing a hand against the wall, catching her breath before she shuffled into either the kitchen or living room. I stood abruptly, pulling Mary up with me, and kicked out a pant leg to make allowance for my conspicuous erection.

She was wearing her favourite green and gold frock, spattered with familiar stains of tea and poultry fat, with a cream-coloured shawl draped across her gaunt shoulders and a pair of balding fuzzy beige slippers distended by her rheumatism. She had nicer clothes; much nicer clothes from recent birthdays and Christmases that were a better match for her current weight, but this was how she chose to dress now, though the frock hung on her with the sloppy indifference of a surgical gown. Her white hair had been flattened upon the right side of her scalp by having rested her head so long in her palm. The left side was still largely in place from her last styling appointment at Lyla's Beauty Salon. It seemed like such a long time since she'd left the house for any other reason.

"This is Mary, Nanny. You were asleep when we came in. We were going to drop down later and visit."

"Eh?"

"It's Mary. You know, the friend Mom and I've been telling you about."

"Pleased to meet you," said Mary, reaching for either or both of my grandmother's knotty hands. Both were promptly stuffed in the pockets of her frock.

"I'm too old for yer stories, mind! I know what yer about!"

"Nanny! Come in and sit down. Don't get all worked up."

"We were just talking. It's nothing bad."

"Well what were you waitin' fer, Christmas?" I knew Mary smiled at that, but I didn't look at her. "Fer gawd's sakes, lad, it's about time you did somethin'. Yer not gettin' any younger."

"Nanny, *please* ...."

"Jus' don' lie to me, me lad. There t'is. That's all I'm sayin' on the matter."

"Well, I'm *not* lying." I felt foolish contradicting her in front of Mary, so I let it drop. "Do you need anything? Can I do anything for you?"

"Clean me glasses. You always do 'em best. Got 'em greasy with the chicken. And don' worry about me. I shan' tell your sister about what you were doin'."

"Mother."

"What?"

"You mean 'mother.'"

"Oh. Gideon?"

"Yes?"

"Me glasses."

"Right."

"If only I 'ad me legs."

Slowly, unassisted because that's how she wanted it, she walked into the room and collapsed upon the couch with a contented groan.

"This is my first time in Toronto," Mary offered.

My grandmother grunted. I lifted the glasses from her nose and, with a glance, assured Mary that I'd hurry back. Mary nodded she was fine and sat beside her. Just as I left the room, I saw a grin of recognition crease the corners of my grandmother's mouth as she opened a benevolent door of memory.

"Me 'n th'other girls used to sing gospel songs Saturday evenin' with our mum, right after feedin' the goats. You wouldn' know it to look at me, but I used to be quite the religious one. Come seven, we'd race down the lane to watch the boys go home from their rugger. They were so young, you'd na think a bird 'ad ever shat on 'em! They'd look over at us, and we at 'em, but we never none of us said a word. We thought they just wanted to play ball, and them .... Well, they all thought that all we thought about was our bloody goats!" She laughed, and her laugh became a cough, but she seemed to enjoy it just as much. "As if goats are anythin' to write 'ome about! But 'ow could they know any different? So anyway, we all just kept, like —" As I entered the room she was gesturing, slipping one waxy palm past the other.

Laughter crinkled her face the way a deliberate spark kindles old newspapers. Standing by the arm of the couch, I sprayed her thick lenses with two or three squirts of Windex and wiped them clean with a paper towel.

"That's a nice story," Mary told her, hoping to catch my eye.

"What the hell would you know?" she snapped.

"*Nanny!* Please, don't talk like that to Mary."

I shrugged an apology to Mary and she signalled it was all right. The ghost of a smile haunted my grandmother's lips.

"You don' know, none of you!" she said. "It's over'n done before you know. Then yer in the grave a million years and who's sorry then, eh? Eh?"

"Here you go." I placed her glasses on the bridge of her nose. Her eyes twinkled. A trick of the light.

"'Ere now, don't hurt our Gid. There; I've said me peace. He was engaged once before, you know."

I shook my head for Mary and silently mouthed the explanation, "My uncle," and turned again to my grandmother. "Aren't you missing *The Joker's Wild?*"

"It's not right. The man's dead."

"Jack Barry," I whispered. Mary nodded, without comprehension.

"I'm goin' to rest me eyes."

"Sounds like a good idea."

"Nice meeting you," said Mary. "Hope we can talk again soon."

"You watch yer step, dearie."

5

"Of course, my friends, we know the greatest lie in the world, don't we?"

Jonathan Keaton paused, flashing a smile like a dog baring its teeth to a fainthearted stranger. Not a big dog — it wasn't a vicious smile — but the smile had a mean streak about it.

Jonathan was still smiling when he stretched for the glass of ice water upon the lectern. Behind him, David didn't need telling or turning about to know that whatever his brother wanted was just out of reach: he could feel his own shoulder tug against Jonathan's. Straightaway, as if it had been his idea, his own thirst, David straightened up and stepped away from the blackboard and his methodical block letter transcription of Galatians 2:20, then leaned backwards to allow Jonathan to lean for the water.

But for their clothes — a pair of charcoal doubleknit trousers, grey silk ties and a single burgundy shirt and a white jacket with four arms, stitched together at the back — they looked as though they might be preparing to demonstrate an elementary judo toss. All their lives they looked like that.

It was a hot Sunday morning, and I'd been sticky with sweat since the offertory hymn, "Stand Up for Jesus." (Not as easy as it sounds, not with the back of my shirt pasted to the pew like a popsicle to its paper wrapping.) Above my head a ceiling fan whirred inefficiently, yet excitedly enough to prove a credible object lesson for any "If you should die today" call to repentance. From our seats near the back of the sanctuary, it looked like more than half the crowd of 500 were fanning themselves with the special crusade edition of the church program, the one with the full colour reproduction of the promotional portrait I'd first seen in the *Calgary Herald*. Mary and I shared a program, and we took turns waving it selflessly at each other's face. Oppie sat to my left with her new boyfriend, a U of T economics student and Youth for Christ apparatchik named Glen something. Oppie and Glen each had their own programs, and they endlessly moistened their mouths by chewing ever-greater wads of grape-flavoured *Freshen Up*.

"Can anyone here tell me the greatest lie in the world?"

We sat in silence awhile, a polite and uncomfortable assembly of born-again Canadians, until it was clear he wouldn't proceed without an answer.

"That Jesus was just a great moral teacher?" Drew Tallboys finally ventured obligingly from his seat beside the empty choir loft.

Jonathan shook his head. "That's good; that's right up there. But no, that's not what I'm looking for."

Oppie leaned heavily into my shoulder, and said in a hoarse whisper with a whiff of sucrose, "How about 'Blessed are the gullible, for they shall inherit a million dollars'?"

I cast a sideways glance in Oppie's direction and threw her a little grin, though I worried it might only encourage her. I shared her misgivings about the Keatons, but I was becoming scared her doubts didn't end there. There were other signs, too. When Oppie found Jesus she'd grown her hair long, and had permed it into a reserved tumble of tight, unnatural curls. Now it was short again, a mannish bob. She'd also begun accenting her delicate sun dresses with black leggings and Doc Martens. Cause for concern. Oppie was the only gem in my soul-winning crown, and I felt some proprietorial interest in her spiritual health.

Mary fanned me a little more briskly, a little closer to my face, and I responded in kind by tightly clasping her free hand. She rubbed my wrist vigorously with her thumb, as though playing a scratch-and-win game.

"That Christ isn't coming back?" a woman called out, rather plaintively, from directly behind us. Jonathan didn't acknowledge her. Perhaps he hadn't heard her clearly.

"That we all come from monkeys?" Johnny Cicero rasped. Keaton closed the floor to discussion.

"The greatest lie in the world is — are you ready for it? — unconditional love."

While we mulled that over, the twins, as if on cue, which it certainly was, spun about. With crablike sidesteps, and with a crab's reasonable, instinctive grace, David, the grizzled-looking "runt," came to face us. Jonathan busied himself by erasing what his brother had just finished writing.

"That's right," said David. "Unconditional love is a foul lie of the devil, straight from the darkest hole of the deepest pit of hell! It's sent untold millions to their doom, and'll send plenty more while the Lord tarries.

"You tell me, 'But brother David, certainly we are supposed to love God unconditionally'. Oh, is that so? Then remember well the Scripture: 'We love him because He first loved us.'"

As David spoke, Jonathan wrote "I John 4:19" on the board in red chalk.

"We don't love God for *nothing*. Do you hear what I'm saying? We love him because he gives us life, and new life in Christ. Do you hear me? That's not unconditional, my friends. I'd say that's about as conditional as it gets."

Someone shouted "Amen!" and David paused. It was his turn for a drink of water. Indulgently, Jonathan moved with him.

"But then you tell me, 'Brother David, surely *God* loves us unconditionally, no strings attached.' Well, let me tell *you*, my friends, that's the worst kind of nose stretcher; a lie that would pervert the Gospel into an unclean thing! To think that the Lord of Heaven and Earth is the original advocate of 'free love!' May God save us! Brothers and sisters, love *always* comes at a cost, and Divine love at the highest cost of all: obedience! Certainly it's a fact He first loved us — a blessed fact we celebrate — but that same holy love will deliver us to judgement should we spurn Him. If, while under grace, we fail to love him who first loved us, we shall bear the brunt of his righteous jealousy in the Great Day to come!"

David's voice broke beneath his passion. Only when worked up like this did a touch of the Amazon escape his lips. Otherwise, both brothers spoke an English inflected only by a suggestion of Southern Baptist gentility. David collected himself deliberately, relaxed the lines on his copper-coloured face, and dropped his voice to a stage whisper.

"Think back for a moment. Search your hearts. Probably at some time or another you've cared for someone who didn't feel the same. Remember how it pained you? It *hurts* to love like that, doesn't it? Does it hurt when your love is not returned? Of course it does.

"Then think how the very God of Love must feel!" Once again, the jungle was loosed. "This God ... this God who saw his own Son put to death by the mob .... What *astonishing* grace is this! What kind of love? Who can know its depths?"

He shook his head solemnly and pulled a handkerchief from his trouser pocket to mop his brow. Feeling uncomfortable, I coughed needlessly, just to hear my own voice for a change.

"You say you love God? Then prove it, beloved, in word and in deed. Believe me — no, believe His Word — that God's love will out. He will not play the unwanted suitor much longer! He will have us! The Lord's advances will not be denied forever!"

Again, the brothers turned. Immediately I relaxed, exhaling heavily, surprised that I'd held my breath for so long. In this grisly good cop, bad cop routine, David was the one responsible for my subcutaneous bruises.

"It's no wonder those who think God's love is 'hassle free' live as though with a licence to sin," Jonathan said, running a hand through his wiry black hair. It looked so barbed I almost wondered how he failed to cut himself. "To them, sin and guilt are out of fashion. They think God will forgive them anything: even, if you can believe it, their not loving Him.

"You know who started such a lie, don't you? Next time you hear it, you know how to respond, don't you? Five little words: 'Get thee behind me, Satan!'"

"Wait a second, brother. 'Get thee behind *me!*'"

The congregation peeled with laughter, grateful for the respite from the hungry licks of hellfire. It was such a good joke it couldn't be the last time we'd hear it.

I hadn't had much to do with the Keatons since their arrival in town the previous Wednesday. A fawning introduction by Filmore, a couple of prayer meetings with the pastoral staff and a little order taking for my run to McDonald's, and that was it. And that was enough. I'd decided I wanted little to do with them.

It's not like I thought them charlatans or hypocrites. They simply embarrassed me. *Face it,* I found myself thinking, rather ruefully, *any way you slice it, these guys are freaks.*

Having someone affixed to your back is not like having, say, a mole on your butt that looks like John Ritter. It's like having fucking John Ritter on your butt. It's not something that could slip one's mind for long ("Oh yeah! *John!*"). It wasn't something I could politely dismiss and turn away from as a courtesy of my civilizing secondary education. This was no harelip or clubfoot or port wine stain. You can't think about Siamese twins in those terms. This was sobering deformity. It marks them. If Jesus had been joined at the hip to his brother James, I doubt very much whether Christianity would have become all the rage.

During our morning prayer time a few days after the twins had arrived, Charles Jesperson asked me whether I'd read anything about the Keaton's Miami crusade. "Not the latest one; the first crusade, five years back."

"Nothing," I replied.

He looked at me slyly. I liked him. Two men can't fudge a daily hour of contemplation and not respect one another's confidence. He was obviously delighted I didn't know the story, just so he could tell it.

"A lot of folk in the Miami church were having doubts about the Keatons being genuine Siamese twins. They thought it was some kind of act. Naturally, it got back to them. So one night, right in the middle of a sermon, they unbuttoned their shirt. Took the thing completely off. No word of explanation! What do you think of that?"

"Yeah ...."

"Maybe so, but it was the beginning of real revival there."

He lowered his voice to a conspiratorial pitch. "These days, though, most ministers won't let them in their pulpits without getting their word that they'll keep their clothes on."

Then, with a jumpcut worthy of Jean-Luc Goddard, Jesperson asked whether I'd seen a documentary the night before called *Ants, the Kingdom at our Feet.*

David and Jonathan were Filmore's guests for the duration of the crusade, which we were lead to believe could run anywhere from a week to the establishment of Christ's millennial kingdom. Filmore had met them at Pearson Airport in the church van, as they'd requested. (Cars, understandably, were too awkward for the Keatons. I don't know what arrangements they'd made with Air Canada.) I went along, and saw that they travelled light, but for some necessary exceptions. The first was something like a collapsible piano bench of varnished pine, with a turquoise seat cushion and cotton bands lashed between its legs. They would sit at opposite ends and lean against each other with fraternal conviviality.

The second was a two-seat commode. They set it up in the practice room, behind one of the gun-grey utility shelves stacked with sheet music (the choir didn't meet in the

summer). The room became their makeshift office and, I presume, lavatory. Until their arrival, the choir room had been
mine. Now I was expected to work out of the balcony. (*Flexible
and eager to please.* My report cards always said crap like that.)
Whether they took it home to Filmore's, I didn't know. I didn't
want to know. I already resented them enough for my shame
at puzzling over the gross functions of their undivided selves.

Those first few days they didn't have a fix on who I was,
what I did or why I was there. I was the guy from the gods
who ran for their coffee. Probably one in every town. In some
towns, maybe one for each brother. I didn't care to explain
myself to them. But whenever I thought of their potty I pitied
them, and felt obliged they hadn't asked me to empty it.

Even before Mary moved in for the summer I usually had
Sunday dinner at my mother's. It made sense, going to the
same church as we did, and she'd become a great cook since
she'd accepted Christ. And Lord's Day afternoons my father
liked to safeguard for Chinese takeout, the New York Times
and "Gilmour's Albums." When I was seeing Mary home
Tuesday evening after a church league softball game, Mother
met me at the door, and blurted she'd just invited Filmore and
the Keatons to join us for dinner ("nothing fancy") after the
Sunday morning service. In the sudden droop of my shoulders,
in the way my heels scuffed the porch, I told her the idea
depressed me, though I said, weakly, "Okay, sounds great." But
she'd received my message. She said I "didn't have to be that
way," but if that was how I felt then I needn't come. In front of
Mary, this was acutely embarrassing. It made her look petu-
lant, and worse, made me appear petty. And how I appeared to
Mary seemed the single worry left me for this life. I lied, saying "What? Don't be silly; it really sounds *great!*" Generously,
which made me feel smaller still, she said I could invite Oppie
and her new friend if it would make me happy.

I called Oppie the next day. She'd love to come. She didn't
even ask Glen.

"Oooh aye, but we're proud of our Gideon!"

Nanny was sitting next to Filmore on my mother's tartan couch, speaking with the ardour she typically reserved for speaking to herself. They'd met several times before on his pastoral calls to my mother. She freely admitted liking him, which was so unlike her it disturbed me, until I realized he reminded her of "that Göring bloke" whom she'd always found amusingly preposterous. I glanced at Filmore as I crossed the floor with a glass of juice for Mary. He was nodding gravely, his neck bulging over his collar like freshly-baked dough spilling out of a bread mould. A resemblance, no doubt.

We were eating in the living room, which drew less attention to the Keaton's seating requirements than if we were at the dining table. Mary and I shared a lumpy beige ottoman that we'd pushed in front of the mantle. Oppie sat beneath the window, across from the couch, on a dainty chair lately reupholstered with golden taffeta and braid. My mother, who was in the kitchen, had a wobbly dinner chair next to Filmore's side of the couch. The Keatons bench was in the middle of the room. Jonathan faced Mary and I; David everyone else except my mother, who sat almost precisely between them.

Geez —I wondered, as I'd wondered since the first time I'd seen them — *how the heck do they go to the bathroom?* I noticed they only took a few sips of their cranberry spritzers, and that, it seemed, just to be polite.

When we arrived, the dinner trays had already been unfolded and dispersed about the room. Most had metal tops painted to resemble Harris tweed, which they decidedly did not, and each aluminium leg was oxidized and missing the black rubber nub of a footer. They'd been wedding gifts from my grandmother. Except for one: shorter than the rest, it had a plastic tray the colour of cherry Lifesavers and a big picture in the middle of Gumby and Pokey.

"Remember that?" My mother squealed when she saw I'd noticed it. "You didn't think I still had it, did you?"

No, and no, since I probably hadn't used it since the first time the Smothers Brothers show was cancelled. And what *was* she doing with it. No matter. When I saw it made Mary smile and sing, to me, "If you've got a heart, then Gumby's a part of you," It was perfect for me.

Mary gave my hand a furtive squeeze as she took the juice and made room for me again. She gestured with her fork I could finish her turkey if I cared to. I was bloated, but I did. It was too provocative to resist eating off my girlfriend's plate.

My mother returned from the kitchen with a serving dish piled high with remaindered dark meat and stuffing. "There's plenty more turkey!" she declared lyrically, and offered up the evidence to the twins before setting it atop the broken console stereo. Then she lifted her own plate from the seat of her chair, scanned the room to be certain everyone still had food, and sat with a sigh.

"So then," she asked the twins, without addressing either in particular, "have you been to Toronto before?"

"He hasn't," Jonathan retorted, winking at us, "but I have."

Oppie laughed, making it alright for the rest of us. Even for my mother, who regarded the Keatons' situation with the polite fiction of disregarding it altogether, giggled behind a forkful of turkey breast. My grandmother laughed as well, though she hadn't heard the joke.

Oppie pushed her tray aside, smoothed the pleats of her egg-shell silk skirt and stomped towards my grandmother in her black leather, red-laced Doc Martens. (Red laces for the blood of Christ, she told me.) She perched beside her on the arm of the couch.

"So, how ya been, Mrs. Frye?"

"Can' complain, I 'spose. Does no good. Who're you, then?"

"Oppie. I know what you mean."

"Mary," said Jonathan, and I missed my grandmother's reply to Oppie. "I hear you'll help out during Focus on Youth week."

"I *am*?"

"Oh, I guess Pastor —"

"Not yet," Filmore interjected. "I was just about to ask her."

"About what?"

"Prayer," answered Jonathan. "Whenever we do one of our youth weeks we like to meet with a small circle of young people, maybe half an hour or so before each nightly service. We find it helps us target the needs of the congregation's teens and college kids."

"We spoke to your Pastor and Johnny Cicero the other day," David continued, over his and his brother's shoulder, "and they both suggested you. You're with *Wise Up!* is that right?"

Mary answered with a nod. Jonathan translated.

"Yes she is, David."

"Good girl. We've heard about *Wise Up!* God's using it mightily. Any*boo*, we'd like you to join us. Gideon will be, too."

Mary glanced at me and smiled. "Sounds neat!" she said.

A brief pause followed, which proved too much for my mother, who blurted, "We've got pie!" We answered with obliging grunts of pleasure and spastic rolling of the eyes which protested *No, I couldn't possibly*, before we fell to cleaning our plates.

Out of our gluttonous calm, with an unhurried flick of her head, my grandmother asked Oppie, "Who's that, then?"

"Jonathan and David Keaton," Oppie answered softly.

"Oh aye." She nodded into a void, squinting at a sliver of remembrance. "I remember a calf our neighbour Mr Blandin had. Born with two heads, poor bloody devil."

The twins excepted — I saw a smile twitch on Jonathan's face — everyone squirmed in their seats. None more so than my mother.

"'Orrible creature 'ad to be put down. Monstrous, it was."

My mother was already at her side, attentively laying a hand upon her wrist. She spoke softly, with concentrated affection.

"Well mother, what do you say? Time you had a lie down?"

She swatted the hand away. "Ya think I'm a mad woman? I know what I'm talkin' about! Gideon dear, can you put the kettle on?"

"Sure."

Before I stood, Mary pulled me close to her teasing mouth. "You always put the kettle on best," she whispered.

When I returned, mother was back in her chair. David was speaking to her in low, reassuring tones.

"... all the time, really. It's just curiosity."

"We understand and honour curiosity," Jonathan appended. "When something departs from the natural order, we
should be curious."

"And what's a curiosity but a living miracle?"

"It's a fact."

"Praise God."

"Amen." Jonathan curled his mouth into a tight smile and
— oddly, I thought — winked again. "Well then .... Should
we, brother? I'm feeling prompted by the Holy Spirit. How
about yourself?"

"You think? I hadn't .... Has everybody finished eating?"

"Should you *what?*" Filmore asked, fidgeting with a cuff.

"Sometimes, for our friends ...." Jonathan paused, shaking
his head to reorder his thoughts. "God's blessed us. He really
has. But I know when I say that there's plenty of people who
think I'm out of my tree. 'Blessed? Siamese twins?' Many people have told us that if they'd been joined to their brother or
sister they'd have probably killed each other long ago."

"That's true," David chuckled.

"But I wouldn't trade this life for any other —"

"Nor I."

"... and the blessing is real. We are fearfully and wonder-
fully made." Jonathan lowered his eyes and smiled sardonically.
"Of course, maybe David and I are made a *little* more fearfully
than most, but we're all miracles of one stripe or another."

"*All* of us," his brother added gravely.

"So then ..." Jonathan cleared his throat, and raised his
hands, palms up. "Would you like to see our miracle?"

"P-pardon?" Filmore stuttered.

"How we're joined."

"*Oh!* Well, I .... Oh!"

Quickly, as though protecting a winning hand of *Uno*, my
mother drew a full house of fingers to her mouth. She turned
to the Pastor in eager hope of counsel, but Filmore said nothing. His jaw was set, though his jowls danced with the nervous
energy drummed up by a pair of his own podgy fingers. Oppie
beheld the twins in wonder, before turning to me with a look
of vulgar expectancy. My blanched face must have been a

rebuke, because when she turned again at the Keatons a faint blush of shame now stained her amusement.

Mary's lips were slightly parted, and her head was cocked at an inquiring angle as though she were trying to process something she almost comprehended. Her stare was screwed into a squint and was fixed upon Jonathan, who returned it with a shit-eating grin. As though to prove how unalike we were and how little we knew each other, Mary was not alarmed. She looked fascinated.

In the first bloom of our astonishment, only my grandmother completed a sentence: "Gideon, be a dear and put the kettle on."

Oppie shrugged her shoulders and blithely whooped: "Go for it!" She pushed herself off the arm of the couch and hastened back to the dainty golden chair, which promised a less obstructed view.

"Jonathan, David," Filmore began with uncommon stiffness, as though he were unaccustomed to public speech. "I'm sure I speak for all .... We think your offer is very .... Don't put yourselves out."

My mother's nodded her head brusquely. Her eyes seemed huge and luminous, and were concentrated upon the brothers' borderland of white polyester, beneath which one twin became the other, or something that was neither one nor the other, but both.

Filmore continued. "It's an honour to think that, after just a few short days among us, you feel comfortable enough to offer us such a ... blessing. But please, you're our guests here. Thank you very, very much, but you *really* needn't."

"Thank *you*, Vern," Jonathan replied. "But it's really no trouble at all."

"We consider it something of a spiritual gift."

"Sometimes — and we give the glory to Jesus — seeing the miracle of the way we're joined helps bring others together. We can't explain it."

"We've seen some marvellous things."

"Lives rededicated to Christ. Drugs and liquor kicked."

"Healings, even," David swooned.

"Seeing us is no great shakes," Jonathan chuckled, as he began unfastening his cuffs. "But God's ways are mysterious."

"'He uses the foolish things to confound the wise,'" my mother softly recited, turning her vague attention to her paint-by-numbers Christ. She looked stricken.

Jonathan tugged his right arm free of the jacket.

"We have a tailor down in Atlanta who makes these for us. Decent man. A Messianic Jew."

The jacket hung like a cape from his shoulders. David hadn't budged. Once more, Jonathan cleared his throat.

"Shall we, then?"

Everyone seemed to draw the same shallow breath. Mary took my hand. We'd reached the crest of a precipitous incline.

"If you think," my blanched mother began, and then began again. "It's a little — I mean, I suppose — if everyone ...." She pulled at the skin of her neck and sighed, then smiled defeatedly.

"Please don't." I'd been silent so long, my voice sounded strangled and strange to me; high and unfamiliar, as on a tape recording. Mary exhaled heavily through her mouth and loosened her grip. My belly relaxed. I felt okay again.

"No, please do," Oppie protested. "It'd be so cool!"

"Jonathan," David said demurely, "I think maybe this isn't —"

The kettle whistled. Jonathan slipped back into the jacket. I left the room and fixed my grandmother's camomile tea.

There we are the following night, lying on my bed next to a bag of barbecue Lays, listening to "Wondering Where the Lions Are" one mo' time. The redolent heat of her chip breath beguiles me. I can feel her breasts against my chest, even the perky forbidden zone of her nipples. The unaffected play of her flesh lies hard upon me, just beneath her untucked lumberjack shirt.

Mary isn't wearing a bra tonight.

If I chose to, I could slip my hand beneath her still-buttoned shirt and cup a bona fide naked tit. I could even take a nipple between my teeth, and love it as I'd long pretended, every bit as deliciously as I'd been taught to love her toes and fingers. If I wanted, maybe, I could discover whether she resembled the alien maps I'd surveyed in the magazines that I'd blistered myself upon whenever my imagination failed the "People" section of *Maclean's*.

Yes, I could do those things. And Mary probably wished me to.

Thank God one of us knows when to stop.

I lifted her hands to my face and kissed her open palms.

"Gotta pee."

I needed to, and badly, but thanked God anyway for the excuse of a full bladder for the chance to relieve a more foreboding pressure. It was impossible to piss through my swollen cock, so I reviewed my Greek vocabulary cards that I kept in a black plastic box by the toilet. *Future active indicative of krino, "I judge":* *krino, krineis, krinei, krinomen, krineite, krinousin.* Worked like a charm. When I returned to the bedroom I headed for the turntable and lifted the needle, then crouched before my record collection.

"What do you feel like?"

"Oh, anything. Nothing."

"T-Bone Burnett?"

"Whatever."

Back in her arms, Mary felt different; cooler by maybe a degree or two. She'd reigned in her passion, just as I'd hoped. Just as I'd feared.

"You know," she said, munching a chip, "you don't talk much about your work."

"Not much to tell," I sighed. "*The Solid Rock* went out today. Secretary's on vacation, so I stuffed the envelopes."

"Oh, come on!" she grinned, playfully pushing me away. "There's more than that, what with the crusade and everything."

"Well, you'll see for yourself next week. I don't have much to do with the Keatons. The pastoral staff pray with them every afternoon, but that's about it."

"Who's your favourite?"

"Favourite what?

"Favourite Keaton?"

"I haven't thought about it." I snorted. "I guess I don't think of them as two people.

She gave me a salty kiss on the forehead.

"Pretty bizarre, wasn't it?" I said.

"What?"

"Them wanting to take their shirt off for us."

"I wish they'd done it. It was so electric. Like magic."

"*Magic?*"

"Not magic. But I felt close to God, or something."

"*Something?*"

"Well, God."

"Hmmm." I held her tightly, listening to her heart and my alarm clock. After a while I said, "Okay, who's your favourite?"

"Hmmm. It's funny. They're *so* different. David seems real quiet, except on stage. And then Jonathan .... I don't know. He's got a real presence, doesn't he?"

"You mean he's cuter."

"No! Well, yes he is, but .... Strange, isn't it, that David looks so much older and everything?"

"Uncanny, I'd thay," I answered, doing a bad Boris Karloff.

Mary giggled, even though I don't think she recognized the voice, and kissed me lightly with pursed lips. Then her mouth opened and we rolled together. I was on top of her, nibbling and slobbering over her neck when she whispered, matter-of-factly, "I want to make love to you."

I moaned softly and smiled, and kissed her on the chin.

"So do I. But we know what that would mean."

Mary nodded slowly. She slipped a finger in my mouth. I could see my reflection in her clear, wide eyes. "But there are, you know, *other* things we can do."

I took hold of her hand and licked the tip of her finger. It was tangy with barbecue seasoning.

"I know. We have to be very careful. There are so many snares, even for Christians. *Actually* ...."

"*Yes ...?*"

"I think it would be a neat idea if we prayed for strength right now. Don't you?"

The prayer circle for Focus on Youth week wasn't much of a circle: just Jonathan and Mary and David and I, sitting paired up in single file, front to front, back to back, front to front. We came before the Lord according to evangelical custom, with head bowed and eyes closed. I found the whole thing redundant and unexceptional, but Mary found it a blessing.

Thursday afternoon, my grandmother complained about a funny feeling on her right side. It wasn't her first or worst stroke, but as her doctor said, "It's best not to have one if you can help it." Mary wanted to come with me to the hospital, but I told her she shouldn't miss the prayer meeting. I assured her I was alright, and that I'd probably see her at the service.

Nanny was sleeping when I arrived at the hospital. My mother was with her, as she'd been with her before, and convinced me the best thing I could do for her was to go to a prayer meeting.

I arrived at the church to the sound of David's intercessions. His cry unto the Lord echoed the length of the rear hallway, all the way to the parking lot entrance.

"... your Word will not go forth void ...."

He was still praying when I reached the door to the choir room. There was a thick pane of frosted glass, about a foot square, set in the door at eye level. It blurred the image, like a Kirilian photograph, but I could see them in a row: David, Jonathan .... Where was Mary? There was something else: a very short, squat smudge in front of Jonathan. No, the thing was crouching. I squinted. Suddenly, I couldn't breathe properly.

"... fill us with your Spirit, that we might be found acceptable in your sight ...."

The thing was between Jonathan's legs, almost doubled over. It was a slender, stooping shadow with an auburn crown, that bobbed up and down like a dribbled basketball.

Not to put too fine a point on it, but things were never the same between Mary and I.

IV

Which is harder: to be executed, or to suffer that prolonged agony which consists in being trampled to death by geese?

Søren Kierkegaard

1

As we said our astringent goodbyes over the waning moments of the Muscular Dystrophy Telethon, I asked her if there was someone else. All she would admit was, "It's kinda complicated." I said nothing, just stared at Jerry Lewis mewling "You'll Never Walk Alone" and wondered what he must smell like.

So long as I called myself an evangelical, and for almost as long as I was called one by others, I told nobody what I'd seen through the frosted window. How could I describe it, and to whom, when even to name such a thing was defiling? I hinted at it, of course I did, but only sparingly and in the most equivocal terms. Oppie, bless her, caught on. No one else had a clue what I was trying not to talk about. Not even close.

I knew what to call it alright, but I couldn't speak its names aloud; not even to myself. *Blow job, cocksucking, head.* Ugly words. I wanted a more amiable obscenity to describe my bride's taking my measure in her mouth. But some day, God willing, I would be able to speak these words and more besides, yet without sin. Some day, should the Lord tarry and I be granted enough time to find a bride, they would speak to me as well. Like a lucid transmission on the wedding band, a burst of shortwave over an exotic, stupefying distance. *What God hath joined together*, and all those other words, too, in a run-on sentence I would vocalize all the rest of my days.

But then one day I'm late for a prayer meeting, and catch my girlfriend going down on a Siamese twin. A thing like that couldn't help but make me wonder whether I was losing myself between the pages of other people's dirty stories.

Mary didn't return to Bible school. (A brittle prayer answered and some consolation, but I didn't exactly shout hosannas.) She mumbled vague justifications, like needing "to think some things through," and I was not disposed to argue. In silence I drove her to Pearson International, where she kissed me, fleetingly, with a closed mouth, and was gone; caught up in the air by an L-1011 and delivered to a life I knew nothing about. *The one shall be taken and the other left.* The first woman I'd thought of as my one and only, just another loop in a neural chain that wounds me.

Three nights later I sat on my bed, my swollen luggage zippered shut beside me, diffidently packed for my senior year. I played Bob Dylan's *Shot of Love* one last time and got unexpectedly weepy during "Lenny Bruce," a track I typically skipped as a profane downer after gurgling along to "Property of Jesus." About 10:30 my father rapped softly on my door, finally letting himself in when I didn't answer. I must have looked especially miserable, since he tried to cheer me in his oblique, backhanded way.

"You know, somewhere there sits a young fellow with a finger up his nose wishing he were you."

He made me smile at least, and given how I'd felt that was almost miraculous.

2

ppie's letter arrived on the eve of my Fall Greek exam. For the longest time I blamed her for my bungling the question on the periphrastic use of the participle.

November 1

Yo! Big Guy!

How goes it, fella? Keeping out of trouble, as if I don't know?

Hear anything from that crazy Mary dame? Geez, I hope not. You deserve better than her, if you want my opinion. (And I know you do!) Anyway, hope you're over her and feeling better and all kinds of other good stuff.

So, got a new babaloo yet? I do, thanks for asking. Name's Kim, but he's a guy. (Kinda like a Johnny Cash song, eh? Ain't love grand?) He works the soundboard at Larry's Hideaway. You'd like him. No, you wouldn't.

Alright, already; enough tiresome banter. Time I got to the reason for this minor epistle. My, my, how to begin .... (Nuts, this is tougher than I thought.)

We've become pretty good friends over the past couple of years, *n'est pas?* You know me about as well as anyone (whatever that means), so you must know I've been going through some changes of late. Well, sorry to have to break this to you, but I've gone through a few more since you've left.

Basically, I've come to the conclusion that this Christian scene just isn't me. (Who knows, maybe some *other* Christian scene would suit me fine, but this one, nope, I don't think so.) I'm still interested in God and faith and all the rest, but it's important for me right now to keep an open mind. (Or maybe what I mean is, I want my old mind back.)

It's not like this is some hasty decision. In fact, in a weird, sounds-like-a-cop-out kinda way, it wasn't even my decision to make. The thing is, it's just not in me anymore, and I won't fake it. Not to you, especially.

Leaving the church hasn't been as easy as I'd expected. Giving up volleyball, for instance, was very hard. (Don't mean to be glib, but the girl can't help it.) I know lots of people are going to say I was never born again, never let Jesus into my heart, never said the right words or whatever but trust me, I did all those things. They'll say I'm lost. Well, who knows, maybe they're right. But they'll never find me, that's for sure.

Hope you're still my pal.
Oppie

PS: I still think you should tell somebody about what you saw. No one should get away with shit like that, least of all that fucking freak show. Kapeesh?

Soon after I read this, during a Friday night hayride (a perk of being a senior classman), I first felt afraid of the sky.

Our destination tonight was a negligible hill in the middle of a field thick with the frozen shit of cattle awaiting their slaughter, where we would spend half an hour or so singing the familiar hymns and Gospel choruses.

As the tractor pulled out of the fluorescent fog of campus, my neck relaxed and my head lolled onto the hay. It smelled earthy, dirty and good. I looked up, and took in stars and star clusters, clotted upon the darkness like sour cream in cold coffee. A Korean student next to me, whose name after four years I still couldn't recall, mumbled something prayerful about the heavens declaring the glory of God. Beside him, Tibo Fung tried to impress a couple of giggly women by pointing out Venus and Saturn.

Saturn. I wrapped my slender arms around me like the ribbons on a special Christmas gift, hugging myself tightly through my wool coat and mock turtleneck sweater. Saturn made me shudder.

I'd recently discovered a library book that didn't seem to belong on a Bible school shelf. An art book, filled with vivid images of gambolling satyrs and wood nymphs. Characters who still carried considerable daemonic weight around campus, but pretty innocuous fare, save one painting in particular.

It depicted Saturn, one of the more demented gods of Mediterranean antiquity. Blood smeared his lips and knotty hands, and his eyes were immense and brimming with monstrous, I-can't-believe-I-ate-the-whole-thing stupefaction. No wonder. God or no god, the crazy bastard had just swallowed his own son.

I remember scrutinizing the gory scene a long while, horrified some, but mostly tickled by a ridiculous question: *What kind of a role model is that for a planet?* It was only later, and only after I'd read Oppie's letter, that I shocked myself with an answer: *Perhaps, after all, a most appropriate one.*

The rings of Saturn. I recalled Voyager 2 sending its pictures home for developing during the summer crusade at Cliffside. They were in all the newsmagazines, most of which still lingered on the shelves of Overcomer's periodical room well into winter. Wheels within wheels of ice and rock in inestimable number; fragments as piddling as refined flour and as big as my father's house, pressed together in hundreds of variegated belts like a vinyl disk with bands of discordant volume and density. They make a perceptible smudge if you know where to look on a clear night. With just a pair of field binoculars, they can be glorious. David Keaton called them "God's signature in the heavens."

It started ages ago, say astronomers (much, *much* more recently, say the creation scientists), Saturn's attraction was too much for one its moons. The satellite was drawn closer, closer — too close — and was granulated by the planet's terrible gravity. The remains of that aboriginal and unmourned world became the rings of exquisite debris that bind the gas giant like a halo that has slipped about its swollen waist.

Maybe the myth made good cosmology.

I rolled my head to the side and scratched my nose on the straw, but uncomfortable thoughts had hold of me.

With the singular, enormous exception of the Holocaust, I didn't find the evil of this world a difficult thing to fathom. (Hearing the odd story of a hollow-eyed Jew accepting Christ in the queue to the showers never much inspired me to worship.) The evil that men do, and women too, was a no-brainer, given the heights from which we'd fallen and the lengths to which Lord would go to prove the worth of His Church. (How far would He go? I heard the voice of an eternally cocksure Pierre Trudeau: "Just watch me.") And there was a scale to human suffering that made sense to me, if only, finally, as mystery. But gross cosmic violence, even with glorious aesthetic consequence, gave me a chill.

There was a pamphlet that had particularly impressed me as a freshman. Titled *The Gospel in the Stars*, it argued God had commissioned a billboard of natural religion for those with eyes to see. Orion was just over my shoulder, and he was supposed to represent Christ, but I forgot why that was and wasn't especially comforted.

By the time we reached the hill I was sitting upright, eyes fixed, unblinking, on the field of snow lying dead before me. My legs dangled over the side of the wagon, my hands clenched fistfuls of straw at my knees. The night was *too* clear, the stars *too* bright. *If only there were a ceiling to the sky*, I remember thinking, and then felt worse for having thought something so mad. My hands dug deeper into the straw, hungry for something substantial to grasp, because I was overwhelmed by the unintelligible fear of falling *up*.

Something terrifying and turbulent was happening to me. I was struggling with a kind of panic I'd never imagined. I'd known greater fear — Filmore falling off the cliff, the hole in Delbert's skull — but this felt more grievous, just because there was no good reason for it. Buoyant and taut, as though my bones were moulded from hollow plastic and braided with pipe cleaners, I felt that one small step off the wagon would be my last, giant leap. I could see myself tumbling forever in zero gravity, like Gary Lockwood's character in *2001*, where it made no sense anymore to speak of up or down, this way or that.

Raptured. With no one out there to catch me.

Our time on the hill was an anxious hell for me, but I didn't let on. I joked, I sang, but I didn't feel the weight return to my arms and legs. The dread of being lighter than air and moorless under all that sky oppressed me, and as much as I could I'd grab at something solid to keep from drifting away into the dark. The wagon's edge, a tractor tire, a tree. Anything within reach that was heavy enough or well rooted.

The faint voice of an Asian girl requested we sing "How Great Thou Art." By the time we reached "I see the stars, I hear the roaring thunder" most everyone's voice was soaring with eyes cast heavenward, but my voice cracked and my gaze stayed fixed on my shoes. I couldn't seem to keep from falling a half-beat behind, and soon I gave up, silently mouthing the words to myself. By the final verse I'd given up on that, too.

For the return trip most of my classmates lay stretched on their backs in the straw, silent, staring straight up into the speckled night. *Jesus,* I thought, *how could they do that?* And then it physically hurt to think how inconceivable that suddenly seemed. Myself, I was sitting tense and erect, arm wrapped around a post, on guard against strange, new thoughts. *God,* if only it had been a little overcast, maybe I could have laid back like the others.

My uncle must have hated limpid night skies, when the tracer fire would have seemed like luminescent scribbles connecting the dots of the stars. I would have been happy for just a few shady tiles of cirrocumulus to hide beneath. It wasn't until I was safe under the dormitory roof that I calmed myself enough to know I wasn't going mad. At least not all in one night. Back in my room, I distracted myself to sleep by watching streaks of light from the odd pair of high beams slip between the Venetian blinds and stretch themselves thin and irregular upon my ceiling stucco. It wasn't the Milky Way, but it was a pretty show.

There were several more hayrides after Christmas, but I was always too tired or busy.

"Apple juice or milk? What's your pleasure?"

"Milk, I think. Thanks."

She spun nimbly on her flat heels for the kitchen, and showed me the honour of not bothering to tell me to make myself at home.

We weren't especially close, Miss Faulkner and I. But close enough. She had unwittingly grafted a few sprigs of her own curiosity onto my pared, desiccated brainstem, and so was largely responsible for my outgrowing my unformed fantasies of the mission field. She was the smartest believer I'd ever met, and I wanted my intellect calibrated according to her factory specs. A hint, perhaps, that God had called me to be a scholar, too.

I wasn't a great student but I wished that I was, and wishing was enough for her, because that was so much better than most everyone else. It meant I received her subtle, ironic smiles that said she was glad I was in the class, because even if I didn't get it all, she knew I knew enough to regret I hadn't.

When I flattered myself, I thought I was her prodigy. When I didn't, I knew I was only so by default.

I sat on the nearest end of her brown corduroy sofa, setting my casebound, chicken-broth coloured yearbook on the cushion beside me. Though I'd had it for three days, I was saving the first signature for Amphora Faulkner.

Pertinax crept from behind the television and licked her paws, then warily slunk towards me to rub her sent glands against my overripe grey socks. With an abrupt, effortless leap she was suddenly on the sofa's arm, meowing luxuriantly, vaunting her teeth, before turning about and lashing my face with her black and orange tail and presenting her rosy pudendum. My gaze fell to the coffee table, which was almost eclipsed by a massive volume of engravings by Albrecht Dührer. I picked it up, with both hands, and opened it at random to the cortege of his Four Horsemen upon the knobby heads of doomed Bavarian burghers.

"Like it?" Faulkner entered the room, her lips pressed into a thin smile. In each hand she toted a stubby glass. "Rathuh grisly stuff, but there you are. Early Reformers were such sadomasochists. But don't say Ah told you so."

"Not much has changed," I readily quipped, with all the plodding and charmless sagacity of an over-reaching undergraduate. Which is what I was.

"Oh no. Now days, mostly we're just masochists."

I grunted my agreement and nodded, as if to say that's just what I'd meant. I tried to stroke the cat but it bounded to the floor and disappeared.

"Ah'm not sayin' that's better or worse. But honestly, it's *much* less interestin'."

I shuddered a little and shut the book. Faulkner sank into the far side of the sofa with an expression of delighted fatigue, just as she might in a warm bath on a frigid school night. She crossed her legs and smoothed the folds of her green poplin skirt, and in the hollow of her lap she cupped her glass of nectar.

"Dürhrer's a favourite Lutheran of mine. My brothuh sent that for my birthday. The postage must've cost more than the book, it's such a heavy thing."

"I didn't know you had a brother."

She nodded. "Khepera."

"The capital of Uganda? Is that where he is?"

"That's his name, Ah'm afraid. He's a high school teacher in Memphis. Five years younguh." She sipped from her glass and mindfully set the glass beside mine. "Funny name, isn' it?"

"What's it mean?"

"It's a funny story." The corners of her lips crinkled but she shook her head, changing her mind. "Maybe a little *too* funny ...."

"Oh?" I grinned, eager and familiar just enough to sportingly egg her on. "How come?"

"Well, it takes some explainin'. See, our Dad was somethin' of an archaeologist —"

"I remember reading about that."

"Yes. Well, he wanted me named Amphora, because he found shards of a wonderful Sumerian jug around the time Ah was ... well, I suppose we could say conceived. Excuse me. That's what Amphora means, you know." I nodded solemnly, not exactly sure what she was talking about. "Mothuh preferred Beatrix, but then she never put up much of a fight when it came to us. When my brothuh came along we were in Egypt. Khepera is an ancient Egyptian god. Quite a character, they say."

"What did he do?"

She lowered her eyes, and so did I. We both watched her index finger trace tiny hoops on the rim of her glass. Her lips coiled in an equivocal smile.

"Are you *sure* you want me to tell you?"

"Oh, of course."

"It's rathuh delicate, actually."

"Oh, don't worry about that," I rebutted affably. "I'm tough; I can take it."

"Well," she sighed. "Khepera, they said, supposedly created the universe by — pardon the expression — spillin' his seed."

"Oh!"

"I don' know what got in their heads. My parents, I mean."
Then she snorted. "The Egyptians too, I guess. 'I had union
with my hand,'" she intoned as in a sonorous burlesque, "'and I
embraced my shadow in a love embrace.' Oh goodness — can
you believe that?"

My face tingled with a blush, which embarrassed me more
than our conversation, and I tried to bore myself pale again by
gibbering some insipid words of sympathy.

"It must have been tough, growing up with a name like that."

"No one knew what it meant. He was always so grateful.
But I don' think it was too bad. Ah'm sure it must be much
worse over here for all those poor oriental boys called Kok
and Wang."

Now her face reddened too, though it looked less scarlet
than mine felt, as she savoured an incongruous giggle which
she tried to hide behind the knuckles of her right hand. I felt
my insides jump; enough to make me think of all those spastic
hausfraus in heritage sitcoms who leap upon their kitchen
tables at the suspicion of a mouse. She'd never, in my hearing,
made such an off-colour remark.

"Oh, excuse me!" she said, still giggling. "It *has* been a long
year now, hasn' it? Ah always get a bit flighty this late in spring
semestuh." She kneaded her brow deeply, and with leisurely
delight. "Anyhow, he's always gone by Kip, so there you go."

She glanced down at her side to my yearbook, as though
noticing it for the first time. She picked it up and cradled it in
her ample lap while she vacantly flipped the pages.

"Ah've always found Ancient Egypt like another planet. It's
so far from us and strange." Her waxy eyes twinkled as she ran
her fingers through her ashen, close-cropped perm. "The
Romans are so much more like us. Ah never really felt that for
the Greeks, except maybe Aristophanes. Ah think it's amazin'
that we can still laugh at their jokes."

I nodded from behind my milk.

Faulkner sighed contentedly, and tapped a stately minuet
on her chin with a pair of plump fingers.

"Do you know what the Emperor Vespasian's last words
were?"

I shrugged.

"'Oh dear, Ah must be turnin' into a god.'" She flashed a broad grin, which I returned unopened, though with a tactful chuckle. "See, there's real wit there. The wit of a good man, too, Ah dare say. Someone who didn' take himself too seriously. Or his gods, for that mattuh. Those were the best kind of pagans. At least so much as you can measure these things." She exhaled heavily through her mouth. Her breath ruffled my pant leg. "Now then, let's see here, where's my picture in this thing .... Here we are."

From a hidden pocket in her skirt Faulkner raised a pen, chewing its silver button as she pondered an inscription for my book. She delivered a little exclamation of discovery when she found the words, then scribbled them down hastily and set the book atop the Dührer.

"Thanks very much," I said.

"My pleasure."

Pertinax reappeared at my feet, startling me slightly, stretching and yawning and demanding attention. She brushed against my calf, and as I bent to scratch her head she twisted her neck, anticipating my touch.

"Hmmm ...." Faulkner's voice sounded mellow and far away. I looked towards her as the cat again tired of me, and saw her toss her head as though trying to dismiss an indecorous thought.

"Ah probably shouldn' ask this ...."

"What?" Pertinax leapt onto the cushion between us.

"No," she smiled obliquely, rubbing her cat's grey belly. "Ah really shouldn't. But this has been botherin' me for a long time —"

She opened her mouth wide to take a deep breath, which persuaded me to take one myself. Almost imperceptibly, her right leg began to swing on the fulcrum of her left knee, twisting like a slab of ham in a butcher's window.

"It's not a proper subject to talk ovuh with a student but, well, it's not like you'll be a student for much longuh, right?"

"Amen!" I boomed, and took a celebratory swig of milk.

"Well anyway, the thing is, Ah've always wondered how you young boys *do* it. It's such a mystery to me, you see."

"Do *what?*"

"How you — goodness, how shall Ah put it ? — control your basuh instincts. Your animal drives. Ah mean, if that's not too personal a question."

I stammered and giggled absurdly. Then shook my head and stammered again.

"Ah'm so sorry! There I go. Forget it. Ah should've known."

"Oh no, no. That's fine." I cracked my knuckles and tried to clear my throat, but nothing was there. "It's just, I guess, I'm not sure I know exactly what you mean."

"Oh. Well, just resistin' temptation and the like. Ah know the urges must be very strong for boys your age; even Christian boys."

"Well," I replied with guarded ambiguity, "I *suppose* that must be true. Most of us just pray for strength to resist. And, you know, like that." Breezily, I chewed a thumbnail.

Faulkner nodded, fingering the collar of her bone-coloured silk blouse that clung to her like the Hindenburg to hydrogen. *Just one spark, and we'd both be history.* Her gaze drifted to her crossed right foot and I followed suit. The toes were dramatically curled back from the sole of her tawdry patent leather sandal, and their nails were painted a sociable candy apple red. I was bewildered. The rules were quite precise about toenail polish.

"I suppose it always works?" She asked, twisting in her seat to better face me.

"Oh ... well, no, I can't say that." I gulped some air but couldn't keep it down. "I can't speak for *all* of us, but I'm sure *some* of us, sometimes, have our moments of ..." I waved my hand senselessly, "weakness."

"Overcomuh's a funny place, isn't it? The powers that be keep you boys and girls apart for four years, and then expect you to know enough to marry sensibly after you graduate. That must be very hard. Ah can't imagine what you all must go through." Then she chortled gruffly. "Well, Ah mean, yes Ah can."

"Sometimes it's hard," I spluttered with moronic candour. "Then sometimes, it's harder than other times."

She nodded her head slowly and began swaying her leg more deliberately, her foot now arcing in my direction as a fold of her skirt fell away, revealing a milky flank of calf. It wasn't much, or even all that much to look at, but after a semester of Bible school it might as well have been her thigh, ass or pubis. I don't think I could've been more staggered by my retarded recognition that there are such wonders in this world. Trembling, I set my glass of milk on the table, then wiped my clammy palm across my forehead.

"You heard the story, Gideon, about the King of Syracuse?"

"No, I don't think so."

"One day durin' an argument, his opponent told him he had bad breath. When he went home that night, the king asked his wife why she'd never mentioned his breath before. She just said, 'Ah thought all men smelled that way.'" Ah answered her sumptuous laugh with an unsteady smile. Then she pursed her lips and absently smoothed the fur of her cat's haunch. Pertinax meowed her gratitude and rolled onto her back. "Ah know it sounds a little strange, and not everyone would agree, especially here, but men and women have got to learn what they smell like."

I nodded reflexively, unsure again of what I was assenting to.

"I think I know what you mean."

"Ideally, Bible school should be the place."

"Things are changing, I think. I hope." I faltered, "I guess."

"Ah'm sure they are," she nodded bluntly. "But are you ...."

Her face broke into an ample grin, literally, as her light foundation began to crack and the fuzz of her cheeks began to poke through like weeds in a broken sidewalk.

"What I'm tryin' to say is, are you gettin' close enough to the young ladies to know what they smell like?"

She waved her hand that I need't answer, and tossed back her head with a hoarsy snigger. Her neck was stretched taunt, and looked thick and creamy like a rain-soaked pine log peeled of its bark. I felt a familiar, lonely tingle between my legs.

"There's a nasty rumour going around," I confided gingerly, undaunted by such a bad idea. "Night watchmen say that they've seen sacks of salt peter in the dining room pantry."

Her eyes swelled comically. "Salt peter? Oh no, Ah'm sure they wouldn' do that. That's somethin' they do to prisoners, don' they?"

"That's what shocked us."

"No, they wouldn'. Or would they?"

"I hope not." I felt buoyed by a capricious joke. "All along I thought my self control was thanks to the Holy Spirit!"

"Hmmm," Faulkner nodded. She didn't laugh as I'd expected. I sank in my seat. I sank deeper when she abruptly asked, "Is there a big problem in the dorm with boys touchin' themselves?"

"*Touching?*"

"Yes. You know .... Oh, Ah shouldn' be askin' such things ...."

"Well, I —"

"No, never mind."

"It's just, no, I mean —"

"It's okay ...."

"No, it's not something we talk about. If I understand you."

"Yes, Ah think you do." Faulkner took a long drink of nectar, and when she was finished wiped her mouth inelegantly with the back of her hand. The cat leapt off the couch, leaving nothing between us. "Do you think that many of them do?"

"Do ...?"

"Touch themselves?"

"Oh, I ...." My voice scattered and vanished like a jet's contrail cloud. Her foot glanced against my shin. She didn't apologize.

"What might they think about when they touch themselves, Gideon?"

"What might they think? About?"

I felt dizzy and anxious, as something old and reptilian — myself, but an inconsonant, swamp-humoured, three-toed self — threatened to snap into life. And something did, as a warm and pudgy hand fell upon my knee, and the blur of another reached for my cheek.

"They think about you, Miss Faulkner."

3

ou like these? You do, don't you? Do you? You can touch them. You want to touch them? Do you ....

Here, give me your hands .... It's okay. They're for you. Pretend it's cookie dough. Uh huh, that's right. Knead me, boy. Hah! Ah made a li'l pun.

There. Feel how hard their gettin'? Feels good. That's right, it feels good when you do that to me. Use your mouth. All over. It's good all over. You can bite me, if you like. Don't be afraid. Gently. But not too gently ....

Come closuh, son. Let's take this off. Yes, Ah want to see .... My, you're so pale! You need some sun. Don' be shut up all day with your books. Shhh. No, that's alright. Kiss me here. Now roll over.

Tickles a little down there, doesn' it? Right here especially, huh? Right at the base, on the flip side. Like that? Tell me you like that. Did you know you taste like red licorice? Anybody tell you that before? Anybody taste you? Any girl slap her titties in your face before? Anyone ever cup your balls like this before? Like hearing me say that? Like your bad teacher talking dirty to you? Look at your hard cock thingy there. Ever seen it so big? I like that.

Ever been with a naked girl before, Gideon?

Try up a touch; right at the top. That little gristly thing. See it? It's not very — oh, you had it for a sec.

It's got a hood; looks like a monk. Remember your Church history. Oh I shouldn' say that... There. See there, down there? You can — Oooh! Yes! Gold star, Mistuh Gast. That's what Ah'm talkin' about. Good. Now don' move.

Ah mean move, but just don' go far from — ahh!

Suck it, lick it, lap it up. You hungry? Show me you're still hungry.

Gentle, now.

Ah think we're doin' pretty well, Gideon. Feel how wet I am? You went to a public school, didn' you? In health class, did they tell you what that means? It means Ah like what your doin'. It means Ah want you to stick it in me.

4

$\mathfrak{IF}$ aulkner was salty and tart, like a formidable cheese. Until she wedged my head between her burly drumsticks I'd no idea women came flavoured, like cornerstore cheddars seasoned mild, medium and old. When the time came to go down on my second lover, I was delighted to discover they didn't all taste so piquant.

Once we'd started (or rather, once she'd unfastened her blouse, and had bountifully spilled out of her bone-coloured corset), I had no trouble deferring my scruples for a while (or rather, for as long a while as it might take). The make-believe temper of the night, and too many nights spent bonding my fingers together with the crazy glue of my lonesome ejaculate, overturned — in the rapturous twiddling of an eyelet — all my learning as though the Lord's good counsel were spiteful droolings.

Inviting her to pray with me for strength didn't cross my mind this time. God knows I was fearful, but once we'd started my fear was only for the performance of my shy, floppy man-root, which surprised me by seeming in no great rush to raise its herbaceous stalk towards the light. If a claque of bookish seraphim must record this in their Logs of Judgement, I hoped at least to give them something worth writing about.

But then, with enough coaxing, enough germane, sympathetic abrasion, I stretched out atop and between her, hyperventilating, palpitating; whisking away with inchoate logic. I tried to look down between us, to glean the gross mechanics of our magic act, but her pale belly, striated with stretch marks, screened everything, and its button winked at me like a cyclopean eye. Then she clamped her jaw on my earlobe savagely enough to make me wince, which loosed a lewd, throaty giggle from her before she licked me down my jaw-line and kissed my lips, roughly, and for the first time.

Predictable as shift work, but more than routine, my guilt punched in as soon as my spermatozoa punched out.

My shame, I knew, would be merciless; a tremendous *Yikes!* written in blood across the sky like a connect-the-dots constellation. This sin was much too grave, too conceivably catastrophic, to be forgiven with a simple Protestant prayer. The remorse and sense of spiritual doom felt, somehow, too Catholic for that. Regrets draped gloomily across my pinched shoulders like folds in the disavowing shawl of a Portuguese widow. *Take it to the Lord*, I tried comforting myself, but it was no comfort. I knew I had to do something before the Lord took it to me.

According to the New Covenant, the sincerity of my goobery sobs for pardon, and the length and inclemency of my extended, scalding showers should have been sufficient to restore to me a sense of my having been set apart to a righteous end. So naturally I was mystified how come I felt, if I were to die and stand before God's wounded, Right-Hand Man, the great *maître d'* at the end of the world, that He would arch a damning eyebrow and say, "Reservation?" What more might be required of me I couldn't tell, and I was petrified of asking further instruction. "If thine eye offend thee, pluck it out," I found a nettlesome text.

Cause and effect: God's making a list and checking it twice. So instinctively, perversely, when my mother called the following Tuesday with the news that Nanny was back in hospital with another of those strokes of hers, I couldn't help think I was to blame. And why not? If I'd crossed the mob and, straightaway, my grandmother received a dead fish in the mail, I wouldn't have called that a coincidence, either. No, this had all the earmarks of a warning from my *Capo e Capo*: smarten up, kid, or the old lady gets it.

"You know, I love that old hymn."

Sluggishly — a tacky smudge of blackened gum and the inky ruts of pious graffiti only grudgingly giving me up — I raised my brow from off the pew before me, and squinted with weary alarm down the long aisle towards the tabernacle's dais.

O for a Thousand Tongues. Jesus, would I ever be able to sing that hymn again? Doubtful, I remember supposing, even as chapel accompanist Bev Derlago played an introductory stanza and I doubled over in supplication, which became a senseless nodding with fatigue. I hadn't slept a night through since my night with Faulkner. I was so beat I hardly even squirmed during Charles Wesley's unfortunate invitation to "behold your Saviour come."

When Dean Blier's voice roused me I had no sense of how long I'd been out. I felt grubby, and had an urge to brush my teeth. His voice quivered with a phlegmy and unfamiliar distress that charged the air of the great hall with apprehension and voyeuristic enchantment, in seemingly equal measure.

"Uh huh," mumbled Blier, absently shuffling his papers. "I really do ...."

With a tremulous bleat — so improbable coming from the Dean it almost physically hurt me — he withdrew a lengthy tissue from a trouser pocket and generously daubed his nose.

"I'm sorry ...."

Suddenly he was sobbing and trembling, taking tremendous gulps, like a lousy swimmer bobbing in breakwater. All about me classmates began muttering their prayers.

"The Lord was just ...." Blier began, before convulsing with another tearful fit. He shook his head, sighed heavily and started again. "Sorry for all this. It's only, God was really speaking to my heart during that song. Don't know why. Maybe the line, 'His blood can make the foulest clean'." He shook his head once more and laughed mirthlessly. "It has to be .... These things .... He ...."

I was wide awake now and chewing my fingernails, even as they tingled with shame at where they'd been and what they'd done. My sin sat in my belly like a knob of indigestible tallow.

"He's showing me something. There's a part of my life that I've lived without his blessing. I didn't know. A real big part, too. And I just .... I don't think the Lord'll let me get on with this until I get it right ...."

Nothing would interrupt him; not a rustling page nor a clearing throat. I tried to distract myself by absently leafing through a notebook. When I recognized my Greek assignments I hurriedly folded it away in my knapsack, which drew a disapproving shake from a head before me.

"Since my sin has been public, so my confession must be. What I have to say is that I've been a ... a negligent parent!" Blier wiped his eyes with his soiled tissue and blew his nose in it. "While I've been so busy on campus, and with the boys in the dorm, I've been forgetting my own. My own dear sons. There's an urgency, I feel, to get it right now, or I'm not a fit parent or counsellor. Forgive me, Lord! And please forgive me, boys." He stretched wide his wavering hands. "Peter and Johnny, your Daddy's sorry!"

A great, liberating moan rolled back towards me from the centre aisle, as I watched senior linebacker Peter, quickly followed by his younger and slighter brother John, leave their pews and race each other to their father's arms. From afar on the girl's side arose an impromptu "Amazing Grace." Someone down front applauded, but it didn't catch on.

After a long embrace — moving and mortifying to sit through, what with Derlago tinkling incidental music as though accompanying a silent film — Peter disengaged and approached the microphone.

"I've got the greatest Dad in the world!" he barked, jabbing the air with a *We're No. 1* sign. "It takes lots of love to do something like that." Peter turned his head and nodded rapturously towards his father. "Thank you, father. But I'd be a hypocrite if I didn't confess — to the school, to you, and most of all, to God — that I've sinned too. I've been disrespectful to you and to this institution. I'm sorry. Please forgive me and pray for me."

To our atonal chorus of amens, Peter backed into the arms of his father. Their wide, red eyes then fell upon John, who made his way forward, more reticently than his big brother. His voice was clotted from crying and his sentiments vague, but I heard some muffled remorse over "impure thoughts," at which the dean clasped his hands together, threw his head back and shouted "Hallelujah!"

Hallelujahs abounded throughout the tabernacle, and I slouched deeper in my Slough of Despond. Moments like this, I sulked, were what made the Holy Spirit seem so full of Himself.

"I was intending to continue this morning with our devotional series on the life of Joshua." Blier was clear-eyed and in control now, and his boys had returned to their seats. "But I want to be sensitive to the leading of the Spirit here. This may be an important moment for us. For *all* of us. What I think we'll do here is open up the remainder of our chapel time, to give us a chance to share as the Body of Christ. If you have something on your heart which you feel the Lord would have you confess — any sins against our fellowship that you need to make right — then this is your chance. Some of us may feel a little raw right now, so I want to be careful not to orchestrate anything. Just listen to God."

From all parts of the tabernacle, students stood and began squeezing their way down the pew to the platform, where they promptly and without direction formed gender-specific queues for the microphone. Those near the rear chose to await their turns on the first row of choir benches.

Harold Jorgens apologized for making a spectacle of himself by eating bugs for money. A one-year certificate student named Gerald Reid made a hazy, equivocal confession that hinted at "effeminate tendencies." Cathy Gilchrist admitted to a thankless spirit. A classmate of mine, a geeky cipher named Syl Holtzkeag, mournfully acknowledged listening to Lionel Ritchie on campus. My ears pricked up. I'd have been up there too if all I had to confess were the likes of that. Several evenings in the Spring I'd been hanging out in Tibo Fung's room, listening to his contraband cassette of my favourite ass-kicking, Christian album, Dylan's *Shot of Love*. Zimmy may have converted, but his music was still too syncopated and his testimony too compromised for the likes of Overcomer.

Fung was up there himself soon, echoing John's halting confession of impure thoughts. (No mention of the Dylan tape, I noted.) That was to prove a popular disclosure; almost every man who followed made some allusion to it. But when Dianna Rempel wept an apology for wearing a non-regulation bra (sheer and "godlessly low on support"), the Dean broke in with the gentle direction to "keep private sins private."

Lois Wong whispered her dread at the prospect of mission service in Kenya, something she'd been preparing for since her first class three years ago in Personal Evangelism. Sam Boswell wept that he'd kept a copy of *Penthouse* in his room since Christmas break, which proved to be the most humiliating confession until Chester Babbs' admission that he subscribed to *Hanging Melons*.

The regular chapel period ended, but by now all eight choir benches were filled. With a quick phone call to the administrative office Blier extended the chapel a further half hour. Thirty minutes later, classes for the remainder of the day were cancelled.

Blier rarely strayed far from centre stage. He nodded prayerfully, with a thoughtful finger pressed to his chin for most confessions. For those who rambled he would lay a hand on their shoulder and, if necessary, shepherd them off stage. He led us through the occasional hymn or a gospel chorus, though unaccompanied. (Early on, Bev Derlago had confessed the sin of pride in her musicianship and left the hall in anguish.)

The catalogue of petty vices made me heartsick. I hadn't read *Hanging Melons*, I'd lived it: in three dimensional, transdenominational living colour. Mine wasn't the oafish sin of Onan. I'd made good to the last drop this time.

I kept checking my watch compulsively, anticipating the noon hour as a welcome respite, but presently we were joined by the dining hall staff and it was announced that lunch was cancelled. Shortly thereafter a student I didn't recognize publicly confessed his hunger as though it were a vice. Blier made the concession that if anyone absolutely had to leave, perhaps to grab a "quick bite" downtown or back in the dorm, that was permitted. I was encouraged, then, to see Nathan Weaver stand and shuffle past me, and was about to follow him when he reached the aisle and turned towards the stage. Nathan, in his turn, confessed a "frivolous" attitude, which was true enough, and wept ruefully over his wasted years spinning stale Monty Python routines. *And now for something completely different.*

Blier nodded heavily, with indulgent compassion. It seemed his recent homily chiding the "mood of frivolity" on campus, specifically the Student Life Committee's "Skits-o-frantic" sensibility, had found its mark.

No one, as I could tell, made for the exits, and I was too self-conscious to leave alone, and too guilt-stricken to have the confidence to know, once on my feet, in which direction I might walk. I didn't even know whether I could walk. This cavalcade of sin was making me so dizzy, I couldn't even roll my eyes. When I tried, the rafters of our cavernous tabernacle hanging high over my head seemed so far away and so ponderous, and behind them, I knew, was just empty sky, it scared me to simply look up. I felt myself losing myself, so I tried to pay attention to my breathing and hunkered down, gripping, white-knuckled, the rack of hymnals at my knees, and refused to let go. I could barely look above pew-height, but I was resigned to riding it out like a nasty patch of turbulence.

By mid-afternoon almost half my class had owned up to something. Some had been to the microphone several times. Most sat smiling munificently at each new confessor. But there were a few who looked confused by an infilling of the Spirit that had left them emptied of themselves.

I felt a colossal itch to put things right, to disgorge the lump in my belly. But what to say, and why to say it before all these people? This wasn't my sin alone, nor exactly had it been all my idea. I wasn't excusing myself, but if I confessed much beyond "impure thoughts" it could end a career, maybe even shorten a life.

With some effort I convinced my conscience that fucking my teacher was a private affair. Nothing good could come of its public admission. It is sensible, and scriptural, to limit confession to the circle of the transgression. I would go to Faulkner quietly and pray with her. Gradually I relaxed my grip on the rack of hymnals before me. *Yes, Lord. Like the woman you found in sin. Discretion isn't cowardly when it's the wisest course.*

And then of course there she was, a blubbering, contrite hulk stumbling down the aisle, moaning with such abandon that she silenced Yuri Panchlow's admittance of intermittent snooker playing. As she clambered to the podium in her wrinkled beige rayon dress, both queues fell back without a murmur, and Blier deferentially surrendered the rostrum to the first faculty member since himself to participate in this Great Awakening.

For a long while she could only weep into the mike. Her cries filled the hall, elbowing aside even the most prodigious "Amen." I dropped my head again to the pew before me. I had trouble organizing my thoughts. Or perhaps I could, but chose not to. I heard a seatmate whisper, "Thank you, Jesus," as my breathing grew shallow and I tried hard not to die.

"Ah've gotta confess," Faulkner finally gasped. "Ah've gotta confess somethin' horrible." Reluctantly, I raised my eyes. She waved a hand in front of her face and again collapsed into thick sobs, regaining composure only once Blier had moved to her side and whispered her some encouragement. "Ah've gotta confess that Ah've done somethin' so wicked ...." Her voice trailed off precipitously. She shook her head and cast a baleful glance towards the distant ceiling's cross-beams. "This is the hardest thing Ah've ever done ...."

I pressed my forehead hard against the wood and recalled the true cross, wishing I hadn't been born the first time, let alone the second. Just beneath the gooseflesh of my back, my spine tingled and slithered like an electric eel.

Please God oh please God please don't let her say it please just please maybe please Jesus please God forgive me you could just take her home right now please just take her ....

"Ah feel so dirty; so ashamed ...."

Sorry Christ sorry Jesus forgive me I didn't mean that but God just please God just make her stop ....

"Ah don't feel good about sayin' this, but there's just no way Ah can keep this to myself anymore. Ah've been feelin' so .... Oh, *Jesus!* Please forgive me! Ah've gotta confess, Ah'm guilty of — *Lord!* — indecent relations ...."

As though it had just been suckerpunched, the Body of Christ emitted a wheezy gasp as Blier laid a hand on Faulkner's heaving shoulder and steered her aside from the microphone. He closed the chapel with a curt prayer and a request that we leave quietly, then motioned for the dean of women to join him on stage. They ushered Faulkner through a door behind the choir loft, which lead to a suite of pastoral offices and counselling chambers. I closed my eyes and gently drummed my head on the pew.

It was only four in the afternoon, but I decided there was nothing left to do but go to bed.

The hallways and toilets of the dormitory were purring with speculation after Faulkner's partner. Suspicion fell chiefly upon "some town guy." A bountifully-freckled sophomore named Ivor Klugman — who, just three hours before, had declared himself a "no good gossip and tattler" — insinuated that perhaps Blier had his own reasons for moving so quickly to silence her. No one else would have that. Blier was unimpeachably married. Fornication was one thing; nobody could get their head around adultery.

There were whispers that it was another woman, but that idea was smothered in the vacuum of consecrated silence as the more devout floor monitors made it clear they considered such conjecture unedifying.

No one I heard suggested a student.

"Hard to believe, isn't it?" Tibo Fung said, massaging his gums with his dry toothbrush. "She taught you Greek, huh?"

"Yeah. Right. Hard to believe."

In my room, I pulled the covers over my curled frame and tucked them tightly beneath my chin. Lights out at six and on an empty stomach, but I astonished myself by promptly falling asleep.

It was the best sleep I'd had in months. In the early morning, rising for a bountiful piss, I found a note had been slipped beneath my door. A red note. The dean wanted to see me as soon as possible. "As soon as possible" was underscored three times in heavy black ink.

After Word

I

Jesus Christ our Saviour, what is it that he saved? Look at our pietists, the most Christian of all Christians, those pale, wicked, terror-stricken creatures, who cannot smile and who look like maniacs. They seem to carry a demon in their hearts and, mark you, most of their leaders end up in prison as malefactors. Why should their Lord have delivered them over to the enemy? Is religion a punishment, and is Christ the spirit of vengeance?

All the ancient Gods reappeared as demons at a later date.

August Strindberg

0

When I was, I think, six years old, I got a bad nose-
bleed at the Canadian National Exhibition.

I was with my grandmother in the children's
midway. I don't remember if my parents came as well that year.
They rarely did, and never went on the rides. Nanny let me
choose my ride, and I picked a sleek, silvery flying fortress
with a chunky red button in the middle of its steering column
that lit up a pair of clattering machine guns on my wings. I
pressed the button often, as did the other fly-boys in my
squadron, until my plane lurched downward unexpectedly and
I struck my nose on the rubberized rim of the cockpit. The
pain and the copper taste of my blood stunned me, and I
began to sob.

While I whirled about the ride's spidery hub, toy guns
metallically pattered away and my drippings stained my polo

shirt, and I could see my grandmother arguing savagely with the carny. The ride couldn't have lasted much longer, but she forced him to stop it early for my sake.

When she came to get me I remember it looked like she'd been crying, too.

1

"**F**orgiveness is free. Not cheap."

That was how Derek Blier spelled it out, three weeks before I was to have graduated. He looked salmon-eyed and sweaty as he explained he had no recourse but to expel me from Bible School for "gross sexual misconduct." He prayed over me, sandwiched my right hand in both of his and wished me well. Then he gave me 24 hours to be off campus property.

"Gross sexual misconduct" didn't need to be intercourse, not even sexual conduct; a simple kiss would have been gross enough. That didn't occur to me until the next morning, on the bus to the Calgary airport, as I recalled one of my grandmother's favourite maxims: "May as well be hung for a sheep as a goat." At long last, I thought I knew what she was talking about.

Amphora Faulkner was relieved of her duties for the balance of the term and took early sabbatical. The Campus Life Committee which decided her case accepted her public confession as a demonstration of genuine repentance. God is merciful, and Faulkner had admitted her sin. I hadn't.

I don't remember precisely when I stopped singing Jesus loves me. It all happened with such little reflection, and so matter-of-factly, that I must have fallen into apostasy piecemeal. My convictions were squandered in such preposterously trifling increments I barely noticed before I was practically spent.

Over the first summer of my post-undergraduate life, bowing my head in blessing before a Whopper combo simply became, one day, a perfunctory bob when the mop boy wasn't looking. Finally that struck me as insulting, to both God and the mop boy, and so I stopped altogether. While I still took communion, my old evangelical partiality for grape drink over the fermented fruit of the vine began to seem lowbrow as well as low church. Come on; even Martin Luther and C.S. Lewis enjoyed the occasional snort!

My prayer life contracted, becoming non-verbal, almost aconceptual. I assured myself this could only mean I was becoming more spiritual.

Dozens of old issues came up for grabs; things I'd thought long settled. Evolution, for one. Was it still *Case Dismissed!* — as I'd titled an essay, ingenuous punctuation and all, for my sophomore course Introduction to Creation Science? Or might it be possible the universe was older — *considerably* older — than the six, eight, ten thousand years, tops, that a literal reading of Genesis might allow? But if that were so, then how could I make sense of dinosaurs? I knew the Lord's ways to be mysterious, but if millions of years worth of doltish, monstrous lizards roaming about somehow helped further the Heavenly Kingdom, then what in God's own name was He thinking? So I struck from my creed the familiar call and response on the matter of First Things. But with a faith grown so fat with doctrine, I had dogma to burn.

Curiously, infuriatingly, it happened just like Dean Blier had always warned us it might, should we eschew one blessed jot or sacred tittle of Holy Scripture. Even seemingly reasonable doubt about, say, Jonah's "great fish" would lead, inevitably, to apostasy's Grand Guignol finale: a bloody-minded denial of the power of the Blood and the Resurrection of the Dead.

I didn't suspect what was happening until finally I threw in the towel on the Book of Revelations. (Seven heads and ten horns? The Whore of Babylon? *Grab a brain.*) Disbelief, when at last I knew it for what it was, felt as veiled and profound as my once Blessed Assurance. I missed faith's intermittent consolations, but the time would have come, even if Amphora Faulkner had never tickled my funniest bone, that I would no longer have cared about whatever the Hell Ezekiel saw way up in the middle of the air.

2

In the bottom of her rattan laundry hamper my grandmother kept a pair of ceremonial Nazi daggers with
gold scabbards and brocade tassels, a runty, rusty Luger
missing its munitions clip and a pair of grey field binoculars
embossed with eagle and swastika that always smelled like
clammy leather. I never asked where they came from or how
she got them, or even why she stored them beneath her beige
heap of foundation garments. I just assumed everyone's grandmother must hang out her washing on the Siegfried line.

> *Whistle while you work*
> *Hitler is a jerk*
> *Mussolini pulled his weenie*
> *Now it doesn't work.*

And teaching Nanny's naughty war jingles at recess made a nice line of credit with my bullying chums, who'd just as soon kick me in the balls as kick me in the ass.

The first time my grandmother confused me with my uncle Gideon I was 11 years old. Young enough to find it curious, old enough for it to scare the bejesus out of me. And vice versa.

I'd just bought Alice Cooper's *Killer* album and felt like sharing it. My parents, however, were not a sympathetic audience for glamrock. They still had hopes for my taking to *Pete Seeger Live at Newport*, which they'd bought me last Christmas, and kept cajoling me each week to stay up late for both or either Smother's Brother. So I hauled my plastic and canvas record player down to Nanny's sitting room, brandishing the album's gatefold of Alice hanging from a rope. I only wanted her to hear "Under My Wheels", which was three minutes of the choicest *sturm und drang* my ears had ever laid eyes on. And it would be years yet before I'd see *Hollywood Squares* and hear the words, "I'll take Alice Cooper to block".

Nanny was annoyed and fidgety; not nearly as intrigued as when I'd brought home the *Sticky Fingers* LP with a functioning fly. Wearily, about halfway through, she waved a hand in front of her face and muttered, "I don't much care for that. Not like them others."

"What others?"

"Them others you used to play."

"Who?"

"Spike Jones. You gone off 'im?"

"*Who?*"

"Spike Jones. Good Lord, me lad, you used to think the sun shone out 'is arsehole!"

"*What?*"

She eyeballed me queerly, leaning forward. Then she simply said "Oh", drawing it out as though she'd guessed the answer to an unexpected question, before sinking back into

her cosy, crumb-lined chair with a distracted look on her face.
I scratched the record in my haste to say goodnight.

The older I grew and the more she had her "little" strokes,
the less likely she was to guess the answer.

I was home from Bible school for nearly three months before I
finally saw my grandmother. I wasn't avoiding her. I was avoiding my mother.

I didn't know what to tell her about my expulsion without
admitting too much, so I decided to tell her nothing; not ever.
I explained it all to my father, because I still shared his house
and I felt that gave him some proprietorial stake in my life.
(Besides, I knew he'd be good for some unaffected empathy
before his inevitable I-told-you-so's.) But the only thing my
mother ever got out of me was that I'd "changed my mind"
about Bible school. After a while, when my spiritual anaemia
became evident to us both, she just stopped asking. "It's your
life," she'd sniff, before promising me that I was in her prayers.
My God, that infuriated me.

In the Time Before Sex I'd wanted to be a missionary. I would
imagine myself sweating litres for the Lord in a shed made of
soup tins by the banks of some unnamed river, growing leeks,
eating grubs and teaching Sunday School to born-again headhunters. I knew that I'd care more about saving their souls than
sparing my scalp. *Precious in the sight of the Lord is the death of his
saints* — and I was ready to make his day. Martyrdom didn't
seem like such a big deal, what with a millennium of bragging
rights in return. ("I was thrown to the lions. Yourself?"
"Covered in wax, impaled and set on fire." "Lucky bastard.")
No pain, no eternal gain.

Of course, if it wasn't any skin off God's nose, I hoped to
get some head before I lost mine (conjugated, naturally, by the
conjugal bed). But in the Time Before Sex I was intending a
thrifty, thirty-year stint in Papua New Guinea, with a trip
home once every five years or so for a tour of church base-

ments armed with slides of grinning, toothless converts. In the Time Before Sex I had wanted sex — I'd always known my heavy thumper wanted to lay down a mojo rhythm — but more still, I'd wanted to be a hero for the Lord. So had Mary, my first and most foolish love, and Oppie Szabo.

I was supposed to be a *missionary*, for Christ's sake. I should have been in my shed of soup tins translating the Gospel of John, not curled on a single bed listening again to old Guess Who records. That's why I'd needed to see Oppie: she was another saint gone soft in the middle.

"Cheer up, Gid. You're not a loser. A loser's some guy who wears an 'I'm with Stupid' t-shirt when he's all by himself. As bad as it seems, I can't see you doing that." Oppie Szabo rubbed her nose and smiled, picking at the crumbs of her falafel plate and called for another Black Label. "Fuck it. I've got a shit-load of work today, but I'd rather get pissed with you."

"Work? Since when?"

"Since, like, *always*," she smirked. "I've got my own drafting table and light box. Well, I share the light box with another designer, but she's cool."

I'm glad for another round — drinking a beer feels so right, finally — but I have no thirst. Not much appetite, either. I've hardly touched my fish and chips. There's a stupid bubble of guilt crowding my brain for having robbed the fish's sacrifice of meaning. The food was supposed to comfort me, but now I wish I could comfort my deep-fried cod fillets.

Oppie's black blouse fell open as she hunched over her purse for cigarettes, and I found myself tracking the shadow between her pale breasts. I shuddered and stared at my plate, and when I mumbled, "It'll all work out," I wasn't sure what I meant.

"Sure it will, but the thing is you should never have been there in the first place. I know you're feeling pretty shitty, but trust me, it may be a blessing in disguise." She struck a match and smiled. "Listen to me. *Blessing*. Sounding like I'm still the goddamned Bible thumper. Geezus, why don't I just tell you to take it to the Lord?"

"Number's no longer in service."

"Directory Assistance?"

"No new listing."

"Bastard." Oppie squinted at a large television perched in the corner of the pub playing music videos with the volume off, and sighed. "I envy you."

"Me? Why?"

"You've got lots of interesting shit to work out. I've just got my same old shit. And boring shit it is."

"Oh, come on. You're being too hard on your shit. I like your shit. You've got cool shit."

"Thanks. You really know how to sweet talk a gal."

"It's just, you've gone through it all already. The deprogramming."

"Could be. But you'll be a tougher nut. It was more like a fling for me. But the Father, Son and Holy Ghost are the three great unrequited loves of your life. Sorry if that sounds too gay." Our waiter brought a clean ashtray. "My last pack," she grinned at me. "Honest."

"Right. Just remember, 'the last shall be first.'" She stuck out her tongue and wagged her head. The honed points of her black bob bounced against cheeks as white as unstirred vanilla yoghurt. "Your hair looks good this way."

"Haven't done anything to it, but thanks. Full of compliments today, aintcha?" Oppie took a long drag and vacantly began peeling the label from her beer bottle. "So tell me something. I never got what you saw in Mary. What was the deal there? Besides the toe sucking."

"Ever tried it? Isn't that enough?"

"Well, under normal circumstances, yeah. But not here."

I shrugged and poked at my fish — sorry, *fish* — tossed in my balled-up serviette and pushed away the plate. "I don't know, but when I was with Mary, at the beginning, anyway, I had no doubts. It was crazy, the way I felt, but I was sure all the craziness was just God's will."

"Then God must have a lot of interesting shit to work out, too."

"Well, that's life, I suppose."

"Life's a joke."

"I'm not laughing."

"I didn't say it was a *good* joke." Oppie smiled vaguely and brushed ash from her lap. How many times have I imagined the body beneath those black natural fibres? Her belly would be as pure as a blank page, and I would hear her draw breath sharply as, with a shaking hand, my ballpoint wrote *Zowie!* below her watermark. I knew, from a hundred salacious dreams, how her breasts would fill my palms; how her nipples would stiffen between my fingers. What I couldn't imagine was her words if she knew of her billing in my fantasy life. What kind of friend am I? What kind of Christian? But God, it must be sweet to lie between her thighs.

Oppie glanced again at the muted television. A girl band I didn't recognise was lip syncing waist deep in a swimming pool filled with what looked like cherry Jell-O. "I guess you really don't need to explain Mary to me. I was a Christian then, but I still knew she was a freak."

"Yeah, well, when you think that your love's been ordained from before the foundation of the world, you don't ask questions. You don't worry about the little things like sex and mental health."

"Trifles, really." Anyway, I'm glad you found out. Imagine if you'd ended up together."

"Nobody ends up with anyone," I spat. Oppie looked puzzled and strangely wounded, embarrassing me. I turned aside and stared vacantly at a table of three silent, porcine men about my father's age. Two were staring intently down the flutes of their lagers as though expecting them to prophesy. The middle third, I noticed a moment later, was looking straight at me. Embarrassed again, I turned the other way and found myself making insignificant eye contact with the lead singer in the music video just as the bartender changed channels to a seemingly perpetual beach volleyball tournament. Two women a side, each wearing tank tops and Speedo shorts. Each with a first name, the electronic caption told me, that ended in a vowel: Debbie. Tracy. Margo. Tanya. Tracy got off a good one, and though Tanya got a palm on it, her set was too wild for Margo's spike. Mary always had a wicked serve, too.

I took a breath and faced Oppie. Now I had my words again.

"Remember those old sermons, about how we can't understand life now because we're looking at it backwards, like the underside of some swell tapestry that God's weaving, and that only after we die we'll see the pattern and it'll all make sense?"

"I remember *you* saying that. Used to be a favourite of mine."

"Well, don't listen to me. There's nothing on the other side. A good thing, too. Then I might have to hate God instead of just ignoring him."

"Christ, I'm glad I decided to get drunk with you."

"I've always wanted things to be wrapped up: just a happy ending, you know? I don't know if it's the legacy of faith or too many Frank Capra movies. I want an eternity like the one of the old Greek Christians, where nothing happens, perfectly, forever. If I can't have that, then I'll live in Bedford Falls."

"*Mr Jones Goes to Washington?*"

"Smith. No. *It's a Wonderful Life.* I was thinking I'd be with Mary when the credits rolled. Thought I'd made my happy ending. It was a big deal."

"Correction: a big *fucking* deal."

"And then, there she is, sucking off a Siamese twin —" I gave one loud, sharp laugh. "Cripes, when I put it like that... Anyway, then it seemed like my choices didn't matter. There was no big picture, you know? Just the ugly little one I found myself in." I stopped myself. "Am I rambling? Do I sound like a crazy person?" Oppie nodded and smiled. I studied her eyes. *Like two chocolate almonds*, I decided, and suddenly craved something sweet. "I read something, once, somebody said —"

"Cool! Me too."

"'All my life I have been longing for something that I cannot name.'"

"Oh yeah, I know that. Breton, I think. André Breton."

The three fat men ambled past us, and each in turn fixed their gaze upon Oppie's Royal Doulton neck and shoulders. I smelled after-shave, stale smoke and lonely farts. One had ink stains on his double-knit crotch. I sighed. I *hated* them.

And I hated myself for being a pretentious twat with just enough wisdom to recognise myself as utterly and irredeemably a twat.

"Well, I hope you get what you want, Gid. I really do."

"Thanks. I just wish I knew what it is. I worry I won't recognise it when I see it. Oh well." I smiled comically, then sighed dramatically. "But enough again of my shit. I guess it'll all work out."

"Hey hey hey! It doesn't work: we do. I mean, we all have to figure this stuff out or die trying, right?" She tossed off her beer and crossed her legs, accidentally sliding a silky foot up my trouser leg. I didn't know she'd slipped off her boots. "Oh, is that you?"

"Um, yup."

"Sorry." Her foot was gone. "Don't worry. It's like the Stones say, 'if you try some time, you just might find, you get what you need.' You know," she smiled, "I'd been thinking *Exile on Main Street* was my new Holy Bible, but that *Let it Bleed* album has got a lot to be said for it."

I nodded and smiled, having nothing to add. I made a mental note to reacquaint myself with my old Stones records.

"So, how's your mom? She never really liked me, did she? I can tell. It's okay. Be brutal!"

"What? No no; of course she likes you! What's not to like? It's just she doesn't really *get* you. She doesn't get me either, though, so don't sweat it."

"She *despises* me."

"Nah, it's just you intimidate her. Since that last time she saw you she calls you my 'Friend with the Tea Bags'."

"Hey!" Oppie snorted. "Those were great earrings! *God.* Cheap, too."

"Yeah, I know! I loved them. But Mom doesn't have a highly evolved fashion sense. I guess that's where I get it. She doesn't know what to make of someone wearing a couple of packets of Lemon Zinger on fish hooks." Oppie stared absently at my plate. "But I think you've got a *great* look." She raised her eyes to mine and smiled. "And for what it's worth, she told me she prays for you."

"Oh yeah?" She gave me a lopsided grin. "What for? Real earrings? To stay away from you? She probably thinks I'm a bad influence, right?"

"Well yeah; there's that. But I think she prays for you to come back to God. The usual repentance stuff. Like for me."

Oppie shook her head and wrinkled her nose. "*Eeeew!* I don't like that. I don't want her to pray for me. Make her stop!"

"I'll pray that she stops, how's that?"

"*Eeeew!*"

"Are you having coffee?"

"Tea. Lemon fuckin' Zinger. No; changed my mind. Another round. You?"

3

I was 22 years old that summer and knew for a fact my life was over.

Ahead of me, stretching unto a Christless eternity, were years and years of joyless scrounging, aiming to sweeten the hand-to-mouth purgatory of this world's routine with those rare brushes with grace I could no longer explain or even name. In other words, a typical 22-year-old, though with a head full of Scripture and $12,000 poorer in student loans, yet without a decent stereo.

Autumn arrived, really pissing me off. For the first time since I was four years old I didn't have anywhere to go. Without a school to return to I felt stupid, and without God I felt preposterous. I awaited a second act, but was beginning to worry this little drama was a one-act play.

I took a sales job at a futon chain called The Tuck Shoppe.

The logo was gold on black, in a flamboyant Gothic font, and the T so resembled an F that the double takes were intentional and the double entendres worthy of hazard pay. The owner, a deep-dish Croatian named Laika Milovic, told me that if I stayed a year I'd get cotton fibre in my veins. "Then, ooh boy, you never leave!"

After four weeks and three resignations I was promoted to manager, which amounted to sole employee, of the prestigious north Toronto outlet. Laika confided, with considerable pride, that Saul Rubinek once came in for a pair of black bolster covers, though I never saw him.

By November I'd saved enough to finally move out of my Dad's place, but only enough for a gloomy basement apartment in a dilapidated Victorian in north Riverdale. The other tenants were all younger than me, or seemed to be, and were either living on social assistance or frittering away student loans. And it sounded like everyone had better stereos. All were paired up, or more than paired, in zesty combinations. I was the sole, *sole* exception. Many nights I couldn't sleep, what with the sound system and the sonorous fuckings from the apartment above me. Usually I didn't mind, and nights that I did, I'd never have thought to rap my displeasure on the ceiling. Since I didn't have cable and couldn't afford quality porn it was a cheap and nasty entertainment, and they provided metronomic accompaniment for my melancholic strokes.

Oppie and I moved the same day. We helped each other; even split the cost of a Rent-a-Wreck for a Saturday afternoon. She was settling into the Harbourfront condo of her new boyfriend, a Mazda sales rep named Lanny Delancey. I helped her move from there, too, about three months later. He didn't leave much impression on her, besides his encouragement by negative example to return to school. I didn't hear from her for a while after that. I expected she had a new lover, as she almost always did.

She had. She'd met Arthur.

II

Life presents itself first and foremost as a task: the task of maintaining itself. If this task is accomplished, what has been gained is a burden, and there then appears a second task: that of doing something with it so as to ward off boredom.

Arthur Schopenhauer

1

rthur Sooterkin was a man of his time. Rather than flaunt the dimensions of his cock he boasted of the dexterity of his tongue. He flexed it, flicked it, curled it and stretched it finer than any man of any woman he'd ever been with. He twice told me that a toffee heiress had wanted it insured for a million pounds, and that a "performance semiologist" named Nor/Ma White had threatened to pull it out with a garlic press when he left her for another lesbian.

Arthur was a cheap and charmless drunk. No more than three beers and he might snigger stupidly about how he was a "cunning linguist." I liked Arthur. So did Oppie; enough to marry him, though he didn't like himself enough to go through with it. So they lived together, more or less happily, more less than more more. He was a clever guy with a tall, decaf latte, but on several pints of brewer's retail Arthur became coarse and cretinous. "Dr Jekyll and Mr Ed," Oppie called him. Mr Ed was a big problem for her.

There was also how Arthur wore his politics. He agreed with Oppie on most every issue that mattered to her (and though there weren't many, they mattered mightily), said all the right things when he was sober and still stumbled alongside her in the Women's Day March when he wasn't. But his politics had no sense of humour, only style, and that without inspiration. He collected grievances aggressively, as though they were nothing but the buttons he wore when he marched, as if he'd judged that they too might be worth something some day.

With Arthur it was always Bridgehead coffee, Noam Chomsky and the latest ribbon campaign, except when he'd had a few, when you couldn't edge a word in sideways past his fuck jokes. When Oppie acted, it was conviction; for Arthur, it was abstemious fashion coordination. If he had a rocket launcher it would be designed by Braun and make a swell conversation piece next to the Espresso maker. "Your lifestyle's okay so far as it goes," she told me she'd once told him, "but that's as far as it goes." This was her second problem with Arthur.

A third was his fucking around; or rather, her suspicions thereof. Arthur had spent a week jobbing around Honduras for *Equinox*, and blamed his duty-free crabs on the linen at the Tegucigalpa Comfort Inn. Oppie didn't believe him ("I don't care where it is, a Comfort Inn is going to change the fucking sheets!"), but generally chose to act as though she did.

A fourth ass-ache was Carl, the brother. Oppie had first met him when she and Arthur drove to a roadhouse at Steeles and the Pickering Townline to see him open for an Alabama tribute band. Following his set, Carl impressed her by getting strafed on shooters and yodelling that "the problem with women today is they want you to suck *their* cocks!" Arthur was shitfaced enough to laugh and slap the table hard, as though it were gagging on its vinyl placemats. Indeed, Carl was a problem.

So why did Oppie stay with Arthur? Although he hadn't much hair left on top he still looked good with a ponytail, which is some trick. And besides, he knew how to make her laugh and come. Which is another.

2

"Can I ask you a stupid question?"

"There are no stupid questions," Oppie smiled, slipping a stocking foot beneath her thigh and sipping her Black Label. "Only stupid people."

"Well, I'm just wondering," I began, smoothing the duvet before I nestled into it on the sofa next to her. "Why there are goldfish swimming in your handbag."

"Ah, shit man — you looked! It was supposed to be a surprise." She reached into her purse and pulled out a knotted plastic bag two-thirds filled with water for a pair of skittish fish the colour of Kraft Dinner. "I couldn't decide between Siamese fighting fish or Kissing Gouramis, so I gotcha guppies."

"Good thinking." I scratched my nose. "Thanks, but, gee —"

"What's the problem?"

"Oh no; nothing. It's just, of course, I don't have an aquarium."

"Should have thought of that sooner, huh?" I must have looked lost, but Oppie chucked me gently on the shoulder with her bag of fish. "Got one in the trunk. Remind me before I go. Just a starter kit. Pump, gravel, food; the whole nine aquatic yards. All you need now is a ceramic Jacques Cousteau to blow bubbles out its ass."

"Really? All *pour moi*? Thanks. You're really, you know, thoughtful." What I didn't say is *What and why the fuck?*

"Fish are relaxing. Better than dope, not that you'd know, and they're not against the law yet. And you probably need a little company right now — someone to talk to, who won't talk back." She broke the seal on a pack of Craven A's. "Anyway, they're not supposed to talk. A dog'd be your best friend, I guess, but you got me, and that would just make me jealous. And besides, you don't need that kind of commitment. But fish, all you got to do is feed them and clean out the tank." She passed them to me and shrugged. "Or not. They're just fucking fish."

"Hey look," I said, gently kneading their bag in my palm. "I've got the whole world in my hands."

"Ooooh, the little one's smiling at you!" She cooed. "Yes, that's your Daddy. *Da-dee.*"

I carried them to the kitchen to find temporary lodgings. Oppie called after me, "So, where do you stand on spicy Thai noodles?"

"Unchanged. Why? How's your beer?"

"Yeah, hit me with your rhythm stick. The thing is, I'd like you to come for dinner Saturday. Arthur's brother is going to be in town and —"

"Oh Christ. This the one you told me about?"

"Yup; one and only. He's staying the whole friggin' weekend. If you're there I'll have someone to talk to. When those two get together Arthur devolves something awful. I'd say it's like watching *Quest for Fire*, but I never saw it. Rae Dong Chong, right?"

"Dawn," I called out. "As in 'Tony Orlando and.' Thanks, but this may not be a great time."

"Why the hell not?"

"Don't think I'm up to a party. Besides, now there's the fish."

"Hardly a party. Think of it as just us kids."

I poured the goldfish into a glass cereal bowl — where'd that come from? Mom's or dad's? — and listlessly fingered the crocodile oven mitts hanging over the sink. Definitely mom's.

"Okay, so let's assume you're coming and talk about something else." Oppie was standing in the kitchen doorway, striking a match. "So, what'd ya do today?"

"Nothing. What day is it? Oh, watched an old *Star Trek*."

"Romulans?"

I shook my head.

She sharply blew smoke from the corner of her mouth. "I hate them bastards. And what'd you have for lunch?"

"Didn't eat."

"Well, we can't have that. Let's make something. What you got around here, single man ...." Oppie sprung past me and threw open the refrigerator. Cigarette still dangling from her lips, she logged my supplies. "Mushrooms, pepper ... a red onion. Yum. Still got some old Ragu I see, and if that Kraft Parmesan shaker isn't empty or more than a year past 'best before' I'd say we're in business. Oh yeah, any pasta?"

"Somewhere. Some kind. You know, you don't need to do this. It's nice, but won't Arthur be expecting you?"

She closed the fridge door and exhaled. "He's got a photo shoot way the hell out in Belleville. Won't be home before eleven. So ...."

"So what?"

"The pasta?"

I opened a cupboard above the stove and yanked out half a bag of cheap dry rotini, and ducked the Pringles cylinders that came tumbling after it. She grinned, looking around for somewhere to stub out her cigarette, and I picked up an empty tube and handed it to her. Hand free, she happily started chopping the onion.

"Now, about Saturday ...."

"Yeah, okay. What the hell." I found a colander and drew water to wash the mushrooms. "Remind me: I haven't met Carl, right?"

"If you had, you wouldn't say okay. No; forget I said that. You know his song? 'It Takes Two to Say Hello, but Just One to Say Goodbye'?" I shook my head no, but she didn't look up from the onions. "Cute title, in a George Jones-ish way. It got some airplay somewhere, he says. But frankly, he's more like Jim Jones. A weird, heavy dude. Fucked up about women."

"Cool," I snorted. "Me too. We should get along just fine."

"No; *seriously*. I don't think he's violent, but he gives off that vibe, which is just about the same thing. Whenever we see him I wind up wanting to run his ganglia through the cuisinart." She punctuated with knife, onion and cutting board.

"No, I don't believe it. You have a cuisinart?"

"The better to emasculate you with, my dear." Oppie glanced towards me and grinned. "Well okay; not you. And it's Arthur's, like everything else in the house except my comic books and tampons."

"You're still doing better than me. All I have are comic books."

"Ah, poor boy. I *bleed* for you"

3

We'd finished the pasta and a six-pack, and had been reduced to a half-bottle of six-dollar port when the doorbell rang.

"Gideon Gast?" There was a boxy, broadly-grinning man in an unabashedly chocolate-brown suit on my landing, draping a grey wool coat over one arm and holding a red leather Bible the size of a waffle iron in both hands. Beside him stood a flyweight, pop-eyed pale woman in a tartan parka, its fur-lined hood thrown back to reveal a head of tightly-braided dull chestnut hair wound into a crown on the back of her skull. She was cradling what I presumed to be a baby beneath layers of blankets, but it could just as easily have been even more blankets. Next to her was an adolescent boy wearing a blue hand-me-down-filled jacket with a black band of electrical tape where it had cracked at one elbow.

"Um, uh huh...?"

"Hello then!" He stuffed the Bible under his arm and gave me his hand. "Jerry Toews, class of '70, the new — well, since November! — Overcomer alumni rep. Whole of Southern Ontario, that's a fact! And this is my wife Rexella and our son, Jeremiah. Glad to know ya!" Toews grinned broadly and I think Rexella smiled, but I blinked and so missed most of it. Jeremiah's eyes remained fixed on his red shoelaces. "We were in the area on personal business — do you know you're blessed with some tremendous carpet outlets? — and I've been meaning to say howdy for a couple of weeks now, so I thought we'd swing by just to introduce myself." Toews glanced uncertainly over my shoulder in Oppie's direction. "But please, if this is an awkward time for you —"

"Well, it's not the best —" I turned my head and looked to Oppie. She had a slightly drunken, seriously mischievous grin for me and shrugged. My liquored-up head thought *Hey, this could be fun.* "But, y'know, it's not the worst, either. I've got a few minutes. Sorry about the mess." I stepped aside to let them pass while Oppie stubbed out her cigarette.

"Great, great; thanks. We won't take up *too* too much of your time. Should we take off our boots?"

"Oh no, please don't bother."

"Say, did you ever get a visit from Perry Emprey?" I shook my head, but he had his back to me, and pulled off his boots regardless. "A real sweet old guy; class of '47? He was your alumni rep until last October, when he went home to be with the Lord. I inherited his old list. We didn't have this address of course, but then there aren't many other Gideon Gasts in the city."

"Ah! That must be it."

"What's that?" Toews asked, as I show them to the sofa. The room stunk of tobacco and beer. Even I could smell it.

"I mean, how you found me. I really didn't expect a follow up."

Rexella smoothed the folds of her skirt and sat on the edge of the couch, laying her small blankets across her knee. There was no baby after all. And neither were there blankets; she'd been carrying carpet samples. Her pinched nose wrinkled and she looked to her husband as if to say *Can you smell it too? That's the stink of sin!* He didn't acknowledge her, but sat beside her, taking her hand, with Jeremiah next to him. The boy reached into his coat pocket and took out a small plastic action figure and contented himself with making it jump from one knee to the other.

"At least we found you, eh?"

"But now you've found him," said Oppie, softly and with tender irony, "what are you going to do with him?" Toews furrowed his brow for a moment before deciding to take it as a joke.

"Oh nothing! Nothing at all. My job is completely supportive. Just to say, you know, we're still here if you need us, now that you're back in the world." He grinned with suggestive naïveté. "In the world, but not of it, eh?"

I set a small cushion on the red plastic Sealtest milk-crate that organized the first third of my rehabilitated, pre-conversion rock collection (Alice Cooper's *Easy Action* to Grand Funk's *E Pluribus Funk*), dragged it close to Oppie who had taken my only armchair, and squat. "Actually, I didn't expect any sort of follow up. I didn't exactly graduate."

"No?" Toews flipped open his Bible to a folded sheet he'd tucked in somewhere around the Minor Prophets and ran a finger down a column. "Ah. Well my list is a little out of date I suppose. Yes ... last March. But you would have had just a few more weeks —" He shut his Bible and looked at me, shaking his head. "Sorry, none of my business. Unless — well, unless it's something you want to talk about?"

I smiled stupidly, and remembered I'd been drinking. "Nah, I don't think so. There's not much to tell." Oppie cleared her throat.

Toews glanced towards her, and his face appeared suddenly bathed in awareness. "I'm sorry, I don't think I caught your name?"

"Oh *geez*," I mumbled. "Sorry about that. This is Oppie." The Toews looked at each other with alarm. *A minced oath!*

"That's a sweet name," said Rexella, just barely, through her papery lips. "Very unusual."

"Thanks," said Oppie. "It's from the Bible."

"So," I jumped in, suddenly embarrassed on everyone's behalf, "what does an alumni rep do?"

Toews cracked a knuckle and relaxed a little into the sofa. "I guess you could say we're something of a lifeline to the school. After years in a place where Christ is lifted up, adjusting to an ungodly world can be forbidding. So don't worry, I'm not here to weasel donations. I mean, not just!" He chuckled at me perched on my milk crate. "Just a joke, obviously"

"So this is your full-time job?" Oppie asked, not bothering to mask her stupefaction.

"Oh no! But I like to treat it as such. I'm also an associate minister at an Associated Gospel church up in Newmarket. Though it's not really in an official capacity yet. We're still waiting on the Lord on that score, aren't we?" Rexella nodded listlessly. "But chasing down alumni keeps me pretty busy." He paused, absently rifling the pages of his Bible as though he was about to deal a deck of cards. "That, and I'm working on getting my real estate licence."

Oppie beamed. "Cool!"

"We only want to know you're doing okay. I'm always reminded of a great quote of Mr Barstowe's: 'None of us graduate 'til the honour roll is called up yonder.' I like that! That's why I wanted the job. It's like a family that way."

"Some family," Oppie mumbled into her shoulder.

"Yes. Sadly, not all families are like a Bible College. Rexella and I met at Overcomer. We were both in the Certificate of Missions program." He looked to Oppie, and then to me, with something like sympathy. "I'm sure I don't need to tell you how tough O.B.I. can be on relationships. Somehow, though, the Lord opened our eyes to each other and worked it so we were able to spend a little time together without breaking the rules. Well, maybe we bent them a wee bit," he smiled, and rubbed Rexella's wrist. She finally had some colour to her face, so she must have been blushing. "I hope she doesn't mind me saying this, but Rexella didn't graduate, either. She missed her last year so we could be married as soon as I finished my certificate. The next Fall we were on our way to Pakistan. We served ten-odd years there with Save Now Millions."

"Formerly Save Now Muslims?" asked Oppie.

"Yes indeed!" Toews looked relieved, as though he'd finally admitted this was the right address after all. "But the old name started giving us hassles getting visas. Are you familiar with it?"

"Not very. An old boyfriend of mine was interested in S.N.M. The mission, of course."

Toews nodded. Of course, the mission. "Did he join up? What's his name?"

"Scott Poors. I don't know what he wound up doing. We sort of lost touch a while back."

"Ah, I see. No, I can't say that rings a bell. Opie —"

"Oppie —"

"You wouldn't by chance be an O.B.I. undergrad yourself, are you?"

She smiled warmly. "Nope, never had the privilege. I leave the theologizing up to my buddy here." She stretched out her arm and tousled my hair.

"Hey!" I squealed, but I loved it.

"So Gideon. What have you been up to since gradu — since you left?"

"Well, hmm. Good question. Not really a whole lot. Right now I'm sort of in the retail sector."

"Oh? That's good. Everyone needs to buy things. What do you sell?"

Dope, my sperm, my ass, I wanted to say. But I answered "Futons." I may as well have said "smack" for his lack of comprehension. "Sort of like mattresses."

"Oh? That's great, great! Everyone needs those. Lots of tremendous opportunities to witness, I bet."

"Yeah," I wheezed. "Pretty much." *For this to be fun, I think, I'm going to need more beer.*

"Your program was what again? — Sorry, I know I read it in Mr Empery's notes..."

"Bachelor of Theology."

"Impressive! That's a tough road to hoe. Had to take Greek, right?" I nodded, heavily. "I guess you had Amphora

Faulkner then." I nodded again. "That was awful what happened. We just heard a short time ago. Terrible, terrible. I guess you must have been there? It was such a shock."

"Pardon me," Rexella said, rising, "may I please use your washroom?" I pointed her in the right direction as she laid her carpet samples carefully on the sofa and excused herself. For an instant I was convinced she meant to do a spot check for rubbers and spermicide.

"We noticed on the way over you're quite close to Pinecrest Baptist. Is that your home church? I know the youth minister; I've heard great things."

"No, I — well..." This was it. This had to be it. I hated to disappoint him, but I couldn't persist in the lie that I'm *that* Gideon, the one he expected to find, even if it meant begging a confrontation with the ghosts of my former selves. "I sort of don't attend anymore."

"Oh; found another church, eh?"

"No. I mean I don't go to church."

Finally, Jeremiah raised his round eyes and stared at me.

They left a polite five minutes later, after Toews asked if he could have a word of prayer with us and I, emboldened, said thanks but no thanks. I was shaking; glad I showed the courage of my lack of conviction, but mournful for my washed-up Saviour and all his old Gideons. I'm relieved, too. Relieved I'm not Jerry Toews. I could have been him. Hell, I had been. I'd been Jerry without the family and the real estate licence to fall back on. But then, what did I have to fall on now?

Oppie and I giggled boozily about their visit until we brought in the aquarium and it was time for her to go. Then, just like that, I stopped laughing.

4

Even in winter, even in February, Oppie and Arthur's neighbours held yard sales. Or rather, one yard sale, in perpetuity. Often, particularly during the peak summer months when they'd sell pet turtles out of a plastic tub on the porch, their business would encroach upon the adjoining properties. First, a toehold of spotty grass close to the road might be commandeered for a carton of eight tracks, then a strip on the wrong side of their common walk could be appropriated for a rack of smoky-smelling double-knits and velour shirts. Oppie and Arthur needed to demonstrate leatherneck vigilance to safeguard the integrity of their frontage. But they didn't.

Arriving for dinner that Saturday night I nearly tripped over a spongy cardboard box of damp Harlequin romances pressed into the slush. I heard muffled "fuck you's" and the clatter of power tools in strange basements as I pressed the buzzer.

Arthur greeted me with a shoulder rub and a hazy smile. I smelled at least three beers in him. The track lighting was muted, sandalwood was burning in a small clay pot as Chet Baker mewled *You Don't Know What Love Is*.

"Yo, Gidman!"

Oppie bolted from the sofa, a neutral blur of black cotton and pale skin, waving a vague Excuse Me to three guests left fidgeting on her abandoned punch-line. One of them, I figured, was Carl. He would be the sullied-looking man with the sandy hair — fairer but thicker than Arthur's — in the drab khaki sweater patched with accents of leather. The busty brunette sitting next to him in the egg-white silk blouse and paisley vest looked like she wore his brand. She fingered the silver tips of her bolo tie and twisted her neck to steal a glance at his wrist-watch, which he wore just below the hand which crowned her knee. Next to her is a woman in black jeans and black T-shirt and hair the colour of bartlett pears. I had no idea who she was, or whose.

I hadn't expected dinner for six. I wasn't thinking of even numbers, of uncut corners. Mary, God and all the rest were still heavy on my heart, and now it was sinking fast beneath the added burden of playing the odd man in. *They can all go fuck themselves*, I thought. *I don't need this.*

"Sorry I'm late," I grumbled, fudging good humour while I kicked off my boots. "Or early. Am I early? Have I got the right day?"

Oppie hugged me and snatched my brown bag of wine. (Hungarian Bull's Blood, six bucks a bottle.) Arthur took my coat, but only to toss it behind me atop the others on an ottoman, and miss.

"'This is the day that the Lord hath made,'" chanted Oppie. "You're just in time. Carl was just going to tell us about Hitler's testicles."

"Hey, good name for a band."

"No, really; this bugs me. Is it like the guy only had one ball? Was he born like that? And how did shit like that get around?"

"You know, doctors can be real blabbermouths," said the blonde I didn't know.

"Yeah, but *Nazi* doctors?" Oppie shrugged. "I just think they might have worried about it getting back to the Führer. You know, like, 'Herr doktor, I could use zee laugh. Vot is zo funny?' She scrunched up her nose and giggled at her own joke. "Oooh, that Hitler! Don't you just *hate* him?"

"Some of his lovers — and let me tell ya, I use the term loosely — they talked before the war." Carl's voice was confident and rhythmically expansive, vibrantly scored with a tobacco rasp. A good voice, I bet, for bad country music. "Confidentially, of course, but you can't keep the good stuff secret. Everyone wants to know how famous people fuck. Did you know he liked women to piss and shit on him?"

"You see," Oppie said in a stage whisper, "it's all terribly fascinating. You thought you were just coming for dinner. We've got the last orgy of the Third Reich happening here." Then softer, this time just for me, she added: "Thank *God* you're here."

"What'd you like, Gideon?" Arthur, already halfway to the kitchen, bounced languidly on the heals of his moccasins while I made up my mind. His black sweatshirt was silkscreened with a fresh bouquet of Van Gogh sunflowers. "Oppie's theme drink this evening is Black Russian."

"I'm not ready for that yet, whatever it is. Beer, thanks."

"Export? Blue? Black Label?"

"Surprise me," I said, though I really wanted a Black Label. *Why the fuck did I say that?* I slouched inwardly.

"So, how are the fish?" Oppie hooked her arm in mine as she walked me slowly towards her circle of guests. "I bet the little charmers are getting into all kinds of mischief."

"Well, one of them's dead."

"No!" She stopped short and drew a hand to her mouth, stricken. I still found it difficult to tell when she's being sarcastic. "How did it happen?"

"I don't know. Found him — her? — this morning, all lifeless and gummy on the kitchen floor. Must have jumped out of the tank in the night. I really didn't think they could manage that."

"Could he have been pushed?" Arthur called out.

"Maybe," I pleasantly allowed, though I hated indulging his drunken comedy. "I probably filled the tank too high. I'm

just glad I didn't have time to name it. Who can flush something you've named?"

"Don't answer that," Oppie called to Arthur, who shouted
back "What?" but Oppie ignored him.

"Geez," she sighed. "Let me get you another. Sorry about
that, I didn't know. Maybe it was suffering. Maybe it's for the
best." She shook her head briskly and flashed a chagrined
smile, as though surprised and embarrassed by how much it
had bothered her. "Well, let's talk fish later; on with the
intro's. You haven't met Carl before, have you? Okay, so
here's Carl. And Carl, here's Gideon, killer of fish. And Carl's
friend, Veronica, and my work buddy Cheryl. I've told you
about her."

"Yeah, I remember." No, I didn't. "Glad to meet you, et
cetera."

"Sure thing," Carl mumbled vacantly before returning to
his Black Russian. He had the rubbery, olive-coloured aspect
of a Medieval bogman. Veronica proffered a broad, generous
smile but her eyes reached no higher than my breastpocket,
and quickly fell again to Carl's wristwatch. She could be 25 or
40; I didn't have a clue. She was so heavily made up I assumed
she meant to compensate for something, but I couldn't make
out whether it was innocence or experience. She rested a hand
atop Carl's, who proceeded to weave her slender fingers with
his own, as thick and as coarse as a lariat. Her free hand kept
playing with the string tie.

"So," I ventured grudgingly, "Hitler's missing ball, eh? Is
this a party game? Who's got it?" Carl snorted, kneading
Veronica's thigh. I noticed he wore a thick gold band on his
baby finger. *Ay carumba.*

"Good question," Oppie reckoned, motioning me to take
the pine rocker while she sank into the sofa next to Carl. "Fess
up, Carl. It might be worth something someday."

"No; he was born that way. Pissed off the crazy bastard.
Made him feel half a man. I don't think he once got a proper
boner."

Breaking the seal on a fresh pack of Camels, Oppie smirked,
"And he probably blamed Eva Braun. Just like an *übermensch*."

"The Jews, more likely," I said. That stops the conversation dead. *Good one, old man.*

My father had made me cry that afternoon. He dropped by with a bottle of schnapps and a jar of mixed nuts and we sat for an hour, watching TV with the sound off, drinking without needless speech. When he left he looked like a smoked ciga-rette. I embraced him gingerly, as though he might collapse into a pile of ash. His moist eyes spoke his longing, but I don't believe he knew what he yearned for. I've been able to tell him I love him, shamelessly, only since the first summer following my expulsion, when I began to notice I was losing my own hair.

I'd hardly talked to my God-struck mother since leaving Overcomer. It had been hard to choke an "I love you" to her without some singsong irony in the back of my throat.

"I like your house," Veronica blurted as Arthur reappeared with two bottles of Ex, one for me. ("Thanks man.") His return prompted me to be bothered afresh by the head count. Six of us. Was Oppie meaning to fix me up with Cheryl? She was kind of cute, if nondescript. But I hadn't come prepared to impress any-one. I would have flossed. I would have worn nicer socks. I would have vetted some conversation topics in the bathroom mirror. I was ready to play a bit part. The fifth wheel: just a spare waiting for a pair-bond to lose its tread. Not the most rewarding role, but not without its rewards if you can't bear the thought of a challenging evening. But now I was uncomfortably tense, and felt my teeth grind and my hands clench the armrests. Still, Cheryl was kind of cute. And one of these nights, I thought, it would be nice to spill myself on a strange, warm belly.

"Really bright and open," she continued while I nudged my rocker to make way for Arthur as he pulled up a dining room chair between myself and Oppie. "But I think you're real-ly brave to live in this neighbourhood." Veronica swung her finger in a tiny arc, like a windshield wiper. "I think it'd be a little too intense for me."

"Think so?" Oppie asked, squinting, after blowing smoke out the corner of her mouth in Arthur's direction. "How come?"

"Well, there seem to be lots of" — her voice dropped to nearly a whisper — "bad graffiti."

"Really? I guess I don't notice it any more."

"And Carl mentioned some kind of gang down the street."

"Oh, that's just some kickboxing club," Arthur answered. "They don't bother us. It's their neighbourhood, too."

"That's right," Oppie added, stretching in her leggings and crossing at the ankles. "If they want to swarm someone they take the streetcar. They don't beat the shit out of someone where they eat. But I know what you mean. Sometimes I think it'd be a nice place if everyone would just move away." Veronica nodded before Oppie appended, "but maybe I'd think that anywhere."

"Well, I still think you're brave. And I still like your place." Veronica took a sip from Carl's glass. She'd already finished hers. "I've thought lots about moving to Toronto, but there are so many crazies here."

"I don't worry about them," Cheryl said. "I've always been able to move faster than a crazy person."

"Yeah," Oppie smiled. "It's not the crazies that scare me. It's the ones who know what they're doing. I worry they know what I'm doing, too."

"Nothing much scares me in Niagara Falls," Veronica straightened up and glanced at Carl, who replied with a pinched smile and a slight shake of his head. "Okay! Except for the Falls. I've got, like, a bad fear of heights."

"Oh," said Arthur. "I thought you were from Brockville."

"Uh uh," piped up Carl, "that was Donna. Remember, the one with the artsie breasts." He held out thumb and forefinger, a half inch apart, to jog his memory. Arthur stifled a giggle like a sneeze. Veronica looked flushed. Could it be with pride? Maybe she'd taken it as a compliment.

"Gideon's afraid of heights, too," Oppie offered without pause or flinch, graciously availing herself of my neurosis to lift the conversation off Veronica's chest.

"And depths, widths, lengths ... all the dimensions," I declared with a loopy smile as I rung the neck of my beer.

"I'm afraid of premature baldness," Arthur groused with a straight face.

"*Darling*," Oppie sighed with a flourish of feigned mid-Atlantic ennui, "you're 36. I'd say it's *terribly* mature."

"Actually," Arthur admitted, "I'm afraid of dying a stupid, freakish death. Anything that makes people laugh. Strangers, that is."

"You better hope it's strangers," added Oppie.

"I know just what you mean," I said. "I'd hate to go out as something to pad *Weekly World News*."

"Ah!" Oppie said, finger raised. "But what if you could get the cover?" I cocked my brow studiously and took a sip.

Carl jumped in. "You mean with something like, 'Man Breaks Neck Sucking Own Cock'?"

"Cocksucking is very important to you, eh Carl?"

Carl's eyes crinkle with a wicked smile and he turned towards Oppie. He opened his mouth to speak, but his leathery brow suddenly creased with shadows and he sank back into the sofa.

"I don't know," Oppie continued, ignoring Carl. "Worse things can happen to you than being killed by a punchline. It might even be kinda cool. We all gotta go, so why not give the gift of laughter? The Grim Reaper *should* lighten up."

"Jesus Christ," Arthur muttered. "I thought you'd put away all your Iron Maiden albums."

"Fear fucks you up," Carl grunted persuasively. "Fuck it. I haven't got time for neuroses — no offence," he added, with a nod in my direction.

"Um, okay. None taken."

"Carl saw his first Woody Allen film last night," Veronica said, as though that explained it.

"I saw *What's Up, Tiger Lily* once, too," Carl corrected her. "That was good stuff, but that fucking Lovin' Spoonful ...." There were murmurs of recognition all around.

"*Annie Hall* was on CityTV last night."

"Great film," declared Arthur.

"She wanted me to watch it with her."

"It's not like I *forced* you or anything."

"I gave it a chance. I watched the whole thing. I hate the guy even more. I could hardly sleep last night, I hate him so much. Neurosis isn't funny. It's just sick. Or not even sick; just an excuse to be weird."

"Woody Allen's not neurotic," I said. "True neurotics make experimental shorts about bad haircuts and nuclear winter."

"No," Oppie smirked, "true neurotics watch them."

"Right," Arthur scrambled to add, "and psychotics *wear* them."

While Carl was still snorting, Oppie excused herself to check on dinner. As she stood and stretched she gave me a fleeting, apologetic glance I didn't know how to interpret. Striding towards the kitchen with an uncommon grace, as though she knew eyes were on her, she called back, "We're having sweet and sour Hitler balls."

You could hardly hear him for the laughter, but Chet Baker was singing *My Funny Valentine*.

When Oppie returned she and Arthur swapped tales of their favourite street people. Over dinner Veronica was reminded of a vintage *Rhoda* episode, and the thought of a young Valerie Harper was all Arthur needed to start talking dirty. Carl told us he didn't think Joan Crawford killed Kennedy to put a Pepsi man back in office, but it was an argument with some merit. Cheryl didn't say much, but I noticed she laughed at my infrequent and lousy jokes.

If Mary Christmas were here she'd hate it. If the Gideon of last winter were here he'd have hated it even more than this year's model. But if our two old, happy selves had been here at least I'd have had a footsie partner. At least I'd have been more than an odd sock. And despite the even numbers, that's how I felt. I found no good reason to keep tuned in, so I dropped the thread of conversation, picked at my food and poisoned my soul.

Picture Cheryl naked. Or picture this: Cheryl and Joan Crawford naked. *Aroogha! Hubba hubba!* Young Joan Crawford, years before *Straight Jacket* and *Johnny Guitar*. Flapper Joan who spread like mayonnaise, seducer of men and women (to name but two), whose lovers could rival the Pope's divisions. They'd complement each other well: a good composition by arc lamp or candlelight, however the mood struck. Joan on top, definitely on top, her thighs shrouding Cheryl's face like a picnic blanket. Both are glossy; slippery with baby oil and emollients more fragrant. Cheryl still wearing her bra. (What would it be? Black lace, strapless. Yes.) Joan bends low, her breasts swinging freely, her nipples scuffing Cheryl's belly. She's leering. Her crazy lips are wet and eager, and her mouth is dry with athletic desire.

I shook my head and sighed softly. I was trying too hard.

I remembered Mary Christmas, pressing my hands between hers and telling me with a robust whisper that she wanted to make love. I remembered admitting "So do I. Let's pray for strength." I remembered the first time I realised that Mary had meant it.

"Anyone care to help the hostess clear the table?" And before Cheryl can clear her throat, Oppie suggested, "Gideon?"

"So? What d'ya think?" she asked conspiratorially as we piled the plates in the sink.

"He's a shithead." I knew that was what she wanted to hear, but I was disappointed I don't hate Carl with her passion.

"*Exactly*. Thanks for coming and putting up with it all. At least Arthur's behaved, more or less." Reticently, I fed the garburator scraps of noodles. "What's wrong?"

I snorted a laugh and shook my head, but began explaining myself nonetheless.

"Dunno. Just feeling a little lost tonight. I didn't know your friend Cheryl was going to be here."

"*Oh*. She's great though, isn't she?"

"Yeah, but — I mean, she's okay — I just — " Suddenly, I didn't remember what my problem is. But I felt uncomfortable talking up another woman with Oppie. "Never mind, it's nothing."

"I'm sorry. I didn't think it would be a big deal."

"No, I know. And it's not, honest."

"I didn't know Carl was bringing anyone until this morning, so I called up Cheryl to even it up. But Jesus, I should have suspected he'd have a date. Carl without a girlfriend is like a tongue depressor without the tongue." Oppie sniggered and wiped her hands on a dish towel. "I don't know what the hell that means, but hell, I *mean* it."

"Nights like this ...." I shrugged and met her eyes. I'd hurt her, and I knew it, but she didn't want me to see that. "I mean, thanks for dinner and everything — you know what you mean to me — but I'm feeling kind of lost right now. A night like this doesn't advance the plot, you know?"

"Cripes, don't worry about the plot. There'll be one waiting for you when you're dead. Just go with the flow, baby. You might one day look back on your life and think, 'That was a damn good read.'"

I leaned against the counter, planting my palm in a smear of cheese sauce. "Oh *Christ*." Silently, Oppie handed me a dishtowel. "Sorry. I don't know. I don't think anything would satisfy me tonight. The even numbers bug me, but then I don't want to always be an odd number, either."

"I see. Phobic about numbers now, are ya, huh?"

"No, no. It's just I'm feeling like a fucking stray."

"Ah, *c'mon* ...."

"No. Well, okay," I smiled. "Guess I'm sounding pathetic."

"No. Well, okay," she smiled back. "If it makes you feel better to be right."

"It's just I want to be essential for someone. Irreducible. And for someone to be that for me."

"Like your boyfriend, God?"

I chuckled grimly. "Yeah. That guy."

"Well, don't know what I can say to that, except 'one is the loneliest number that you'll ever do.'"

"I suppose you'll try to make me feel better by saying 'two can be as bad as one. It's the loneliest number since the number one', right?"

"Well, tell me about it. Or no; let me tell you about it."

"Maybe I should move on to threesomes."

"Like Three Dog Night?"

"Like evangelical dates: me, God and the girl. But God always got the girl."

"Ah! A *menage à Dieu* ...."

I turned on the cold water tap to rinse my hands, even though they were clean now. "Jesus Christ, Oppie. Thanks for inviting me and all, really, but a night like this makes me wish I were still agoraphobic."

"Ohhh ...." Oppie moaned warmly and dug a thumbnail into the small of my back, and I turned to accept her tender smile. "Don't say that, ya big lug. Have a lousy time if you want, but I'm glad you're here."

"Yeah? Thanks. Me too, now."

She bumped her head gently upon my shoulder, then drew a deep breath before she began again. "You know, I went to work today — big surprise, right? — and like everyday, the office was full of career receptionists in shiny pant suits, with shoulder pads broad enough to shelve a Time/Life series." I turned the tap off and faced her again. She shook her head slowly and forced a smile. "Cheryl's great. She makes going to work fun. But that's about it. And then I remember when living forever was something to look forward to. Now I think, when I'm dead, just leave me the hell alone." She drew both hands slowly through her hair, front to back, as she pressed her eyes shut and stretched her lips into a broad smile. "Some days I'd kill myself if only I could live to regret it."

"Oppie —"

"Made you forget *your* troubles, didn't I? Fuck, why can't genius drop like shit from my ass? Oh! Just remembered. This afternoon I thought up a cool companions ad to run if Arthur and I ever break up: 'A woman only a necrophiliac could love. Any undertakers?' Like it?"

"Yeah," I giggled, though too girlishly. "That's great. I could see myself responding to something like that."

"I bet I'd get some cool replies. Almost worth breaking up just to see. Now hold the friggin' door and I'll grab the cranberry cobblers."

5

I walked Cheryl home. It was late, and it was almost not really out of my way.

"So, what's it like working with Oppie?"

"Oh *gawd*! She's just the best. It'd be soooo boring without her; I couldn't stand it. She tells me everything."

"Really?" I was taken aback, and slightly embarrassed, by how loud she was now. The street was as quiet as she was at dinner.

"Oh yes. I know *all* about you."

"Really? So tell me something about myself."

"Well I know you two used to be big-time Bible thumpers."

"Oh *Christ*. She told you that?"

"Nothing to be ashamed of. I used to smoke maybe three packs a day. Gave it up like that. I can relate to addictive personalities."

"I never thought of God as the Big Pack of Smokes in the sky."

"It's all the same shit, though." I nod, without comprehension. But it's too dark to see, so I grunt my approval. "She told me about what happened at your school. That sounds horrible. You should have sued."

"Thanks, but I'm not the suing kind of guy. I'm the let's-pretend-it-never-happened guy."

"Can I ask you something personal?"

I nodded, but she couldn't see me, so I added, "Sure."

"Are you in love with her?"

"Who? *Oh!* Oh no no *no!* We're just friends."

"Okay, okay. Just wondering."

"Why? I mean, what makes you think I do?"

"I don't think anything. I just think you should be in love with her. Everyone should. I think she's great. And she talks about you all the time."

"I think she's great too, and I hardly talk about anyone else, but we're just friends. And she's living with Arthur."

"When I met her first I thought she must be with you. It was always 'Gideon said this,' 'Gideon did that,' 'Me and Gideon went here.' She hardly even said a word about him."

We walked in silence another two blocks, the clatter of our footfalls stifled in grey slush.

"Now can I ask you something personal?"

"Ask away," she said.

"We're pretty close to my place. Would you like to maybe, you know, stop by for some coffee?"

She patted me on the back. *She pats me,* thought I, *on the fucking back?* "Thanks, that's nice, but I don't think so."

"Oh. Okay, sure."

"No; nothing personal. I'm even a little drunk and horny — maybe a lot drunk and a little horny — but I'm sort of exploring celibacy these days. I don't want to mess around with a guy again until I know it'll be something special. You mind?"

"Sure, no, that's cool. But I should warn you. I've pretty much mapped celibacy; there's nothing left for you to discover."

She threw back her head and loosed one loud, hacking

laugh. "Shit, you do make me laugh. Another thing Oppie was right about. And there's the best reason why we shouldn't fool around."

"What's that?"

"Op-pie and Gi-de-on, sitting in a tree, k-i-s-s-i-n-g —"

"Hey!"

I spat a venomous gob upon last Sunday's *Star* that carpeted the transit shelter. I cursed Mary because the streetcar's late. I cursed her and Amphora Faulkner for my crippled heart, its lacerations as long and as rich as menstrual lips.

I've walked Cheryl home, but now I'm cold and need the dubious comfort of a streetcar. It doesn't come. So I cursed Cheryl with ten thousand *fuck you's* for not coming home with me. And I cursed Oppie for her part in my awkward deaths; for not letting me be her dearest friend, her greatest love.

God, I'm just a bitter troll with Jesus breath, hexing fig trees for the hell of it.

It's past one when I reached home. I meant to find a dirty Italian movie on channel 47 and jerk myself to sleep, but I see that Matt Helm is on CityTV. *Which one is this? The Ambushers?* I didn't know why I cared, or how I even remembered the title, but it was important for me to watch at least until I knew for sure. I sat on the arm of my one comfortable chair and slid down slowly onto the cushion. A corner of Carl's latest cassin-gle, "Life is What I Want for Breakfast," dug into my thigh, reminding me that I'd had neither the heart to decline it nor the head to offer to pay for it.

Dean Martin's on the screen, making googly eyes at Janice Rule. *Then it is The Ambushers.* And Christ, I thought, she looks so hard and smart and sexy, maybe I don't need channel 47 after all. I wondered whether Dino ever came on to her off the set, and what she might have done about it. Somehow, it was suddenly important for me to believe she wasn't a pushover. And I wondered, whatever happened to her?

Everybody Loves Somebody Sometime. Oppie once told me she'd been an ugly kid. The kind who's cute to adults, but bony and

wan, awkward and toothy, and set upon by peers. When puberty struck the teasing stopped, and soon she began receiving
another kind of attention which she welcomed as much as she
had being called "Poopy." Her first real boyfriend was a high
school bassoonist who, once he persuaded her to lie down with
him naked, dumped her for a flutist built like a cello. When she
found out, she scratched all her Jim Croce records.

   You're Nobody 'til Somebody Loves You. It's just another song so
long as you can sing *Jesus Loves Me.* But it's problematic when
you're home alone on a Saturday night, getting hard watching
a Matt Helm movie, wanting to smell, for a change, the prosa-
ic vulgarity of someone else's farts.

6

The next morning I did what I unfailingly do whenever romance is undone by farce. I began another journal.

I rifled my desk for a pen of suitable gravitas, and for the notebook that I'd meant to fill with other journals. That I had no fresh bagels for the toaster oven helped concentrate my mind, but once I'd slipped *My Aim is True* out of its sleeve and onto the turntable I didn't need any more encouragement.

I sucked pensively upon the silver button of my Schaeffer pen, opened the book and prepared to astonish myself.

It took me until "Waiting for the End of the World" to fill a page, and that mostly cribbed from Elvis Costello lyrics. Just one cup of Lemon Zinger tea and my memoir was decaying into doodles, cross-hatches and word strings. Depressed and needing to forget myself, I dressed and hurried to Blockbuster to rent something whimsical. I browsed leisurely, and finally settled upon *A Night at the Opera*. I was enjoying it, even smiling occasionally, until I unaccountably burst into tears when the orchestra struck up "Take Me Out to the Ballgame." This so exasperated me that for the first time I purposefully declined to rewind.

Cutting my losses, I was in bed by 9:30, but the thought that I'd pissed away another Sunday, let alone squandered my life anticipating and recalling embraces, kept me tossing until after 1 a.m., when I began to feel worse. My anticipation/recollection ratio was way out of wack. At last I fell asleep trying to begin again, and for at least the fifth time, *The Pickwick Papers*, still feeling bewildered by the coincident burden of my pre-, mid- and post-life crises.

If I dreamt at all, I don't recall.

In early spring I got a call from Delbert Moon. It was long distance, all the way from Hamilton, so naturally we couldn't talk long. He said he'd be in Toronto the following Sunday and asked if we could get together. I said yes. He gave me an address where we could meet, but wouldn't tell me what it was. I checked it out the night before. It was a bar called Pandora's Box. Silhouettes of preposterously-titted women frog-marched beneath the pink neon exclamation, "No Strings Attached!" Looked like a classy joint.

Gentlemen, take your hands out of your pockets and put them together for ... the lovely Mannndeee!

Gasps of steam shot from aluminum spouts at stage left and right as Mandy wobbled into the amber spot, chaperoned by a debonair Gino Vanelli tune. She looked bored, though perhaps her intention was to be sultry, and wore a Catholic school uniform over fishnets and red stilettos. She pouted as she chewed a wad of grape bubblegum, which cannot be an easy thing.

It was mid-afternoon and you could tell. The mood lighting was bi-polar, the patrons sparse, and the dozen or so strippers walking the floor must have been toting those stools on their heads for the sheer aerobic joy of it. I stood at the back, next to the bar, and let my eyes adjust to the dark by fixing upon the lone table dancer.

The room was painted black, with thick bands of brushed chrome that squeezed it about the corners and a few slender, random accents of pink and lime neon. The stage, configured like a giant scallop, was lacquered whipping-cream white with — in a departure from bivalve physiognomy — mirrored tiles pasted to the interior of its raised upper shell.

Out on the street, above a Plexiglas case brandishing publicity stills of women boasting tits bigger than my head, a placard had congratulated me upon arriving at Toronto's "party central." Inside, except for the cheesy music and the muted sports bloopers playing over and over again on the bar television, there was a languid air that suggested indifferent contemplation during a shoddy organ prelude. Even where men sat together, they rarely spoke except to order more drinks. Let the good times roll over and play dead.

Delbert was the only one who looked like he was having fun. Just as in chapel, he'd passed up scores of empty seats for a stool front and centre on perverts' row. I wouldn't have recognized him if he hadn't craned his willowy neck to tuck a few bucks into Mandy's garter with his teeth.

I slunk onto the stool beside Delbert and waited for him to notice me. It took until the stripper noticed me first.

"Gideon!" he cried. "Fuckin' A!"

He'd grown a scraggly beard and his hair was over his ears; not long, but longer than was ever allowed at Overcomer. So many alumni let their hair grow out. It didn't matter whether long hair was fashionable; what mattered was that they could do it.

Delbert's hair had receded so precipitously on top that the trepanation scar couldn't be camouflaged by an ingenious comb over. It was purple, and resembled a welt of caramelized skin. A scrunched up Tilley Hat sat at his elbow, next to an empty shooter.

"So what do you think of my beard?"

I'd forgotten what our conversations could be like.

"Looks great." It looked cemented with spirit gum, as though Delbert were a 12-year old Wise Guy in a Christmas pageant. It was a lot like what I had grown, briefly, my last year of high school. I was proud of it too, until I realized that left to itself, even a strawberry can grow hair.

"Ever been here before?"

"Nope."

He wagged his head disapprovingly. "If I lived here, I'd be here every fucking night."

"Such language!" I smirked, recoiling with sham astonishment.

"Remember that movie *Night Dance?*" I shook my head. "I never saw it either — it came out, like, you know, back *then* — but it was based on this place. The women are really proud to work here. They put on a Helluva show. And let me tell you something." His knee nudged mine, and he smiled expansively. "They make you believe in angels again."

"So Delbert ...."

"Hmm?"

"What the Hell happened?"

"What do you mean?"

"I mean this," I said, jabbing a thumb towards Mandy's burning bush. "I mean, *Jesus Christ*, how the hell did we wind up *here?*"

"Funny old world, eh?"

"Okay, small picture first, Delbert." Bob Hope's nose. That's what Mandy's breasts reminded me of. "Why Pandora's Box?"

"I'm *testing* you. And I'm just Del now, alright? Just Del. See, anyone who can't come in here," he said, resting an elbow on the narrow lip of stage that was our table, "I don't want to fucking talk to."

"Been through some changes, eh?"

"You don't know the half of it," he grinned. "The fucking *half!*"

I nodded bluntly, because I believed him, and ordered an Ex I didn't really want without lifting my eyes to the waitress who'd suddenly appeared between us. "Another Orgasm?" she asked Moon without enthusiasm. "Please," he chirped. Then I looked up at her.

I looked *way* up. Good Lord, she was a tall one. Five eleven or six foot something, maybe my height. A crew-necked black velvet top was stretched taut over her tulip bulb breasts. Its sleeves were hiked up past her elbows, revealing her slim forearms as more generously freckled than her face. Black horn-rimmed glasses yoked a pair of hazel eyes. Her hair, as ruddy as late autumn leaves, was rolled into a flip at the collar, and her bangs were crowned with a plastic silver hairband. This was "Where the Boys Are," and it would have been caricature with anyone but her and Connie Francis.

"So," I said absently to Moon as she turned to leave and I kept watching, "I guess I passed your test."

"Well, you're here. Surprised?"

She was wearing a pair of tight, tan slacks which bared her ankles and about a third of her calves above beige canvas flats. When finally she was out of sight, I couldn't remember what Moon had said.

"Pardon?"

"Surprised?"

"Oh yeah, right. No, actually. Not really."

Moon wrinkled his brow. "You *gotta* be!"

"I guess I don't shock so easily any more."

He sniffed. "But this must be just about the last fucking place you'd expect to see me."

"Yeah, well, not so long ago, this is the last place I'd have expected to see myself. Second last, after Chippendales."

"Know what you mean," he sighed, and returned his attention to Mandy, who signalled her designs on earning another tip by grinning and swinging her breasts like a pair of semaphore flags. "Been through some changes yourself?"

"Things change. I don't know that I have."

Moon snorted and watched the stripper. "Know what you mean." Then he squinted and turned back to me. "Sorry. No, I don't."

"I feel the same. I don't know how else to explain it. And I don't mean just the same as when I was at, *you know* ...." He nodded sympathetically. "I'm just the same guy I was in high school, in grade school, in daycare, even. Probably more so than at ...."

"Got ya."

"... because *there*, it wasn't me, but Christ living in me, as we used to say." Moon flinched. "I wasn't *supposed* to be me. I couldn't think of anything more discouraging. But of course I was, anyway — I mean we all were, really, weren't we? — but ...." I groaned heavily and shrugged. "Geez, it's been awhile since I've talked like this."

Moon chucked me on the shoulder with a scrawny balled-up fist. "You're doing just fine."

"So what's your story? Bet it's a doozy."

"Oh, I don't know. Been here and there; done this and that. Got a job. A fucking good one too, eh."

"What?"

"What I do."

"What *do* you do?"

"I work at the university."

"Really? McMaster, I suppose, eh?"

He nodded. "Atomic waste management. They've got a reactor and everything."

"Really?"

"Abso*fucking*lutely. Best job I've ever had."

I laughed abruptly, and immediately wondered what was so funny. "So," I said slowly. "You work in an atomic reactor?"

"Technically, no. I take all the leftover radioactive shit from the medical labs and put it away."

"'Put it away'?"

"Solid waste I stuff in fucking long cardboard boxes. They're like caskets for cheap, skinny people. I pile them up in the back of a garage on campus. All the fucking liquid shit I pour in big fucking metal drums that get rammed in the basement of a classroom until the fucking truck comes from, you know, Chalk River. Then it gets buried for like a fucking million years. One time, the fucking lift on back of the truck broke and a couple of fucking drums split open on the ground. I stood there while a fucking pumper hosed it all into the sewers —"

"Sewers?"

"Yeah. I had to stand there warning everyone not to step in the shit while it ate clean through the fucking asphalt."

He clucked his tongue and nodded thoughtfully. "Greatest fucking job."

"Don't you worry about, you know ...."

"Dying?"

"Right."

"Oh, it's real, real low level shit. No problem. I'm monitored. I wear a *badge*. My boss checks what I'm exposed to. He knows what's going on. It kinda scares you a little at first, but it's funny how fast you get used to it." He leaned closer, and dropped his voice to a clandestine level. "Now, sometimes, late in the afternoons when there's not much to do, I head down to the garage and make kind of a loft out of the boxes. I just curl up on top and take a nap. Boss doesn't mind. I've caught him doing it himself." His lips curl into a contented grin. "It's cosy."

"On top of the radioactive waste?"

"What you can't see can't fucking hurt you. That's what I say these days. Unless — and get this — unless you *let* it hurt you." He tapped at his wound with a slender, arthritic-looking finger. "That, I learned the fucking hard way."

"You sound like a Christian Scientist."

Moon squinted again, first at me and then at Mandy. "But that's a cult."

"Sorry. Just joking," I explained flatly, with a wave of my hand. "But what happened to you? And what *are* we doing here?"

He brightened perceptibly, and swivelled his stool to better face me while the stripper bumped and ground it out.

"It's funny. It just occurred to me one night, maybe three or four months after I left O.B.I.: 'Holy *shit*, I drilled a hole in my fucking head!' I saw it, like, for the first time, and it just kinda clicked that what I'd done was, I dunno, nuts or something. The really wild thing was I even thought those word — 'shit' and 'fuck' — and I didn't beat myself up for it." He shrugged. "I was in therapy at the time. You get the picture."

"So, fuck minced oaths, I guess, eh?"

He tossed back his head and roared. "In*fucking*deed."

I scratched the back of my head and tried to unscrew my bloody-minded grin. "When did you move to Hamilton?"

"I came to spend some time at a kind of clinic, and when my treatment was over I just fell in love with the place."

"Huh. So when did you —"

"Hey," he gushed, "I just remembered! I read a great fucking book last month in the garage. It's called *The Outsider;* heard of it? By Camus," he elucidated, rhyming it with hummus. "You gotta read it. I'm just like that guy! A real existentialist. And Pink Floyd's *The Wall?* Seen that? A*fucking*mazing."

"Could you excuse me for a sec?"

I didn't need to piss, but Moon had spent my patience, and listening to him rave like old times was making me claustrophobic. Nothing, I hoped, a splash of cold water on my neck couldn't help.

As I pushed open the door to the men's room, and sighed softly with gratitude for even this brief recess, a young Korean in a white blazer sprang from a folding chair, clicked his heals and barked "Sir!" My washroom attendant. I'd read about this sort of thing in "Talk of the Town."

"I'm just going to, um ...."

He clasped his hands behind his back and bowed stiffly from the waist. I could feel him watching, waiting for God knew what, though I was thankful that he was still only waiting, while I stood at the urinal and pretended to pee. He allowed me to flush it myself, but when I approached the sink he spun the hot and cold taps with such élan that for a moment it seemed quite sensible to leave this to a professional.

"Thanks, but I can, you know ...."

He squirted my palms green with soap gel, and once I'd rinsed, snapped free a pair of paper towels and wiped my hands dry. I didn't remember to douse my neck, but was so eager to get the hell out and so worried about what else he might do that I wouldn't have bothered even if I had. For the both of us, I felt embarrassed, and although my hands felt damn good and I supposed that deserved a gratuity, I didn't want to encourage him. He held open the door for me, belching loudly in my ear as I bolted for it.

"I heard about what happened," Moon said when I returned.

"What? Just now?"

"No," he laughed cordially as I sat down. Another stripper, a boxy Hispanic with muscular thighs wearing an lemon-coloured negligee, was listlessly treading the stage to "She Works Hard for the Money." "At Overcomer."

"So, you know about my dishonourable discharge?"

Moon nodded. "That's why I looked you the fuck up."

Our drinks arrived. We both reached for our wallets but he waved me off, explaining I could get the next round. But there was no bloody way I'd linger long enough, so my irksome scruples compelled me to pick up the tab. Besides, and more than besides, I relished the chance to tip our waitress.

"Thanks a lot; that's fine," I told her. Ten bucks on her platter and I felt like Charles Foster Kane.

"Well thank you, too," she said sweetly. And just stood there.

"I don't need change."

"Well then, you should count your blessings."

"I'm sorry?"

"No, I'm sorry. The tab's $10.60."

I handed her two more dollars and apologized excessively, although she never stopped sounding awfully sweet. As she turned away and walked towards a party of three beefy blue suits extending their working lunch, my eyes followed her pale, lean ankles until they disappeared into heavy shadow. So many naked women, and those ankles were all I cared to ogle.

"How'd you find out about it?" I asked Moon, when all of her was again out of sight.

"I hear things."

"Just like old times, eh?" His face crumpled. "Shit. Sorry Del, I didn't mean to —"

"That's okay." He smiled wanly. "I *was* nuts, wasn't I?"

I snorted, not without affection. "You were a fucking maniac."

The stripper's first number ended to scattered, inattentive applause. She was down to her scuffed, pink, four-inch heels and black leather thong. Briefly, during the intro to "What's Love Got to Do with It," she trooped off the stage to fetch a remnant of golden shag carpet.

Unexpectedly, Moon leaned his shoulder against me, and would have laid a hand across my wrist if I hadn't moved it in time. Hoarsely, he whispered, "I want you to know, you weren't alone."

"What?" I smiled vacantly. "About what?"

"I mean about Faulkner, and all that."

"I still don'— *Jesus Christ!* You mean ....?"

"Yupper."

"No way!"

He nodded, and reclined on his stool, satisfied, and almost toppled over. For a long time I just gaped at him. Godammit, he kept finding ways to astonish me.

"But I ... but, *you?*" I finally stammered. "And no one found out? When was this?"

"Freshman fucking year; middle of the goddamned second term. She kept having me over for dinner, and you know how good her cooking was. I didn't know why she kept inviting me. Fuck. I did like the food, though."

"It's just so ...." My voice dwindled and died, as if by shaking my head I'd snuffed it out.

"Thought you were the first, eh?"

"I don't know. I guess I did. I hadn't thought of it. First in years and years, anyway."

"Me too, the first time."

"First time?"

"Fuck, yeah!" he enthused, emptying his glass. "Every fucking week until fucking summer vacation." He wiped his mouth with the back of his hand. "I was a fucking mess, let me tell you."

"Every *week?*"

"She liked doing the doggy thing the best. You find that? What a cow, eh?"

The doggy thing? I took a deep breath, which felt awfully welcome. "I still can't believe it."

"Oh fuck, yeah." His eyes flashed. "'Believe it, oh, receive it', brother!"

"So, tell me," I asked, raising the bottle of beer to my lips, "was that, you know, your first time?"

"Posi*fucking*tively! Hadn't even kissed a girl before. Not properly. And certainly not down *there!*" he chuckled. "God, the taste. *Jesus!*"

"Pungent, wasn't it?" I smiled weakly, trying to get in the spirit.

"Well, you got used to it. I remember, that fucking summer of my freshman year, fucking her was all I fucking thought about. I was playing it over and over in my fucking mind, you know? One minute I was wringling the eel, the next it was God forgive me this and Lord have mercy that."

"'Waking the wizard'?"

"You know: waxing the knob."

"You mean waking the wizard?"

"Got it! Gawd, were we fucked up or what?"

"So you never told anyone?"

"Jesus no!" he recoiled. "Not at school. Scared to. Good reason, eh? Look at you. I had to take a fucking power drill to my skull to get out of there. And you just fucked once."

"Yeah, well, there's a reason for that ...."

"It was fucking killing me! All those times ...."

"... it was *awfully* late in the year ...."

"... sometimes repeating two, three times a night ...."

"..."

"But I was so fucked in the head when I went back the next year. You know, I couldn't even go near her! Changed my fucking program and everything."

"You never did like talking about her."

"But then, when she didn't try to get close to me either, I *really* got confused." He brooded over his empty glass, twirling it around in his hand, before turning to me and saying, "But you know where I'm coming from."

"I do."

"So ... you only banged her once, eh?"

"Okay, okay! Just once. You're the king."

"God only knows how many others there were. What a fucking slut, eh?" He stared hard at the stripper. She was lying face down on the rug, vaulting her hips, arching her perfectly tanned ass in our direction. "Sometimes, I think, maybe drilling the hole really did the trick."

I squinted, and studied his face for clues. I didn't know what he was talking about.

"My life sure turned the fuck around afterwards, that's for damn sure."

I guzzled my beer, and dimly realized that when I left here I'd need a few more. "Jesus," was all I could say.

"But who knows, eh? Maybe it worked."

"Not like you expected."

"Fuck no!" He beamed. "Not a fucking bit!"

Fifteen minutes later, on our sixth stripper, we left, upon my excuse that I had to cook for the house. We passed the table where our waitress was taking her break. Spread out before her was a spiral notebook, a pencil, a half-emptied bottle of cranberry juice and a crinkled bag of corn chips. She was reading a spindled copy of *Between Man and Man*.

"Did you see that?" I whispered hoarsely, unable to contain myself. "Our waitress reads Buber."

"Shit, I like Buber," Moon replied, thoughtfully. "I really fucking do. I cried so bad when Cornelius died."

7

The following evening I returned alone to Pandora's Box. And again the next Tuesday. And Thursday night they had 99 cent nachos.

Jesus wept. Or maybe there was something in his eye. I was feeding a hunger nobler than my unforgiven urges, but even if I behaved like I'd believed a year before and still expected that his New and Holy Jerusalem might, at any moment, drop from the clouds and ferry me into the Happily Ever Afterworld, I wouldn't have expected the sweet benefit of his doubt.

I wasn't there for the prodigious bosoms, landing strip pubes and flawless bums. Or rather, God forgive me, not just for that. I'd fallen in love with the waitress.

I wanted to tell her honeyed, giddy things, like Jimmy Stewart told Donna Reed in *It's a Wonderful Life* ("You want the moon? Just say the word and I'll throw a lasso around it and pull it down"), but after four visits my craziest ejaculation was, "Say, these are *great* nachos!" At least that helped me learn her name without needing to ask her for it. She scribbled it on the bottom of the bill in dull green ink: "Swell nachos, eh? Grace."

Grace, to begin with, was just a daydream. Another casual fantasy for my make-believe favours to rub up against. With the kind of common logic that proves man's perversity — at least this man's — she commanded my attention in a roomful of strippers because I could only imagine her naked. She was a serendipitous object of desire — which was nice and welcome but nothing special, given how I found them all the time, every day, especially at rush hour on the subway if I was caught without a newspaper or an interesting book. These fleeting lusts of the heart, especially since my expulsion, seemed as volitional and worthy of reflection as a blink.

It became a different game when I saw what she was reading.

My third year of Bible School I'd been warned away from Martin Buber as though he were the class bully or queer. ("Jewish mystic (1878-1965) Panentheist: God in everything. Transcendental relation displaced by temporal I/Thou. Jesus just good person." Those were all my dodgy notes on Buber from the half-semester elective, "Modern Philosophy and Biblical Faith.") Half a year after graduation, inspired by having picked my way through much of Paul Tillich's *The Courage to Be* and having several times picked up *Fear and Trembling* to read the same first few pages over and over again, I figured I was as ready as I'd ever be to take on a panentheist. For two bucks at a used book store on Harbord Street I bought a spindled, scored copy of *I and Thou*.

I hadn't started it yet, but I liked the man's face: a hermitic Santa Claus whose sack was filled with coal, but that was perfect because he looked as though he expected a hard winter. I'd shelved it at the end of my row of Fontana editions of C.S. Lewis, and expected to get around to it once I'd knocked off the Penguin omnibus of Father Brown mysteries.

When I spotted *Between Man and Man* on Grace's table, it was as if a light bulb — one of those cartoonish Bright Ideas

— had suddenly materialized, but not over my head: it hung above her copper-coloured, aloe-conditioned crown, shining like 2,000 watts of xenon. *She knows.* That was my resolution, though I couldn't justify it, nor even explain what it was that she knew. All I could do was affirm the tickle in my lungs and the tingling in my palms and the soles of my feet. She'd left her impression upon my body like a stigmata of pins and needles. Whatever this was, it was Big.

I didn't know her schedule, so since she could be there almost any time, naturally I had to be there lots. And just as I'd begun to notice other friendless regulars, so she couldn't fail to notice me, and maybe, somehow, misread my own particular desperation for "strong silent, spiritual type." That was the plan. I didn't get my hopes up.

The little note she'd added to my bill seemed affable enough, encouraging even, perhaps, but I didn't want to hope against hope.

I couldn't see Grace returning my affection, precisely because I wanted it too much, but I had to try. Not as a feasible shot at happiness, more as a vaguely-realized opportunity for self actualization. The whole "what doesn't kill me makes me stronger" school of dating. I presumed she had a boyfriend, maybe a girlfriend, and that either way or even neither she wouldn't give me the time of day, let alone that time of the night. Such thoughts lightened my heart. Having already given her up as lost, I had nothing left to lose by pursuing her.

And so I rubbed my hind legs together, spritzed the air with heady pheromones and took up the sprightly courtship samba.

For my fifth visit to Pandora's Box I decided to turn up the heat. I took along my own slim volume of Martin Buber.

Settling on which to bring was something of an issue. *I and Thou* had the advantage of being the only one I owned, but it just seemed too obvious. I still hadn't read it, and that hurt my pride. I should, I reasoned, at least pretend that I'd started it.

She was reading *Between Man and Man*, but I was too self-conscious to carry that into a strip club. The only other one I knew was *Good and Evil*, but I quickly discounted it as sounding too censorious. So, by unhappy default, *I and Thou* it was, and despite my misgivings its title did have the kind of erotic frisson that I associated with a clutch of Edith Piaf songs I might misunderstand equally well. It was my wish that such romantic signifiers would win me points with Grace, should she be keeping score.

Cradling the book's broken spine in my palm, I sauntered into the club the following wing night. I loitered near the bar until I discerned that Grace was working, then hurried to a freshly-swabbed table for two in the middle of her section. To distinguish myself further from the shy, florid fat men nursing empty bottles and the clerks from Revenue Canada in sweat-stained Arrow shirts who clustered around the dancers, I had the inspiration to sit with my back to the stage. A smug smile doodled on my lips as I scratched my chin and randomly opened the book. *I contemplate a tree*, I read.

Grace greeted me with a cheery "Howyadoin'?" and asked what I'd have. A fresh lime-coloured butterfly clasp pinned back her red hair, and she wore a loose-fitting, white rayon blouse bedecked with pale green polka dots the size of coffee rings. The tails of her oversized shirt lolled in the draft of the club's tireless ventilation above a tight pair of black polyester slacks. I ordered twenty-four suicide wings and an Ex (veggies and dip; no fries). Apparently Grace hadn't noticed my book. I would make sure she did when she returned with my food.

I was squinting over the top of page 57, watching for Grace to swing through the kitchen door, when "the very lovely, very luscious Ginger" took the stage to "The Boys are Back in Town." It was during Ginger's floor routine to Nazareth's "Love Hurts" that I spotted Grace, heading for the far side of the section with a tray of beer for a party of five middle-aged Filipinos in matching blue and white rugby shirts. It was another couple of minutes, after another visit to the kitchen, before I saw Grace with my order. As she approached my table, I dropped my eyes to the unfocused print and raised the book higher.

"Here we ..." she began, and so ended.

I set the book at my side, folded open as though I actually cared to keep my place.

"Oh great, great. Thanks, Grace."

I looked up at her. She drummed her fingers lightly on the bottom of the tray, blew a stray lock of hair from her cheek and screwed up her face in a grimace.

"Mind if I sit down?"

"Pardon?"

"Mind if I —"

"Oh no no no. I mean, no. Please."

She sighed heavily and set the tray aside, then pulled back a chair and sat down.

"Here's your stuff," she said flatly, gesturing absently to the bottle and basket of wings. "Go nuts."

What are you doing? Why are you talking to me? That's what I wanted to ask, but all I could say was a strangled, "Are you sure?"

"Of course. Now, what's the deal?"

"Deal?"

Grace rolled her eyes and nearly smiled. Clearly, she was enjoying this, but I wasn't yet convinced that was good news for me. She had me alarmed and disarmed; so rattled I felt like throwing up, and yet so charmed I hoped it wouldn't come to that.

"Fess up. You're in here all the time. Always in my section. And now you're sitting here reading Martin bloody Buber with your back to the stage."

"Oh, you know Buber? He's a bit of a favourite of mine. I appreciate how he, ah, supplanted the transcendental, you know, rela-"

"*Please.*" She shook her head slowly. I'd disappointed her.

"No, you see, it's like ...." I surrendered with a dinky shrug and reached for my beer.

"What gives?"

"About wha—"

"About what is it you want?" She folded her arms across the table top and said, in a hushed voice, "Come on. If it's any incentive, our bouncer's name is Gerhard."

"Huh? No, I don't — that's not — I mean — now look, I'm *totally* harmless!" My voice broke as I stared at her with wide, wet, I-hoped-to-God puppy dog eyes. She smiled.

"Relax. Have a wing."

Straightaway I reached for one, and impulsively gestured for her to join me. She shook her head.

"Vegetarian?"

"Hell no. It's just the food here sucks."

I nodded vacantly, then dunked the wing in sour cream and said, as I raised it to my lips, "So I guess that note you wrote me was all lies."

"What note?"

"About the nachos. You said they were swell."

"Really? No; never tried them. It's processed cheese. Hate that stuff. Probably just a little sarcasm. Not something I'm proud of. Sorry."

I nodded again and bit into the chicken. I chewed slowly, and waited for her to say something.

"Alright then," she finally said, as flatly as before. "If you've got nothing to tell me, I guess I'll get back to work."

"No no, wait. I noticed you reading Buber the other day —"

"Ah *hah!*"

"And I suppose I thought ...." What *had* I thought? "I thought, like, 'Wow!', you know?"

Grace removed her glasses and squinted hard at me. She took a deep breath and puffed up her cheeks, first one and then the other, letting the air out slowly in a low hiss.

"Okay. With you so far."

"Well, so, I thought that could be something to talk about, to break the ice." I twiddled the neck of the beer bottle, nearly overturning it. "I suppose I should tell you, I'm not so good with small talk."

"Hey, small talk's not much to be proud of." She rubbed a thumb across her cheek, then propped a freckled elbow on the table and balanced her chin on her fist. Then she smiled. "Mind you, it *is* something. Anyway, consider the ice broken."

I scratched the back of my head and grinned bashfully into my basket of wings. "Wow, how about that? Broken ice."

"Like, 'wow'."

"I'm glad we're talking, sort of."

"Sort of glad, or sort of talking?"

"Talking. Sort of."

"Yeah, well you didn't have to stalk me to do it, you know."

"Was I? Sorry. Didn't mean to creep you out or anything."

"Hmmm." Grace nodded blithely, the tip of her tongue poking between her teeth. "Of course, that totally reassures me."

"Well then, hooray for me."

She spanked the table with an open palm and sat bolt upright. "Now what do we do? See, my break's only ten minutes."

"Now what?" I stared at the blackened ceiling above her head. My hands and feet were tingling, like on that first day. "Now what? Geez, I don't know. I didn't think you'd talk to me."

"Sometimes I surprise even myself."

"So, what can we do in 10 minutes?"

She shook her head and smiled softly. "Is it always so hard for you?"

"What?"

"Asking someone out?" *Showers of blessing.* "Where *are* you from, anyway?"

"From here. From Toronto. But ...." *But.* Why muddy my life with dependent clauses? "Never mind."

"But *what?* Never mind *what?* Just broke out of the slammer?"

"No, it's nothing, it's just .... I don't want to tell you my story before you know me better." And I hastened to add before she did, "If you want to hear it, that is. It's not like I spent my formative years chained in a closet, but that's in the ballpark."

She returned her glasses to the bridge of her nose. "How intriguing, and yet so extremely disturbing."

"Sorry," I muttered, waving my hand as though erasing a blackboard. "Bad joke. Do you think maybe you could forget everything I've said so far?"

"Why?"

"Because you must think I'm an idiot. I might be a fool for you, but I don't want to be an idiot. Can I just start again?"

"You're doing fine. And my break's almost over."

"I'm Gideon, by the way."

"Like the Bible? I'm Grace."

"I know. Like the Bible."

Playfully, almost shyly, she offered me her hand. Her fingers were tapered like votive candles, but her handshake was firm.

"Nice to meet you. Anything else you should tell me?"

"I'm not the kind of guy who hangs out in strip clubs."

Grace sniggered and leaned back in her chair. "No, of course you're not. You're just researching your novel, right?"

"No, I mean, like —"

"It's okay. Where do you think I am? I'm not the kind of woman who works in them, either."

I laughed, but she corrected me.

"No, seriously. The crazy truth is, I'm researching *my* novel. That's my excuse, anyway."

"A novel? No kidding? That's so wild!" I winced. I sounded maybe ten years old. Well, fuck it; that was a good year for me. "What's it about?"

She shrugged. "Don't know yet. Better find out soon; I'm nearly finished."

"Sounds interesting," I said senselessly, leaving me wanting to bury my head beneath my chicken wings.

"So, now what?"

"Now what, *what?*"

She made tick-tock sounds with her tongue and glanced at her watch.

"I dunno. Gee ...." I chuckled, and suddenly felt faint with good fortune. "Well, how about dinner, maybe, sometime? How abou —"

"Tomorrow night? Le Select?"

"Yeah. Okay." I put a finger to my lips and cleared my throat. "Um, where's that?"

"And *Holiday's* playing at the Nostalgic. Cary Grant and Katherine Hepburn. Seen it? Want to see it again?"

"Okay. Yeah. Sounds great."

She lurched towards me, over my basket of wings, over my sour cream and carrot sticks, and gently poked my collarbone with her index finger. "You're one of those guys who knows what he wants and just goes out and gets it, aren't you?"

"You've sure got my number."

She smirked and pushed back her chair. "Alright, gotta go. And for goodness sake, please turn and face the stage. It's really insulting to the dancers."

I pushed back my chair as well, as if I was about to follow her to the kitchen. "So, speaking of numbers ...."

"I'll write it on your cheque."

"Listen ...." I felt emboldened by her scent — Laura Petrie catching her breath after a USO show — and pushed my luck. "How late do you work tonight? You want to grab a coffee?"

"Tonight?"

I nodded, grinning softly.

"I dunno. Maybe." She snorted and shook her head, smiling to herself as she stood and collected her tray. "Just tell me, if I say yes, how big an idiot will I be?"

III

We ought not to let ourselves be satisfied with the
God we have thought of, for when the thought slips
the mind, that god slips with it.

Meister Eckhart

1

My problem — I once wrote in a journal before ripping out the page, throwing away the journal and trudging to the beer store, cursing — *is that I want every day to be like the last 5 minutes of* It's a Wonderful Life. *No matter how good it is, it's just never enough until Clarence gets his wings.*

Clearly I was pretty damn full of myself. Most days it was sufficient to have a fresh bag of barbecue chips, a big, fizzy bottle of Coke and something tolerable to watch on television. Still, long after I'd given up on the Lord, I held out for angels. I had hope, and hope against hope, that an apple-cheeked cherub, a literally God awe-full seraph or some other officer of the Host Invisible might at last open up the world for me. It seemed it would take at least that much to show me the simple riches of life among the elements: the wonders of the flesh and every fragrant emission.

For a short while I thought I'd found one. She was all I wanted and all I'd hoped for — everything I'd given up as being too right and too good for me. She made little more than a cameo appearance in my life: no more than a walk on and a run away. Still, just as my grandmother had been devout until her son failed to come home, so I, when my angel of the Lord departed, knew that God no longer existed for me.

Not Mary. Never Mary. I mean Grace Wilby.

Whatever Mary and I had, and at times it seemed considerable, it never had the "I Found It!" zing of new-found salvation. That almost convinced me that she must be the one, because she didn't rival the Lord for my affections.

Grace, though, God help me, had powers. Older than Jehovah's, or at least the Jehovah with whom I'd been acquainted. If she were an angel, she was a stranger to my immaterial heavens and hells. Her smells were of garlic and wild roots, forest beds of shed oak leaves and freshly turned sod. And she was my greatest, death-defying fuck. My Anäis Ninja.

When we made love we made God from the clay we clawed from our backs. I scratched that in my journal for Grace. I still can't believe the shit I wrote for her. I can't even believe I tried again to keep journal. How about this: *My Emmanuel/Emmanuelle — both Christ and Syliva Kristel.* Geez; I guess it was love. It had better have been.

Naturally Christ was a hard act to follow, but my *Penthouse* iconography could be a tough bastard, too.

2

It's a shame, really a goddamn shame, when love's Toblerone begins to melt. Its treacly file of shark's teeth, decaying and fusing together into stubby bridge-work, is not a pretty sight. But I'd rather make a spectacle of my chocolate bar than leave it wrapped in its factory foil, preserved in the deepest pocket of my linen trousers that hang in the darkest corner of my walk-in closet. If the Toblerone of my love must dissolve — and it must — I'd rather that it dissolve on my tongue, where I can taste its sweetness before it makes my breath stink.

Grace was late, by maybe 20 minutes, for our coffee at the designated Donut Castle, and for half an hour before that I'd been asking myself, and not once rhetorically, *Just who the hell*

am I trying to kid? Until I saw her over the hump of the muttering tramp who sat by the window, I doubted she would show
at all. There she was, though, waiting beneath a street light on
the far side of Queen for a grubby streetcar to pass. Right then
I had my answer. *That woman, there, the one jay-walking towards me,
grinning over God knows what. That's whom I'm trying to kid.*

We sat together for 90 minutes, maybe more, me nursing a
short, black decaf and a heart clotted with worry over either
boring her or scaring her away, and Grace blithely chugging a
double-double plus two refills and laughing every time I hoped
she might. We talked about how we both preferred frozen raspberries to fresh, about her novel and my haircut, and how much
we preferred *Manhattan* over *Annie Hall*, and *Stardust Memories* over
both. (Coincidence? Not likely.) Eventually we split a leathery
baklava — two forks, one plate: her idea — and that was that.

We didn't fall into bed right away like I'd suddenly thought
possible, but give me an inch and I'll take that inch, piss myself
with gratitude and drown in my stinky pool of good fortune.
Not that I was easily satisfied; it's just that since God passed
away, my perspective *vis-à-vis* godsends had been shot all to
fuck. Water into wine or raising the dead: what's the diff?

Friday night, like Grace suggested, we dined at Le Select,
scarfing chicken linguini and foregoing dessert to cab across
town to catch *Holiday*. We were a couple of minutes late,
though with time to spare for *Angora Love*, a baffling Laurel and
Hardy two-reeler. ("What were they thinking?" Grace whispered with a hateful shiver when it was half done. "Did people
ever laugh at Oliver Hardy? Thomas Hardy seems funnier." I
grunted meaningfully.) When the feature began, we squeezed
a large, oily bag of popcorn between our thighs (my right, her
left), and — even more significant, I silently enthused — we
shared the same straw for our soda water.

"I guess this is kind of a date, huh?" Grace said afterwards,
as we raced for the subway through a downpour, stooped
close together under the broadsheet movie program I held
over our heads.

"Uh huh. I mean, I was kind of hoping —"

"Then I suppose it's okay if you put your arm around me."

Fifteen minutes later our train drew into Bathurst station; my arm, half asleep, still spanned her shoulders. Grace announced it was her stop and we kissed awkwardly. It could have been the big wet one I'd been rooting for Cary to plant on Katherine, or Hardy on Laurel, and for an instant my lips tasted the moistness of the tip of the tip of her tongue. But I pulled out of it, astonishing and dismaying myself. That old born-again hysteria over "rushing things." Despite months of inadvertent exorcism, a puritan ghost still rattled about the perilous circuitry of my brain.

When we might see each other next was left undecided; an ambiguity which normally chills my blood to Sangria. I didn't know I was happy until hours later when I still couldn't sleep, couldn't eat, couldn't even jerk off.

The next morning, about 8:30, I answered on the first ring and she asked if I felt like breakfast.

We met at College and Bathurst, outside a crammed Mars Diner, where we gave up on a booth and walked for a while, neither of us really hungry, until we found a small, unpopular place on Queen Street a little after eleven: late enough, we supposed, to order a pitcher of beer with home fries and scrambled eggs. The food was alright and I should have been hungry, but I had such a craving to go down on her, to just hitch up her calico checkerboard and drop to my knees for the sacrament of her gooseflesh, that I couldn't tuck into pork sausage with my usual gusto.

"I got something to ask," she said, sopping up her yolk with a wedge of white toast.

"Ask away."

"Well, since I guess we're kind of dating, and because I already care about you ...." A heavy sigh. "I think now's a good time we —"

"*Hmmm?*"

"— talked about the fate of your soul."

I laughed uncertainly, like a lottery winner stumped by the skill testing question. I found my packet of strawberry jelly and began picking away at the seal.

"*Huh!* Good one. You're kidding of course. Ah, aren't you?"

Grace squinted at me, cocking her head at a *What-the-fuck-do-you-think?* angle. "A boyfriend told me that in high school. We were parked at a Harvey's. I let him eat my pickles."

"Asshole."

"Thanks, man," she nodded, and refilled our glasses. "You used to be like that, didn't you?"

"No way. I would never have dated a non-Christian."

She hooted into her glass of draft. "And you're *not* kidding, right?"

Sheepishly, I nodded.

"So, how long was this phase of yours?"

That's what it was now. A *phase*. Like wanting to wear leather pants or live on the Moon.

"Oh, I don't know," I sniffed. "Two, three years? Maybe more." Like two, three years more. "Geez, it was all so long ago." Hardly.

"Do you go to church now?"

"Oh God no!" I gagged, almost giddy. "Nope, not me. No way. I'm no Churchie McChurch." Grace nodded, but her expression clouded and she drew herself back into her chair. "But of course, that's not to say .... I mean, spirituality's a very, *very* big part of my life. It's just that church, in my experience, hasn't been all that, uh, nurturing. That's not to say it *couldn't* be. That's just, like ...." A deep breath and a wobbly grin. "So ... how 'bout you?"

She shrugged. "Oh, you know; sometimes. Not often. But there's sort of a circuit that I do. If I just need to deal with the usual liberal guilt I go to Bloor Street United. But the best place to keep abreast of boycotts is Trinity-St Paul's. And once in a while I get a craving for some high church — I mean *nose-bleed* high — so I might drop by Smoky Tom's." I shake my head, not comprehending. "St Thomas. Got to hand it to those Anglicans; they've got a real soap opera going. A spin off, you could say. Seems like I can stay away for months and months and not miss *anything!* And then there's the little Zen temple in Chinatown when I'm feeling especially obscure. But mostly, Sunday mornings, all I hear is the sound of one hand making coffee."

I nodded, spearing blackened ends of sausage. "I can relate."

"So what do you think about things?"

"Things? Which things might they be?"

"God. Why we're here." She shrugged again. "Just asking."

"Oh, *things*. Well now, let me think." I cast a glance to the ceiling, trying to recall the last book I'd really read. "I don't know; how about you?"

Grace smiled indulgently. "Asked you first."

"It's just hard for me to articulate these things. The God talk seems so ... *debased*." I shuddered. "I find I don't want to talk about God anymore. Maybe about the God *behind* God."

She nodded, but asked, "What do you mean?"

Damn. "Oh, you know: the Wholly Other, the Ground of Being, the Absolute Thou. All that stuff. The Ineffable, the Transcendent, et cetera, et cetera. The more you talk about it, the less sense it makes." The more I talked, the more I remembered how much I loved this shit. "Theology, keeping my doctrine pure and all that; it used to be the most important thing in the world to me. But life's a puzzle we're not expected to solve." I stopped babbling long enough to listen to my heart. It surprised me. "Hey..."

"Hey, yeah?"

"I'd like to go to church with you sometime."

"For real?"

"Really real," I grinned. "I haven't wanted to go for a long time. But you ..." *You could make me love God again,* I wanted to say, and wisely didn't. "You make it sound, I dunno, natural. Just a part of the routine of things. That's good."

"Glad you think so. Me too. Sure, let's go sometime. I'll introduce you to all the best priests."

"Cool."

"So, you were telling me your theology. What's God to you?"

"God? Well ..." I took a drink and tried recalling my notes from O.B.I.'s False Doctrine class. "I try not to limit God by a definition these days. I mean, you can't really conceptualize divinity; all you can do is encounter it."

"Have you?"

"Oh, sure! Everyone does now and then." I glanced at her suddenly downcast expression, and gulped. "I mean, don't they?"

She just stared intently at her homefries and arched her eyebrows.

"So ...." I wiped my lips on my napkin, then balled it up and dropped it on my plate. "What do you think?"

"You want to know what I think?"

"Absolutely."

"I think you're full of crap. But I think that's sweet."

I almost laughed, but my throat closed around it and I coughed instead. Grace set down her fork and stretched both arms across the table, where she found my hands and unclenched them.

"You're trying too hard. That's all I mean. You don't need to pretend so much."

"But I —"

"Maybe you're not, but it doesn't sound real. Sorry. I'm a stickler about this kind of stuff. Don't say things just because you think I want to hear them. It's sweet, I guess, but it gets stale fast. You'll probably get it wrong, anyway; I'm a bitch to pin down. But I like you, okay? I can tell you're decent, and I know you're funny and smart and I like your dimples when you smile and all that shit. So just be real."

I breathed again, letting out a faint, sputtering whistle. My palms tingled with her touch.

"No one's talked like that to me before. Well, maybe *one*, but she's just a friend. You know, I really want to say .... That is, I want to ...." I wove my fingers together with hers, and my pulse, thick with appetite, thumped a muggy *Babaloo* in my ears. "I was just wondering .... Would you like to come back to my place for some, uh, tea?"

She shook her head slowly and smiled. "I guess I'd like to fuck you, too, but I've got to work. Thursday night?"

"I'll put the kettle on."

Thursday night she cooked dinner at her place: lamb chops with bacon and eggplant in a heavy cream sauce, with clam chowder and sausage rolls for appetizers. I'd never seen a woman eat meat with such relish.

She taught me Yahtzee over Creamsicles and Ovalteen, then a little later, dropped the needle on a grainy pressing of "The Girl from Ipanema" and coiled barefooted and cross-legged beside me on her flannel tartan sofa, and opened her first volume of family photos. My arm, slipping behind her back, cupped a bony, bare shoulder and she snuggled closer. It just felt the thing to do.

Prostitutes don't like to kiss you. They'll suck you, fuck you, and piss in your mouth if they're paid to. But kiss? I don't think you can buy that. You can pretend she's coming with you after a three-minute tug of love, but you can't make believe she cares if she won't part her lips for your tongue. Or give you a peck on the cheek. I'm not talking anilingus; just a little peck, like a checkmark from a quality controller that says you've passed inspection. It's easier to kiss ass than to fake that.

We slid together to the ceramic floor, pushing aside her photo albums and spilling our half empty mugs which she told me not to worry about. There was no rushing things; it felt like we had until the end of the world to map each other's sweet spots. I soon learned she didn't much care for being bitten on the nose, but her neck was extremely sensitive; especially close to the collar bone, which was where my nibbling earned me my first merit badge. A good boy scout: that's what I felt like, when I heard her breathing grow ragged and short and she purred, "*Hmmm*. I already think that's my favourite thing."

The music stopped, and our only accompaniment were her upstair's neighbours fighting over pizza toppings.

"Maybe I should put on another record," she mumbled.

"Where's the stereo?" I asked the gooseflesh of her belly.

It seemed a long time before we took things to the bed-room. Until then, besides the occasional sally southward to suck a toe or stroke a calf, we'd lingered pretty well above the waist. I'd already grown quite familiar with her little breasts, which had become as slippery as pickled eggs with our sweat and my slobber. I waited for her on the bed while she was in the bathroom, breathing in the sweetness of her beeswax candles and exhaling slowly through my lips. Noiselessly, I teased the air with my tongue like a bugler preparing to awaken company C. And when at last she came to bed in an untethered kimono, and I saw the vivid scarlet of her pussy curls for the first time, I went down on her like a dog to a water dish who had been left all morning in a Lincoln Town Car with the windows rolled up. She tasted as happy as lychee fruit.

Eventually, we got around to fucking. Condomless, after I'd come for the first time, inside her with her pale feet twined behind my neck. The moment before the initial penetration, with her painted toes pointed to the ceiling and her long legs spread wide as she stuffed me into herself, she asked, "Can you call in sick tomorrow?" Right then I resolved I'd be up to her double dares of "Deeper," "Harder" and "Don't stop."

I knew it was early, but I told myself I was writing vows between this woman's legs, never to be spoken — "I pledge you my eyes, that I may always see you as I do this day." She would be my last woman.

That first night was a small, sticky bubble of contentment that still felt momentous enough to redeem a respectable chunk of the world. It was too good to be too good to be true. It was our whispered goodnights, and our finding each other again with another probing caress.

"God's a verb," Grace said, astride me, in the early morning light. "God's what we do here."

She kept legal size folders of her lovers and friends in a drab olive filing cabinet next to the fridge. They were indexed alphabetically by given names, from Alexandre to Zoë. She said I couldn't look at them. I hadn't asked. Though frankly, I was curious about Zoë.

Drinking Ovalteen our first morning, after I'd called in sick, she wanted to know what colour folder I wanted. Red. A propitious choice. ("My favourites always choose red. I couldn't have seen you again if you'd asked for yellow.") With a black magic marker she squeaked my name onto its tab, filing me between Edward and Gunther.

"Now you have to write me poems," she smiled.

3

I needed a good night's sleep.

But Jesus, just *look* at her. I wanted to pull an all-nighter just to study her nostrils dilating in sleep, or spend the wee hours hunched over her to catch all those soft, REM-cycle mutterings or to stroke her menstrual-coloured hair splashed back across her fluffy hypoallergenic pillow. How could I sleep, with this brand new broken record in my head that sounded so preposterous and sweet: *Grace Wilby is my girlfriend .... Grace Wilby is my girlfriend ....?*

Buy me a pint and I could pretend the whole thing with Grace was an elaborate prank; maybe a contrived piece of living performance art. But buy me a coffee, black, and I'll confess I loved Grace desperately, just like Jimmy Stewart did Kim Novak in *Vertigo*, and then again later in *Bell, Book and Candle*. She wasn't my last great hope for romantic closure — I'd already given up on a happy ending in a world without end — but I thought, just maybe, she might at last be my last happy beginning.

It's not even as if we were dating; not in the sense of going out together. I did introduce her to Oppie, who'd been demanding to meet the reason I wasn't calling so often, and Grace took me to a birthday party for a stripper friend. ("Electra" was a York psych major named Carla Rosenfeld. Her boyfriend's gift was a pair of green hiking boots from Trailhead. Grace gave her Mahler's *Lied von der Erde*). That about cleared our social calendar. We were only together for a couple of months, but after we broke up I wished we had seen more people, so they at least could bear witness to our having looked like happy lovers.

What we *were* doing was pressing ourselves together as though waiting for the glue to set, on either my twin Sears box spring or her queen-size futon, almost every night of the week and many daylight hours on weekends (and once on my lunch break in the store). The more time we spent coiled together, staring deeply into each other's eyes like a pair of self-taught hypnotists, the more she reminded me of a psychic healer from Manilla I'd once seen on *That's Incredible!* I used to think that shit was bogus, but while Grace loved me she seemed able to pluck out my sick heart muscle without breaking skin or spilling blood.

All I want, I wrote in my journal, *is to be the favourite book by her bedside, the one with a fractured spine and ears moistened by salty fingertips. The funny one she'll hate to finish.*

"Do you really think I'm beautiful?" What a tender, fucked-up thing to ask. And she asked it with such aching delicacy, as though she truly didn't know.

"You're the most beautiful woman I've ever met." The right and true answer, before adding, ineptly, "I'm not joking!"

I can't shake it from my head, the *this-is-itness* of one queerly-charged night in my room, sitting naked on my bed, both of us short of breath, pronouncing our desires to make a baby and maybe other forever things. I haven't forgotten her limber, calming lotus, our trembling hands and the glass of milk we shared to settle our nerves. She told me I was the first man she felt she could live with. "You're the one," she whispered and, well, I thought that was that.

Sometimes, I remember, we ate; ordering in a pizza, or maybe I'd cook an omelette. ("All single guys are proud of their omelettes," she said. "Not all should be," I replied, and felt so bloody clever.) But mostly we lived on domestic beer, Ovalteen and diminishing reserves of body fat.

When she was about to fall asleep, which was always before me, we'd link up like a pair of premium dessert spoons, and I would press as much of myself as there was against the sleepy warmth of her back. My tongue felt sore only after she'd fallen asleep, as if all our kissing and sucking had nearly pulled it out by the roots.

A Thursday morning, dark and early. Grace had been sleeping soundly since 1:30, while I'd been enjoying my usual leisurely swoon over her candid body and our consummate love. But she didn't need to get up; her shift began at noon, and I had to be up by half past seven to open the store by nine. About 2:30, I began to worry. *Enough's enough. Go to sleep; she'll be there tomorrow.* But I couldn't turn myself off.

Four in the morning and I was still wide awake: over-tired and hyper-stimulated, heart riven with palpitations; belly, arms and legs tingling with that same, unstable current from my Bible School hayride. My mind raced with crazy thoughts, one of which was that I couldn't book off work, not if I had to explain I was literally lovesick.

Stealthily, about 4:30, I peeled myself from Grace and tip-toed to her bathroom for a quiet nervous breakdown.

I closed the door and sat on the toilet, planting my fore-arms like tent pegs upon my knees and cradling my head in both palms. I moaned softly, while a snippet of agitating Scripture about how no man can see God and live kept flooding my thoughts.

"Gideon?"

Shit.

"*Gideon?*" A rustle of linen as she climbed out of bed.

"In here," I replied, croaking.

"You okay?"

I grunted viscously. "Just taking a, you know, dump."

"Sounds bad."

"Oh yeah. No more strip joint food for me."

"Need anything?"

"Oh no, no. I'm okay."

Her feet padded closer to the bathroom door. "I thought I heard a funny noise."

"Really?"

"Sure you're alright?"

"Fine. Just fine."

Grace returned to bed. I shuffled after her 5 minutes later, after having talked myself into taking a genuine bowel movement. I didn't sleep that night. *All things work together for good.* But what about the catch? That nutcracking dependant clause about loving God.

More than anything I wanted to be with her, but I didn't know whether I could survive it.

It was her idea that we move to Spain.

She just said one night, "How about we move to Spain?" I pursed my lips reflectively and nodded. "Yeah. Spain sounds okay."

I didn't think she was serious. I was just thrilled to be included in her fantasy.

Grace had been twice before. The first time was the summer of her senior year of high school, when she'd left her virginity in Barcelona with a brooding photo-journalist she called "Bongo." The second time was four years later, right after university. She'd meant to stay three weeks but was there six months, "exploring celibacy" this time, waiting on tables in Madrid and writing a novel. Grace grew bored of it after 300 or so pages and abruptly wrapped it up with, "And then they all died." Her current work

in progress was completely different. She'd reworked one chapter of it into a children's book called *Victoria's Secret Garden*, which
she hadn't tried to sell. And which wasn't really for children.

When we got together the next night, Grace enthused
she'd applied for a visa, called her travel agent and had two or
three leads for subletting her apartment.

"What's wrong?" she said, looking up from our favourite
pizza delivery menu.

"Nothing. Not a thing. It's only ...." I puffed up my cheeks
and exhaled extravagantly, hoping to play this for comedy,
and sat beside her on the couch. "This is moving pretty fast."

She set the menu on her lap and squinted at me, as though
she were peering through a microscope.

"Don't want to go?"

"Sure I do. It's great — it's a *great* idea. But I haven't travelled a lot. Not like you. So I ...." I shrugged, and gave her a
little smile. "Just getting up and going .... I mean, it takes some
getting used to."

She folded her arms and sighed, settled her head on the
back of the couch and lifted her eyes to the low stucco ceiling.

"What's wrong?" I asked. The tremor in my voice sounded
like everything slipping away.

"This is me," Grace said. Her voice was broken, too. She
swallowed hard, then looked at me. "I can just get up and go.
I'm not going to change."

"I don't want you to. Change, I mean." I wanted my arms
around her, but for the first time since we'd slept together I
knew that might not always be a good idea.

"Do you want to go to Spain?"

"I want to be with you."

She closed her eyes and shook her head.

"That's not what I asked."

I discovered, when I crawled home early Sunday for a nap,
that my mother had been trying to reach me since nine the
night before. I tried her, but she wasn't in. She called just after
I'd fallen asleep.

"Your grandmother's had another stroke."

"*Another* one?" I said, as though it was unseemly of her.

My mother was silent for a moment, and then explained, without inflection, "The doctor says we might lose her this time."

"Oh."

"If she lives, she may be a vegetable."

"A *what*?" I was too groggy for this. The thought of a turnip in my grandmother's frock almost made me laugh.

"There's been some serious damage this time."

"Oh, *shit!* Sorry ...."

"I tried calling last night. I guess you were out."

"Yeah, well ...." I shrugged to nobody. "Yeah."

In an hour, I was with my mother at the hospital. Nanny was still in intensive care, plugged to monitors and drips, her eyes closed and mouth open, her head resting at an awkward angle. She was asleep or unconscious. Or, maybe, a vegetable.

She'd been dying incrementally ever since my uncle died all at once.

"I just pray the Lord'll forgive her," my mother sighed.

"I'm sorry," Grace said, holding me, stroking my forehead. "I know she means a lot to you."

I kissed her between her breasts and didn't say anything.

"I guess you like the idea of Spain even less now."

I sat upright beside her, traced her jawline with the tip of my index finger and looked her in the eye.

"No. I've been thinking. I really want this. I *need* to do it. Getting up and just *doing* something has always been so hard for me." My eyes reddened. "I don't know if I ever told you. I used to think I was going to be a missionary." I brushed my nose with a finger. I wiped it on my sleeve, then took her hands in both of mine. "Now I want to take risks. With you, I do."

"Shh," Grace said hurriedly, pulling away. "Don't say anything." She pressed a finger to my lips. "Not right now. I've written you a letter." She handed me two sheets of paper.

This isn't easy .... It's me, not you .... I've enjoyed our time together ....
I'll never forget .... I'll always care ....

I couldn't make sense of it, first time through. Like my grandmother, the vegetable. Grace took back the letter. Probably for the red file folder.

"You okay?"

I wheezed a bitter laugh, and looked away.

"I'm sorry," she said softly. "I just have to do it for me."

My head snapped back. "But I — did I *miss* something? I thought this was —" My hands beat the air, as though trying to conjure our bliss. "So, you're going alone?"

She nodded.

"But it's supposed to be *our* trip!"

She smiled indulgently. "Gideon, we've barely known each other a month."

"*Six weeks!*"

"Are you counting from the first time we slept together, or from when we met?"

I slapped my forehead. "*What?* What the *fuck* difference does it make? You said you wanted to have a baby with me."

She crossed her legs, arched her eyebrows professorially, and gave her head a tiny rattle. "No, I didn't."

"Yes!" I shouted, slapping my thigh and wagging a finger at her nose. "*Fucking* yes! You did so! *I* remember."

"Sit down," she cooed. "Don't be upset, okay? I'm sorry if you misunderstoo —"

"I understood you fine. I just don't now, that's all."

"I don't mean to hurt you."

"Well —," I smirked, stood, and began to pace.

"I still care about you. More than it must seem to you right now. But I've got to get away, and it's got to be just me." Grace uncrossed her legs. "I'm sorry," she shrugged, and gave a goofy smile. "That's the way it is. Sit down, okay?"

I folded my arms. "No."

"What do you want from me?"

I want you to wake me again with a kiss, and move your hips with lewd intent. I want to taste you, neck and toes, till we forget whose is whose and which is which. I want your grit between my thumb and fingers and fresh nibbles on my neck. I want you to take me in your hand and mouth, and to paste your painted lips with myself. I want you wet again. I want you, without my telling, to know precisely what it is that I want.

I plunked down beside her.

"I guess I just want to be with you. Pathetic, eh?"

Grace shook her head, and smiled pleasantly enough. "No, it's not. It's flattering. It's just —" She dropped her head on my shoulder. I didn't like it there, but left it alone. "I don't think I can be with anybody right now."

"But the intimacy —"

"Intimacy takes time."

"No, it doesn't."

She just sniffed.

"Okay, well, suppose it does then. Let's take the time."

"It would just be harder later."

"Why? Why would it?" I took a deep breath and doubled over, clasping my hands. "Sorry if I sound like a crazy person."

"It just can't work. I'm sorry." Grace absently kneaded my shoulder. I wished that she wouldn't. "The trip —"

"But I *really* want to go!" I sounded like a child on the way to the dentist, watching the Niagara Falls exit recede through the rear window of his family's sensible sedan. If this is what's best for me, how come it's not my tooth that aches?

"You want to go to be with me. I just want to go." She shook her head solemnly. "That's the difference. You'd be too much responsibility. I'd come to resent you. You don't deserve that."

I scratched my nose for time — I was running out of things to say. "What about your telling me I was the first man you thought —"

"I meant it, whatever I said. It's just —" Grace pulled away sharply. "Don't try to make me feel guilty."

"I only want to know what happened."

"Nothing's happened. I'm not sorry about anything." She smiled again, more broadly now, and set her hands on my knees. "You need to know that. It was fun."

"*Fun?*"

"Okay; more than fun," Grace nodded. "But honestly, this isn't about you at all."

"Huh." My mouth was dry. "I know you're trying to make me feel better, but I kind of wish it would have *something* to do with me."

"Shhh. Now come here. Let's not talk any more about this now. Just let me feel you, lest old acquaintance be forgot."

4

All the miserable things I do to defer that hollowing-out moment when I know we've given away too much; when my lover looks at me one morning as though scales have dropped from her eyes and she finds herself lying next to Barney Fife instead of Sheriff Andy. I'll make absurd excuses and impossible promises, convince her if I could I'm the cure for cancer when she gets that look in her eye that says she'd rather rent a Shelley Long movie. I'll stretch the truth as thin as gold leaf before I'll bear that look, before I'll watch that movie, before I'll hear the words "Depart from me, I never knew you."

But what should I do? There will always be some character flaw I've forgiven myself, some hoary smudge on my soul to which I'm blind until it's reflected in another's disenchantment, when the thrill is gone from all my endearing quirks.

Apologies all 'round, I suppose, and then on I trudge, grilling myself on what I've learned. Too late to save a lost love, but maybe soon enough to safeguard the next.

Some things, thank Christ, I've never needed telling. I knew by Grade 10, about the time of my first kiss, that I would not worm my way further into Judy Lieber's heart by admitting I thought her mother was "hot." Other things have taken time. Often I've needed a partner to teach me, whether she wanted to or not, or suspected she was teaching me, or even knew she was my partner.

To distrust happiness and believe in sour ends: Mary Christmas taught me that. "God sent you to me," she whispered, and I thought that settled it. Early the summer of my junior year, shortly before she came to Toronto, she wrote, "You're the first man I've loved who's deserved me." That was something I'd always wanted to hear, and hadn't known it. Then, when she was gone, I worried she'd been right. Like a good comparison shopper, I'd learned from her that if a girlfriend were too good to be true, she probably was. As Sophia Faulkner might say, and did with her hips, *amator emptor.*

Thanks to Grace I became conscious of the fat content of my yoghurt, and saw the virtue of trimming my nostril hairs. Because of Grace I stopped turning on the television before I'd taken off my coat. On her account I read enough James Joyce to convince her I knew more than the dirty bits at which my *Ulysses* would forever fall open. Thanks to Grace I gave all my beige corduroys to Goodwill.

Not much, maybe, in the big picture, but it was the making of a pleasant miniature.

Grace was a good woman, but that's all she was. If she'd really been my saviour and had gone to prepare a place for me, she'd have commended my wanting to savour our love, to suck it thin like the last, sweetest sliver of Toblerone. But Grace was a good woman, and she dreamt of other appetites.

Until she left we slept together intermittently. Regrettably, sleeping much better than before. My palate had wised up, and no longer could I confuse common bread and wine for the Body and the Blood. Then, as departure time approached, she began withholding more of herself from me.

A little at a time she said goodbye. First I couldn't finger her ass, then nestling my head between her legs was off limits, then dawdling too long on her nipples was a no no. Pussy gone; hips, breasts going, going gone. She started wearing panties and a flannel pyjama top to bed. Her topography was becoming alien again. Finally, only her mouth was left, mostly just to explain how things had changed. Except for the last night. Then, and for the last time, she was naked for me.

I was so mad, later, when she fell asleep. Time wasted, of so little time left for us. I wanted to wake her and tell her some wounding thing: words to be a spigot of blood and water, tapping her like a pickled baby pig from high school biology. But I didn't know what to say; I just wanted to make her cry. So, I let her sleep. For a while, listening to her snore and her odd brassy fart, she seemed no more cryptic than a *TV Guide* crossword puzzle. I even wondered, *what's all the fuss about?*

Her cat crawled between us, curling around the crown of her head to lick her salty scalp. She shifted towards me, and I felt the chill of her bum against my hip. For the first time I thought it necessary to note that she had two small moles on her stomach. I gauged them at three and eleven o'clock to her belly button. She'd be gone soon, I knew, and before she left I needed to finish inventory.

Memory, like an oyster's grain of sand, becomes more than an irritant, if you give it time.

She slept late. Around nine her breathing became laboured and wheezy, and then seemed to stop altogether. I would have nudged her then, but she started whistling through her teeth. Now, it sounded so warm and homey to me I nearly sobbed. When finally she awoke, she asked if I was still mad at her. She didn't want to feel guilty, she repeated. No, I lied, I wasn't angry at her

Grace smiled. "Maybe we'll end up together after all."

She'd given two weeks notice to the club, another week to me, sublet her apartment to a stripper and was gone. But before that, just before she crossed into the "passengers only" section of the departure lounge, she whispered, so softly, or maybe did nothing more than shape the words with her mouth, that she loved me.

Then I stood there and watched her walk away. Once she was out of sight I scratched my head, giggled and cried.

Who dat?

Like a phantasmic game of Clue: my grandmother, in the kitchen, cooking fish.

It's how I would dream of her, always. The haddock sputtering grease on her mangled hands, "Pack up your Troubles in your Old Kit Bag" on her splintered lips. Her fingers painted pearl from batter she drops more fish in the Crisco, making it sputter and pop like a George Formby 78. She mutters that the power's "low," as though Ontario Hydro were teasing our GE range, before she spears some scrump for me to test. (All batter, no fish. Yum.) I'm always 12 years old in the dream. Though there's no one else in sight I know my family's together, and the batter is crisp and bubbly, glistening with rendered lard. Yum.

When I'm done with a sclerotic idyll like this, it's no wonder I skip my morning crueller.

That's why it's a mystery what Winston Churchill's doing here, hunkered down at the kitchen table, filling his cereal bowl with my Grandmother's All Bran. It had never been an issue before. Nanny's back is to Churchill, watching the stove, warbling what sounds like the theme from *Baretta*. "You going to eat or what?" grouses Winnie.

When I awake, amused and perturbed, I switch on the light and roll onto Grace's side of the bed. (I can do that, now she's two weeks gone.) The pen I fell asleep with pokes me in the ribs and specks my chest with blue ink. I open my journal at its last entry: *Still awaiting the second coming (or is it the first?)* I don't recall writing that and, though I'm still slightly drunk rather than hungover, don't care for it, but can't think of anything better to say. I absently doodle a few spaceships and tits, then close my eyes for another slumber party of one. I know I'll be asleep soon but leave the light on regardless.

Tenish, maybe ten fifteenish I awake again, for the third or fourth time this morning, and decide enough's enough. My skull still rattles with last night's empties as I shamble naked and woozy to the bathroom, where I flick on the light and brush my teeth vigorously. I expect my gums to bleed these days. They've receded again. (When, exactly, did that happen?) *Really must buy some floss,* I resolve, as a cherry-stained foam of Crest Freshmint Gel slobbers onto my hand and slops down the drain. The basin is still polluted with several weeks of my sheddings: dried glops of toothpaste and whiskers and the occasional crooked limb of a Daddy Long Legs. *Really must do something about that,* I counsel myself. *There's so much; better write it all down.* I fetch the nearest pen and paper and return for a fecund, self-centring dump.

1. RINSE SINK
2. RETURN VIDEOS

I cross out number 2. *Apocalypse Nude* and *On Golden Poon* are already overdue, but I won't take them back until they get me up and off just once.

It's hard for me to believe, sometimes, that my experience adds up to much, but there it is.

"How are we doing here?"

Still breathing, albeit laboriously. The air in this sepulchral Queen Street crawlspace is clotted by so much smoke and attitude I made a face with each inhalation. I needed to pee another amber yard or so of flat ale, but between me and the washroom stood a near-prohibitive crush of several dozen skinheads. I can hold my liquor a few minutes more.

A typical Thursday night/Friday morning at the Club Foot. So Oppie told me. I'd been here before but never on a weeknight, as if such a notion of how we portion out our lives still had some correspondence to my world.

Against her advice I ordered nachos. Disconsolately, I poked the corn chips with the stir stick from my cold coffee, check my wallet (how are we doing *here*?) and decided to switch back to beer.

"Another round?" Oppie nodded, she thought that sounded good.

"I can't believe where it all goes," I wheezed.

"Huh?"

"My unemployment insurance."

Oppie had been late, which was as predictable as my early arrival. When she showed five minutes into the first set she sat between me and a guy with abraded knuckles and a brow as busy as the grill of an uncertifiable Lincoln Town Car. With the casual fraternity of a longtime smoker she bummed a light from him and shared his copper-coloured ashtray.

Either Emerson, Lake and Mengele suck, or I'd aged beyond the psychographic for this scene.

"You like?" Oppie squealed, louder than she needed for a change, over something called "Greek Salad Surgery."

I nodded, and began drumming the table manically with both hands. I didn't want to disappoint her. The night, the club, the band: all her idea. The week before, after I'd told her my Winston Churchill dream, she said I needed to get out more. I didn't tell her that all I might need was to watch better television.

"We're gonna take a little break, an' ...." The lead singer left it at that, as his band spilled off the stage and stomped to the bar.

Our beer arrived and we took salutary gulps before Oppie leaned into me, setting the tips of her ebony bob whirling. She was dressed, naturally, in black: a spaghetti-strapped bodice, a mid-thigh skirt with fringe, elegantly ripped mesh stockings and a pair of dressy Docs. Her skin was luminous. The only respite from her monochromania was that gleaming coat of candy apple lipstick for which I — and, I think, the stranger at her left — had already complimented her. Nights like this, when Oppie looks like this, it was consolation enough to think we might be mistaken for lovers.

She looked as though she was about to tell me something funny when the stranger tapped her elbow and lurched drunkenly towards her ear. She turned half way to meet him, answered his whisper with a garbled laugh and a pair of wide, startled eyes in my direction, then offered a few soft words I could make out. I looked away and drank deeply. Vacantly, I rubbed at the blue ink of admission stamped on the underside of my arm, making a blurry dotted line across my wrist. I turned back towards them when I felt the table rock from his hands planting on its edge. With an odd and off-putting smile towards me he reeled about and tried for the toilet. Oppie looked at me with an astonished grin.

"What was that about?"

"That guy ..." she mumbled, shaking her head. She reached for her purse. "Where's my cigs?"

"What?" I grinned humourlessly. "What'd he say?"

Oppie shook her head dismissively and lit a cigarette. She took a long drag, blowing the smoke out of the corner of her mouth, away from my face.

"Boy/girl bullshit. You remember, surely."

"Barely." I was still smiling, but stopped when I pictured what I must look like. "So, what'd he say?"

"Oh, you know. Thought I looked 'hot', or something. Wanted to get together. Crock of shit. Don't mind hearing it once in a while, though. Like an old Rod Stewart song."

"'Spread your wings and let me come inside'?"

"Older than that," she added quietly with a smile, her voice trailing off as though she'd been distracted by an indecorous thought.

"So, how did you get rid of him? Must be a tough job," I added in a cartoonish *basso profundo*, "for a sexxxy lady like yourself."

"You've *no* idea."

"So what did you say?"

"Said I was with you. Of course, this means you may have to fight for me. Sorry, buddy. Still, he made it a pretty tempting proposition, in a grisly kinda way."

"Oh, *puhleease!*"

"I've always had this soft spot for big dumb guys with lousy complexions. The sensitive slash dangerous type I guess

you'd call it. They've got a 'shut up, let's fuck' kinda thing happening, which isn't altogether a bad thing." She sloshed beer
on her chin. "*Believe* me."

"I don't want to hear about it."

"What? *What?* Does a fantasy make me a slut?"

"No, of course not. It's only — " With mock horror, though
I felt the real thing, I scowled and shook my head slowly.

"Oh, lighten up. You're getting as bad as Arthur. And I'm
not even sleeping with you."

"Yeah, well, you know ...."

Oppie nudged closer, her eyes softening as she cocked
her head. If she knew she'd hurt me, this was her saying she
was sorry.

"Actually, I don't know. It seems like, the longer I go without sex, the weirder the whole thing seems."

"With me, the more I do it, the more I can't believe it."

"I'm serious."

"No shit. So am I. You first." She pats my hand with
comic, tender insouciance. "Zo, vhat zeems to be zee problem,
Herr Eddipus?"

"It's just ...." I stared absently past the blunt end of her bob
to the crimson neon Budweiser which overhung the bar. One
morning recess in grade five, Gary Tartaglia told me how babies
were made by the pee of mommies and daddies. I didn't believe
it then, either. "It's just, do people really *do* that to each other?"

"Well, it's in all the papers." She made me chuckle, gen-
uinely, and her eyes crinkled with relief. "Very serious shit, this
beast with two backs bullshit. It fucks us up. Or wait: is that
our mums and dads?"

I nodded slowly and turned the bottle between my palms.
I'm surprised, suddenly, by how little I want to talk about this.

But Oppie hadn't finished. "It's lonely on the top, eh? And
the bottom. And every which way but loose."

"I can't remember."

"Grace hasn't been gone *that* long."

"Two months. That's long enough."

"Not long enough to want her back. For Christ's sake, you
don't still want her, do you?"

"I want a big, dumb love. Something obsessive and sick-making. So yeah, Grace could do nicely. We weren't together long, and I can't say I really knew her that well, but I miss her. I thought the other day of how her favourite conditioner made her hair smell like raspberries. Burst into tears! But then there's other times. Then, it's almost like I miss someone else."

"Who?"

I took a pensive sip of beer and sighed wistfully. "I don't know yet .... Me, maybe? Nah, that's just crazy talk."

"Fucking right. Ah hell," Oppie immediately stammered. "Sorry, I'm such a bitch." I hadn't noticed especially. She leaned back in her chair, just as I have already. We drank silently for a couple of minutes before she appended, in a sudden hurry, as though she'd forgotten to say it long ago, "So tell me, why is it that encouraging you depresses the hell out of me?"

I smiled, bashfully, and scratched the nape of my neck. "Guess I'm sorry, too. It must be a real drag to be friends with someone so strung out on himself."

She grinned warmly. "You've seen me in some bad times, too."

I wanted to hug her for that. I was afraid my eyes might redden if I didn't say something silly, so I muttered, "It would be much simpler, wouldn't it, if we were all just big brains in jars?"

Oppie giggled. "'I bid ten thousand quatloos on the newcomer.'"

"Wouldn't that be great? We could spend our days sloshing around our jars, wagering on bloodsports."

"Yeah, but you'd probably still envy Kirk for pulling that sweet space poon."

"Guess so. That 20th Century testosterone made him look so stupid, eh?" I snorted. "Hell, they make me look stupid."

"Testosterone, estrogen: they make *everyone* stupid." Oppie drew a deep breath and curled both hands about her bottle. "Buck up, big guy. You've lost a girlfriend, but you're still relatively young and employable. Shit happens, but you know what? Then it's *happened*. This too shall pass. I remember the shape you were in after that stuff with Mary."

"Mary?" My voice broke. Maybe I was a little startled to hear her name. It always startled me, even though Oppie mentioned her often.

"Grace was a goddamned saint compared to her. You were right to be fucked up over Grace. Not Mary. *Jesus*," she snorted. "Mary Christmas and Grace Wilby. You sure do go for those didactic names. Didn't you go out with Pussy Galore for a while, too? No wonder we never hooked up. 'Szabo' just means 'tailor' in Hungarian, and 'Oppie' means — shit, I forget. Let's pretend 'cute.'"

"I'm surprised you think I should have been fucked up over Grace."

"Grace did some good stuff."

"I didn't think you liked her all that much."

"Well, not *that* much. Just much-*ish*."

"I guess your standards have dropped."

"Nah, I'm just grading on a curve now. And it wasn't that I didn't like her. It's just I didn't think she was your type."

"Maybe not. But I wasn't looking for a blood transfusion."

"So, why don't you go running after her? Maybe she's ready for you this time. Why don't you fin—"

"No no. No way."

"How come?"

"I won't pursue a woman twice."

Oppie nodded, though she again asked, "How come?"

"First time's tragedy; second time's farce. If that's the choice I've got, I'll take the mystery box that Carol's showing."

"*A new dining room suite!*" She chortled into her chest, then looked up and said "You still think about her, right?"

"Who? Ah, it doesn't matter; I still think about *everyone*."

"Hmmm." She stubbed out her cigarette. "Don't mean to turn metaphysical on you, *dood*, but I figure, at the end of the day and all that shit, it's better to be proven wrong hoping for the world, than proven right expecting the end of the world. Even" — sweepingly, Oppie waved a fresh, unlit cigarette for emphasis — "even if it breaks your goddamn heart." She settled back in her chair and grinned, so pleased with herself that she's actually flushed. "So tell me: am I, like, wise or what?"

"You're the Karnak of our generation."

"I've often thought as much."

"Seriously though, thanks. I like the cut of your jibberish. You're probably right, but my life's really boring the hell out of me these days and I can only imagine how you must feel. Let's talk about something other than my misery for a change, okay?"

"Okay. So, how's your folks?"

"Try harder?"

"The night's still young."

"Oh, they're okay," I replied, exhaling heavily. "Same as ever, I guess. No — I'm not being fair. It's been bizarre talking to my Dad since the Bible School thing and all my fucking broken hearts. He seems younger now, somehow."

"Maybe you're just feeling older. Or more like your own age."

"Whatever. Our relationship seems reduced — elevated? — to playing old war buddies. When we get together it's like vets getting together at the legion and swapping tales of our amputations."

"Love is a battlefield."

"It doesn't make me feel much better, but feeling sorry for someone else makes a nice change of pace sometimes."

"That's what I love about you. And your mom?"

"*Christ.* She's still after me, if you can believe it, to go to that frigging Keaton Crusade. You'd think she'd know by now."

"She probably thinks the same about you."

"Don't depress me."

"Let's go."

"Yeah, right." I sniggered, then met her eyes. "No. No *way!*"

"Ah, c'mon on! Just *think* about it. It's perfect."

"*Perfect?*"

"What're you afraid of?"

"It's not about that."

"So what's your problem?"

"I can't. This is .... I don't believe you could sugges —" I threw up my hands like I was directing traffic.

"Just for fun."

"*No!*"

"We'd sit at the back; no one would know we were there. You wouldn't even have to tell your mom. It's at a big place, right?"

"The Coliseum."

"Goodness, how positively first century."

"And we'll be the lions, right? Hell no. I wouldn't even rent the video."

"We could brown bag our own communion wine — maybe a decent scotch. That has a nicely dissolute, trailer park ring to it."

"Yeah, but I'm not —"

"We could *out* them! You could pretend to get a word from the Lord and start speaking in tongues. I could interpret for you: 'God's telling him his girlfriend gave you a blow job.' That'd put a Pentacostal chill in those hard fundie hearts, doncha think?"

I chuckled. "That, I like. But I'm not changing my mind. Now, can we please talk about the Leafs? The Jays? What the fuck: the Argos?"

"Hey, maybe they'll take their shirt off this time. Holy shit, Gideon, we've just gotta gotta go! Get with the program; this is high concept!"

"Take Arthur."

"No way. He'd call it morbid religious mania, even after a few."

"He'd be right."

"But he has no idea how much *fun* that can be! No, it's gotta be *you*. You'd understand. He never learned the lingo. You're fluent. Hell, you taught me everything I know."

The band began ambling back to the stage. The drummer carefully nestled a half-emptied bottle of Black Label against his stool and kicked it over as he sat. He cursed, bent to right it and struck his head on a cymbal.

"You really like these guys?" Oppie asked incredulously.

I shrugged. "Not especially. Great name, but I could've had as much fun reading the club listings. Nice idea, though," I added weakly. "Thanks."

She tossed her head. "They bite. Let's make like toast, and jam." She was already pushing back her chair and tugging her black leather waistcoat about her bare shoulders. "I just want to drink and talk. Whadya say? Let's drink and talk, 'kay?"

Five minutes later, once I'd finally threaded the crowd for a piss, I join Oppie on the street beneath the club's awning. She was two thirds through another cigarette. According to the digital clock across Queen, the one above the burgundy-tinted window of the Wang Ho Funeral Parlour, it's ten past eleven. Later than I'd thought, but earlier than it feels. The lightly falling snow made the sidewalk slabs look like freshly-pressed cookies dusted with icing sugar. There were no beggars, no sirens.

"So where to, Magellan?"

"Where?" In that neighbourhood, at that hour, I felt most at home in donut shops, and only when I got it to go. "What do you feel like? Coffee?"

"Fuck that noise." Oppie squinted east, then west. "Should we grab a taxi? Where are we going?"

"I don't know. Chez Guevara?"

"Here's one." She waved both arms turbulently at an east-bound Diamond cab, which braked for us on the far side of the street. "Come on," she called, stepping off the curb. "Hell, opportunity knocks me out!"

I was right behind, bare hands thrust in my pockets. "Don't you have to work tomorrow?"

Oppie turned about and scrunched up her nose. "*Friday?* Hardly counts." She raised her hand to hold up a streetcar. Its bell clanged furiously, but it stopped nonetheless. "My weekend started yesterday."

She flicked her cigarette down a sewer grate and clamoured in, calling out "Danforth and Chester, please and thank you." The cab arced into an ample U-turn as I closed the door. "It's around there somewhere," Oppie mumbled with a swirl of her hand.

The meter clicked over. Two twenty, two forty. Even when I have money it's as transfixing as an intravenous drip, but especially when I don't. I rubbed my eyes and thought of sopping black hair and fresh raspberries.

After a few blocks of silence, Oppie spurted, "Widow's Hump is at Larry's Hideaway next Friday."

"Oh?"

She nodded. "Might be good. Arthur wants to go. Interested? Maybe I could call one of my promiscuous soul sisters."

"Just one?" I smiled out the window and relished the words "*Chez Guevara.* Glad I thought of that. Been meaning to go there for a long time."

"You just like the name, you ol' commie. My bung-holing fuckwad of a brother-in-law — pardon my French," she lobbed towards the cabbie's reflection "— he's been there. Hated every minute. Said it was like — God, what was it now? It was all bullshit anyway. We'll like it."

Four sixty. Four eighty. "You know, I hate to be a drag, but I don't think I've got much mon—"

"And this Winston Churchill shit," Oppie interrupted. For the first time tonight, she sounded decidedly drunk. She rocked lightly against my shoulder as we turned a sharp corner onto University Avenue. "He's dead, right?"

"Sure. Long time"

"Huh." She was quiet for a moment, and then says softly, "Don't worry about money," she said quietly. "I'm positively *awash* ce soir."

As we approached Dundas and Yonge traffic slowed. We found ourselves behind a bruised and dusty streetcar, loading claques of shrieking teenage girls and unloading dour shift workers. On the southside of Dundas, outside the entrance to the Eaton Centre, a street preacher was declaiming the Gospel to an audience of two dozen souls.

Our taxi was idling, waiting for the light to change and the last commuter to clear the street. The evangelist's strident tone bled through the glass, though it was muffled by the clatter of the cab's heater. His back was to us, one hand on his hip, the other pointing up, down, all around. I didn't pay much attention to him. Jesus Christ, you see that shit all the time.

But Oppie ogled out the window, transfixed as though she'd never seen such a thing. Or maybe just once before. Talk of the Keatons had got her in the mood. She playfully chucked my shoulder. "The memories, eh?"

"My misspent youth," I wheezed, labouring for a joke and giving up. I closed my eyes and let my head loll back onto the vinyl seat.

As finally we accelerate, Oppie made a gasping, gurgling noise and I turn towards her. She was twisted about, gawking out the rear window. Her eyes were wide with disbelief, but narrow quickly in concentration.

"*Jesus H* ...."

"What? What is it?"

"I think that was Scott."

"Scott ...?"

"Scott."

"Scott Baio?" I yammered drunkenly, believing it passed for wit. "Montgomery Scott? F Scott Fitz-"

"*Scott!*" She sounded wounded. "The guy I was with when we met. We were born again together. Remember?"

"Fuck *off!* Scott?"

"I think so. I really, really think so."

"But it's —"

"Why not? Maybe he stuck with it. Not everybody's as bright as us, eh?"

I wrenched my neck, glancing over my shoulder. But we'd already reached the next intersection, and there was nothing back there now but headlights and hazy fluorescence.

"I didn't get a good look, but ...." Oppie took a shallow, fluttery breath and sighs "Geez." Then, violently, she shook her head and grimaced — "*Born again!*" — before striking my shoulder once more; harder this time. "And it's all your fault!"

Earlier that evening, when the phone rang during the "Silverman Helps" segment of *CityPulse News,* I'd had a hunch it was my mother. I picked it up anyway. That's just like me.

"Should I come over?" she offered, after I told her about Grace. "Do you need anything to eat?"

"No, please. No, thanks. I'm okay."

"What a shame. You and Grace. I'm *so* sorry, dear. You seemed to get along so well."

"You think so? Thanks. I didn't think you'd say that. I guess we did. But that's got nothing to do with it."

"You know, maybe I shouldn't say anything —" She hesitated, waiting for my permission to continue, but I said nothing. She continued anyway. That's just like her. "It's nothing against Grace. I didn't know her well but I liked her. It's just, remember: an unequally-yolked couple has the cards stacked against them from the get go. Just look at your father and I."

"That wasn't our problem, believe me."

"Grace didn't profess Christ, did she?"

"You got that right."

"Now lookit." Her voice sounded sharp and inappropriate, as though she were honing the Sword of the Lord to butter an English muffin. "I won't have that nonsense. You gave your heart to Jesus years ago. There's nothing you can do about it now, my dear. Don't ask for it back. He doesn't work that way."

I allowed myself a grin that surprised me by its guilessness. "Gee, I didn't know you were such a Calvinist."

"You bring it out in me."

"Sorry. You can't imagine how much I hate this."

"Alright then. But you know what I think." We lapsed into an awkward silence, which felt more comfortable than our awkward conversation. Then, as though this was her best effort to change the topic and I had better like it, she said, "You know, the Keatons haven't been to town since. It's going to be great. Everyone down at Cliffside is really excited about their coming back."

"That right?" With a shallow sigh, I mustered enough guilt and grace to affect interest. "Where's the crusade this year?"

"The Ex. The Coliseum, I think. They're much bigger than they used to be. And you know they used to be *big*. I hear they're going to put the stage in the middle, so they can preach in the round."

"Cool," I shot back like a smart ass, but she didn't catch me at it this time.

"Isn't it? Very snazzy, I figure." I could hear her smile now. "I think a lot about that first year they came to Cliffside. Especially the nights you and Mary got involved. You both looked so natural up there." She paused to savour the image. "I liked Mary. Whatever happened to her?"

"Jesus *Christ*, how can you say something like that?" My mother caught her breath, then sucked her teeth disapprovingly. Both good indicators that she'd begun praying silently. How I must have disappointed her since I shared a stage with the Keaton twins. I'd heard so many breaths caught, so many teeth sucked. "Sorry, mother. Sorry about yelling, and taking the Lord's name, and all that. You just kinda bring it out in me." I punctuated the last remark with a laugh, but she wasn't in the mood to reciprocate in kind. She was still sucking those teeth.

"Right. Sorry. Look, let's just leave it, alright? I've got to go. Take care. Talk to you soon. I'll call you next week."

"Don't put yourself out on my account."

IV

I, I am godless,
and I am the one whose God is great.

The Thunder, Perfect Mind (Nag Hammadi)

1

y mother was in grade 6 when her brother died. Just an 11-year old carrying a torch for Perry Como. When I was a child she seldom mentioned Uncle Gideon, so I sometimes wondered why she'd given me his name. Only on Remembrance Day would she reveal at least the presence of his absence, when she would watch the cenotaph ceremony live from Parliament Hill and shed tears between her fingers.

I never knew my grandmother to cry for her long dead son, but she never stopped talking about him. Whenever I showed the mildest curiosity, even if it were nothing but an adolescent fetish for shiny helmets and pretty explosions, she would fetch her grey strong box and let me sift through the jaundiced letters he'd mailed her from England. The last one was dated April 30, 1943, and was the shortest of them all. All he said was how sorry he was to hear that the Maple Leafs hadn't repeated as Stanley Cup champs.

My uncle's Lancaster bomber was 69 feet, 6 inches long (approximately the distance from blue line to goal crease), with a crew complement of seven (too many men on the ice). He was a mid-upper gunner, which meant he hunched exposed inside a glass bubble atop the drab olive fuselage. He worked nights, miles high above occupied Europe, looking to point a pair of machine guns at anyone who might be pointing a pair back at him. His plane was one of eight lost the night of May 16, during the famous dambuster raids on the great barrage works of the Eder, Möhne and Sorpe. The dams portioned out water to power the generators of the great armament industries of the Ruhr valley. The Eder and Möhne dams were breached, and though arms production was not appreciably hampered and the dams were soon repaired, better than a thousand Germans drowned, some of them undoubtedly fascists.

The movie stars Michael Redgrave.

2

"I can't believe you talked me into this."

"Betcha can."

Oppie fidgeted with her leather handbag, making room for a flask of scotch wrapped in a crinkly paper bag and her old Scofield Reference Bible. The scotch slipped and almost strikes the pavement.

"Holy shit," she gurgled, and let the Bible drop to catch it. A dozen or so of the neatly groomed heads in our queue swivelled in our direction, some to stare disapprovingly, others just to hear us more distinctly. I scooped up her Bible for her, and she tucked it beside the flask.

"Right," she mumbled. "Language, language."

At least she looked the part. Beneath her coat she's wearing an ivory blouse and ankle-length caramel skirt I remember seeing her wear to church. She'd left her Docs in the closet for a scuffed pair of vinyl taupe boots with modest heels. She had her last cigarette less than an hour before, while we waited for the streetcar to take us to Exhibition Place. Since then, she'd chewed half a pack of Clorets.

"I wish you hadn't brought that Bible."

"How come?"

"It's just too —" I waved my hands, trying to catch a word I used to know.

"Gotta follow along in the Word," she explained with born again bonhomie.

"Please," I gently hissed. "Don't talk like that."

She yanked my elbow, pulling me close to her mouth, and whispered gruffly, "All part of my fiendish disguise."

The line was moving faster now. *We'll be in the lobby soon.*

"This is horrible," I groaned.

"Cheer up. It's not the end of the world."

"Well, you never know."

"Knock knock."

"'Armageddon Outta Here', right?"

"Heard it before?"

"Bible School. Freshman year. We told jokes, too."

A distorted selection of *Praise Strings III* fed on itself over the public address system as we settled upon the Coliseum's west side, fourth row from the front. That was pushing the envelope of my proximity tolerance and Oppie knew it, so she didn't begrudge me taking the aisle seat. Below us, the arena floor was covered with ranks of metal folding chairs that fanned out about the centre stage. They were already taken, except for a roped off block of seats three rows deep on the floor's west side. Between those seats and the stage, the musicians huddled together, heads bowed in a quick word of prayer. Each wore a three-piece-suit. Drummer, guitarist and organist, just like the Doors.

The stage was a wooden dais, maybe 30 feet across and four feet high. A Plexiglas lectern rose on the south side, with four high-backed, wooden chairs with crimson seat cushions arrayed in a semi-circle behind it. At the opposite end of the platform, a dozen or so folding chairs marshalled in choir formation. Two stubby stairwells were cut into the middle of the stage, on the east and west ends. In the very middle of it all I saw a curious dark hole, about 10 feet in diameter. From where we sat, it looked as though there were a purple drape rimming the hole's circumference. The scene vaguely reminded me of a vanilla donut, and when that image occurred to me I heard my stomach rumble. Oppie must have heard it as well, because she offered me her second-to-last Cloret.

A pair of young and solemn-looking Caribbean women, cradling enormous black Bibles and wearing vivid orange and blue frocks, sat directly before us. Their straightened hair was pulled taut to the nape of their necks, one using bobby pins, the other, a plastic butterfly clasp. A few rows in front of them a wheelchair was parked in the aisle. I made out a sandy shock of hair from a head twisted violently to the left.

Oppie and I stood to let a tremendously fat man in a dark green jacket and blonde trousers join his attractive wife. She'd been standing in her place, waving her arms to draw his attention since we arrived. "Praise the Lord," he gasped, his sweaty chops dissolving in a grin, when "Excuse me" might have been more appropriate. Oppie nudged me. Rather than look at her directly, I arch my eyebrows a touch and felt guilty for even that. So far I'd resisted the temptation to mock all the ugliness and bad taste in order to confirm our set-apartness. It just seemed too pathetic.

"How ya doin'?" she asked softly, reaching between her legs for the handbag beneath the seat.

"Fine, fine."

Astonishingly, it's not such a lie. My pulse was steady and trustworthy; no faster than it might have be for golf on TV. I breathed deeply, enjoying the cordial swelling of my chest. My thoughts weren't painted, as I'd feared they might be, with pictures of derangement and damnation. No, I wasn't going to panic; I wasn't going to Hell. I wouldn't be clenching my armrests, fighting the urge to march down the aisle in answer to an altar call. No, I was alright tonight. I didn't belong here anymore.

A reassuring thought, even as it depressed me.

Oppie gave me another nudge.

"Want some?"

She was offering me the scotch. She'd already taken a snort. Reflexively, I glance behind us. A young couple, possibly high school seniors, had their heads bent together over the biographies in the Keatons' program. The young man's arm spanned his friend's back, and his hand lay gently on her far shoulder.

I shrugged, "What the hey?"

I returned the flask as the lights dimmed and a scratchy recording of "Come Thou Fount" was cropped at the first stanza as a choir of two dozen men and women, clad in red robes, entered handclapping and singing "When the Saints Go Marching In." Without instruction, people rose from their seats, and began waving their hands high above their heads or clapping them together in and out of time. Oppie and I didn't sing or wave or clap, but we stood to get a better view, and she gave her fingers a few sarcastic snaps.

"Fucking Charismatics," she muttered.

The choir stretched single file as it circumscribed the stage, snaking like the world's soberest conga line between the dais and the first row. A stocky, tanned man in a three-piece lime-coloured suit of shiny crushed velvet and a slim Asian woman in an ankle-length, emerald-green dress woven from some novel polymer followed the choir and strode purposefully, hand in hand, towards the stage. The man's hair is long and wavy, impeccably moussed, the colour of hearty bowel movements. Behind them strode Pastor Drew Tallboys of Cliffside Baptist and a very old and thin man. They side-stepped a pair of gawky choir members and climbed the stairs to the dais and took the four wooden seats. It's then I noticed something stirring in the hole in the stage's middle. The tops of two heads — one bald, one kinky, and back to back — slowly rose from the inner darkness, as though they belonged to a pair of lazy gondoliers navigating the birth canal who both think it's the other's turn to steer.

"David and Jonathan." I spat their names like cherrystones. "The original Jesus Freaks."

The singing continued, now with more gusto as the crowd fixed on the twins. David looked pretty much the same, and though our view of Jonathan wasn't good he appeared paler, balder and more stooped than I recalled. David was wearing a cordless microphone, so I assumed as much for his brother. They looked to be sitting on their same old bench.

The song ended, but the Keatons kept rising until they were maybe six inches above the platform. Their elevator gave a little shudder and that's it.

"God bless you, Toronto!" David raised his arms stiffly, stretching them wide apart with open palms. Jonathan's hands still rested on his Bible.

"'How I want to be in that number'." David threw back his head and nodded expansively. "And you know what? I know I will be."

"By the promise of God!" Jonathan shouted. At least his voice was animated. And painfully amplified. I hoped someone thought to turn it down.

"The assurance of infallible revelation." David chewed his words slowly as though each was a sticky, sweet toffee. "Will you be in that number when *your* number's up?"

"Or aren't you sure, but you want to be?" jumped in Jonathan, though more soothingly this time. "Or maybe you are sure, but you wish you weren't."

"Go to Hell?" cried his brother. "I wouldn't care for that!"

"No thank you, devil!"

"Well praise the Lord, tonight's going to be special!" David clasped his hands together with a loud smack and stamp of his feet. "*Oooeee!* I can feel it! Are you feeling it, brother?"

"The anointing of God! Hallelujah!"

The Coliseum resounded with a flurry of thank-you-Jesuses. Oppie took a sip of scotch and I gestured that I'd like some, too. I was still doing okay, but I'd never before heard a preacher squeal like a pig and I can't say I much cared for it.

"But we don't want to get ahead of ourselves," said David. "I'd like to ask our dear friend, the Reverend Duncan McComish of Allan Road Free Presbyterian, to ask the Lord's blessing."

I closed my eyes, and Oppie nudged me. I smiled, but I kept my eyes shut. Even though I couldn't pray, it was still a quiet mystery I couldn't joke about. Besides, I liked

McComish's voice. It reminded me of Sunday night chicken broth and a Wayne and Shuster special. It was a burnt-orange voice — not, like the woman's dress ahead of us, vibrant and sunsplashed — but old and fruity and seemingly good for me.

McComish climaxed with a throaty "Amen," daubing his lips with a tissue he must have pulled from a hip pocket while our eyes were closed, as he returned to his seat. Then the pair dressed in lime and emerald stood. I referred to the program: "The melodious husband/wife ministry of Kyle and Akido Nixon."

"There's an interesting tale, told in Acts, chapter 10," David Keaton began, following Kyle and Akido's salsa-tinged *Oh Happy Day*. "You needn't turn to it." Almost everyone with a Bible, which was almost everyone, did so anyway, except Oppie. "I'm sure you know it. We read how Peter was to take the Gospel to the gentiles, to the house of a man called Cornelius in the city of Joppa."

Jonathan picked up the story. "The night before, Peter was up on the rooftop praying, and he was hungry — famished! — and the Scripture says he would have eaten, but he fell into a trance."

"What the fuck ...?" Oppie muttered.

Below us, to our left, through the arena's eastern gate, an angel had entered the arena. Its white-robed back was to us and it wore a cowl pulled over its head. Two large, flimsy wings — coat hangers and tin foil, by the look of it — quivered on its shoulders. Both hands cradled a huge grey scimitar which glimmered with the dull reflectivity of bargain plastics.

To the increasing distraction of the crowd, the angel walked towards the platform steps.

"And while Peter was in this trance," continued Jonathan, ignoring the angel and the murmuring crowd, "he saw Heaven open, and a great sheet came down to him that held all manner of food to nourish him. But the Bible says it held 'wild beasts, and creeping things, and fowls of the air'."

"Not quite kosher!" David chipped in, winking I suspected.

"And a voice called out of heaven to the Apostle, 'Rise, Peter; kill and eat."

The angel was now at the foot of the steps. Like a wave across the arena, friends leaned into each other, whispering. Some pointing, some others shaking their heads, a few with fingers at their mouths looking desperately alarmed.

Oppie's hand fell upon my forearm, which she squeezed hard.

"What the hell?" she grumbled, and cleared her throat.

"Peter was famished," David continued. "Simply *starving!* And along comes God with all these things that had been forbidden for him to eat. Peter had been born again, saved by grace, walked with the Saviour. But he still ate like he was under the old dispensation. He was proud of it. He said, 'Not so, Lord; for I have never eaten any thing that is common or unclean.'"

The angel was on the platform now, standing between the brothers, who still hadn't acknowledged its presence. Tallboys and the Nixons were smiling, and following with soft, indulgent eyes the wobble of the angel's rickety wings. Reverend McComish fished for a pair of chunky eyeglasses in his jacket pocket. He held them upon the end of his nose, gripping a thick black rim between thumb and forefinger. He squinted, curling his bottom lip nearly enough to bare his gums to the first row. But I wouldn't call that a smile. Someone, I assumed, had neglected to mention this part of the act to him.

Oppie clutched my arm violently.

"You want to go?" I asked. "You okay?"

She exhaled, relaxing her grip. "I'm okay. Okay enough. It's just getting a little freaky."

"But the food was from God," said Jonathan. "And He wanted Peter to enjoy it."

The angel's face was lost in the shadows of its cloak. Still, by the rustle of its robe and a subtle air of hesitance, it seemed to take a heavy breath before it lay one hand atop the other on the hilt. Then it raised the scimitar above its head, high above the heads of the twins. Women's voices shrieked, and some men's. From directly behind us, a baritone called "Hey, look out!"

"The Lord said to Peter," quoted David, his voice rising to a shout from deep in his belly: "'What God hath cleansed, that call thou not common!'"

The angel's arms arced down swiftly, drawing the sword between the necks of the Keaton twins. It struck the fabric of their common jacket, pulling it down, bunching the material up around their shoulders. The brothers gave a little tug and the jacket fell away into two halves as though torn along a perforation. With a hollow thud the plastic sword clipped the bench, and in another moment the twins were standing, back to back, and unattached.

"Holy Christ!" I blubbered. Or maybe that was Oppie. Perhaps both of us. Probably both.

There were some shouts of praise and scattered, baffled applause, most of which was strangled by nervous laughter and fits of coughing.

David wheeled slowly about the raised platform, both arms raised palms up. Whether worshipping or preparing to surrender, it was hard to tell. The angel lay the sword across the bench and fell back a step. Jonathan began to unbutton his shirt, starting with the cuffs.

"This isn't magic," David cooed. "And we haven't been fooling you. It's the truth, my brother and I were joined since before we were born. And we always thought it would be that way."

"We were happy with the life the Lord gave us," said Jonathan. He'd pulled out his shirttail, and was working top to bottom on the buttons. "We couldn't even *imagine* another life."

"God knows what He's doing. If we'd been like everyone else, we wouldn't have reached so many for the Lord."

"That's right," nodded the woman dressed in orange to her friend in blue, who nodded back at her.

"It wasn't until God ..." David paused, looking to the arena's rafters, "invited us to eat, of that which we'd denied ourselves for so long — the common fare we'd thought unclean — that we decided the Lord had made for us a new thing."

"The doctors couldn't promise we'd both survive."

"But we got a second opinion from the Great Physician!"

Jonathan raised his hands to his collar to remove his shirt. "The proof is in the pudding," he said, chuckling and flashing his teeth. "And since the operation, I tell ya, that's pretty much what our backs look like. You know, whenever I read how the

Lord told Thomas to feel his wounds, I can't help but get a little queasy myself. So we won't take offence if you choose to
look away."

Not pudding; more three-cheese pizza two days cold,
topped with extra scar tissue. Two slices were missing from his
narrow shoulder blades, where the skin appears pale and
unruptured. Jonathan turned slowly on the heels of his feet, so
all assembled could get a good eyeballing.

"I'd show you mine," grinned David, "but Jon's the pretty
one."

Oppie snorted, as does the young man behind us, which
earned him a "Shhh!" from his girlfriend.

"Seriously," David continued, "tonight you're to be our witnesses — in a sense you can't even *imagine* — to the end of a
long, yet blessed, journey."

Now *I'm* uneasy. Something we can't imagine? I took a second swig of scotch before handing it back to Oppie.

"Toronto has a special place in our hearts," David said
breezily. "Mine especially. It goes back a couple of years, when
we were here for a crusade at Cliffside Baptist Church." A
smattering of applause from proud congregants at hearing
mention of their place of worship. "The Spirit was moving, let
me tell you, like we've rarely seen."

"The Spirit?" groused Oppie, softly into my shoulder. "Is
that what the kids call it nowadays?"

"Throughout the crusade, my brother and I were blessed
with a youthful team of prayer warriors with whom we wres-
tled against Principalities and Powers for the salvation and
sanctification of souls."

"Hey, that's you." Oppie poked my ribs with an odd but
unaffected pride. I nodded, senseless, barely taking it in.

"Lives were changed." David paused, nodding, before he
added, "Not least of all, my own."

"What's he talking about?" I mumbled, gnawing a thumbnail as though peeling wallpaper.

"It was at Cliffside, ten years ago, that the Lord introduced
me to a prayer warrior. My angel. And tonight, God willing,
I'm going to make her my wife."

David beckons to the angel, who had been standing silently with head bowed next to Tallboys' chair. The organist softly, almost playfully pecked at the Wedding March as the shrouded figure glided towards Keaton, who lifted his hands to the hem of its cowl and threw it back.

"Holy ..." I whispered hoarsely. "Holy ...."

"Is that —"

"... shit."

The lanky chestnut hair I'd known for a time had been domesticated by hot curling irons, but the elegant nose and cheekbones were precisely as I still barely remembered. It's her.

"This is Mary," David said, beaming. He took her hand and she smiled bashfully, and with her free hand nervously tugs at her angel wings. "Mary Christmas, until tonight. Then it's Mary Keaton, until Jesus takes us home."

Oppie twisted towards me, bouncing in her seat. "Jesus Christ," she rasped, "I can't believe this! Those fuckers are getting married? Right *now*? And we're supposed to just *sit* here?"

"Pass the scotch," I giggled.

Oppie gave me a queer look. I couldn't explain why suddenly I feel so giddy.

"It's been a long road ...." David paused, and his gaze fell to the strong, slender hand he held. He breathed heavily through his mouth and gently swung Mary's hand, then glanced up and slowly scanned the crowd before him, finally fixing upon an especially tender-faced, blonde-wigged old woman in the third row. Almost guilelessly he returned her artless smile. "I tell you something," he said, wagging a lazy finger. "This is the happiest day of my natural life, but I don't know if I'll be able to get through it without balling like a baby."

"*Yeesh*," Oppie shivered. She turned to me, and I turned to her wearing a sloppy, bone-headed grin. "Um, you alright?"

"Sure? Why shouldn't I be?"

She opened her mouth to tell me why, but right then Mary said, in a clear, unamplified voice, "I'd like to say a few words, if that's okay."

David quickly unclipped his lapel mike and fastened it to the collar of her robe.

"First off, I've got a confession: I'm not really an angel."
She smirked, and jiggled her crinkled wings. The crowd
relaxed, and seemed to be warming to her. "I know, I know, it's
hard to believe ...." *Lordy, Lordy, that sweet toaster oven of a toe-suck-
ing mouth.* I felt a tweak of physical memory at the tent flap of
my Stanfield's. "It's nice for David to call me one, but he knows
better. After ten years, in and out of each other's lives, we both
should know, right?"

Mary raised a fist to her lips and cleared her throat, briefly
glancing at David. He smiled, closed his eyes and — just barely — nodded twice.

"But it hasn't been easy for us," she continued. "Ten
whole years, struggling to figure out what we want — let
alone what God wants — can't help but change a couple.
God, too." I squint, unsure of what that means. She scratches
her nose with a thumb. "It all seemed rather complicated, as
you can imagine —"

"*Hah!*" Oppie snorted. And so did Mary.

"— loving a Siamese twin is not for the faint of heart."

There was a rustle of suddenly uncomfortable people,
crossing and uncrossing their legs, clearing their throats or
again laughing uneasily. Oppie gave me another funny look
but I ignored her.

"Or, well, maybe you don't need to hear about that," Mary
tossed off.

Jonathan's lips began moving silently as he bowed his
head, pressing his hands flat together before his face with his
fingers forming a steeple that reached the tip of his nose. His
brother was nodding again, more conspicuously now. Behind
them, Reverend McComish was glaring first at one Keaton and
then the other, his brow creased like so much corrugated cardboard. He cast a baffled glance to Tallboys, who whispered
soft words that only made him wince and seem to sputter
something to himself.

"All I want to share is, that this has been a hard love for us.
Harder for me, I suppose. I mean, I love and respect Jonathan
as a brother —"

Jonathan raised his eyes. "And I you," he mouthed.

"— but we all knew, so long as they remained joined, David and I could not be joined, not *really*, as man and wife." A spark of jealousy — *Cripes, they'll be banging tonight!* — which promptly burns itself out. My kindling's too seeped in years of come and tears for me to get worked up about this sort of thing. "So believe me, it's been hard. And something this hard can give a person plenty of reason to be angry at God. It didn't seem fair, you know? I sure was pissed —"

"'Pissed'?" Oppie mumbled, as though waking from a dream. "What did she say?"

"You heard right," I whispered. "Just look at the whites of McComish's eyes."

"— until I realized that was okay. I was angry at God, and that was perfectly alright. Sometimes, I think, He must want us to be." Mary shook her head with wonder, and grinned. "I mean, just take a look around, right?"

But people were already looking around, trying to find comprehension in friendly faces. Of those who looked as though they were actually listening to her, none gave much indication of knowing what the Hell she's talking about. Just the Keaton brothers. A thin-lipped smile was fixed to Tallboys' face, but I couldn't believe he was actually listening.

"What I'm saying is, Jesus isn't frail, like all the pretty stained glass implies. We don't need to be on our best behaviour. If we're angry, we can let him have it. I don't think we can do a single thing that could shock him, or make him stop loving us. I tell you, the guy can take it." Mary grinned, and stretched her arm towards David, who took her hand. "Believe me, if He couldn't, I'd be shit out of luck."

The crowd made a rude sucking noise, like a vacuum cleaner whose eyes were bigger than its dust bag. McComish began wringing his hands and surveying the ground, looking for an agreeable place to fall on his knees. Oppie grabbed my wrist and stammered, "What the *fuck*? What the fuck is this?"

"I'm not trying to be shocking — well, maybe just a *teensy* bit," she smirked. "And I'm sorry if I've offended anyone. But the thing is, I've learned that God's been around; He's heard it all before. All He wants to hear now is the truth, and I think nothing would make him happier if we just admitted right here, right now we're all full of shit. And Christians should be the first to admit it. Because you know, the most profound thing in the world is this: that Christ has redeemed our shit."

Oppie and I stood to let the fat man squeeze past us, followed quickly by his wife. (This time there's no congenial "Praise the Lord!") All over the arena floor and in the stands there was motion, as people gathered their coats and coaxed their friends to join the spontaneous columns forming for the exits. A couple of choir members got up and left, as well as a musician, who unplugged his guitar and brushed by the incredulous organist, instrument cradled proudly in the crook of his arm.

The two women ahead of us remained seated, listening, nodding their occasional agreement.

David took a step towards Mary and dropped her hand, and gently pressed the small of her back. He smiled warmly at the blonde-wigged woman in the third row who'd kept her place. "Of course, we all know the Word, 'Blessed are they that hunger and thirst after righteousness, for they shall be filled.' We *all* know that, right?"

The sound of his voice checked the flight of some toward the exits, and they stood in their place, listening.

Oppie whispered, "Let's go, okay?"

I wrinkled my nose. "You kidding?" I snorted. "This is so *cool!*"

"No, it's just weird. And you're crying."

So I was. Not balling, not weeping, but my eyes were wet, no doubt about it.

"Well, do we?" David asked. There was a buzzing of assent. "Amen, then, right?"

I daubed my eyes with an index finger. No big deal; just a couple of swipes. "All better."

Oppie sighed and arched her eyebrows. "Tell me if you start cracking up, right?"

"I'm fine, fine," I gasped. I was so improbably fine, it was worrying me. I wished I felt a little worse.

Jonathan scratched his chin and squinted at the Coliseum's far corner, trying to look as though this thought had only now

occurred to him. Oddly, now they were separated, I could at
last see the resemblance.

"You want to know something? I'm not so sure we do.
Does the Bible say, 'blessed are the righteous'? No! It says
'blessed are they that *hunger* and *thirst* ....'"

I felt a sudden, cool breeze from somewhere — from all
around me, as though the air conditioning had just kicked in
— raise gooseflesh on my arms and the back of my neck. *You
cold?* I was about to ask Oppie, but she had already tugged her
coat across her chest and was rubbing her hands together.

"God doesn't want you to be good," David sniffed. "Do
you hear what I'm saying? Hey, I don't write this stuff!"

Oppie flipped open her Bible. "Fuck it," she breathed. "Is
that New Testament?"

"Gospels," I suggested. "Try Matthew."

Something was tingling in the back of my throat. It felt
like a sweet slice of cherry pie and two scoops of ice cream, or
what I used to call the Holy Spirit. It landed in my belly,
brushing the suede underside of my flesh. I shifted in my seat.
Not such a bad feeling, that cherry pie.

"What am I trying to say? That God wants you to *want* to
be good. That's all."

"That's right," the woman dressed in blue murmured to her
friend in orange.

"Don't *try* to be good," David said.

"God doesn't want that," added Jonathan.

Just then, there was a startling cackle from the row behind
us. Oppie and I flinched, then together, turn in our seats, and
see the young woman doubled up, shaking with hysterical
laughter. Her boyfriend's arm was draped across her shoulders,
and he was cooing his concern in her ear. She gave a loud hoot
and threw back her head, bumping his. Tears were starting to
stream down her face. She stamped her feet and hooted again.

"Just *want* to be good," David crooned.

A sudden bark of laughter drew our eyes to the floor,
where a large black man was upsetting a couple of empty
chairs as he fell, clutching his sides and howling gleefully.
Nearby, a young man toppled, helplessly giddy, into the lap of

his neighbour, an elderly Asian woman. She gave a loud and long snort through the lattice of fingers she'd held to her lips. Patches of giggles began breaking out on the stands opposite.

"What the fu—," Oppie began to say, but stops as though she'd swallowed her tongue. I turned towards her. Her lips were pursed, and her eyes wide and confused. She shook her head fiercely, pounding her fist first on her knee, then on mine. "What's wrong?" I mumbled, but I know just by looking at her. She was scared and excited and angry, but finally she had to laugh, in great heaving gulps that took away all her breath. And in a great, weird chorus, Oppie's laughter rolled together with all the others.

"Gideon," she eventually managed to gasp, "what is so fucking *funny?*"

"What would the Father want with your righteousness?" Jonathan wanted to know. "What do you think God Almighty would do with it?"

"Burn it up!" bellowed David.

"Isaiah 64:6: 'All your righteousness is as filthy rags.' Does the Lord of Heaven need that?"

"No!"

"Does He dress in filthy rags?"

"*No!*"

After a struggle, Duncan McComish had managed to push himself out of his seat. He looked unsteady; unsure of why he's standing or maybe even where he is. But he danced a little jig nonetheless.

"You feel it?" Jonathan asked us, beaming. "You feel the anointing?"

My belly didn't tingle anymore. I didn't feel giddy. Not now; not when everybody else does. Now I had absolutely zero compulsion to laugh. Many are called, but few are chosen. That must be it. I'd been visited, but the Spirit had departed. Almost, almost, almost. Ah well; them's the breaks.

All about us were whoops and titters, giddy hallelujahs and amens. Splotchy, pudgy, bony, unclenched hands were dancing overhead like a fleet of kites on the beach the first good day of summer.

"God wants to bless you," David declared, stressing each word, even the preposition. "And believe you me: He doesn't give a *shit* if you deserve it!" If anyone was still listening, no one was especially shocked.

"All God wants is that you *want* to be good," repeated his brother.

"Just want it. Hunger and thirst after it. *Want* it! That's all."

"Amen," I reluctantly mumbled.

"Fuckin' A," sputtered Oppie through her spiteful giggles. She's punching her wrists, as if to make herself wake up.

David stepped back, and swabbed his forehead with his wrist. Then he slapped his thigh and turned to Mary, who wore a wide, swampy grin.

"Okay, baby — let's get hitched!"

3

Before my mother took her home, Nanny had spent
nearly a month in the hospital.

She wasn't a vegetable. She was still her, but she
couldn't read, couldn't talk, couldn't get out of bed.

Nanny needed a caregiver now, to feed her and help her
pee, though she couldn't tell us she needed or wanted anything
anymore. Mother hired a nurse to watch her during weekdays.

I'd visit a couple of times each week, sit at her bedside for
10 or 15 minutes and hold her gnarled hand, telling her I
loved her and that I was doing well, even if she was asleep, and
even if I wasn't so well. She looked through me, as though she
didn't know me. Or did, but no longer cared.

I spent most Sunday mornings there, so my mother could
go to church and pray for me. Eleven Sundays after Grace had
departed, a week after the Keaton crusade, mother asked if I

might stay a little later than usual. It was Pentecost, which normally wasn't a big occasion at Cliffside, but Pastor Filmore had proclaimed this "The Year of the Holy Spirit" and a retired professor from a college in upstate New York was expected to lead an after-worship seminar on spiritual gifts. ("I've got an open mind," she said, "but tongues ceased in the first century.")

About 11, Sunday morning, I lined up Nanny's pills and fluffed her pillows so she could sit up properly. She didn't look at me, didn't acknowledge me at all; just stared at the distressed chestnut dresser opposite her bed, and the small black and white television atop it, which I wouldn't turn on because there was nothing but Gospel and *Star Trek*. She stuck out her tongue for her medicine, and then I held out a glass of water, but her hand bumped mine and her nightgown got badly splashed. Nanny needed to be changed.

She wasn't embarrassed. She wasn't anything at all but naked, as immodest as a two year old who'd wet herself, but unlike the two year old, wouldn't cry. I dressed her blind, staring at a particular corner of ceiling, and poked her in the eye when I pulled the nightie over her head. When she was dry I escaped to the basement to maybe dig up a forsaken *Jimmy Olsen* comic.

Three cinder-block sized cardboard boxes packed with childhood's detritus were stacked along one wall of the walnut-panelled laundry room. I enjoyed poking through them, picking up and laying down again my old school papers and doodle pads, Radio Havana program schedules and water damaged copies of *Famous Monsters of Filmland*. I didn't find an *Olsen*, but I discovered a *Jerry Lewis*, issue no. 99.

Beneath my boxes was a blue fibrewood footlocker with three brass-plated buckles. It had belonged to my uncle. Now my uncle belonged to it. The key, as always, was in its centre lock. Before I restacked my boxes I turned it, unbuckled the buckles and lifted the lid.

First of all were the photographs, scattered like confetti over everything. Dozens of sepiatones of my uncle Gideon as a kid, rolling on a lawn I'd never known, being watched by my grandmother, and a bald fat man I'm told was my grandfather. A few grey portraits as an adolescent, gangly holding his newborn sister. And there was a snapshot of him and his fiancé, looking square at the camera, laughing, holding hands in the front seat of his pre-war roller coaster. You couldn't tell by the picture whether the ride had just finished or if it hadn't yet begun.

And there were his letters home, the ones Nanny used to keep in the strong box. I didn't know why they weren't still there. Here also were documents of his service and death, a deep pile of neatly folded clothes and two pairs of shoes. And next to the shoes at the very bottom, swaddled in the front pages of a *Toronto Telegram* from 1964, was a black porcelain cylinder with its lid sealed with brittle yellow tape. My uncle?

I pulled out a dull orange shirt and matching pants: boyish flannel pajamas. They felt heavy with years and smelled musty, and were so small it made me heartsick. And there were other clothes. Adult clothes I recognized from the pictures here and others I recalled: a crisp white shirt, wide-wale, brown corduroy pants, a copper-coloured wool sweater and black oxfords.

As I found a piece, I laid it atop the washing machine. They were all here. Then I began to undress.

There were two white shirts, and the best fit was still an inch too short in the sleeves, but the trousers — though not to my taste — were a perfect fit. The shoes were too small to wear, but I liked the sweater Nanny had knit him, back when everyone still called Eddie Cantor "Banjo Eyes."

With the sweater buttoned, I brushed my hair with my fingers and climbed the stairs. If I had stopped to think — even if I hadn't stopped, but had only thought a little — I wouldn't have done it.

I opened the door to Nanny's room.

She was lying on her back, her hands folded together at the belly above her paisley duvet. She was neither asleep nor dead. Her eyes were blinking sluggishly, their lids beating a dull semaphore. She didn't bother turning her head towards me.

I crossed the room and sat on the lip of her lavender bedspread.

"How are you doing?"

She looked at me, with a look that said that even if she could have spoken, she wouldn't have likely bothered. Then she let her head droop to the side of her pillow, the side at which I sat, and it stayed like that — simply very old and bored — until her face steadily screwed into something like a squint. She had noticed the sweater. Her dentureless mouth began to open, slowly, and I noticed a shiny band of spit that spanned her gums.

She smiled suddenly, as though recalling something important.

"How are you?" I asked again. "Are you alright?"

She reached for the hem of the sweater.

"Nice, isn't it?"

She grasped a patch of wool, and rolled it between a rheumatic finger and thumb.

"You made this, didn't you? You did a good job."

She lifted her head. Her eyes were watery and beginning to redden, but as her head fell back to the pillow her mouth suddenly split wide with a lopsided grin.

"You did good," I said, nodding spiritedly. "A *really* good job. I like it a lot."

Her eyelids fluttered, and she lost a tear in a wrinkle. I took hold of her hand, and she squeezed mine back with twice the vigour with which I'd squeezed hers.

It would be another year before mother would call me at three in the morning to say that Nanny was gone. She didn't say where.

4

ppie left Arthur the day after the Keaton crusade, though she didn't move out for another week. And another week passed before I heard about it.

In the days following the revival meeting I'd wanted to be left alone, and but for the rare wrong number and medium-rare telemarketer my wish was granted. When at last I called Oppie, Arthur sounded surprised she hadn't told me she'd gone, and embarrassed, he found himself mumbling, "It was a mutual thing."

"Y'okay, boy-o?"

Oppie and I are sitting in the window of a septic coffee shop at Dundas and Ossington, two blocks from her new-found flop at the home of a pair of friends I've heard about for years but never met. Arriving first, I'd found only one donut on display. It was plain and plainly stale but I bought it regardless, and was picking at its crumbs over a second cup when she arrived.

"Why didn't you say something? You could stay with me."

Oppie snorts and smiles, breaking the seal on a fresh pack of Camels. "For a while, anyway. I'll have to find something cheaper soon."

"Wouldn't want to cramp your swingin' single lifestyle."

"No no no." I'm shaking my head as though palsied. "I would love it if you did." Still smiling, she taps out a cigarette and cocks an eyebrow. "I *mean* it. I've been thinking. After — maybe it was seeing Mary, or all that —" I take a deep breath, puffing out my cheeks, then exhale slowly through flapping lips.

"Yeah, I know."

"What *was* that?

"Yeah. I don't know."

"Anyway, I'm doing better. Or different. Not good, exactly; but not bad. Just more like me." I snort. "My old joyless self."

Oppie nods and reaches for her lighter. "'Welcome back'," she sings softly. "'Your dreams were your ticket out.'"

"Don't know about Mr Kotter. It feels more like the Petticoat Junction of the soul. Like my whole life's been spent in anticipation and remembrance of sex. But enough about me —"

"Never. So, how'd you manage it? Enquiring minds, you know."

"I just thought about what my Mom said when my Dad proposed. Did I ever tell you?"

Oppie shakes her head, but I suspect she's indulging me.

"Apparently she said 'What the hell?' Can you believe that? How could anyone be expected to live happily ever after, in the shadow of such a big 'what the hell?' My life's compromised enough with all the little ones."

"Yeah. Like, 'Do you want onions with that?'"

"Exactly. 'Onions? Ah, what the hell?'"

"That may be okay for a turkey sub, but not a marriage."

"My thoughts exactly. I mean, that's *waaay* too much indifference. So I've promised myself: whatever I do, whomever I'm with, there's gonna be no big 'what the hell?' And let me just say, I'm not indifferent about onions."

"No," she shrugs, raising a cigarette to her lips. "But the theory's still pretty fuckin' sound."

"It's just like, after a while, you start to wonder: 'Why this life and not some other? Why her and not somebody else?' It bugs me I haven't become necessary for anyone yet. But I guess the reverse is true, too."

"You don't know that."

"Hmm?"

"Nothing."

I gaze absently at an empty streetcar stopped outside the window. Oppie is trying to light her cigarette with a stubborn Zippo, and has said nothing by the time it pulls away under an amber light, so I continue.

"Anyway, I asked myself, did it kill me to get expelled? To break up with a couple of girls?"

"Actually, sort of. Yeah," she nods to herself. "You got whacked good a few times there. But you got born again, again."

"*Hey!* I like that."

"Thought you would," she grins. "I can read you so easily. You're like a talking book."

"Thanks," I snort, and think *You're like Braille. I don't know what you mean, but I'd like the feel of those little bumps.* "Anyway, so now I think, if I'm not dead yet what's the worse that can happen? I'll be depressed for a while and eat tons of shit. Big deal. I was doing that even before I got saved."

"Yeah. But the difference now is, if you eat that fatal bag of chips, you don't get to go to heaven."

"Hmm. True. Maybe I should start monitoring my fat intake."

"Hmm *indeed.* Well, glory to God and all that. Sounds like you've gone and got yourself healed, sort of. Shitfire," Oppie mumbles past her clenched cigarette. "Lighter's fucked. Back in a jiff." She pushes back her chair and jogs to the cash for some matches. When she returns, grinning, she leans across the table, cupping her elbow in her palm, and smokes exultantly.

"Enough, finally, of me. What's with you?"

"Cripes. My turn, is it?"

"It's only fair."

"Oh, I don't know. Like I said when you called. Nothing special. Arthur's not a bad guy, really. Not if you keep up with your booster shots. But eventually you start building up a resistance."

"That explains it. I never got inoculated."

"Besides, he didn't want kids."

"Oh." She's never mentioned wanting children before. "So, you do?"

"Not especially, no. But I want a boy to want kiddies with me. Goddamned estrogen. Biology is a fucking outrage."

"I think you'd be a great mother."

"Think so?" Oppie squeaks, so strangely vulnerable. "Thanks, man," she murmurs, glancing to her mug with a shy, unlikely grin. "Anyhoo, I've thought about leaving him like *forever*, even before we moved in together, but it hurt too much. Not *too* much: not compound fracture hurt; more a sprained wrist kind of thing. But you know me: low pain threshold. But then staying suddenly started hurting more, so here we are. I left 'cause my heart was feeling too ouchy. What a wimp."

"No; it's more gutsy than that. It takes guts to leave." I sputter a laugh. "Listen to me. You'd think I might have ever left someone."

"Give it a few more months and you'll think you have. But it takes guts to be left, too. That's the disgraceful truth about being a grown up."

"It's nice, though, to think things work out sometimes. Like for Mary. It's kinda nice, even if I'm not in the picture."

"Or in the picture, but with your head cut off by a thumb."

"Right." A heavy sigh. "It would be good, though."

"What's that?"

"A happy ending. How come I can't have a happy ending, too?"

She smiles sweetly, blowing smoke away from my face. "Possibly, my dear, because this isn't the goddamn ending."

Author's Acknowledgments

Writing a novel is a very solitary endeavour, blah blah blah.

I mean, *please*. Spare me. I'm sure it hasn't seemed solitary — not nearly enough — to the many patient friends and impatient former friends who indulged my monomania as I searched, oh so importantly, for *le mot juste*.

Enormous thanks is due to the first of my enablers, Malcolm MacRury, without whose encouragement and sound judgement I doubt I would have begun the first chapter, let alone finished the last. I'm deeply indebted as well to Christine Purdon, whose enthusiasm and advice upon each instalment of my first crummy draft motivated me to write the next, and then promptly rewrite it.

I'm forever grateful for indispensable friends like Charles Stuart, Patrick Renouf, Natalia Moskwa and Paul Slansky who, by asking "How's the novel coming?" and simply being in my life, compelled me to have something more to say than "Er, I dunno."

Thanks to Michael Bate for the wonderful sheltered workshop that is *Frank Magazine*.

That my manuscript improbably became a book I owe to the faith and hard work of my agent, Dean Cooke. And heartfelt thanks to everyone at Dundurn who has made this experience so much more pleasurable than I'd dared hope. Special thanks to my editor, Barry Jowett, who both read what I'd written and knew what I should have, and to my copy-editor, Julian Walker, for making me look better than is my right.

Thanks to my family, in advance, for recognizing fiction when they see it.

Most profoundly, thanks to my sons Aarrow and Jacob and my wife Raina, without whom everything would be just too ridiculous.